FALL FROM GRACE

FALL
FROM
GRACE

ANDREW M. GREELEY

PIATKUS

Copyright © 1993 by Andrew Greeley Enterprises, Ltd

This edition first published in
Great Britain in 1994 by
Judy Piatkus (Publishers) Ltd of
5 Windmill Street, London W1

**The moral right of the author
has been asserted**

*A catalogue record for this book is available
from the British Library*

ISBN 0–7499–0228–0

Printed and bound in Great Britain by
Mackays of Chatham PLC, Chatham, Kent

For Jason Berry, who has fought the good fight.

"The old things have passed away; behold, new things have come."

II Cor 5/17

INTRODUCTION

While the political and ecclesiastical realities of the City and the Archdiocese of Chicago in this story are real enough, the characters are all creatures of my imagination and not based on any real person, even when they bear the names of real persons. The lawsuit described is a composite of different cases around the country, most of them even worse than my fictional case. The names of the principal characters—Kieran, Kathleen, Maeve, Brendan, Brien, Leary, Brigid—are all from the legends of sixth-century Ireland. This book was drafted before the explosion of the pedophile crisis in the Archdiocese in the winter of 1991–1992 and is not about that crisis.

PART I

KIERAN

"I need a personal favor, Kieran." Her eyes were ice-blue; Lake Michigan under a cold, sunny sky.

"Name it, Kathleen. Whatever it is, you've got it. No questions asked."

We were both from Chicago political families; we knew what a personal favor meant. No matter what our past conflicts had been, we understood that the request for a personal favor must be granted.

"An AIDS test for me." Her voice did not waver. "And for my children."

I could have argued that I was not the kind of doctor to administer the AIDS test. But I knew better than to quibble when the request had been presented as a personal favor. Not in Chicago.

I opened the door to my inner office and stepped aside so that she could enter. She was wearing a black, double-breasted trench coat. It was soaking wet, as was her flaming red hair, which she wore pulled back into a tight knot.

"I didn't know whether you could do such tests," she said, untying the belt on her coat.

"I am an M.D."

She winced as I removed the coat from her shoulders as if she was in pain. "I know that, but I thought you might leave the tests to others."

"Most of the time I do, but occasionally I test some of my patients who don't want to go to another doctor or clinic. You understand that you'll have to sign an authorization—both for you and for your children?"

I had not seen or spoken to Kathleen Leary Donahue, as she now had to be called, in almost twenty years. She hadn't changed much, save for the splashes of silver streaking her otherwise flaming red hair and the tense lines around her eyes and jaw, although those signs of strain may have had more to do with the stress of the moment than with the years between our last meeting and the present one. Kathleen's face was much the way I had remembered it: slender and sharply etched, with only an endearing touch of softness beneath her chin. Her body, neatly sheathed in a gray knit dress that only ran as far as her thigh, was clearly as sleek and lean as it remained in my memory. Her elegant breasts, though not large, took my breath away as they always had.

"Do you want me to sign the papers now?" she asked.

"Sure. Sit down while I find them."

She glanced at the couch and then sat primly on the only chair in the small room other than the one behind my old battered desk.

"Here they are." I had rummaged through two drawers. "Four of them."

She drew a fountain pen from her purse and signed her name with brisk, businesslike strokes. "There you go: one for me, and one each for Meg, Maeve, and Brigid."

"I'll be looking forward to meeting them."

She nodded. "You won't have any trouble knowing whose daughters they are."

"You will accompany them?" I began to prepare the syringe.

"Of course." She rolled up the right sleeve of her dress.

"Will you tell them what we are testing for?"

"I never lie to them, Kieran."

As I tied the tube around her arm, hoping that my fingers would not tremble, I pushed up the sleeve of her dress. I caught a glimpse on her upper arm of what looked like a deep bruise. I pretended not to notice it. Before I had a chance to judiciously weigh the evidence, my street instinct had confirmed a suspicion: Kathleen had been battered by her husband, a husband who was engaged in risky sex with other men.

"You understand that we recommend four tests—one every three months—for anyone who has been exposed to the virus?"

Her shoulders slumped. "Really?"

"I'm afraid so." I injected the needle into her vein, skillfully if I do say so myself.

"You're pretty good at that."

"Maybe just lucky." I applied the traditional ball of cotton and Band-Aid.

She rolled down her sleeve and stood up. "I suppose you wonder why I chose you."

I removed her coat from the hook behind the door. "No questions asked."

She went ahead and answered the question I refused to ask. "Because I trust you. We're public figures; my husband, as you know, is running for the Senate. It would be very hard to keep these tests secret."

"I understand."

She slid her arms into the sleeves of the soggy coat which I held for her. "I knew I could trust you."

"That's a change of mind, isn't it?"

As soon as I said those words I regretted them.

She turned away from me, her head down.

"If it is, I was wrong before. . . . I'll see you tomorrow, Kieran. Same time?"

"Same time . . . with Megan, Maeve, and Brigid?"

"You've got it."

She walked into the outer office without turning back toward me.

"See you tomorrow," I said.

"Thank you, Kieran," she said with a catch in her voice. "Thank you very much."

After she had left, I collapsed into my chair, swiveled it around, and stared out the window. The rain continued to beat down with angry fury on the trees in Grant Park. I was not to ask questions of her, but there was no tribal code against wondering to myself.

I had left Chicago a long time ago, swearing that I would come back and reclaim my reputation and my woman. The reputation was now unimportant. I was a tenured member of the Department of Psychiatry at the University of Illinois, a Fellow of the Institute for Juvenile Research, a Training Analyst of the Chicago Institute of Psychoanalysis, author of more than two score professional papers, and two well-reviewed monographs on the use of self-hypnosis in the psychoanalytic treatment of the young.

Whatever had happened, or was alleged to have happened, on that Labor Day weekend at Grand Beach in 1972, was long since forgotten, most of the time even by me.

My redheaded woman was another matter. As the lightning cut across the dark sky above Lake Michigan, splitting it into jagged fragments that could easily fall apart, I decided that I might want her as badly as I ever did.

I had long told myself that she was irrelevant too. Only now, worried, fragile, appealing, she didn't seem irrelevant at all. I still wanted her. I had deceived myself all along, as my own training analyst at Cornell Medical Center had insisted. My denials, he'd told me, were repressions.

He was right, damn him.

I tried to shed my hasty conclusion as to Kathleen's apparent troubles and considered the evidence anew: rib injury, massive bruise on her arm, AIDS tests. What did they mean?

Careful analysis only confirmed what my street instinct told me. Kathleen would not be the kind of woman who would play around outside her home. So the injury and the threat of AIDS must be Brien's doing.

A man who is inclined to beat his wife is especially likely to do so when he is under great stress. According to the papers, Brien was about to run for the United States Senate. That would mean tremendous stress. Arguably, Kathleen was in grave danger. Women had died in lesser danger.

The next day, as promised, Kathleen returned with her brood of red-haired maidens. Her daughters, aged sixteen, fourteen, and twelve, seemed to be sweet and vulnerable young women with shy smiles. They were much more diffident than I remembered their mother being at the same ages. Their hair was as red as hers, and the bodies of the older two as well developed, but their eyes were green, a deep but gentle green, instead of the icy blue as were hers.

"Good afternoon, young persons," I said with my own shy grin that seems to work with kids.

"Good afternoon, Doctor O'Kerrigan," they replied in chorus.

The rain had swept out the night before. The autumn reds and golds of the Park under a shimmering blue sky seemed an appropriate background for so much young loveliness.

Their mother beamed proudly, as well she might.

"Brigid, why don't we try you first? You look like the bravest of the lot." I led her into my office, leaving the other three Donahue women in the waiting room.

Although I have no kids of my own, I'm good with children and teenagers—perhaps because I don't have any. Or perhaps because I've never grown up, I'm also a pushover, as I found when I taught Junior High during my training analysis. I have to watch it when I'm treating kids. I'm especially sympathetic to young women between the ages of ten and sixteen. I find their energy, enthusiasm, and hope—none of which are yet blighted by experience—quite irresistible. I feel sad when I see them bounding enthusiastically down the street on the way home from school because I realize how much suffering lies ahead for most of them.

"Do they call you Brigie?" I asked the twelve-year-old twisting nervously on my chair, a child about to burst into full womanly bloom.

She grinned and nodded.

"Never Biddy?"

She shook her head and frowned as if to say, "Who ever heard of such a silly name."

I rolled up the sleeve of her parochial-school blouse. "Did you know that long ago 'Biddy' or even 'Bridie' were what people called young women named Brigid?"

An expression of candid disbelief, as she looked away from the syringe I was preparing.

"There is even a song about a girl named Biddy Donahue. I suppose we could change it to Brigie:

"*Brigie Donahue,*
I really do love You!
Though you live in Beverly
To You I will be true!
Brigie Donahue,
I'll tell you what I'll do,
If You change your name to O'Kerrigan,
I'll change mine to Donahue!"

I made up the stanzas as I went along. I reached the second chorus just as I slipped the needle into her thin vein. She joined in with a lovely young soprano voice.

> *"Brigie Donahue*
> *I'll tell you what I'll do,*
> *If I change my name to O'Kerrigan*
> *You'll change yours to Donahue!"*

We sang all the way to the door and were greeted with applause by her mother and sisters.

Kathleen's smile was radiant. Could it be for me? We had sung love duets for many years, and although we'd only been acting out parts in school musicals, we actually meant the scripted words we sang.

But that was long before I left Chicago and before she married Brien Donahue.

"I'm Maeve," said the second sister. She instantly struck me as being more her mother's daughter; she was much more self-possessed than Brigid.

"I know that," I said. "It means passionate."

"I know *that*. . . . Did Mom tell you that Brigie sings?"

"No way."

"How did you know?" Her soft green eyes considered me, not suspiciously but very carefully.

"I'm good at guessing."

"Megie is on the Saint Ignatius basketball team." She rolled up the sleeve of her blouse. "They lost the championship to Mother McAuley last year, but they think they're going to win this year."

"She'll know you know you told me."

"No, she won't."

When I put the needle into her arm, she didn't so much as flinch.

"Thank you for the tip," I said, dabbing the spot. "Do you play basketball, Maeve?" Maeve shook her head. "I do Taekwando. You know, Korean Karate. I can break a two-inch-thick board with a kick. I'm a black belt."

Somehow, it didn't surprise me.

Sixteen-year-old Megan proved the loquacious one.

"Are you guys going to beat McAuley this year?"

"We're going to totally destroy them. I've already warned my mom; when we're finished, there'll be nothing left of her alma mater."

"And she said?" I tied the tube around her arm and she twisted uncomfortably.

"Well, she's like loyal, but she's more loyal to her family than to her old school . . . ouch."

"Sorry."

"Well, it didn't hurt much . . . anyway, my mom plays twenty-one sometimes with us when the boys are around. They flirt with her."

Somehow I wasn't surprised.

I said goodbye to Kathleen and her brood with a heavy heart. When I'd had her by herself she was a woman whom I had lost, one who had been unfairly taken from me. With her daughters, she was a mother and a wife whose familial ties I had no right to trespass.

I had once promised Kathleen that I would protect her always. For all her intelligence and determination, Kathleen had seemed then to require protection. I hadn't been able to keep my promise as things turned out, but then there was no statute of limitations on that kind of bargain. With Kathleen's unexpected arrival on my doorstep and her even less anticipated request for a personal favor, maybe I would at last get a chance to make good on my promise of long ago.

KIERAN

We all knew that the Donahues and the Learys were moving into the north end of the neighborhood, the "Ravine"—prehistoric sand dunes from an earlier Lake Michigan—squeezed against the south fringes of the Ryan's Woods Forest Preserve. We were already calling their homes, one in back of the other two, "the Compound" in imitation of the Kennedys.

"They're not Harvard types," my father said with his usual gentle smile, "but they are the best we Chicagoans can do in the way of an Irish political aristocracy."

"I feel sorry for them." Mom looked up from her book. "It must be difficult to be prisoners of that sort of tradition."

"Do they fool around sexually as much as the Kennedys do?" I demanded.

Both my parents laughed. It was impossible for me to shock them, no matter how hard I tried.

"I'm sure they're as prudish as the rest of the Chicago Irish." Dad laughed.

"As some of them anyway," Mom said.

They both blushed slightly.

"How come they don't hold political office like the Kennedys?" I asked.

"Jim Lenihan was state senator for a while," Mom observed, putting a finger in place in her book and closing—a sign that we were to have a conversation. "And Marty O'Brien was a county judge before he died."

"Small-time." I snapped my fingers.

"It's not for want of trying." Dad closed his book too, putting a bookmark in place. "Somehow they don't manage to win."

"Don't make no waves, don't back no losers," I observed, citing the title of a book about Chicago politics.

"In Chicago"—Mom removed her thick glasses—"we don't tend to vote for aristocrats, especially when they're only a generation ahead of the rest of us."

"The Kennedys weren't much better than that," I said.

"Sometimes"—Dad leaned back in his vast easy chair—"I think they're too clever by half, always plotting for political influence, but never making the decisive move."

"Unlike Dick Daley, who will be mayor forever."

"And who is not an aristocrat." Mom laughed. "For which thank God."

"Yes, he is," Dad replied. "He courted Sis by taking her to the opera. He reads history and biography and Dickens to his kids at night. The difference between him and Jim Lenihan's bunch is that he doesn't think of himself as an aristocrat."

"They tend to be snobs." Mom put her glasses back on. "I know some people say that because of envy, but I think it's pretty true."

"They drink too much." Dad closed his eyes as if imagining our new neighbors bending their elbows. "Especially Red Hugh O'Leary, as he calls himself. Yet he's the most likable one of the lot. Finest criminal lawyer in town."

"I'd drink too." Mom opened her book. "If I lived with that woman."

"Mae?" Dad opened his eyes.

"Of course not, she's pretty and sweet. That terrible mother of hers, Maud."

"The last of the great Irish puritans," Dad added and picked up his book. "All the children are older than you, are they not, Kieran?"

I was named after the Irish saint, his name pronounced KEY-ron, on whose feast I was born, a real saint despite the nuns in school, who had never heard of him and were skeptical even when I brought in the missal printed in Dublin and showed them the feast.

Kieran—or Cyrnan or Ciernan—was founder of the abbey of Clonmacnoise, if you please, and he had a pet dun cow after whom the monastic manuscript called *The Book of the Dun Cow* was named. He died in his middle thirties, an ill omen, I sometimes thought.

"I believe"—Mom looked up from the book—"there's one grammar-school child still, in your grade, I think, Kieran. A cute little redhead who sings."

"All we need," I protested loudly, "is a cute little redhead who sings. . . . If she plays volleyball it might be another matter."

So it was for the cute little redhead that I was looking when I wandered by the Compound the next morning after Mass.

There were nine of them standing around in front of Jim Lenihan's sprawling house, five Learys and four Donahues, tall, handsome, self-satisfied young men and women. One of the girls, Mary Anne Leary, I would learn later, was not especially attractive, but she compensated for it, or so it seemed that brisk late-summer day, by her poise and self-possession.

Standing apart from the others, hands on hips as if considering the whole situation with fastidious dismay, was the "cute little redhead."

I fell in love with her on the spot.

Heaven help me, I have never quite recovered from that reaction.

So I did some research on her and lay in wait for her the first day of school. I carried her books that day, a faithful slave for an Irish queen.

A frightened and fragile queen, terrified that her new classmates wouldn't like her.

So she needed a knight protector as well as faithful slave.

Her gratitude when I assured her that we'd like her melted my already lovestruck heart.

"They'll adore you, Kathleen Mavoureen. You'll be the queen of the class within a week."

"Don't be silly," she said, pleased but still anxious.

"I'll bet on it."

"Really?" She seemed to relax. "Why?"

"Because you're sweet and good."

"I am NOT." She blushed furiously. "I'm a little bitch."

"All right, you are a little bitch."

"I am NOT . . . and I'm not consistent either."

We both laughed and in that laughter our love affair began.

How could I have ever lost her?

I'm fascinated by the difference between our self-images and our reality. Kathleen Leary saw herself as tough, outspoken, independent. In fact she was sweet and fragile and gentle—a truth that everyone in the class knew after the second day.

"Isn't she nice, Kieran?" Jenny Cahill asked me.

"Tough little bitch," I replied with a dismissive wave of my hand.

"She is NOT."

"I know, but that's what she thinks she is."

"She's the sweetest girl I've ever.known."

"Hot-tempered redhead."

"I think you like her already."

"No way."

"You can't kid me, Kieran Patrick O'Kerrigan!"

I never could kid Jenny.

Kathleen Leary was a fierce competitor who did not like to lose. During a close volleyball game, her blue eyes hard with determination, her maroon St. Praxides uniform soaked with sweat, her compact and curving body tense and poised for battle, she did look like a warrior queen.

And sent my imagination running wildly and my heart beating furiously.

But after the game was over and we had won, which we did with disgusting regularity, she would chat with the girls on the losing team, hug some of them, and win them over with her grace.

Such savvy came to her as naturally as breathing.

She should run for president, I thought.

She did run for president of every class she was ever in and always won easily, the last of the politicians in the Lenihan Compound.

And the most effective.

"Great game, Kathleen Mavoureen," I'd say to her, uneasy and embarrassed as I always was in her presence.

"Oh, thanks, Kieran." We'd shake hands. "And thanks for coming and cheering for us."

"Wouldn't miss it for the world."

Kathleen in sweat-drenched T-shirt and gym shorts was something not to miss.

"The other team played well."

"Almost too well."

"Not quite," she'd grin impishly.

"And you were gracious to them after the game was over."

"That's called sportsmanship, silly."

I suppose it would be sportspersonship these days.

"You're very good at it."

"They're nice girls. I don't hate them except during the game. They might be neighbors or friends when we grow up."

"Or voters."

"Weird little boy." She would wave me away and then head for the showers, if there were showers in the gym.

Then, careful not to hurt my feelings, she would add, "It was really very nice of you to come."

I was a voter too.

And a lover.

LEARY

Martin Roder, Vicar for the Clergy, shifted his massive bulk in the chair across from my desk. "Father McNulty is not a very good priest, Bishop Leary. As I told him, himself, he is selfish and demoralizes other priests."

Most of the staff at the Pastoral Center don't call me "Bishop." I'm "James" to them or, if the Cardinal is present, "Jim." The Boss thinks that's my name and I don't bother telling him that it's a nickname I detest.

Martin is a pious, dedicated, hardworking priest, but not what one would call flexible. The Cardinal appointed him as Vicar for the Clergy because of his loyalty and his popularity with other priests. It's not an appointment I would have made if it had been up to me.

"I hope you didn't say that to him, Martin."

If he had, and I was pretty sure he had, he had violated in one fell swoop all qualities of prudence, charity, and truth.

"And you know what he said? He said that we tolerate drunks and loafers and active gays and we should leave him alone unless we were willing to specify in writing why he was worse than they are."

"And you replied?"

Martin was only about one-third as quick-witted as Brendan McNulty.

"I told him he was violating canon law by appearing as a lawyer in a suit against the Church!" Martin's mouth curled into a frown of disdain.

"I understand," I said with a sigh. I would have to hear Martin out. I hoped that it wouldn't take him much longer to vent his frustration with Brendan McNulty. I had yet to prepare my invocation for the Ireland Fund Dinner that night. It was an important event, honoring our old family friends Tom and Sheila Donahue. Moreover—and this was the reason Sheila had arranged for the award to herself and her husband—it would serve as an informal launching pad for the senatorial candidacy of their son and my lifelong friend Brien Donahue, one of the finest Catholic laymen I have ever known.

Moreover, I had received a tip from a trade union official that some of the laymen on our staff were accepting kickbacks from nonunion contractors. I didn't believe the charge, but I would have to investigate. The Archdiocese has a sorry history of such corruption among trusted laymen. I had hoped there would be time to begin to investigate the matter that afternoon.

"I have these terrible dilemmas," Martin continued doggedly. "I'm supposed to protect the rights of the accused priest and at the same time defend the alleged victim. How am I supposed to do that, how am I supposed to get treatment for the priest and get him back into his work, if another priest, who does not have permission from the Cardinal to be a lawyer, appears on the side of the enemy in a civil suit?"

"Enemy?"

"The parents of the alleged victim."

"I wouldn't call them the enemy, Martin."

"We know that their son was not victimized. His is a case of child neglect, not pedophilia."

"I understand."

In this particular instance Martin might well be right. Our psychiatrical consultants, I had been told, had given Gerry Greene a clean bill of health. We would be much better off, however, if Martin were not so dogmatic about everything. But he was the sort of priest to view the world and all that transpired in it as a contrast of extremes: black and white, good and evil. Everything was clear to a man with no self-doubt like our Vicar for the Clergy.

"I told him we need priests for parish work," Martin continued grimly. "We can't permit them to pursue other careers in this time of dire shortage."

"And he said?"

"That I wouldn't have approved of St. Paul making tents."

"I understand he does a lot of work out of St. Praxides, much more than the pastor in fact."

"Misery" Casey, the Pastor of St. Praxides, spent most of his time on vacation or playing gin rummy at the Beverly Country Club.

"That's not the point, Bishop," Martin insisted. "He's not a full-time parish priest. I told him that all the other priests are saying that he studied law and practices it because he wants to escape from real priestly work."

"I see."

"In the Cardinal's name I forbade him to continue on the case."

"I don't think that was such a good idea, Martin. We don't accomplish much in the Church these days by giving orders."

"I confronted him with this letter that was sent to the Cardinal."

He handed the letter over to me. It was unsigned, naturally. Most critical missives from purportedly concerned parishioners were sent anonymously.

"Someone at the party asked Father McNulty about whether the liturgies that some nuns were presiding over were really valid masses. And he said that in God's eyes they were probably as valid as a Mass said by a drunken pedophile priest. He shouldn't have said anything like that, Bishop." Martin pounded his fist against his thigh. "Those kind of remarks shock the laity."

"And Brendan refused to respond to the anonymous letter?" I asked, already suspecting the answer.

"Absolutely. He said the Cardinal should tear up all anonymous letters."

Good advice. And the kind of remark that Brendan McNulty might have made—"Half fun and full earnest," as my father, Hugh Leary, would have said.

"He says that if we don't deal with the 'pedophile epidemic' as he calls it, there will be a tremendous scandal in the Archdiocese. Bishop, there isn't an epidemic." He began to tick off his guidelines on his fingers. "We send men back to parish work only if they have been cleared by the police and the Department of Children and Family Services and only if we don't find the accusations credible, and only if the consultants say there's no firm evidence of perversion. There can't be a scandal if we stick to these guidelines I worked out with you and the Cardinal, can there?"

Sure, guidelines prevent scandal. And laws prevent crime. If I had my way I would make Brendan McNulty Vicar for the Clergy.

"Let's hope there's no grave scandal," I said.

"And he hints at some silly nonsense about Satanic cults!"

"Involving priests? That doesn't sound like Brendan at all."

"You have to do something about him, Bishop. He won't listen to me."

"I'll talk to him, Martin." I sighed again.

That's all an auxiliary bishop does these days—talk to people, or rather listen to them.

"I wish you would, Bishop. I find him impossible to deal with."

I smoothed Martin's ruffled feathers as best I could. Without promising to do anything, I managed to persuade him that we were of one mind and that I, too, would attempt to restrain the errant McNulty. And I would, too, though in my own way.

Although I believe the Church could use more priests as bright if perhaps not as plain speaking as Brendan McNulty, I shared Martin's wish that he would focus his intelligence and zeal on some other problem besides the victimization—alleged victimization as our lawyers have taught me to say—of children by priests.

We have a serious problem in the Church with priests who are also pedophiles. It is not as serious as the national media make it seem. It's a problem that affects only a handful of priests, but as few as a case or two a year costs the Archdiocese an enormous amount in legal fees and settlements.

There have always been sexually active priests in the Church—straights and gays—bishops, popes, and even some who eventually became saints, as far as that goes. Some priests have violated their celibacy vows. Most have not. And then there are some priests who have preyed on children.

Most gay men, I repeated to myself, are not pedophiles. It's a completely separate issue psychologically. Most pedophiles are not gay, though most priests who prey on children, for some reason, pursue males instead of females.

"Fine," I said aloud to myself. "I have it all down. I know exactly what to say. But we can't keep these cases out of the papers and off TV forever, especially not when our brightest young priests are on the other side."

I would have to talk to Brendan McNulty myself, I resolved. I'd have to try to persuade him to sit this case out. I only hoped that Martin Roder's ill-tempered remarks hadn't already pushed him beyond the brink of forbearance. Priests like Brendan were too important for us to risk driving them out of the priesthood.

BRIEN

Dear God, I am glad I made it back to the washroom here at the law office before I vomited. The smell and the filth in those high-rises are unbearable. It's not right that men and women would have to live that way. So much suffering, kids my daughters' ages with two children already. Thirty-five-year-old grandmothers. Drugs, rape, and murder are all commonplace. How can anyone live like that?

I'm going to vomit again.

There's too much pressure in my life as it is. It keeps building up and building up. I feel that I'm almost out of control.

The stress is killing me. I can't take it anymore. Something inside me is tearing me apart. I knew when I took this advisory job with the Housing Authority that my stomach would rebel. Mom and James insisted that I take it. They're right that it's good public exposure. Maybe I can do something to help the poor people in those projects. I want to do that, even more than I want to be elected to the Senate. Why should my life be so good when theirs is so bad?

But I won't help anyone by vomiting into a television camera.

KATHLEEN

I could not have told Kieran that my life had ended at five o'clock in the afternoon the night of the Ireland Fund Dinner Dance.

It had been a hard day at the University as I struggled to narrow down the focus of my dissertation with little help from my pompous dissertation committee member—who did not believe that an attractive mother of three was appropriate scholar material, not at *the* University anyway. He had been more interested in trying to catch my eye than in listening to my theories of the history of the Irish-Americans in Chicago politics.

I was tired but I didn't have time for a nap. But the dance would be fun. I'd get my second wind. My husband's parents would be honored and that would make them happy, my brother the Bishop would tell his unfunny jokes and my husband and I would come home and make love, an activity which was more than a little overdue.

So, tired or not, I looked forward to the evening. I had taken off my suit and had hung it up in the closet, deciding I'd have to make do with a quick shower instead of a long nap. I had just reached back to unhook my bra when the phone rang.

Until that moment I would have said that I was a reasonably happy woman, wife, mother, and scholar in the making. I had three lovely daughters of whom I was terribly proud; I lived in a nice home in Beverly and spent the summer in an equally nice home in Grand Beach; I drove my own Mercedes 350; my husband, kind in his own bumbling, self-obsessed way, was better than most men in our crowd, at least when he was sober; he was running, informally so far, for the United States Senate, a job at which he would be reasonably good, considering the potential opposition; I was studying for a Ph.D. in history so I could do something useful with my life once Brigie went off to college. What more could a woman ask for? It was not what I had expected from life, but it was a lot more than many of my friends had.

Then, with a single phone call, it all collapsed, the whole house of cards came tumbling down. Only then did I realize how total my self-deception had been.

"Mrs. Donahue," said the hoarse male voice.

I was surprised not to recognize the voice of someone calling on my private line. "Yes?" I replied.

"I suppose you think your husband is going to fuck you tonight."

"Who is this?" I said, terrified.

The caller ignored my question and went on to describe, in the most excruciating detail, a specific act my husband had a habit of engaging in whenever we were intimate. Still stunned, I managed to cry, "What do you want?" But the caller had his own agenda.

"The last time he fucked you was after the dance at your Club, wasn't it? He can only get it up for you when he's had too much to drink, isn't that true?"

"Who are you?"

"Even then it has to be pretty rough sometimes, doesn't it? Course, you don't mind it rough, do you? You kind of like to be pushed around, huh?"

"Why are you calling?"

"I just want you to know I've fucked him fifty times since you have!"

"You're insane!"

"Insane, huh? Well, let me describe exactly what he did to you last time!"

He then recounted a detailed, explicit—and utterly vile—description of my words and actions in the advanced state of sexual arousal, a portrait of my pleasure that only my husband could have given him.

The truth stung me with its utter plausibility as only the truth can. Years of infrequent sex with Brien suddenly could be explained: the whole time Brien had been engaged in sex with another partner, maybe many partners. Through the years of our marriage I had occasionally wondered if there was another woman in Brien's life. Never had I suspected there was another man.

I remember clinging to the receiver for a full minute or two after I'd stopped listening. The caller continued to speak, but whether he filled me in on additional details of my marital relations or details of his own intimate contact with Brien, I couldn't say. I'd heard enough, more than enough. I couldn't take it anymore. For a few moments, I forgot to breathe. When at last I took a gasp of air, I smashed the receiver into the phone. When the phone began to ring less than a minute later, I picked it up and hung up again without checking to see who it was.

Forgetting, for the moment, my shower, I went over to my bed and lay down. My head was spinning. Brien's and my lovemaking became clear. All too clear. Somehow he never seemed attracted to me. He'd never felt that desperate pull of allure other men seemed to feel for their women. For a long time I'd thought the problem was me. Wasn't I pretty enough? Sexy enough? With maturity I'd come to realize that I wasn't at fault. Brien was just Brien. Some men just had weaker libidos and Brien was one of them. I could learn to live with that. But now the horror of betrayal—a betrayal so complete—of what I had regarded, until that phone call, as my happy, content life.

As the initial shock began to wear off, I felt a surge of rage. I took it as a healthy sign. I still had enough self-esteem to feel that I deserved better treatment than this. Then I thought of our girls. I couldn't live with Brien anymore, that much I knew. But how would my three little redheads feel about being separated from their daddy? How would they react to divorce?

Thinking of them made me consider other risks. Had Brien jeopardized his health and mine by engaging in risky sexual behavior? I hoped to God not. A day ago I would have said it would be impossible, but then, a day ago I would have sworn that Brien was as faithful to me as I had always been to him. With a resolve even I felt was steely, I decided to get an AIDS test in quick order. At the same time, I'd get one for my girls. Oh, I knew it was extremely unlikely that any of them could have contracted the virus even if both Brien and I had it. But I also knew I would never feel completely safe until I knew for sure. A mother is entitled to be a little overcautious, after all. Until this moment I had prided myself on not being the hysterical sort. But with the real terrain of my marriage suddenly so baldly revealed, I'd been knocked off my usual even keel. So I would indulge myself in the AIDS test, ease my mind on one subject.

Fearing AIDS, irrational though it was—at least as far as my girls were concerned—put me in the proper frame of mind. I had to be a grown-up. I had to form a plan. I would say nothing to Brien about what I had learned until after the dinner. There was no rush. I would have to think through my demands.

It was hard to believe that I'd as much as settled on a divorce. Until this evening, divorce had always struck me as being something for other people, certainly not for me. For a brief instant I was tempted to pretend I had never received that phone call, that I'd not heard the searing truth about the man I called my husband. But I'm not the sort to keep up appearances that way. I'm not made of that kind of mettle—luckily, probably. But as I forced myself into the shower and began to compose my plan, lucky wasn't exactly the way I was feeling.

I found myself wondering if I'd be able to find another man after Brien and I parted. On balance, I decided that I was probably still attractive enough and certainly wealthy enough to get the cream of the available crop, which might not be all that creamy. But I'd tried marriage once and wasn't inclined to try again.

I thought briefly about Kieran. How had it gone wrong between us? Could something still be salvaged of our eight years of love?

That's when I decided that I was a complete fool. As the hot water sprayed hard against me, I tried to drive all nostalgic whimsy from my brain. Brien was running for the United States Senate. He could hardly afford the scandal of a messy divorce. I was hesitant to rob him of his shot at getting into office. Despite the sham of our marriage, I still knew that Brien Donahue was a caring man, a sensitive man. He wasn't as sharp-witted and conniving as so many of his fellow political aspirants were, but I'd always felt that what he lacked in savvy was greatly compensated for by what he had in heart. Though this particular evening I was loath to admit it, I still knew that the U.S. Senate would be a better place if Brien was in it.

Both Brien's family and mine had long thrilled on the notion that if Clarence Wagner hadn't died in 1954, Dick Daley would not have been elected chairman of the Cook County Democratic Committee, and the Donahues and the Learys would have been the kingmakers of Chicago politics for the rest of the century. In Brien's candidacy for the U.S. Senate, both the Donahues and Learys saw a chance to grab the political mantle they felt fate had cheated them out of. The aspirations of both our families rested with Brien.

Sheila Donahue, Brien's mother, had groomed her son for political candidacy. Throughout his life the strong-willed woman had steered him to choices that could only enhance his image once he finally did find an office for which to run. Some of Brien's assets—his blond good looks, his great build—came by genetics. The rest of the package—Notre Dame football star, a year at the London School of Economics, experience in the law as well as from serving on several important commissions and boards—were as much an inheritance, thanks to his mother, as well.

Brien Thomas Donahue had come to be, through careful manipulation, just what the Yuppie and suburban Democrats were looking for: an articulate and telegenic, fiscally responsible liberal with interesting ideas, a nondogmatic Catholic (Brien was pro-choice) who had some understanding of foreign policy and deep roots in Illinois (not just Chicago).

Rounding out the picture was me, a devoted wife with her own political pedigree, and our three lovely daughters.

Objectively, Brien had a fighting chance at getting elected, particularly if Rich Daley did a little more than hint at his support. If he backed Brien, there would be no primary race and my husband would have a fighting chance against the dull Republican incumbent next year. I'd have put the odds at three to two in Brien's favor.

For all his mother's conniving and ambition, Brien really was more than just another suit. He did indeed care about the minorities and the poor all around the world. He was indeed a liberal Catholic; he could even, on occasion, sound like a feminist. He had enough understanding of fiscal policy to get the kind of advisers who could explain a budget to him.

None of his convictions ran very deep, but they were sincerely held as far as they went. He was quick on his feet after he had been properly prepared with deft answers, and exuded honesty and charm. Some political columnists had fun comparing his syntax to Rich Daley's. You always knew where Brien Donahue stands, they said, while with the Mayor you needed a couple of clarifications from his press secretary and even then you might not be sure.

I knew that public discussion of a divorce at this time would as good as scotch his chances at getting elected, perhaps even at winning a primary. The instant a flaw like a failing marriage became public record, Democratic challengers would undoubtedly surface. So much for the dynastic aspirations of the Donahues and Learys!

Although that mischievous streak that runs so deep in me was tempted to thwart Brien's candidacy just to spite our power-hungry families, I knew deep in my heart I couldn't jeopardize his chances. I couldn't honestly say that Brien T. Donahue was Illinois' last best hope, but he was certainly the best man in the field for the U.S. Senate. Despite his personal failings as a husband, he would still be that rare, caring politician. I knew that whatever I decided to do, I'd not do anything too rash before the election. I guess politics was deep in my blood, too.

But even if I played the part of the good, loyal wife through to November—as I knew I could—what would the terms of our marriage in the privacy of our own home be? That is what I had to determine. As far as negotiations went, I was in the catbird seat. Brien would have to agree to my rules if he wanted my public cooperation. I just had to settle on what it was I really wanted, both for me and my three girls. Ever since that phone call, I had a hard time thinking of my daughters as anything but "my" girls, not "ours."

I was still mulling over the situation when Brien entered our bedroom.

"How were the Henry Horner Homes?" I asked.

"Pretty terrible. We've got to do something about them. . . ."

"Easier said than done."

He wasn't even looking at me, though I still hadn't dressed. How could I ever have persuaded myself that he found me sexually attractive?

"At the housing project this afternoon, the reporters asked me today about the report on more runways for O'Hare."

The politician in me triumphed over the outraged wife.

"How did you respond?"

"I said I understood how bad the noise was in the suburbs, but that I had concerns about flight safety and the costs of delays and called for more study."

"You didn't say that O'Hare was vital not only to Chicago but to the whole region?"

"No." With that, he went into the bathroom and closed the door.

Of course not. No one had planted that sentence in your head beforehand.

I sat at my vanity naked and ashamed. How could I have let myself come to this point? Most men found me alluring. My husband did not.

As I dressed for the dance, I thought about the other love of my life, maybe the only real love, the one I had lost.

I could still remember our first tentative kiss back in the early summer of 1964.

KATHLEEN
1964

"Don't be afraid, Kathleen." Kieran's arms, surprisingly strong, encompassed me firmly. "I won't hurt you. I'd never hurt you."

"I'm not afraid," I said, even though I was quivering and my knees, always my weak point when I was scared, were turning to mush.

We were in the outdoor stairwell leading to the basement of a Dutch Colonial house on Hamilton Avenue. We had been consigned to this secret place, as twilight turned to dusk, by a kissing game at one of our eighth grade graduation parties, two weeks of mild depravity—beer and "making out"—marking our rite of passage from grammar school to high school. The phonograph inside was playing music from "Hello, Dolly!" I remember the sound like I heard it yesterday.

"You are too." He laughed gently. "And so am I and we won't argue about who is more scared."

"All right," I gulped. "And I know you won't hurt me."

"I love you, Kathleen," he said solemnly, "I'll always love you. I'll always take care of you."

That was a bit too much for my early adolescent woman's body and soul to take. Always? That was a long time. I was concerned only about the kiss in which we were about to engage.

"Just tonight will do," I giggled.

"Tonight and forever."

I didn't know much about boys, less than many of the other girls in the class, none of whom were as good as I was at pretending that I knew all about them. But I did know that Kieran O'Kerrigan was a strange boy. No ordinary boy talked about "forever" at an eighth grade party.

He drew me closer or I drew him closer or whatever and we began our kiss, a tentative exploration of two sets of lips, both of which wondered what the other would be like.

I was trembling. He didn't seem to be.

He was, I realized as our lips met, a skillful kisser, much better than I was. Kieran, our class had joked, was not good at much of anything except studies and being nice.

He was also a good kisser and probably with no more experience than I had, which was precious little.

"Oh, Kieran," I sighed as our lips parted, "that was nice!"

"Only the beginning." He now gathered me firmly against himself. "I've been wanting to do this since the first day I saw you."

The second kiss was sweet and gentle and then became firm, challenging, demanding. I collapsed against him in a kind of preliminary surrender.

"Wow!" he said.

"As good as you'd thought I'd be." I fought to control my voice.

"Always the competitor." He laughed. "But you're astonishing, Kathleen Anne Leary, just astonishing. Eight and a half."

"Ten," I insisted.

We laughed together, nervously but happily, satisfied with ourselves and our tentative transition toward greater sexual maturity.

He released me and helped me down the steps toward the basement door and back into the party.

I'll never forget the kiss. Never. I can still taste its richness now.

"Before we open the door and face the hoots and hollers of our disgusting classmates, Kathleen Anne, I meant what I said." He brushed his lips against mine. "I'll always take care of you. I'll always be your friend."

I determined then and there that someday he'd be my husband.

I met Kieran for the first time when I was walking down Hoyne Avenue toward St. Praxides, laden with all my books for eighth grade, cool and defiant in my external attitude toward my initial encounter with the snobs in St. Praxides eighth grade.

My knees were preparing to betray me, but I'd never let on. I'd show them. I'd let them know that I didn't give a hoot about the whole eighth grade class at St. Praxides.

And their parents. And Beverly Country Club. And the 19th Ward. And anything else they thought important.

I had absolutely refused a ride to school. I was not about to arrive for my first day in a chauffeur-driven Lincoln Continental. However, the books were heavy and I wasn't sure I'd make it all the way to St. Praxides without dropping them.

I could see myself crying in fury and rage if I did that.

This funny-looking boy, short, sandy-haired, skinny with a weird smile, suddenly appeared next to me.

"You're the new kid?" he said.

"So what if I am?" I demanded defiantly.

"I'm Kieran O'Kerrigan."

"That's a dumb name. It rhymes with moron."

Real charmer, the little redhead, huh?

"I admit that 'Kathleen Anne' is prettier. Kathleen rhymes with mavoureen."

"Humpf," I snorted. This creep had no right to know my name, much less to add what I dimly suspected was an Irish endearment. "Are you in sixth grade or something?"

"I'm in your class." He chuckled, not at all offended.

"Boy, am I the lucky one!"

"You don't have to worry about the other kids . . ."

"I'm not worried about them," I announced fiercely. "I don't give a shit about them."

"Give me some of your books." He reached over and grabbed the top layer.

"I will NOT. Boys don't carry girls' books anymore."

"This boy does, at least when the girl is a pretty and frightened redhead on her first day in a new school."

There was no way I could fight him off. If he wanted to carry the books, all right, let him carry them.

"Creep," I muttered.

"They're prepared to like you," he said. "All their relatives over in South Shore say you are a real neat girl and that you don't have the hot temper that you pretend to have."

I felt very embarrassed, like he had taken off some of my clothes.

I also felt enormously relieved.

I would show neither feeling.

"They lie," I said haughtily.

Then my good humor took over. "Actually I'm a terrible, hateful bitch!"

We both laughed at that. He laughed first and I couldn't resist his laugh.

I was never able to resist it.

"The girls will all like you," he continued, "even if they resent you, because you're the kind of kid that's always popular and they'll want to be on your side. They also have heard that you're good at volleyball and they need one more killer for their team. The guys will like you because . . ."

"Because why?" I prepared to blow up again.

"Because you're so sweet and kind and patient and soft-spoken."

We laughed together for the second time.

I decided that maybe this kid wasn't a creep after all. He was still weird.

And Kieran *did* rhyme with moron. But I never said that again.

What would they think when I walked into the schoolyard with this weird character in tow?

He was right about the warm welcome.

"Ladies and gentlemen," he announced, "I present to you the secret weapon for our championship volleyball team, fresh from triumphs in South Shore, Miss Kathleen Anne Marie Leary . . . Miss Leary, the eighth grade of St. Praxides, eagerly awaiting your reactions to us."

They applauded!

"Who is that weird boy?" I asked one of my new friends, Jenny Cahill, when Kieran had drifted away.

"Him? Oh, that's Kieran. He IS weird, but he's also kind of neat. Everyone likes him."

"What does he DO?"

"You mean sports? Kieran isn't good at anything, except schoolwork. He makes fun of himself a lot. Well, I take it back. He's awfully good at being nice."

"Yeah," I said. "Why?"

She shrugged. "I guess because he likes it. My daddy says if Kieran isn't running for office he should."

"He is STRANGE!"

"Oh, sure, but he's kinda cute, isn't he?"

I considered her suggestion. Yes he was kinda cute. My heart jumped a beat. Very cute as a matter of fact.

"I suppose so."

I glanced across the schoolyard. Kieran was talking to a group of boys, all of whom were looking at me.

I strode over to them, ready for battle. As I suspected, Kieran, still carrying my surplus books, was making fun of me.

"Then she said," he sounded like me and he had twisted his face so he looked like me when I was telling someone off, "Who is this weird boy? Is he a sixth grader or something?"

I was breathing very rapidly, more to keep from laughing than to control my temper.

"I did NOT say weird," I insisted, hands on hips in my most authoritative manner.

Laughter from the boy animals.

"You thought it!"

Perfectly true, but how did he know?

"What I THOUGHT, Mr. Mind-bugger," I shouted, pretending to be furious, "was who is this weird, pushy, obnoxious little boy who is nice enough to carry my books?"

Then, my face as hot as a boiling tea kettle, I turned on my heel and walked away.

The universal laughter was cut short by the bell.

"How did he know I thought he was weird?" I whispered to Jenny as we filed into the school.

"I dunno, Kathleen. Kieran seems to know *everything.*"

In the eighth-grade classroom, he dumped the books he was carrying on my desk, with considerable display of weariness and a loud sigh.

"Well, Kathleen Anne Leary," said our teacher, a woman about my mother's age with a pleasant smile, "you seem to have been welcomed already to St. Praxides."

"Kieran O'Kerrigan made fun of me, Mrs. Keeley," I protested.

Laughter.

Kieran fell back against the blackboard dramatically as though someone had stuck a bayonet in him—a picture of unjustly affronted innocence.

"Did he really?" She smiled. "He's a terrible boy, Kathleen. He makes fun of me too."

More laughter.

"Well . . ." I sighed even more loudly than he and sunk into my chair. "I think he's really weird."

"But nice." Kieran jabbed a finger at me. "Weird but *nice!*"

Yet more laughter.

So began the Kieran/Kathleen act which kept the eighth grade amused for the whole year. We were a great comedy team, especially because no one thought that we really disliked each other.

"Hi." He appeared next to me on Hoyne two mornings later. "I told you they'd like you."

"Humpf!" I sniffed, nonetheless glad to have him to myself for a few minutes of conversation.

"No books to carry." He grabbed a notebook away from me. "So I'll have to carry your notebook."

My face became warm again, its normal state when I was with Kieran O'Kerrigan.

He was, I observed, definitely shorter than I was. And I wasn't all that tall.

"You'll tell them," I mimicked him mimicking me, "that I'm the spoiled kid from South Shore who *makes* you carry my things."

"Spoiled rich kid," he agreed, ducking a swipe of my hand which was intended to miss him by a light-year or two.

"Do you *like* Kieran?" Jenny asked me one day, just before Christmas, as I remember.

"Everyone likes Kieran." I tried to dismiss the question as absurd.

"I mean more than that," she said.

"I might, Jenny," I confessed. "I'm not sure but I might."

"That's not wrong." She was watching me closely, sympathetically.

"I know," I agreed.

I didn't have the words available then and if I did I would have been afraid to use them: with Kieran I felt disconcerted, defenseless, vulnerable—but delightfully so.

"Is your Uncle Tom Donahue going to run for Mayor as a Republican?" he asked me one cold winter morning after we had met on Hoyne Avenue as we usually did.

"Grandpa and Aunt Sheila want him to run."

"Do you think he'll win?"

"As a *Republican?* Against Mayor *Daley?* You gotta be kidding."

As usual, Grandpa and Sheila Donahue (who did the political thinking in their family) had been too clever by half. There may have been smart politicians in our family somewhere back in the distant past, but my family had no political instincts at all. Except for Dad.

Grandpa did serve in the State Senate for a term and Martin O'Brien was a judge, but they ran in uncontested elections to fill vacancies. However, as Dad said to me, they had too much money to dirty their hands in the political game.

"A lot of men in this ward have money," I said.

"But they don't think they're aristocrats, Katie, my love. Your mother's clan haven't voted for a Democrat since Harry Truman. The Seventh Ward has had a Republican alderman for ages. If they were really smart they would have jumped to the Republicans twenty years ago when it still meant something in this city to be a Republican. Before the party was taken over by hacks and nonentities and crooks. If Tom runs now, he'll look like a pathetic turncoat."

I repeated that observation, close to verbatim, to Kieran O'Kerrigan without admitting that I had heard it all from my father.

"So you're interested in politics?" he said.

"Of course. Isn't that obvious?"

"And a Cub fan!"

"How did you know that?"

"I have my ways," in the voice of a Gestapo officer in an old movie. "Why are you a Cub fan?"

"Because everyone else is a Sox fan."

"You really are a weird little girl."

"So that makes us a good pair!" I said, living up for a moment to my familial reputation for boldness.

I stopped Kieran cold with that comment. Good enough for him.

"I'm a Cub fan too," he stumbled. "But would you vote for your uncle if he ran as Republican?"

It was a nice change of subject, for which I was very happy at that moment.

Why had I ever said such a stupid thing?

"Certainly not."

"Why not?"

"Because I am a DEMOCRAT!"

"But your Grandpa Lenihan is a Democrat too and you say he votes for Republicans."

"I'm a REAL DEMOCRAT."

"A real Democrat and a real Cub fan."

"Yep." I decided to revel once more in my power to disconcert this silly, pushy, weird, and very nice little boy. "Just like you. We're a minority group. So we'd better stick together, Kieran Patrick O'Kerrigan."

Even now I am embarrassed to think of how forward that silly little redhead was.

Kieran's face was crimson. "Maybe you're right, Kathleen Anne Leary. We share the same enemies."

"Right!" I was blushing too.

That year we won the C.Y.O. city volleyball championship. My kids think volleyball is a "geeky" game, not a real sport like basketball. But they are ready to acknowledge that my maroon and white championship jacket (which I still wear on occasion) is "pretty cool."

Kieran organized the boys to come and cheer for us at the semifinal and final games. For the apes that they were, they were pretty civilized.

My face was as red as my hair through the final games because of their cheers for me. The other girls giggled at them, but didn't seem to mind, especially because in my fury (mostly pretended of course) I was an even more efficient "killer."

At the end, when we were finishing off our last opponent, the boys, led by Kieran naturally, sang, woefully off key, "I'll take you home again, KATHLEEN!"

"Serves you right, Kathleen," Jenny Cahill told me. "You make up all those crazy cheers at the football and basketball games."

"This is DIFFERENT!" I insisted.

So at the end of that schoolyear—one of the happiest times in my life—Kieran O'Kerrigan, weird, funny little first love that he was—enveloped me in his arms, set me on fire with a couple of spectacular kisses, and promised me that he would take care of me for the rest of my life.

He broke the promise. He let me down.

Maybe not. Maybe I let him down.

KATHLEEN
1992

My nostalgic reverie was shattered by Brien. "Kathleen, when are you going to be ready?" he called.

At my vanity, I began to brush my hair with renewed vigor and forced all thoughts of Kieran O'Kerrigan from my mind. He may have promised to be my friend forever long ago, but he'd broken that promise. He'd let me down.

As I walked down the grand staircase of our grand house, I couldn't help but wonder: Maybe I was the one who'd let him down.

"Outstanding, really!" Megan announced when I came down the stairs.

"Ooooh!" exclaimed Brigid. "So pretty, Mommy!"

"It could be cut just a little lower," Maeve observed.

"Maeve"—I felt my face turn hot—"it would fall off it were any lower."

"Not off of you," she replied and hugged me.

At least my daughters admired my evening gown. My husband did not seem to notice what I was wearing. As we drove downtown on the Dan Ryan Expressway, he babbled on about how someone had told someone else that the Daleys had agreed to support "cautiously" his bid for the United States Senate.

"Did the contact use the word 'cautiously'?" I asked. I couldn't curb my political instincts, despite the afternoon's revelation.

"I think so."

"There's no one more cautious than they are when they want to be."

"I'm sure they'll help," he murmured. "We'll see what Rich says tonight."

Brien babbled about how friendly Rich had been recently as we entered the Chicago Hilton, oblivious to how I looked. The appreciative ogles I received from the cops, cabbies, and doormen were small consolation.

My feminist colleagues at the University would have said that with my décolletage, which was attracting the stares, I was "objectifying" myself. They could not, however, "objectify" themselves if they wanted to. As I told them bluntly one day when I was fed up with their bullshit, breasts are meant to attract men; women are meant to attract men. Needless to say, they didn't go for my argument.

As we stepped out of the car, I took a deep breath. I had to play my part as the good wife of the political hopeful this evening. I'd thought I'd get through this dinner swimmingly; I hadn't counted on the deep feelings of hurt and betrayal that surfaced whenever I looked my husband's way.

The cocktail party before the dinner was a whirl of Irish faces and a thunderstorm of Irish blarney. The instant his eyes fell upon me I could tell that my brother the Bishop did not approve of me, though he had the good sense not to express his disapproval.

"Hi, Kathleen." He gave me a quick kiss on the cheek. "How are the children?"

As a general principle, my brother doesn't approve of me. He never has. To him, I'm the family wild card. In me he's always seen a potential black sheep. I don't hold his ill opinion of me against him. He's a great and good man and I love him. I don't know why his success isn't enough for our mother. But it isn't.

My big brother is as dark as my husband is light. They made a striking contrast in the days when they played basketball and football for St. Praxides grammar school. They are both tall, over six feet, but James is slender and sinewy whereas Brien is thick and solid. James's dark hair and skin led some of the Roman bureaucrats to think he was Italian. His close-set brown eyes made them think he was as suspicious as they were. By nature, he's not, except where I'm concerned.

His hair is turning gray now, much too rapidly for a man in his early forties. And his high, distinguished forehead is always furrowed in an anxious little frown. His thin shoulders are already slightly bent.

I blame the Church for that.

When I was a little girl I adored the ground on which James walked. I still love him with all my heart. I think he loves me, though I don't know for sure.

But we can't talk to one another. When we try to, he slips into the role of the admonishing older brother and I into the role of the rebellious little sister. It's always been that way and it always will be.

After James's tacitly critical reception, I exchanged pecks on the cheeks with Brien's two sisters, Janet and Marian. One was married to a schoolteacher, the other to a commodity broker. They both had hated me as long as I had known them. They've been as disapproving of me as the rest of my family. For some reason, despite my achievements at the University, despite the fact I've raised my three girls lovingly, my immediate and extended families view me with suspicion. My father, Red Hugh, was the only one who loved and accepted me for who I am. He even approved of Kieran.

I'll never know what I did to earn the mistrust of my relatives. I never had done anything wrong despite all their fears which had turned into predictions. I did not drink, I was careful with money, more careful than they were. I was a good mother, a truth they could never admit. They were always picking at my lovely, well-behaved kids, finding the smallest faults and magnifying them beyond recognition.

I had been a virgin on my wedding night, an experience I'd rather not remember, and I had been faithful to my husband for seventeen years.

At least I was appreciated beyond the ranks of the Learys and Donahues. Maggie Daley, the Mayor's wife and a member with me of the St. Ignatius board, told me she'd told her husband that I was the most beautiful woman there that night.

I overheard the Mayor calling my husband "Senator," a title which would make the poor man's evening.

To me the Mayor whispered, "We'll always remember where you were when we needed friends, Kathleen."

It was the third time he had said that to me since he had been elected. He could never say it too often as far as I was concerned.

"If someone isn't loyal to their friends," I whispered back in the time-honored dictum of Chicago politics, "who will they be loyal to?"

"Right!" Rich's magic grin exploded, a grin which seemed always reserved especially for whoever he was bestowing it upon just then. "Isn't it the truth!"

As I whirled around the dance floor that night I figured that the Daleys would be perfectly happy to have my husband—my soon-to-be ex-husband—in Washington. That would get him out of Chicago and out of their hair. Safely tucked in the nation's capital, Brien would no longer be perennially named as a possible mayoral candidate. He'd never win such a race, of course, but his candidacy could be troublesome to the Daleys. Whatever happened with Brien's senatorial candidacy, the Daleys were sure to win. Win or lose—Brien would be out of the running. He'd either be far-off in Washington or—if he lost—he'd be deemed a loser and would therefore pose even less of a threat for any city office.

I felt confident then that Rich would support Brien, but not so forcefully as to take any heat if he lost.

People who don't understand Chicago politics think that the Irish pols are vindictive, neither forgiving nor forgetting. They couldn't be more wrong. Vindictiveness is something that the smart Irish politician knows he cannot afford. Ever.

Rich Daley is not your typical Chicago-Irish politician at all. Neither was his father, despite what you might have heard. Both of them knew better than anyone else in town, however, that forgiving and forgetting are irrelevant to the political game.

You don't forget, of course. No one does, but you don't let not forgetting influence the way you play the game.

When the Mayor died and Mike Bilandic, his successor, was beaten by Jane Byrne in the snow-removal election, both our families, figuring that the dynasty was finished, jumped to the Lady Jane. They supported Ed Burke against Rich in the State's Attorney's race and then Jane against him in the three-way mayoral race which put Harold Washington in City Hall.

Clearly they had underestimated Rich's own political talents and skills and, more importantly, his managerial ability. So had almost everyone else.

I was one of the exceptions. I infuriated my husband and our families by contributing to both the State's Attorney and the mayoral primaries and working for Rich in the latter. My contributions were absurdly small, five hundred dollars, but they would mark me forever as a friend.

Did I think the Daley dynasty would rise again? Yes, I did, but that didn't matter. You have to be loyal to your friends, a simple political truth that my family and my husband's family never understood (save for Red Hugh, when he was sober), which was the reason they had slowly fallen from eminence through the decades.

So, sure, the Daley clan would support Brien Donahue for the United States Senate, albeit cautiously, because they had nothing to lose and something to gain either way. But they'd never trust him again or anyone in his family or his wife's family.

But, as for me, the crazy redhead, she would always be a woman approved because she'd been there when it counted.

Later, when he appeared next to me as I was drifting back to our table from the dance floor, I said to the Mayor, "I assume you consider my daughters friends, too?"

The well-fed, well-scrubbed Chicago Irish, dancing in the palatial grand ballroom of the Chicago Hilton and Towers, might not be quite as elegant as the court of the Sun King at Versailles. But, from what I've read, we smell a lot better.

Rich seemed startled by my question, but he didn't have to ask what it meant. "They go to Saint Ignatius; do I have any choice?"

We both laughed, but the question had been answered. Rich's comment told me that he assumed that I had raised my three girls to understand the importance of loyalty.

"Will you like living in Washington?" he asked.

My reply was the evasive kind of Chicago political answer which said nothing and everything. "I can't imagine trying to take Megie and Maevie out of St. Ignatius."

"That's true," the Mayor agreed.

But he had filed away in his head a question mark about the Donahue marriage and family. It was just as well that I had given him some advance warning: the question marks would become more numerous long before the election.

"How's the dissertation coming?" he asked as the orchestra began again. I was already thinking that I might dance with that cute Father Brendan. Maggie had set him up with the questions just as Sis would have set up the Mayor in the old days.

"It's getting there, now that I have a happy ending to the story— you're the mayor, Ed is the chairman of the finance committee, Dick Phelan is county board president, my neighbor Tom Hynes is assessor, my other neighbor Jim Sheehan is sheriff, Phil Rock is president of the

State Senate, Mike Madigan is speaker of the General Assembly, Jack O'Connor is State's Attorney, even if he is a Republican, Kelly Welch is corporation counsel . . . should I go on?"

The Mayor was laughing enthusiastically. "I don't know anyone better qualified to write the story, Kathleen."

"Thank you, Your Honor."

BRENDAN

"Could I have a word with you, Father McNulty?" Bishop James Leary whispered the question in my ear. We were standing in the lobby of the grand ballroom of the Chicago Hilton and Towers.

"Sure, James," I replied to Bishop James Leary. "Maybe even two words."

I had been admiring the Bishop's sister, Kathleen, a member of St. Praxides parish where I work. I won't say I was ogling her minimal black evening gown. Ogling implies disrespect; and I had nothing but respect for Kathleen Leary Donahue. I was also half in love with her and she knew it and she treated me with amused affection—just the right technique to keep the erotically aroused young priest in his proper place: adore but don't touch. That style would not, I thought, preclude one dance at the Ireland Fund Festival. Possibly two.

"I heard that you had a long dialogue with Father Roder this afternoon."

"Monologue, James."

It was said of James Leary when they made him a bishop that he raised the average IQ of the American hierarchy by fifteen points. It was also said that somehow the Vatican had made a terrible mistake: just because James was a dutiful and hardworking priest, it did not follow that he was on their side.

I didn't think the Vatican had made a mistake. For all his ability and charisma, James was loyal to the Church. So far he had swallowed everything that the Cardinal and the Vatican had demanded of him, even the pathetic plea that Father Gerry Greene was not a pedophile.

The strain of "going along" had taken its toll. James now looked like a handsome British officer in *The Raj Quartet* who was beginning to go to seed.

"It was my mistake," he said gently, "to ask him to speak with you."

"There's nothing wrong with Martin Roder," I replied, "except that he is a stubborn, self-righteous, stuffed-shirt cement-head."

I continued to study the curves of Kathleen Donahue's figure. She was easily the most astonishing woman I'd ever met.

James chuckled. "You were never one, Brendan, to make cautious statements. . . . In any case I hope that we can speak about this matter later on, perhaps tomorrow or the next day. All I wanted to say tonight is that there is no question about your ability to perform prodigious amounts of priestly work. If in the heat of argument, Martin seemed to suggest that, he really didn't mean it."

"Thanks, James." I stopped—for the moment—admiring his sister.

"If we had more priests who work as hard as you do," James continued, "we'd be a much better Church."

It was soft soap, but James meant it. Unlike most bishops these days, he believes that one of his most important tasks is to encourage priests. He's quite good at it, as he is at almost everything else in his job.

"You must have swallowed the Blarney Stone on the last trip to Ireland."

We laughed together.

"I think I see a way out of this Gerry Greene problem. But we can talk about it later. . . . Incidentally, that's a neatly fitted tuxedo you're wearing."

He didn't approve of my showing up for the Ireland Fund Dinner in a tux, but would never say so. Yet he would let me know that he had noticed it.

"There's two ways to go, James. Either a tux or a cassock and cloak and a cummerbund. I'd go that way if I was entitled to purple, like you are. But a clerical suit . . . as your delightful nieces would say, barf city!"

"Maybe they're right." He smiled genially.

"Incidentally, speaking of those charming young women, their mother looks spectacularly attractive tonight, doesn't she?"

"Kathleen?" He glanced at her. She was engaged in an animated conversation with the Mayor. "Yes, I suppose she does."

"She's kind of a heroine at the parish for her spunk in getting a doctorate at The University of Chicago."

"Really?" He seemed both skeptical and uninterested.

I did not pursue the subject. I had figured out months before that there was something amiss in the relationship between the practically perfect bishop and his sister, the practically perfect—and devastatingly attractive—matron. It was difficult to comprehend why two talented, sensitive people who happened to be related to one another were not closer. I was curious about the apparent rift between the two of them.

For as positive and bright as James Leary could be, he was being pretty willfully obtuse in the case of Father Gerard Greene (code name "Lucifer" to his contemporaries in the seminary). A three-time loser in pedophile charges, Greene had physically and sexually abused a third-grade boy in the Catholic school in his last parish, unwittingly aided and abetted by the nun who was the principal of the school and who had sent the boy to Gerry for "discipline."

Gerry wasn't gay in the ordinary sense of the word. The only males he was attracted to—if attracted was the right word—were young boys. But he presided over a group of sexually active gay priests at his summer home at Goose Lake.

On the other hand, he also seemed a zealous and dedicated priest, a reasonably good preacher compared to the abysmal levels that are the diocesan average. He was kind and sympathetic to elderly people and punctilious in his visits to the sick. After one of his escapades, the Archdiocese had sent him off to one of the rest homes the Church reserved for such priests. After six months he was pronounced "cured" and reassigned to parish work.

The Archdiocese's routine response to such incidents is to cover up, stonewall, intimidate. No police force has ever brought formal charges against a priest within the Archdiocese. The media seldom report the charges. With financial deep pockets, the Archdiocese is able to overwhelm the parents of the victims (referred to as "enemies" by Ignatius Loyala Keefe, counsel for the Archdiocese), especially by having countersuits for libel filed in the name of the accused priest. The clerical grapevine spreads the rumor that men like "Lucifer" are "cleared" by the police and even that they win suits against the parents of the victims, who are described as drug addicts and alcoholics.

To those of us who criticize this record, the response is that while there have been public scandals in many other dioceses, there have been none in Chicago. They dismiss our response that they are merely postponing the scandal and that when it finally explodes it will be a catastrophe.

Even priests like James Leary actually seemed to believe that Gerry Greene is the victim of reckless and untrue charges, the wish perhaps being the father of the thought. After an incident before the most recent set of charges, Gerry was left in place in his suburban parish until his term was up and then reassigned to another suburb. Martin Roder insisted that the "alleged victim" was not credible. No surprise. Martin never seemed to encounter a victim who was "credible."

So James was unhappy with me because I was serving as junior counsel for the family of the latest victim of Gerry's amusements. The parents in this case have deeper pockets (thanks to the sale of their summer home and a second and third mortgage on their home). They refused to settle even for a sum substantially larger than the twenty-five thousand dollars that the Archdiocese routinely dispenses to the families of victims to shut them up. They want the Church to agree to set up an independent board to review pedophile cases, a board that would act as advocates for the victim and decide whether the priest should ever be reassigned to a parish again.

This would be a pretty good deal for James and the Cardinal because it would free them from responsibility for simultaneously ministering to the victim and protecting the priest. But it would also mean giving up power. From the Church's point of view, if this went through, the power to close parishes arbitrarily and the right to grant construction contracts to firms whose wages and benefits were beneath the negotiated industry standards would pass out of clerical hands too. The powers-that-be saw an erosion of power and authority as a threat to all power and authority.

Because I have a reputation in the clergy for being a "nice guy" (the highest compliment a priest can pay to another priest), James Leary thought he could talk me out of being an adversary to the Archdiocese in the Greene case.

He was about to find out that I wasn't so nice after all, though I wasn't about to tip my hand at so public an occasion as this very sweet affair.

On the way into the dinner I encountered the Bishop's brother-in-law, Brien—the pronunciation of his name recently changed from "Brian" to "Breen"—a big, handsome, genial jock who might be the next United States Senator for the great Prairie State of Illinois.

"Caught you on the tube this afternoon, Brien," I said as we shook hands.

"Hey, Father Brendan, you look great in the tux."

"That's what the Bishop said, more or less. What did you think of the Henry Horner Homes?"

Brien shook his head and his genial face clouded over. "They're terrible, Father Brendan, just terrible. It's sinful that we should live like we do"—he gestured at the dazzling Grand Ballroom—"and they live the way they do. We've got to do something about it." He might have been a politician, but he sounded sincere.

"I agree, though I don't think our party tonight causes their suffering."

"I know. I know. But it's still not right. We should be able to eliminate that kind of poverty in a rich country like this. I understand the complications, but I don't think we're doing enough."

"You'll get no argument from me about that."

"Anyway"—his smile returned and he shook hands again—"great to see you here, Father Brendan. And I just want to tell you what a great job you're doing with the kids out in the parish. Thank God we still have some priests who like to work with kids."

"I'll keep trying, Brien."

Brien, I figured, was probably the only person at the whole dinner who was genuinely worried about Henry Horner Homes. More power to him. Moreover, he was one of the few lawyers I knew who did not find it necessary to ask how I had managed to go to law school and practice law, sometimes against the Church, and not get thrown out of the priesthood.

The answer was that I paid my own way and there was a shortage of priests. Sometimes I'd add that it was a grace for the Church to have a priest on the other side who would keep the institution honest.

Later I risked a waltz with Kathleen and struggled mightily to keep my eyes away from her splendid breasts, about which her dress left little doubt.

"What's the rosette you're wearing, Father Brendan?"

"It's from A.E.O.H.S.J.—the Ancient Equestrian Order of the Holy Sepulcher of Jerusalem—I'm actually a Knight Commander of the Holy Sepulcher!"

"Really! How wonderful!"

"It takes only clout and money, Kathleen, and it flummoxes the conservatives when they want to go after me."

"Speaking of which, my brother had you cornered, Father Brendan." Her eyes twinkled with mildly flirtatious mischief. "Were you on the carpet about showing up in a tux?"

"Not at all. He admired it."

"I bet."

"Except on one or two issues, Kathleen, he's the best bishop in America. He did an astonishing job turning around the poorest Afro-American parish in the city after he was ordained. Most of us respect and admire him. The Cathedral is deluged with phone calls from people who want to know what Mass he will say, because he's such a fine preacher. He keeps the diocese from sinking into Lake Michigan."

"I know," she said. "I love him as much as anyone does. He's a wonderful priest." I didn't detect any sarcasm in her tone.

"Another dance, Father Brendan?" She grinned like a woman leprechaun.

"How can I say no?"

What was with her and her brother? There might not have been a trace of sarcasm in her remark, but there was clearly more than met the eye to this relationship. I warned myself not to probe too closely. After all, what Kathleen Leary Donahue and her brother thought of each other was hardly my business. I resolved not to inquire any further, at the same time resolving to resist a third dance with the striking redhead in my arms.

What was my business would be the confrontation with James about the pedophilia epidemic in the Archdiocese, an epidemic whose existence he steadfastly denied.

LEARY

I did not like the man who cornered me as I was leaving the dinner. I feared he would ruin my evening.

He did.

"Could I have a word with you, Bishop? My friends have a concern."

On his lips the word "friends" had only one meaning: the Outfit bosses.

He was Irish, not Italian, a smartly turned-out, tastefully perfumed, white-haired, pink-cheeked vice-president at a major Chicago bank—the VP in charge of dealing with the Outfit.

That position made him, by my definition, corrupt.

"What are they worried about now?" I asked curtly.

The Archdiocese does not deal with the Outfit. These days there are no longer any priests who have connections with them. Sometimes I wish for the old days, when all we had to worry about was an occasional cleric we had to send off to South America for a couple of years because he had become too "hot."

Nonetheless the Bosses (in Chicago we don't call them "dons," much less "godfathers") occasionally feel the need to send a message to us. It's always through this man to me, never to the Cardinal, perhaps because he is a northern Italian and they trust him less than they trust the Irish. Normally I simply ignore the message as irrelevant.

"About this election." He rolled his eyes, indicating that they were very worried.

"What about it?" I snapped.

"They're afraid the story will come out, some reporter will snoop around and dig it up."

"That was a long time ago—twenty-five years."

"My friends know that, but with all the problems they have now, they don't need another one."

"Brien doesn't know about it. Neither does Kathleen. I only found out because you told me. What do they expect? He should drop out of the race because of a story that's twenty-five years old and may not be true?"

"It's true, Bishop. Believe me, it's true."

"I repeat, what do they expect? Are they giving orders? Making threats?"

He extended both his hands as if smoothing a tablecloth. "My friends are old men now, Bishop, they have lots of problems. They're not making threats. Most of them would like to see your brother-in-law in Washington. They just wanted me to tell you that they're worried. Nothing more."

"I don't see what there is to worry about."

"The kid is back in town."

"He's the last one to worry about. He wouldn't dream of asking any questions. He's a success in his own unimportant world and content in it."

"Yeah, that's what everyone says."

"You can count on it. I had several long talks with him when he returned. It's all part of the past as far as he's concerned. He's a nice boy, but he's naive and weak."

"That's what they say too. My friends will be happy you agree."

"They can count on that."

"Red Hugh, your father, wrote a letter, they say, before he died."

I felt my blood turn cold. "Who says?"

He shrugged his shoulders. "Some people who claim to have seen a copy."

"Who did he write it to?"

"Whom, Bishop."

"All right, who was supposed to receive the letter?"

He tilted his head to one side. "No one knows. They say it wasn't addressed to anyone."

"Probably doesn't exist anymore."

"You don't have it?"

"Good lord, no. If I ever did, I would have destroyed it."

"That's what I told them." He eyed me intently. "Your sister?"

He nodded across the room. Kathleen and Brien were leaving. She was wound up, tight as a drum, and not from drinking either. She could be dangerous during the campaign if she tried to tell our consultants how to run it.

I had to admit to myself that Brendan McNulty was right: she was a knockout. Not very modest perhaps, something of an exhibitionist in fact, but very beautiful. I had a soft spot in my heart for her since the day my mother had brought the cute little redhead home from the hospital. Somehow I had never been able to tell her how much I loved her.

"Come on, you know what she's like. Everyone does. No common sense at all. If she had the letter, she would have blown the whole thing sky-high. Remember, she thought she was in love with the boy at one time."

"Yeah . . . well, like I say, my friends wanted some reassurance, and I think you've made it possible for me to reassure them."

"I'm happy to hear that." I turned around and walked away from him, feeling tainted even by the conversation.

Reassure the Cardinal. Reassure the Bosses. Reassure everyone.

I had not been responsible for the problem, if indeed there ever was a problem. I wanted no part of it now. But my mother and Brien's parents were too old to cope with, much less answer truthfully any questions I might be foolish enough to ask.

So I had to absorb the worry, just like I had to absorb the Cardinal's worry and the worry of half the priests in Chicago.

I looked around the Grand Ballroom as the guests streamed out, most of them more sober than my mother or the Donahues. The younger generation of Chicago Irish somehow seemed to be able to keep their public use of the "creature" under better control than their parents, at least in public. Few of them, however, had given it up altogether as Kathleen had.

Dear God, what would she be like if she were a drunk? She was provocative enough as it was, stone cold sober.

We Irish had made it big in America and in Chicago. We still ran the city, more or less. Maybe more even than when Rich's father had been mayor.

It would be hard to tell that this well-dressed, good-natured, and marginally sophisticated crowd were the grandchildren or great-grand-children of illiterate and impoverished peasants. Probably none of them considered that they were celebrating their families' liberation from thousands of years of rural misery.

Yet as I kissed my mother and Sheila Donahue goodnight, wincing at the smell of booze on both of them, and congratulated the Donahues on being honored for their generosity and civic concerns, I wondered whether maybe we were not better off as illiterate peasants.

"You were wonderful tonight, Bishop James." Sheila Donahue's voice was slurred. "So funny and so generous in your praise."

"Richly deserved, Sheila."

"The next big party will be when Brien wins the general election." Tom sighed noisily. "Won't that be the day! It looks like Rich is going to support him to the hilt."

"I'm glad to hear that," I said carefully. It did not pay to trust the Daleys too much.

"James," my mother said wearily, "I wish you'd have a word with Kathleen. She doesn't listen to me anymore."

"I'll try," I replied.

It was an exchange in which we had indulged a thousand times. No one in the family could have a word with Kathleen anymore. The years at The University of Chicago had made her even more arrogant than she was by nature.

"I thought that dress tonight was shameful, didn't you, Bishop James?"

I'm always Bishop James to my mother.

"Yes," I agreed. "But very attractive."

"She was always a wild child."

They all agreed.

I drove back to the Cathedral rectory on Wabash Avenue, where I live, with a deep sense of foreboding. It was all coming apart, I thought. Just at the moment of victory, it was all coming apart.

Somehow God had decreed that I must bear the weight of all my own sins, which torment me every day, as well as the sins of my family and Brien's family.

It didn't seem fair.

Father, if it be possible, I prayed in the words of Jesus as I turned off the Inner Drive, let this chalice pass from me. But not my will but Thine be done.

On my lips, I thought, that prayer was almost blasphemy.

If Kathleen had that letter from Dad, or if she ever found it, there would be an apocalypse. She simply didn't understand how things worked—and that, as Jesus said, we should let the dead bury their dead.

Kieran O'Kerrigan, however, was still very much alive. He had not been at the dinner; or if he had been there I had not seen him. Had he and Kathleen spoken since he had returned to Chicago? I wondered uneasily.

If the Outfit were to eliminate anyone, O'Kerrigan would be the obvious choice. He could be shot in an apparent gang-bang by drug addicts. That's the way it went down nowadays. That way the press couldn't call a killing Mob-related.

Not that I wanted Kieran to die. I was only a realist, thinking about what the Bosses might do. Yet my realism was sinful, especially when coupled with the thought that such an action would solve a lot of problems. I told myself that I would not think about such an end for Kieran O'Kerrigan. I wanted him to say alive. I wanted him to find happiness at long last.

But not with my sister. Not then, not now. Not ever.

I wondered if she had seen him. He never once asked about her during our conversations which had led him back to the practice of his faith.

All we'd need would be a rebirth of that foolish love affair.

I thought about the wonderful times we had all had together at Long Beach when we were young: the Learys and the Donahues rushing along the lakeshore, diving into the water, climbing on our boats, ignoring the heat and the humidity, reveling in our youth.

Brien and I leading the way, Terry and Steve wrestling with one another, Mary Anne proud and regal, Kathleen a pretty and reckless little imp. Then, as the years went on, Kieran would be trailing along behind us, clumsy and slow, but always witty and cheerful.

We would never have so much fun again. Of the seven young people in my tableau, three were already dead, Kieran had drifted away, and Brien, Kathleen, and I somehow did not quite seem to fit together in a happy and healthy triangle.

Brien was the closest friend I ever had. So much depended on his election. It would put meaning in all that we had lost. It was the only thing that could.

KATHLEEN

"Please take your hands off me, Brien," I said when we got to our bedroom.

He had pawed me tentatively in the car and then a little less tentatively coming up the stairs. I waited till we were safe in our bedroom where curious little ears would not hear what was coming.

"What do you mean?" He recoiled, astonished that I had, for the first time in years, rebuffed him.

Beneath his macho bluster, Brien Donahue is a timid man. I figured that I could control the confrontation completely.

I was dead wrong, almost literally.

"I had a phone call from your lover today." I leaned against my vanity and folded my arms. "It was a very interesting conversation."

"I . . . don't know what you're talking about." Befuddled and surprised, he sat on the edge of our king-size bed.

"He seemed to know all the details of the last time we made love."

"I . . ." Brien turned white. "I don't have any lover. There isn't any other woman, Kathleen—really there isn't."

The poor pathetic bastard could not even lie convincingly.

"I didn't say 'she,' Brien. I know that your lover is a man."

"I'm not a faggot," he shouted. "Goddamn it! I'm straight."

Leave it to Brien to put more stock in labels than in the fact of his betrayal. I sighed. "At least now I understand why we make love so rarely. To think I took it personally all these years. So has this been going on a long time?"

Brien buried his head in his hands. "Not long. I've only been with him once or twice. It doesn't mean anything." He looked up at me with a puppy-dog plea in his eyes. "It's just something men do sometimes. It isn't important."

"Not important when you reject your wife for a man? Not important that you could be exposing me to AIDS . . ."

"I don't have AIDS!" he shouted.

"How do you know? Have you had a test?"

"I don't need a test."

"You goddamn well better have one! Tomorrow! I have a right to know what you've brought into this house."

"It's not that way, Kathleen, it really isn't. I mean, it's all over now. It won't happen again. I promise you."

For a moment, I believed him. Maybe I thought we could salvage something. For the kids' sake if not our own.

"Will you go into therapy?"

"Won't you ever stop that stuff?" he whined. "There's nothing wrong with me. I don't need therapy. Besides, I can't go in for therapy when I'm running for office. I'll get myself squared away without professional help. I promise that."

Tears began to well in his eyes. I had to steel my heart against him.

"Either you promise you'll go into therapy tomorrow or I want you out of the house. I want a divorce. I want an annulment. I want to be rid of a man who loves another man more than he loves me. Is that clear?"

Now he sobbed. "Don't do this to me, Kathleen. I beg you. Don't do it to me. If you only understood the pressure I'm under, you'd be ready to give me another chance. It happens when the pressure is too much. If there was more encouragement here at home, these . . . these things wouldn't happen."

"You could make love with me anytime you wanted and you know it."

Again I felt the temptation of sympathy.

"It's not sex, Kathleen. It's not about sex at all."

"Then what is it about?"

"Don't you see what he's doing?" He tried to choke off his sobs. "He wants to ruin our marriage. He called you to punish me for ending it all."

I hadn't thought of that. It had not occurred to me to wonder the reason for the phone call.

"He did me a big favor by telling me the kind of man I have for a husband."

"I'm not that kind of man," he shouted.

That should have been a warning to me. The way he shouted should have brought back memories of shouting years ago. I was too angry to remember, especially since I had buried the memories as deeply as I could.

"Face the facts, Brien. You'd rather be in bed with another man than with me."

"It's not that way, Kathleen," he moaned. "It's not that way at all. I love you. You just won't listen. I do love you." He was weeping again. "I do. Just give me another chance. It's over. I promise it's over. It will never happen again. We . . . we can make love a lot from now on."

I could tell that he did think he loved me. And perhaps by his own dim lights he did. The poor man was a mess. I felt sorry for him. But I also felt sorry for my daughters and myself.

I knew I had to remain firm. "Brien, if you have any hope of salvaging our marriage, you have to go into therapy."

"I can't!" He looked up at me in pitiable supplication. "Not now. There's the campaign."

"Is that more important than our marriage?"

"Of course not. Just give me a chance, some time, only a little time."

"It's therapy or divorce, Brien. No other options."

"You can't divorce me before the election! You'd ruin everything!"

A crazed light began to shine in his eyes. I should have noticed it and backed off, but I was too angry to heed the warning.

"Can't I? You just watch me! Now which is it going to be? Are you going to get out of this bedroom or am I?"

"Please," he begged. "Please forgive me. Only one more chance! I beg you!"

My shame and anger ripped away my common sense.

"Sorry, Brien, but you're out of chances. You should have thought about consequences before you took up with that boyfriend of yours."

I saw immediately that I had gone too far. Brien rose from the bed, his shoulders hunched, his hands clenched. As he advanced toward me, his face twisted in diabolic rage, I knew it was too late.

Twice before in our marriage, years ago, I had seen that expression of contorted rage on his face. Twice before he had beaten me into submission and then raped me. Twice before he had begged me on his knees to forgive him. The second time he'd raped me was probably the night we conceived Maevie—fifteen years ago. I had forgiven and forgotten.

My mistake.

"Cunt!" he shouted, slapping my face with his open hand. "Now you're going to get what you've been asking for!"

I flew across the room and banged into the television set. It toppled over. I knew what was coming. Humiliation, pain, more humiliation, terrible pain. The whole scene unrolled before me in my mind's eye. My normally diffident husband would become a cruel and vicious maniac, a demented torturer who would hurt me every way he could, short of putting me into a hospital. I would fight back, kick, scratch, claw, but he would be too strong for me. Then I would fear for my life and stop fighting. Then, laughing hysterically, he would force himself on me. After he had violated me, he would beat me some more before he fell into a complacent sleep.

Brien was a clever wife-beater. He would break no bones. He would leave no marks on my face or arms that anyone could see. The rest of me was another matter. He knew all the tricks of torturing a woman without doing any permanent damage to her.

Brien Donahue enjoying a woman.

Might he have killed me those first two times?

He was so out of control anything could have happened.

"Please, Brien," I begged. "Don't do it!"

He grabbed the top of my gown and yanked me away from the ruined TV. Then he slapped me again, hurling me toward the bed.

"You've been asking for this for a long, long time, bitch," he said, now calm, cold, and deliberate, despite the glow of madness in his eyes. "I'm going to love it."

He tore off my dress and ripped my lingerie. Then he yanked my breasts like he was going to pull them off.

I fought back. I kicked and scratched and jabbed and punched. My attempts at resistance amused him.

"I enjoy it more when you fight," he cackled, then punched me in the stomach.

I bit my lips to control the screams of pain. I did not want to wake the girls, not to this scene.

I tried to kick at his crotch. He avoided my aim, but I managed to slip away. I thought about the Taekwondo I had learned, but none of it came back to me. I tried to escape to the bathroom. I made it inside the door, but Brien shoved his body against the door so I couldn't slam it.

"You might as well stop fighting, bitch." He got the door open and pulled me out of the bathroom. "You're just making it harder on yourself and more fun for me."

I kept on fighting as best as I could, but he was much too strong for me.

He tore off the rest of my clothes and settled down to the serious business of systematically beating me, imposing as much pain as he could. I was too frightened and I hurt too much to continue to resist. I gritted my teeth and swallowed my screams. I prayed that he would not kill me.

Then he raped me, savagely, brutally. He seemed to enjoy every moment of it. He laughed, babbled like a happy baby, shouted with joy. *He's a sadist*, I thought as I struggled with wave after wave of pain and desecration.

Soon it will be over.

I was wrong.

He tried a new ending this time.

When he had finished raping me, he rolled me over on my stomach and began to spank me with one of his shoes.

"This is what we do to naughty little girls." He laughed hysterically. "Do you like it, bitch? Isn't it fun?"

Then he sodomized me.

After he was finished, I lay there on my marriage bed in an agony of bloody pain and degradation and despair. I had been used, used up, I was a dirty paper napkin, fit only for the garbage heap. There was nothing left. I decided that I would kill myself.

I lay there for I don't know how long. The minutes must have crept to hours. My thoughts drifted the way they always did when I felt so alone or afraid. Before I could stop myself, I was thinking again of Kieran. . . .

Kieran and I were not a romantic item during our high school years. I dated a lot of boys and started going to junior and senior proms when I was a sophomore. Kieran attended St. Ignatius and hence was on the top of the social scale when compared to the Brother Rice boys—St. Rita's and Mount Carmel didn't count in our world—and was thought by most girls to be "cute." But he seemed uninterested in dating.

Some people said he was thinking about being a priest.

My opinion, kept to myself, was that he was sensitive about his height. I had learned that Kieran was not only tuned into the hurts of others, but hurt easily himself. I don't remember how I learned that, but I knew it to be true. Kieran O'Kerrigan was not quite the paragon of self-possession and maturity that he pretended to be. So I loved him all the more because I knew he needed someone to take care of him. Me, for example.

I didn't stop kidding him—I couldn't do that. But I avoided kidding him about being short—until his junior year, when he finally caught up with me and surged to the towering height of five feet nine inches.

"Now," I said, looking up into his gray eyes at the one dance we permitted ourselves at every high school social—to the music of "Strangers in the Night"—"I can kid you about being short."

"Why?" He blushed as he often did when we were in each other's arms—at a discreet distance of course.

"Because even with heels on, I have to look up to you."

"Oh." He blushed even more. "But the truth is, Kathleen Anne Leary, that no matter how tall I get I'll always have to look up to you."

What can a sixteen-year-old possibly do with a boy like that?

Love him all the more, I suppose. Anyway, that's what I did.

It was the same year, I think, when we were engaged in that one dance to which I looked forward every other week, that he said to me, "You're a cupcake, Leary."

"A what?" I prepared to put on my outraged face.

"A softy, a pushover, a melting snowball, a bowl of tasty mush."

"If you're suggesting I'm promiscuous . . ."

"Come on, Kathleen, you know better than that."

"Then what DO you mean?"

I felt his hands tighten. "I mean your hot-tempered redhead act is just an act—mostly to fend off that goofy family of yours."

"It is, is it?" My knees began to flutter.

"Yeah."

"So what's beneath the act?"

"A sweet and thoughtful and caring young woman."

"Bullshit!"

"You can't fool me."

"I don't want to fool you, Kieran." I changed my tune rapidly. "I've never tried, not really."

I felt naked, like he had taken off all my clothes. It was a wonderful feeling.

"Just so long as you know that I know."

"I figured you knew all along."

"Mush," he said, with a touch of male triumph in his voice.

He was entitled to it, I guess.

"So long"—I freed my hand to punch his shoulder, very lightly—"as you know that it's sweet-tasting mush."

"Did he tell you that he loved you?" Jenny Cahill asked me later at Red's, the hot dog stand to which we all fled when the priest banished us at eleven.

"Who?"

"Kieran. Who else?"

"Oh, HIM."

"Come on, Kathleen, don't try to fool me."

"What made you think he did?"

"You turned very red, then very pale, and then very, very red again. And you looked, like, terribly happy."

"Did I?"

"You did."

"Do you think everyone noticed?"

"Only those of us who were watching you."

"Why would anyone want to watch Kieran and me?"

"Don't try to avoid the question."

"No, he didn't say he loved me. But he was very sweet."

"Oh." She sounded disappointed. "Do you think he loves you?"

I felt very dreamy. "Yes, Jenny." I sighed. "I'm sure he does."

But then I'd known that for a long time.

My family unanimously disapproved of my social life as a teenager. Unlike Kieran—and my other friends—they were convinced that I was promiscuous.

"You're getting a reputation, young woman," Grandma Lenihan told me in the presence of the rest of the family, "for being terribly fast."

"I don't care!" I wailed.

"They say you're very free with yourself," my brother James said, a seminarian who knew nothing about anything when it came to teenage dating.

"Let them say it!"

"You're too pretty for your own good," Mom chimed in.

It was true that I had acquired such a reputation, but the reputation was wildly inaccurate. As my dates found out early on, I was a virtuous young woman, especially by the standards of the opening years of the sexual revolution.

However, someone had spread the rumor that I was "almost a whore" all around the neighborhood. The young people knew it wasn't true; in fact, they found it very funny and couldn't understand why anyone would take it seriously.

"Like you're the all-time ice goddess," a date said to me.

"I am NOT."

"OK," he said agreeably. "After a certain point."

"That's better."

But the adults in the parish believed the story. "Too pretty for her own good . . . the parish hooker . . . real Jezebel type."

In those days I suspected Mary Anne had launched the rumors, especially since they seemed to come from Loring, which was her school.

So it was a never-ending battle with my family all through my high school years.

"We've never had a woman in the family with your reputation," Mom said sadly.

"Ask any of the kids whether it's true."

"They wouldn't tell the truth," Grandma declared.

"Ask Steve or Ter."

"They'd be on your side."

Anyone who rejected the rumors, you see, was automatically disqualified from testimony.

"Don't take them seriously, Katie, my Celtic princess," Dad would console me when he was around. "They don't know what they're talking about."

"I don't take them seriously!" I wailed. "It's all a lie."

The fact that I wailed showed how seriously I did take them. They were unable to curtail my social life. All they wanted to do, I told myself, was to ruin it.

I would not let them do that.

I'd show them!

I really hated Mary Anne during the last year of her life, poor thing,

especially because she smiled triumphantly every time Mom grounded
me. Or tried to ground me.

Then Mary Anne died. She and Steve and his date were killed in an
accident on U.S. 12 outside of Michigan City when they were seniors,
only a few weeks before graduation from high school. Their car swerved
off the highway, apparently in the wrong lane, to avoid an oncoming
car. Her date, who was driving, survived. His blood-alcohol content was
.2. My family never learned what every teenager in the neighborhood
knew: Mary Anne was already an alcoholic. That night she had been
forcing vodka on her date.

I was devastated. Now there would never be a chance for us to be
friends.

And Steve too—a nice, friendly brother, who always liked me and
tried in his bumbling adolescent male way to support me.

The wake was terrible. Mom lashed out at everybody. It was like she
blamed the whole world for the death of her two children. Or that she
was using the terrible tragedy as an excuse to settle old scores, most of
them imagined. I had never seen that side of her before. Looking back
at it, I supposed it was Grandma Lenihan exploding inside of her.

James was almost as bad. He sulked around silently as if disapproving
of everyone and everything.

I've since learned that grief is eased if you have someone to blame.

Dad and Grandpa tried to keep alive the Irish tradition for the cordial,
friendly wake. But they too were too battered to cover for Mom's
furies—and Grandma's hard-eyed silence.

So, without thinking about it, I found myself, at the ripe old age of
going-on fifteen, presiding at the wake.

"You're good at it, Katie," Dad whispered to me. "A real Irish
political pro."

Despite my grief, I was enormously flattered.

Through those horrible days—Sunday, Monday, and Tuesday, a real
long-distance Irish wake—Kieran O'Kerrigan was next to me all the
time. He kind of appeared on Sunday night and lurked in the background through all that terrible time in the stuffy funeral home which
smelled of women's perfume, mums, and death.

James accused me of having no respect for the dead.

"You're flaunting yourself," he said, "at the expense of your dead
brother and sister."

I walked away from him.

"What an asshole," Kieran murmured.

"He's heartbroken," I replied. "Everyone expresses grief differently."

"You didn't kill her."

"I know."

Later on that evening it hit me what Kieran meant. Somehow I was being blamed for Mary Anne's death. I would always be blamed for it. She was the good sister and I was the bad sister. I was the one who should have died.

I was too young to think it all out that way. But somehow I knew it.

Kieran walked me home each night.

The second night, a dark, stuffy, humid evening with thunder throbbing in the distance, I burst into tears.

He put his arm around my shoulders.

"She hated me and she said terrible things about me," I sobbed. "But I didn't want her dead."

"I know."

"I hoped that we'd become friends later on in life."

I knew as soon as I said those words how foolish was my hope.

"I know."

"I'm not relieved that she's dead."

But I was in part relieved. I would not have to endure that hate anymore.

"She doesn't hate me anymore, not in heaven."

"No, Kathleen, she doesn't hate you anymore."

"I'm sorry that I'm relieved that I won't have to live with her hate."

"How could you possibly feel any different?"

"But they'll all be mad at me because she died and I didn't."

That stopped him.

"I didn't think of that." His embrace tightened.

"But it's true. Especially James and Mom and Grandma."

"But not your father."

"No." I stopped sobbing. "Not Dad."

In front of our house he kissed me on the forehead.

"You're a wonderful and brave woman, Kathleen."

"Dumb kid." I sniffled and reached again for my pack of tissues.

"That too!"

I poked at his shoulder, landing very lightly of course. We both laughed and I felt better.

But not enough better so that I was able to sleep that night. I woke up about five, just as dawn was beginning to break. I sensed something funny in the room as I struggled out of bed to head for the shower. I turned around. Mary Anne and Steve were both standing in the room, smiling at me, still wearing their prom clothes.

I groped toward them, thinking that the wake had all been a nightmare. They waved goodbye and then they were gone.

I've told no one about this experience. I'm sure it was my imagination. But it wasn't a dream. I was wide awake . . . just as I was when Grandpa Martin O'Brien checked in with me when he died.

It was an hallucination, I tell myself. So was the experience of seeing Judge O'Brien. But I didn't know when it happened that Great-Uncle Martin was dead.

I don't believe that Mary Anne came back to make peace with me, not really.

But I do believe that there is peace between us.

I'm not one of your regular psychics. Such experiences have happened only three times in my life. So far.

Dad insisted that I sing *"Panis Angelicus"* during Communion at the funeral Mass. So, after receiving Communion myself, I hurried up to the choir loft of St. Prax's and did the best I could with that aging and liturgically inappropriate chestnut.

Everyone in the church seemed to be weeping when I came back to the front pew. I thought to myself that, without intending it, I must have revealed the grief I felt in my song.

Grandma Lenihan's back was as stiff as a mother superior's when I crowded back into the pew. From the altar where he was assisting at Mass, James was frowning darkly. I glanced at Mom. She shook her head and sighed.

I must have blown it!

They delivered the usual one-two punch.

"You must teach that child not to use an occasion like this to show off," Grandma whispered to Mom, loud enough for me to hear.

And in the limousine on the way to Mount Olivet Cemetery, James lectured me sternly. "You don't seem to understand, Kathleen, that a funeral Mass for your sister and brother is not a time to call attention to yourself. You should have more respect for the dead."

Other people told me that my song was more moving than the Monsignor's sermon, which was not much of a compliment because the Monsignor was always insipid; however it was intended as a compliment because the parish mythology demanded that everyone praise the Monsignor as a great preacher.

In those days, maybe even in these days, other people's praise did not make up for my family's criticism.

Dad hugged me and told me I was wonderful, but somehow his opinion didn't count.

My family life didn't become any worse through the rest of the years of high school. But it didn't get any better either. The stories Mary Anne had spread about me now had a life of their own. I tried to ignore them and sometimes succeeded, but it was hard to accept the fact that some boys were forbidden to invite me to their proms because of my bad reputation.

It's a wonder that my family's attitude towards me did not become a self-fulfilling prophecy. A couple of kids I knew, good kids at that, became pregnant before they graduated from high school because their parents had treated them like they were whores.

They showed their parents: they became whores.

Fortunately for me, I chose to show my parents by being just the opposite.

I loved proms, the fancy dresses, the music, the dancing, the fun at the Lake the next day. I didn't have to fend off my dates because they already knew my reputation among young people.

"You're vain," Grandma said. "You like to flaunt your half-naked body in those scandalous dresses."

The dresses hardly left me half-naked, but they were, I admit in retrospect, a little daring.

The more they complained, the more daring the décolletage became. . . .

"Like WOW!" exclaims my Megan as she looks at the pictures. "Really foxy, Mo-THER, really foxy."

"Did you wear THAT?" Maeve demands.

"I did. Don't you approve?"

"Oh, yeah, it's you know, YOU. Only don't complain when we dress that way."

"I wouldn't dare."

Brigie hugs me. "You're even more beautiful today, Mommy."

It's not true, but I love to hear her say it.

My children think I'm daring, but acceptably so. My own family thought I was vulgar and perhaps sinful.

And I was determined to show them that I could get away with even more.

For reasons which I don't remember, I was forbidden to attend my own prom.

"I HAVE to go," I wailed. "I've already asked Kieran O'Kerrigan."

"WHO?"

"He's inviting me to his prom, too."

They were two blatant lies. I hadn't asked Kieran, but I intended to; and I hoped against hope that he would return the favor.

"He's such a quiet little boy," Mom mused.

"Not so little anymore," Dad said.

Thank God he was home for that argument.

"You spoil her, Hugh." Grandma drew her lips into an even thinner than normal line.

"Well," Dad said judiciously, ignoring Grandma, "I see no harm in her dating him."

I wasn't dating Kieran, but that was no time to argue.

"She should not be permitted to attend those dances with anyone." Grandma always lost her arguments about me with Dad. However, she never learned when to beat a graceful retreat.

Dad ignored Grandma. "I don't want her disappointing Joe O'Kerrigan's son, Mae."

"I suppose you know best, dear," Mom admitted reluctantly. "But mind you, young woman, I don't want any drinking."

Suddenly everything changed. I no longer saw Mom as an enemy but as a mother who had lost two children. I threw my arms around her and wept.

"Oh, Mom, I won't leave you. Not ever. I don't drink. Kieran doesn't drink. Neither does Jenny or her date."

We wept in each other's arms, for a minute or two anyway a mother and daughter who loved one another, no matter what the rest of the family did or thought.

As soon as I could get to the phone, I called Kieran.

"Hi, Kieran, it's Kathleen."

"Who?" he seemed surprised, as well he might have been. I hadn't called him since we were in eighth grade.

"KATHLEEN!"

"Kathleen Leary?"

"Do you know another Kathleen?"

"About a dozen, but none so special."

This was not the occasion to be coy.

"If you haven't been asked by someone else, I want to invite you to my senior prom."

"You're kidding!"

"No WAY!"

"Really?"

"Really."

"Gee." His astonishment seemed genuine enough. "You've made my decade."

I was soaring into the skies looking for my own special cloud of bliss.

"You'll come with me?"

"Is the Pope Catholic? . . . And, hey, you've solved a problem for me."

"What problem?" My heart was pounding because I knew darn well what problem.

"Whether to go to the Ignatius Prom."

"Of COURSE you'll go to it."

"With you as my date?" He sounded worried.

"I'd kill you if you ask anyone else."

Silence for a few moments.

"Thank you very much, Kathleen."

"Thank YOU, Kieran."

I was ecstatic. Not only had I routed Grandma and Mom. I was going to two proms with a boy I truly loved.

A young man I truly loved.

Would he kiss me again the way he had that night when we were in eighth grade?

He'd better!

I don't show my kids pictures of the dresses I wore to those two proms. I wasn't half naked exactly. Maybe only thirty-five or forty percent.

I was the only one in the house when Kieran came to pick me up. Dad was away somewhere on a drunk. Mom was over at Grandma's. Neither wanted to see me, as they said, in an obscene dress.

Kieran whistled.

"KIERAN!" I protested, feeling acutely embarrassed—and very pleased with myself.

"An expression of unqualified admiration." He kissed my forehead. "May I take you up the street and show you to my mother and father?"

"If you want," I said nervously.

"I want."

"You look wonderful too, Kieran."

And he did, in his white formal with a pink cummerbund to match my slinky, skimpy dress. For the first time in my life I realized that Kieran O'Kerrigan was handsome.

"I don't look weird?"

"SURE you look weird. You'll ALWAYS look weird—but now handsome-weird."

It was his turn to be flustered.

"I'm being overwhelmed. Come on, let's show you off to Mom and Dad before we pick up Jenny and her date."

His parents were much older than mine. They had married when she was in her early forties and he almost fifty. Kieran was their only child. They lived quietly in a small house on the edge of the Ravine, a half block from us.

I was impressed that they always held hands in church. You never grow too old to love, I told myself, filing that bit of information away, just in case, as seemed unlikely then, I should ever grow old myself.

They certainly raved about me that night.

"You'll have the prettiest date at the prom," Mrs. O'Kerrigan said.

"How come our son"—Mr. O'Kerrigan chuckled—"is invited by a young woman of both beauty and excellent taste?"

"It is in perfect taste, dear," his wife agreed. "Your mother and grandmother must be very proud of you."

"I invited your son," I replied in kind, "because he's the nicest boy I know."

"A little weird, but nice." Kieran was now the color of his cummerbund.

"And, all of a sudden," I continued, now on a roll, "I find that he's become the best-looking boy in the neighborhood as well as the nicest. So you're the ones who should be proud."

"Irish political family." Kieran winked. "Touch of the Blarney."

"Sometimes Blarney is truth," I insisted.

Maybe, I thought, not without some pride, as we walked back to his Mercury, I am really a whore. What kind of woman says something like that about a shy young man on his first prom date?

A young woman who is very much in love, perhaps too much in love for her age.

Kieran opened the car door for me, went around to the other side, climbed in, put the key in the ignition, and then turned toward me.

"They loved you."

"I'm glad."

My own family didn't love me, but his did.

"It's been a long time since I kissed you properly, Kathleen Anne."

"Four years. Almost."

"I think I should make up for lost time."

"I won't fight you off, Kieran."

"I hear you fight most boys off."

"You're not most boys."

He certainly wasn't.

It was a much longer and more passionate kiss than the earlier one. We were older, our hormones more demanding, and I was somewhat more experienced.

But I had never experienced such a kiss before. Again I still remember its delicious taste.

"Well," he said as if weighing my performance. "The mush is sweeter than ever. Ten this time. Unquestionably!"

"*Kieran!*" I went through the motions of poking at him in mock anger.

He caught my hand and kissed me again, even more effectively.

"This won't be the last one tonight," he said when we parted.

"I'm glad to hear that."

It wasn't. I remember every one of those kisses.

Never in my life have I loved or been loved as I was during that prom season.

We didn't make love. We didn't, to tell the truth, even come within a million miles of making love. But I belonged to him just the same. And he to me.

Despite the chill weather the next morning at Grand Beach, I wore as minimal a bikini as you could purchase at a reputable department store in Chicago—and my high school volleyball championship jacket over it. Open, of course.

Was I teasing this young man, whom I had suddenly discovered to be so wonderful?

I admit I worried a little about that. I was, after all, still a parochial-school-educated Irish-Catholic.

But Kieran seemed delighted rather than teased.

In the afternoon we walked down the beach to be by ourselves. It was much warmer, so I had an excuse to toss aside my jacket and stretch out on the beach.

Seductive?

Well, yes.

But so what!

We began to kiss and caress one another, slowly, gently, lovingly.

He brushed aside my halter and continued his affection.

"I'm lucky not to have my arm broken," he laughed.

"My mixed reputation."

"Mixed?" He paused.

"My family thinks I'm a whore."

"Assholes." He shook his head in dismay.

"On that subject anyway . . . The only boys that can kiss me the way you do are those that I want to."

"Who else?"

"You know the answer to that."

"I guess I do."

The world stopped in its tracks. The wind, the waters of the Lake, the sun moving across the sky all paused. Time stood still. We were caught up in the seemingly endless magic of our love.

He could have done anything he wanted to me. Only I knew I had no reason to fear him.

"Have I said lately that I loved you?"

"In eighth grade."

"Pretty dumb, huh?"

"I knew you loved me."

"Still . . . didn't I say then that I would always love you and always take care of you?"

"Yes, in so many words."

"Do I get a chance to renew my promise?"

"If you want to."

"I sure do: I'll always love you and I'll always take care of you. . . . Now let's go back to your beach and you lead the others in song."

The two proms were interludes of enchantment, rapturous enchantment.

It is fashionable for young people to say that they will never forget prom experiences. But usually proms are really pretty dreadful—tense, demanding, boring. The McAuley and Ignatius proms that year, however were for me periods of unbelievable joy. I thanked God for them many times that summer of 1968. I still do. They proved that joy was still possible in a world filled with evil and ugliness and death.

I opposed the war, alone I think of all my family. I had campaigned for Robert Kennedy in the cold and the rain of the Indiana primary. I wept when he died. Over my family's objection, I marched in protests although I stayed away from the Democratic convention demonstrations because I thought the whole thing was stupid.

I was part of the Vietnam generation, even if I did miss Woodstock, for which thank God. How could I explain that to my daughters, who think the sixties are "like totally gross."

At Boston College I helped lead protests after the Kent State killings. I helped stop traffic on Mass Avenue. I managed to avoid being arrested, which must mean that some of my Chicago instincts survived.

I quit the whole protest business when McGovern agreed to exclude Mayor Daley and the other elected Chicago delegates from the 1972 convention, the week after we learned of poor Terry's death, six weeks before Kieran vanished from my life.

How did McGovern think he was going to win without Chicago?

For all my "activism" until 1972, I still loved proms and I still loved Kieran O'Kerrigan.

So maybe I'm not part of the sixties era at all.

Now the activism seems foolish. We prolonged the war by unintentionally helping to elect and then reelect Richard Nixon, an especially dumb thing for a Chicago politician—which is what I fancied myself and maybe still do.

My love for Kieran was real. The memories still are.

He said he would love and protect me. I trusted myself to him as I have trusted myself to no other man.

He didn't keep his word. He left me. Or did I leave him?

I don't know how it all happened. Suddenly he was gone and my life has never been the same.

Why did I lose him?

Someday I must talk to him, perhaps when we are old and gray, and find out what happened. I was sure he'd call me back after he hung up on me, and he never did.

LEARY

"You realize, Brendan," I said to the young priest, "you're violating both civil and canon law."

Brendan McNulty grinned happily. "Come on, James. You're not really that pompous."

When I was his age I would not have dreamed of calling a Bishop, much less the Vicar General of the Archdiocese, by his first name. I certainly would not have told him that he was being pompous—which at the moment I knew I was.

"You're violating canon law because you are involved in a civil action against the Archdiocese without the permission of the Cardinal. You're violating civil law because you are an employee of the Catholic Bishop of Chicago, a Corporation Sole, and subject to his rules and regulations."

"As to the latter, James." Brendan smiled benignly. "It won't hold up in court and you know it. As to the former, the Cardinal isn't going to take any action against me and you know that too. And, as for being an employee, you don't pay my salary, Elias and McDermott does."

"We pay your benefits, don't we?"

"Nope."

Brendan McNulty is in his early thirties, a strikingly handsome young man of medium height with the dark hair and the pale skin of the Irish. His smile reveals a set of perfect teeth (unusual in our ethnic group) under a trim black moustache. His blue eyes dance with mischief and he has the quick movements of the accomplished athlete—golf and tennis, I believe—and the quick tongue of a precinct captain who may also be a criminal lawyer. He has a first-rate mind. A generation ago he would have been chosen for graduate study in canon law and destined for the episcopal purple. Now he works during the day for a law firm specializing in medical ethics and at a parish in the evenings and on weekends. His biggest problem, it seems to me, is that, in addition to his lack of respect for the Church, he is fundamentally not serious.

"You know that the Cardinal has set his face strongly against you working for a law firm?"

Brendan crossed his legs and clasped his hands behind his head. "Come on, James. If he doesn't fire all the active gays he's got on his hands, he's not going to go after a straight just because he practices a little law on the side."

"Consulting on a suit against the Archdiocese?"

"You send a guy like Greene into a parish, you deserve to get sued."

"Father Gerry Greene," I said wearily, "is a zealous and dedicated priest. He was an excellent administrator under the previous Cardinal. He has been falsely accused. We have reason to believe that it was the child's father who abused the boy. He was cleared by the police and by our consultants."

"There is a quasi-official policy among the law-enforcement and criminal-justice agencies in this country never to arrest, much less indict a Catholic priest if it can possibly be avoided."

"Not everyone would agree with that view," I said firmly.

"Only those who are cops or Assistant States Attorneys," he replied tersely. "The Archdiocese must do its own investigation."

"We do, Brendan." I spread out my hands. "How many times do I have to tell you that."

"A committee of priests decides that a priest like Gerry is innocent and sends him back to the parish because the police have 'cleared' him. It's a circular argument."

"I respectfully disagree," I said in a tone indicating that I thought we should get off that point. "Our advisory board is very careful in its decisions."

"What about the case ten years ago?"

"Nothing has ever been proved about that allegation. There is not even a police report."

Normally I support the Vicar for the Clergy when he removes a priest accused of sexual abuse of children and sends him to an institution for several months of therapy. But neither the Vicar nor I had taken the charges against Gerry Greene seriously. Neither did the Department of Children and Family Services or the State's Attorney. So now we had a massive civil suit on our hands, which had already cost us a half million dollars in legal fees.

I fear these sorts of problems will never end.

"There is too a police report. You've seen it."

"Made by a policeman who was subsequently dismissed. Moreover, there is no evidence that the report is authentic. Why did he wait all these years?"

"Because Monsignor O'Connor had him fired and he was afraid he'd never get another job in law enforcement."

Louis O'Connor was the pastor of the suburban parish where the first charge against Father Greene is supposed to have been made.

"A charge made after the Monsignor has died and can't defend himself. Look, Brendan." I struggled to control my temper. "I don't doubt your sincerity in wanting to help a victim. I'm only suggesting to you that, in fact, Father Greene is the victim in this case. We've had him tested at the Crain Institute and they see no sign of personality disorder, much less of pedophilia intent. Believe me, their tests are thorough."

"Hired guns." He smiled contentedly and shrugged his shoulders.

"Are you suggesting corruption?" I shouted at him.

"Calm down, James." He grinned. "No, I'm not suggesting corruption. But they're your paid consultants. They share the institutional Church's concern to protect priests, to avoid litigation, and to put accused priests back in parishes whenever you can—otherwise they wouldn't be your consultants. They're not exactly objective. Neither are the nuns who heard the complaints first before your arbitration board, nor even the police, who have never charged a priest in the Archdiocese with sexual abuse. Moreover, I'd be very surprised if they ever told you flat-out that you could return a man to parish work. No sensible doctor would ever do that. You and Martin are reading that into what they say because you want to hear them say it."

"You sound like you're against the Church."

"In this case"—he continued to smile benignly—"I sure am. Adversarial law, you know."

I sighed. "The problem is that you don't understand any psychology. You've never had a course in these areas, have you?"

"These areas?" He cocked an eyebrow.

"Paraphilia."

"So that's what they call it. Not perversion anymore . . . a rose is a rose, I guess. . . . No, James, to be perfectly candid, I haven't."

I had an idea.

"Do me a favor, then. Our psychological advisers are convinced that the father is the one who abused this child. Will you consult with an independent psychologist—no, I believe he's a psychiatrist, I can never keep those straight. Anyway, he's an M.D. and a specialist in the problems of children." I wrote out a name and found a phone number on my computer screen. "Discuss the case with him and tell him what our people say."

"A friend of yours?"

"In a manner of speaking. We grew up together. He moved away. When he came back to Chicago two years ago, I counseled him about returning to the Church. He's . . . well, his integrity is beyond any doubt. There were certain problems with his father a long time ago, but everyone has forgotten that. Some charges against him too when he was a boy but they were unfounded. You can trust him totally. I promise I won't talk to him about this case before you consult him."

"He came back to the Church?"

It was a priestly question. Brendan McNulty, for all his relaxed defiance, was still a priest.

"Oh, yes."

"Interesting. Kieran O'Kerrigan, huh?"

"He is affiliated with the University of Illinois and some research center for children and I believe the Chicago Institute for Psychoanalysis."

"O'Kerrigan? They're all Jewish over there, all good analysts are Jewish . . ."

"He tells me that he's an exception."

"Irish-Catholic Freudian . . . Hell, yes." Brendan stood up. "I'll drop by and talk to him. Sounds like a fascinating guy."

"He is all of that."

We shook hands as though there were no conflict between us.

"If you wish, you might let me know what transpires between you."

I would be able to report to the Cardinal, who is, in all candor as he would say, a timid incompetent, that I had a successful dialogue with Father McNulty.

"Why not?" He put the card in his jacket pocket. "Well, James, if you don't mind I have to run. Teen-club dance. Your niece Megie lets me help her run it."

I had almost forgotten that he was assigned to St. Praxides, the parish where our family had moved after racial change had forced us out of South Shore. Kathleen insisted that despite his trips downtown to the law offices of Elias and McDermott, Brendan McNulty did more parish work than the other three priests put together.

"I'm afraid they're pretty undisciplined young women."

"Megie, Maevie, and Brigie? You gotta be kidding, James. They're great kids. Three sweethearts and smart little politicians too. Course that runs in the family."

"Well, we hope their father will be elected to the Senate."

"Oh, yeah, Brien too. But I meant Kathleen. By the way, she is a real knockout."

"Wouldn't that be categorized as a male chauvinist comment?"

Brendan McNulty merely chuckled. "The problem, James, is not the priests who notice Kathleen Donahue, but those priests who walk by her and never give her a second look."

Unfortunately, he was right.

I thought of her at the dinner the night before. Kathleen was indeed striking, a red-haired, blue-eyed goddess out of Celtic antiquity, though her dress was too low cut and too tight for my tastes, an observation I did not make to her.

She seemed so reckless—I might even say abandoned—on the dance
floor with men other than Brien—with whom I did not see her dance—
that I thought she might be drinking, although she is the only one in
our family who stubbornly refuses even a glass of wine.

I began to worry about her. There are so many people to worry
about these days, to say nothing of the poor battered Church.

After Brendan had left, my thoughts turned to the summer that Terry
was killed in Vietnam and Kieran was accused of stealing the money.

That summer before I was ordained I knew that I had to do something
about Brien. I also had to do something about Kathleen. During that
busy and worrisome summer after Terry's death the answer became
obvious to me. Brien and Kathleen ought to marry one another. She
would be a challenge to his strength and power. He would contain her
flighty immaturity. . . .

"Our family is a distinguished and honorable one, James," my grandfather Lenihan used to tell me at our summer "cottage" in Long Beach,
removing his cigar from his mouth to make the point. He would remove
his straw hat, wipe the perspiration off his bald head, and then replace
the hat. After a pause, during which I was presumably reflecting on
wisdom I had heard many times before, he would add in his opulent
baritone voice, "Never forget that. We are not shanty Irish like a lot of
these people around us. We have a reputation to protect and enhance."

There was a storm brewing on the Lake, rushing across from Chicago.
Dark wisps of cloud were racing by above us, footsteps rushing by at
night; and the surface of the Lake was as smooth as a trial lawyer's
voice—and as deceptive.

Even then I sensed that Grandpa Lenihan was suggesting that our
reputation—that is to say the Lenihan reputation—needed protection
from the depredations of his son-in-law, Hugh Thomas "Red Hugh"
Leary.

Grandpa Leary, long since dead of an early heart attack while working in the sewers of Chicago, had been born O'Leary, the name changed
by *his* wife, my grandmother, at the time of her wedding to distinguish
the family from the biddy who was responsible, according to legend, for
the Chicago Fire, not that she or her husband were much better off

economically than the fabled Mrs. O'Leary. She was a domestic servant
and he a common laborer.

"Red Hugh," my father, named both after his red hair and a figure in
Irish history, was, not to put too fine an edge on the matter, a rogue,
a rascal, a scoundrel. He was also a winsome charmer, a red-haired
leprechaun with dancing eyes and a mobile mouth from which one
expected song to burst forth at any minute—an expectation which was
often realized.

He was also a brilliant trial lawyer, "even when I'm sober," he'd say
with a laugh, "which is not all that often."

"And," he would add with a wink and another irresistible laugh, "as
far as that goes, all the good trial lawyers in Chicago are short Irishmen
with inferiority complexes, loud mouths, and a compulsion for the
'creature.' "

"I hardly noticed an inferiority complex in you, Hugh." Grandfather
Lenihan would snap his suspenders in displeasure.

"Ah, it manifested itself for the last time in 1935, or was it 1945?
Funny, I can't remember. Isn't that strange, Jimmy, I can't remember
which year."

Grandpa Lenihan viewed the marriage of his only daughter to this
"gombeen man" (as he called him) with even more dismay than he and
my mother would view Kathleen's possible marriage to Kieran O'Kerrigan.

I had once thought that Mary Anne and Brien would make an ideal
match. But Mary Anne was dead. She and my brother Steve and Steve's
date had been killed in a tragic car crash. Alcohol had been involved,
though in those days people were too polite to say so. Poor Mary Anne
had suffered from the family weakness for liquor even as a teen. Only
Kathleen was left to bring together the political aspirations of the Learys
and Donahues. I knew that Brien hadn't failed to notice her all-too-
obvious attractions. Brien often said that my sister was "the most
beautiful woman I've ever met. In a bikini or not she stops traffic."

"You mean fully clothed?"

He howled. "You have such a prurient mind, James! Either way if it
comes to that! But you know what I mean."

"I know, but you should be careful about your language."

She for her part was always polite to him, but nothing more.

"That was a nice article in the *Trib* last week, Brien," she told him once.

"Did you read it?" He seemed surprised and happy.

"Of course I read it. Your solutions seem a little simple, but they point in the right direction."

I was provoked. He was flattered.

"She's so bright." He sighed. "And so pretty."

I did not know much about romance, but it did not sound like the kind of conversation that signals the beginning of romance.

Then, oblivious to the terrible tragedies which had struck our family, Kathleen, just twenty-one, became very serious about Kieran O'Kerrigan. How serious I never knew and don't want to know today. For all I care now they may have slept together that tragic summer.

Like Kieran, she was drifting. She had graduated from Boston College with honors, to everyone's surprise, and had no definite plans for September. She might teach in a Catholic school. She might go back to college for an MA. She might do volunteer work somewhere. Or, as she brazenly threatened, she might marry Kieran O'Kerrigan.

There was no doubt in my mind that it would be an unsuitable marriage. To begin with, Kieran's family was not as distinguished as ours. Grandpa and Mom considered them to be "new rich," parvenus from Englewood who had "made it" after the war and thought that a move to Beverly in the early nineteen-fifties and a purchase of a house at Grand Beach made them "somebody."

To make matters worse, Kieran's father had died in jail after having been convicted on a conspiracy and bribery charge, of which my father and Tom Donahue had been acquitted.

Finally, Kieran was a strange, dreamy young man, nice enough, heaven knew, but devoid of athletic ability and innocent of political ambition.

"Can't you see what your relationship is doing to your mother and your grandfather?" I was perpetually trying to make Kathleen understand.

"I haven't said I will marry him." She waved her hand. "I just said I'm thinking about it. I thought I ought to tell everyone. Maybe I'll go off to New York with him and help him get through medical school."

"Or help him launch his vocal career in Irish bars?"

"Maybe. What would be wrong with that?"

"I suppose you'd sing with him?"

"I might if he wanted me to."

"Dear God in heaven, Kathleen! Have you no sense of who you are?"

"I'm Kathleen Leary, Red Hugh's daughter, that's who I am."

"Has he agreed to marry you?"

"Calm down, James. It's not that far along. We haven't even talked about marriage."

"So it's all in your mind?"

"And my body."

"What a vile thing to say!"

"Didn't they teach you in the seminary that the body is a sacrament?"

"That's not the point."

"What is the point?" She remained cool and collected, an unusual mood for one of her arguments with me.

"The point is that you can't do this to a family which has borne such grief in the last few months."

"Kieran has suffered a little grief too . . . but I would think that a marriage would bring a little light back to the family, wouldn't it?"

She was provoking me again, but now without shouting.

"The right kind of marriage," I muttered.

"What kind is that? Oh, don't tell me. I know. A 'suitable' marriage, huh?"

"Yes."

"And Kieran's not suitable? Why?"

"You know the answer to that."

"Do I? Well, perhaps I know your answer, but perhaps I don't agree."

"When do you propose to decide about this . . ."

" 'Unsuitable match'? I don't know. There's no rush. I suppose before the summer's over."

"How do you know that he will marry you if you decide you want to marry him?"

"Oh, that's no problem." Her eyes widened. "Of course he'll want to marry me."

"Why?"

"Why? Because, brother, he loves me! And I think I might love him."

"Is that all that's required for a happy marriage?"

"No, but it's a good beginning."

Somehow that marriage had to be stopped. Somehow I had to

protect my sister; I had to protect her from a disastrous marriage, one in which she would always be unhappy. Kieran was a nice boy, but he wasn't nearly good enough for my beloved Kathleen. But how could I stop it?

Dad, frivolous as always, encouraged Kathleen.

"He's a grand lad, Kath, me dear. You'd never be unhappy with him. Never at all."

Grandpa refused to discuss it. If he was at our house—either in Beverly or at the Lake—he would stomp out when the subject came up. Mother, still shrouded in grief over the deaths of her children, bitterly and tearfully opposed the marriage and swore she would not come to the wedding.

Kathleen remained unruffled. "I'm still thinking about it. I won't make up my mind hastily."

Brien was no help. "They're a real cute couple, James. I think Kieran is a lucky, lucky guy."

I began to resign myself to accepting once again that which I couldn't change. Then Kieran solved our problems for us by refusing to defend himself when he was accused of stealing twenty-five thousand dollars.

There were explanations, excuses. He probably took the money in a momentary fugue, overcome by grief and anger. But people knew he took it just the same.

And when he wouldn't give it back, Kathleen was shocked and began to have her doubts about him. Even then, she might have married him, if Kieran had not asked my advice.

Even in retrospect, I think I gave him good advice. I hope I did. I'm sure he's much happier now than he would have been if he had not followed my instructions.

Yet the advice fit so well with my plans for Brien and Kathleen that I wonder if I should have withdrawn from the adviser role because of conflict of interest.

I played judge, prosecutor, jury, executioner, and even God in the case of the People of Grand Beach against Kieran O'Kerrigan.

Even at the time I had my doubts about what I was saying, but I believed sincerely that what I suggested he do was in everyone's best interest.

What happened was this: There was and is a Calcutta Golf Tournament at Grand Beach every summer. It is not as big as the one at

Beverly, where hundreds of thousands of dollars are alleged to change hands. At Grand Beach only about fifty thousand dollars is involved. The gambling is illegal, naturally, but the police do not interfere with Calcuttas at private clubs.

Dave Regan, who was in charge of holding half the pot, stored it in a cabinet in his house, not so foolish an action as it sounds, because no one had ever stolen anything from Grand Beach until then.

The O'Kerrigan house was right next door to the Regans'.

Everyone knew that Kieran needed the money. His parents had left him virtually nothing since they had been wiped out by legal costs.

Moreover, Father Pat O'Connell, a priest who hung out at Grand Beach a lot those days, a cabin hunter it was said, actually saw Kieran come out of the Regan house on the Saturday night of the Labor Day weekend.

The next morning, Pat, his boozy face and bleary eyes solemn, showed up at our house for a "private word with James."

The poor man is dead now, but I never did like him. He was a hanger-on, a parasite seeking patronage from the rich or the presumed rich who liked to have priests around them.

"What's up?" I demanded, as soon as we were seated on the porch facing the Lake. It was already an unbearably humid day, the kind of end-of-summer day when the hate meters turn crimson.

"Your friend Kieran O'Kerrigan"—he spoke the name with a sneer— "is in real trouble. Last night he took the pot for the Grand Beach Calcutta from Dave Regan's house. Everyone knows he needs the money, but he's too young to be imitating his father's crookedness."

"I don't believe it."

"I tell you I saw him come out of the house. Dave came home from supper at Maxine and Hymie's and found the money missing."

"Maybe he was just walking by the house."

"I said I saw him coming out. I thought of him as soon as Dave noticed the money missing."

"Have they called the police?"

"They're giving him till noon today to return it. Then it's the Michigan state cops. Grand larceny."

"What does he say?"

"He denies everything. No one believes him."

"What do you want me to do?"

"Talk to him. Tell him not to ruin his life. Tell him to give the money back."

I nodded. "I'll do that. This morning."

"He doesn't have much time."

I thought about it. I would never need money in all my life the way Kieran needed it at this minute. I was his friend. He needed help.

"Wait a minute," I said to Pat.

I went back into the house, found a ball-point pen and a piece of stationery with my name on the letterhead. I scrawled out a note to Dave Regan, promising him negotiable bonds for twenty-five thousand dollars on Tuesday morning at the First National Bank in Chicago—part of my bequest to me from Grandma Lenihan.

"I'll cover it." I returned to the porch and gave Pat the note.

"You'll do what?"

"I'll replace the money."

"Will he give it back to you?"

"That's between him and me, isn't it?"

"If you cover it, I guess it is."

"They'll accept my word?"

"Sure they will. You're a Lenihan."

"Fine. Then it's done."

He rose to leave. "Actually, it's only $24,835."

"Tell Dave to keep the change."

Later in the day, after playing eighteen sweltering holes at Long Beach, I drove over to the O'Kerrigan house, a small place on the Lake, remodeled from a 1915 Sears portable.

Kieran greeted me at the door with his usual slow, appealing smile.

"What did you ever do that for, James?" he asked. "Come on. Want a lemonade?"

"Sure."

I would have much preferred a beer.

The house was impeccably neat. Kieran had not permitted it to "go to the dogs" as Grand Beach gossip had rumored.

We sat in a shady corner of the lawn overlooking the beach, protected from the direct rays of the sun by trees which would be wiped out by high Lake levels and a winter storm before the year was over.

"I heard what you did, James," he began, head bowed, eyes turned away from me.

"You can give me the money now or pay me when you get a chance if you need the money that badly."

"You shouldn't have done it, James," he continued. "I didn't take the money."

"Who did?" I asked skeptically.

"How do I know?" He hung his head, a picture of dejection and misery. "Would I be so stupid as to do something like that up here where everyone thinks I'm the son of a crook?"

"No," I had to admit. "I don't think you're stupid. But Father O'Connell . . . ?"

"I was just walking along Lakeview in the dark. He was driving by in the Kearney Mercedes, drunk as usual, and I hopped out of his way into the Regan driveway."

"But why would he blame you?"

His argument was a weak one which would never convince anyone.

"He saw me in the driveway. He's never liked me much." He closed his eyes and leaned back against the lawn chair. "I don't know why. Now he thinks I'm a bad influence in the village—as if he were a property owner up here instead of a—"

"Cabin hunter?"

"Yeah. But why use your money?"

"Because they were going to call the police. I'm your friend, and I have the money and I don't need it. That's enough reason."

"I still don't understand."

A strong man who believed he was innocent or at least wished to pretend that he was innocent would have stood up, defied the whole Grand Beach community and fought back. But Kieran, as sweet a person as he was, lacked the strength necessary for such heroic defiance.

"As Grandpa always says, if you don't stand by your friends, who will stand by you?"

I sounded as unctuous as an undertaker expressing his condolences to someone he's never met.

"Well, I owe you the money for covering for me. I'll pay it back someday."

"We won't talk about that, Kieran."

He stood up and, hands jammed into the pockets of his Bermuda shorts, walked slowly to the edge of the dune, and stared pensively at the Lake.

After a few minutes he returned to our chairs.

"Do you think I ought to leave?"

"Leave what?"

"The neighborhood, the beach, everything. Go to med school and never come back?"

"Why do that?" My heart leaped because this would be the perfect solution to our problem—unless Kathleen decided to go with him and also never come back.

I had to take that chance.

"I'll never live this down. I'll always have the reputation around here of being a thief and the son of a crook."

"But you believe that neither of those charges are true, don't you?"

"Sure, but what good will that do?" There were tears in his eyes.

I then said the words which even now trouble my soul.

"If you want the honest truth, Kieran, I think that's just what you should do. Cut your losses and get out of here. None of it's your fault, but these problems will haunt your life if you stay in Chicago."

"Leave forever?"

"Twenty, twenty-five years, anyhow. I'll miss you. A lot of us will miss you. But you'll be much happier away from this cruel place."

"It's been cruel to me, all right. How soon should I go?"

"The quicker and the cleaner the break, the better."

He nodded. "You're right, James. Like you always are. Thanks for the advice. I needed to hear something like that from someone. Otherwise I would have dithered for days or weeks. I'll leave and never come back."

He was gone by the next morning.

With the money, people said. My money.

They marveled at my generosity.

"Did he take the money, Jimmy?" my father asked me several weeks later.

"He denies it."

"Do you believe him?"

I shrugged. "If he was innocent, wouldn't he have stayed and fought?"

"Maybe." My father's eyes narrowed. "Most men would."

"He's not a very strong man, Dad."

"There's different kinds of strength, Jimmy."

"His father was not strong either. Kieran was a nice fellow, but we're well rid of him."

"Do you think so?" He cocked one eye and glanced at me.

"I do."

"Mark my words." Dad's eyes took on that dreamy, mystical look that always baffled me. "We haven't seen the last of him."

I don't know whether Kieran ever said goodbye to Kathleen, or whether there was ever any communication between them after that weekend.

She was quiet and tense for a few weeks. Then she seemed to forget about Kieran O'Kerrigan. She began to teach at a Catholic school in a black neighborhood. She took night courses at Loyola toward an MA in history, a pointless waste of time, it seemed to me. More importantly, she also seemed interested in Brien's preliminary courting. He had, at my urging, moved in to fill the emptiness in her life.

"Poor Kieran," he said when I suggested that now was his opportunity. "I think he's innocent, too."

"He's gone, Brien," I said. "He'll never be back."

"I guess not. Well, she sure is a nice girl and I suppose you're right, it is time for me to settle down."

I married them the following June, the week after my own first Mass. Grandpa and Mom were delighted. Even Red Hugh seemed pleased.

In the later years, as I received checks from Kieran at odd times, I tore them up.

He apparently did not watch his bank records very closely because he kept sending them until what he presumed was a debt had been paid. I have often told myself that if I had to do it over again, I would do the same thing. Whatever has happened to her marriage with Brien, a marriage to Kieran would have been a disaster—or so I often reasoned.

Now I'm not so sure.

BRIEN

I wish I were dead. I wish I had the guts to kill myself. There's a demon inside of me, a monster. I can kill him only by killing myself.

I know I don't have AIDS. But I can't tell her that he insisted on being "safe."

I didn't hit her last night. I couldn't have hit her. Yet, I guess I did hit her. I don't remember much; some harsh words, that's all. But she's a mess. I must have done it.

Dear God, I'm sorry. I didn't want to do it. I hate myself for doing it. Forgive me. Help her to forgive me. Give me the strength to bring the demon under control before he destroys everything in my life.

I worship her. She's a wonderful woman, fine wife and mother, intelligent, beautiful.

Forgive me, please, please, please! Help me never to hurt her again, I beg you!

BRENDAN

"Do you permit your son to watch you and your husband engage in sexual intercourse?"

The three women lawyers who represented the Archdiocese, three wicked witches I called them, had been badgering Helen O'Malley for fifty hours. They were not about to let up.

"Certainly not," Helen replied.

The two not posing the questions just then laughed. That was part of the routine. One of them would ask a question and the other two would deride Helen's answer with their giggles. Thus does the Archdiocese of Chicago play adversarial law with its own people.

"How often do you engage in intercourse?" the wicked witch went on.

"You don't need to answer that question," Ron Long advised our client.

"Do you refuse to answer that question?"

"Yes, I do."

"I'll certify that," the lawyer said crisply, meaning that she would ask the judge to order Helen to answer under pain of contempt. There was no chance that the judge would issue such an order. But the Archdiocese didn't care. It was concerned only with drawing out the process of harassing its "enemies" (the families of pedophile victims) till they broke under the strain.

"Has your son ever accidentally seen you and your husband engage in sexual intercourse?"

"No."

More laughter.

"Are you sure?"

"Yes, I'm sure."

"Not even once?"

"No."

"You've testified that when he was younger, he used to sleep between the two of you when he was frightened by thunderstorms. Did you and your husband ever engage in sexual intercourse under those conditions?"

"No."

The questions were absolutely outrageous. We could easily cite the three lawyers for unprofessional behavior to the Illinois Supreme Court's ethical office. They knew we could. They were also quite certain that we would cave in and accept a monetary settlement and that we would therefore not charge them. I wondered as Helen maintained an utterly serene exterior in the face of their seemingly endless assault whether they were beginning to have any doubts.

"Probably not," Ron had said to me when I asked him. "The Archdiocese has won every other contest by playing hardball. They think the Cardinal and his friends are invulnerable."

"Do you permit your son to fondle your breasts?"

"No."

"Are you sure?"

More giggles.

"Yes."

"Do you take showers with him?"

"No."

"How old was he when you stopped bathing him?"

"I don't remember exactly."

"A year or two ago?"

"No, no. Before he went to grammar school."

"How often did you manipulate his sexual organs when you bathed him?"

"I never did."

"Are you sure?"

"Yes."

"Not even to wash them?"

"When he was still a baby."

"You manipulated them?"

"I washed them."

"Did you find it sexually stimulating?"

"No."

Giggles.

"Was it sexually stimulating to breast-feed him?"

"Not in the usual sense of that word."

"What is the usual sense of that word?"

"Erotically attractive, I suppose."

"You suppose?"

"Yes."

"Well, what did it feel like?"

"Counselor," Ron Long interjected patiently. "I will take this opportunity to warn you on the record that your line of questioning is offensive. You pursue it at considerable risk to your professional career."

"Are you trying to intimidate me, Mr. Long?"

"I wouldn't dream of that, Ms. Taylor. I'm merely pointing out the consequences of your line of questioning."

"I appreciate your wisdom," she said sarcastically. "Now, Ms. O'Malley, will you answer the question or must I certify it for the judge?"

"Anyone who has breast-fed a child understands how God feels."

"How God feels?" Ms. Taylor did not try to hide her incredulous amusement.

"To be the source of life for someone."

"Do you really believe in God?"

Yet more laughter.

Helen opened her mouth to respond, but Ron interrupted. "We're not going to answer that question, counselor. Certify it to the judge if you wish. And let the record show that I assert that counselors for the defendant giggled derisively through this entire session."

"Let the record also show that I deny that allegation."

"Let the record also show that I have asked the court reporter to save the audio tape she is making."

Ron did not bicker with them often. He knew that such challenges merely served the Archdiocese's goal of delay and harassment. But he interrupted occasionally to suggest that eventually there might be a day of reckoning.

Smarter lawyers might have backed off. But the Archdiocese's invincibility had made this crew recklessly arrogant.

At the lunch break, the court reporter, an Italian Catholic from Oak Park, whispered to me, "This is the vilest deposition I've ever recorded, Father. It makes me ashamed to be a Catholic."

Dark-blue suit or not, I was still "Father."

"Judas Iscariot was one of the first Bishops. And it's been downhill ever since."

She laughed. But she took my point. Neither the Cardinal nor his legal representatives were Catholicism.

Would Bishop James Leary read this shameful record?

Probably not. And if he did, Ignatius Loyola Keefe, senior partner in the law firm for which the Archdiocese was a cash cow, would undoubtedly assure him that it was necessary for the good of the Church, especially since the parents the Archdiocese were harassing were trying to cover up their neglect of their child.

Keefe was pure sleaze. Most lawyers in Chicago knew it. But the Cardinal and James were convinced that he was the best in the business and that the Archdiocese was lucky to have him as their senior legal representative.

If Keefe were really smart, he would know that the O'Malleys would not quit and that the Chicago scandal, once it broke, would make all the others seem pale by comparison.

For a long time I had hoped that the scandal could be avoided. As I listened to the witches attack Helen O'Malley, however, I had begun to pray for an explosion.

LEARY

"She's always been a spoiled brat, James." Brien sighed wearily. "You of all people know that. Now she's going to ruin everything."

Brien had pushed his way into my office right after Brendan McNulty had left.

I felt my stomach churn. I had sensed at the Ireland Fund Dinner that something was wrong in their marriage. Trust Kathleen to do something foolhardy at just the wrong time.

"What has she done now?"

I was late for a meeting with the Cardinal about closing more parishes and schools, a critically important meeting. But I had no choice: I had to listen to Brien. He was closer to me than any brother could have been. Moreover, he was one of the finest Catholic laymen of our time. I disagreed with him on abortion, but, with that single exception, I knew him to be the kind of man who could restore a sense of moral values to public life.

I did not, however, offer him coffee. He had walked up Michigan Avenue from his firm's office without calling for an appointment. Our meeting had to be brief.

"She wants a divorce."

"Oh, my God!"

Brien was wearing the usual carefully fitted three-piece brown business suit which, along with a green tie, had become his trademark. But he looked rumpled, almost disoriented. As we talked he dabbed at his

forehead with a large, slightly soiled handkerchief which matched his
tie. Normally it would have remained untouched in the breast pocket of
his suit. He reminded me of a professional athlete trying, after a bad
defeat, to explain to a television camera why his team had lost.

"I don't know what to do about her." He twisted his hands like he
was trying to dry them off. "She's always had everything she's ever
wanted. She's never had to work. I've given her everything, absolutely
everything."

I am a realist about the Sacrament of Matrimony. Brien and Kathleen
were at a time in their marriage when a rift of some sort was inevitable.
The forces that tear marriages apart in our society are almost irresistible,
as the divorce rates show. But the rates are one thing and your own
family is something else.

"It was a mistake to let her go to The University of Chicago, Brien.
I told you that. They have no morals out there."

"I know . . . I know. But I figured that if she wanted to go over there
a couple of days a week it was all right with me. Hell, she didn't need
to teach college. We have plenty of money. It's a silly game, but if she
wanted to take it seriously and it made her happy, well, why not?"

"It's one of these feminist 'identity crisis' things? She wants to be her
'own person,' that kind of thing?"

"I suppose so, James." His chin sunk to his chest. "When you get right
down to the bottom of it. But I guess I made a mistake or two, nothing
really serious, but it gave her some ammunition."

"Someone else?"

He looked up at me and nodded sadly. "Yeah, one of those things.
The pressure's been so great the last couple of months." He rubbed his
hands across his face. "Unbelievable pressure. And I never get any
encouragement at home. Anyway, it didn't mean a thing. It's all over.
Finished. Done. I love my wife and my kids. I don't want to lose them."

"She's not willing to forgive you and give you another chance?"

"Absolutely not! I can't even live in my own house. I sleep in the
coach house and cook my own meals."

I shut my eyes. Everything was falling apart, just as I had feared it
would.

"A fine preparation for an election campaign! The papers will have
a field day! I can see Sneed's column already."

"I know." He seemed on the verge of tears. "But that doesn't matter.

My family is more important to me than the damn United States Senate."

"Is she serious about a divorce?"

"Is she ever serious about anything, James? . . . I don't know. She hasn't seen a lawyer yet."

"That's a good sign."

"She wants an annulment too. She says you guys grant them to everyone these days."

She was right. The matrimonial tribunal was out of control. But a bishop's sister! The Vatican wouldn't like that if they found out.

"That's a long way off, Brien."

"She blames it on my drinking. You know what kind of a fanatic she is on that subject. She says our parents are alcoholics and I'm one too. Shit, James, I'm no alcoholic. You know that."

For the first time, I began to fear that Brien would fall apart on me—and myself already late for a crucial meeting with the Boss.

"I know, Brien, I know. But she's obsessed on that subject." Our parents did drink too much. But Brien and I both knew how to drink in moderation. Neither of us were alcoholics. Kathleen was probably well advised not to drink: she wouldn't have been able to handle it.

"I even promised her I'd join AA. It wouldn't mean anything, but it would keep her happy, know what I mean?"

"I think it's all a tempest in a teapot, Brien. She'll get over it." I was trying to end the conversation so I could rush off to the Boss.

"I don't know, James—I don't know. She's terribly angry."

"The, uh, affair is definitely over?"

"Huh? Oh yeah, that didn't mean a thing. You know how it is, James. Just one of those things that happen. Nothing important."

No I didn't know how it was. A woman is very properly incensed when she finds her husband cheating. I couldn't blame my sister for that, even if she probably had driven him to it. But none of us is perfect. She should be ready to forgive. Let those who are without sin cast the first stone. Had she been faithful to Brien? That was a tough question. I had always assumed that she was, but after she went to The University of Chicago I wasn't so sure.

"She has every reason to be furious at you, Brien. Women don't like it when their husbands cheat."

"Dear God, if I told her I was sorry once, I told her thirty times. I begged her on my knees to forgive me. What more can I do?"

"You've got to be very contrite and considerate, Brien. You have to court her again."

"I know." He sighed. "I know . . . It's hard . . . You see . . . Well, I did have too much to drink at that Ireland thing; and I lost my temper and I might have hit her once or twice."

Dear God, a battered wife. That's all we needed! "You should never have done that, Brien. Never. Men can't do that to women nowadays. It's wrong."

The tears began to roll down his cheeks.

"I know. I know. It was terrible. I'm ashamed of myself. It was like I was in a trance and watching someone else, someone I hated, hit my wife."

"Damn it, Brien," I shouted. "You might have killed her!"

"It won't ever happen again. I swear it. She doesn't believe me. Or maybe she just wants an excuse to dump me."

"At just the wrong time."

"That doesn't matter, James, that doesn't matter."

But it did and he knew it did.

"I still think it will work out. You know Kathleen, she has her big ideas but she never finishes anything. Divorce is like that dissertation: it will never happen."

I stood up. I had to get to that conference. The Boss needed me.

"You'll come out and talk to her for me?"

I should have guessed that was why he had come over to the Chancery Office. I was supposed to persuade my featherbrain sister to forgive a husband who had cheated on her and then had hit her to top it off.

I was profoundly disappointed in Brien, but I suspected that much of the problem was in her, not in him. If a man is driven to another woman's bed, it is often because there is no satisfaction in his own bed. I dreaded trying to talk sense to her. But I didn't have much choice.

"Of course, Brien. I'll drive out to the neighborhood tomorrow afternoon."

KATHLEEN

So I didn't kill myself.

The next morning, Brien denied that he had done anything more than "slap" me "once or twice."

I suppose that he thought he was telling the truth. The other two times he'd beaten me he'd claimed that he had no recollection of what he'd done to me. He had been out of control, literally beside himself. All the rage he felt toward his mother and grandmother—and me too, I guess—had unleashed the savage inside him.

Yet he had enjoyed battering and violating me too much for it to be just a temporary psychotic interlude.

He didn't *want* to remember. He wouldn't look at my bruised and bloody body. Rather, he fell on his knees and begged me to forgive him for "everything."

I said three things: "therapy," "AA," and "HIV test." He agreed to the last two, but it wasn't enough. I sent him packing to the coach house that stood behind our late-Victorian landmark, as I had done when he had drunk himself into a stupor a couple of other times in our marriage.

Intellectually I knew that I was in grave danger. So were the kids. Brien could explode again at any time under the pressures of the political campaign. He might kill someone. However, there was no question in my head about the danger. I could feel it in my gut. I was afraid, terribly afraid, but I was still numb and unable to react. My husband might kill me, I kept saying.

And I would reply, yes, but you must get on with your dissertation.

I don't know what the children thought of this exile of their father to the coach house. They never asked about such banishments. But they were too observant and too smart not to notice it and think about it.

I dosed myself with Advil and—pain and rage notwithstanding—turned on my computer to work on my dissertation.

I was a survivor and so were my kids. We would show them all.

Looking back on it now, I should have called a divorce lawyer that morning.

Why didn't I?

I told myself I'd give him a few days more to decide about therapy and then I'd call the lawyer.

So why didn't I find myself a good divorce lawyer?

I was afraid to, that's why. I was afraid of the publicity and the shame and the conflict of a divorce. I was afraid of destroying Brien's political future—and being blamed for destroying it. I was afraid of the suffering it would bring to the kids and to my parents and to my brother the Bishop. I was afraid to break completely with the life I'd known for almost eighteen years.

I knew it had to happen. I knew I shouldn't put it off.

But I did. Just for another couple of days, I told myself.

So I ate Advil like it was candy, excused myself from Taekwondo class, and tried to sort out my future life.

The first thing I had to do, I told myself, was find out about a possible HIV infection. If my husband had a gay lover, there was a reasonably good chance that he was infected. I didn't know the percentages, but I knew they were high. True, we hadn't made love for almost two months; but I did not know how long his "affair"—if that was the proper word—had lasted.

I knew it was crazy to fear our girls might be infected, but at the rate my world was falling apart, I couldn't be sure of anything. I resolved then and there to have them tested as well. That meant telling them the truth eventually. But I wouldn't worry about that just now.

The question was, where could I find a doctor whom I could trust? We were public figures. It would be hard to keep anything secret. What if word of our being tested leaked out?

Immediately my thoughts ran to Kieran, and not just because he was a doctor who could keep a confidence. Whatever Kieran's problems might have been—and might still be—there had never been any doubt about his physical craving for me. With Brien's betrayal so irrevocable, was there any wonder I wanted to see a man I knew had cherished me only too well?

He had never married. I had heard that there had been a woman in New York for many years but that she had left him. Poor Kieran, deserted by two women. That would destroy anyone's confidence and especially the confidence of someone as gentle as Kieran.

I didn't let my fantasies go any further than seeing him and that genuine gleam of appreciation in his eye. I was not an adulterous woman and was not intent on becoming one. Or so I told myself.

So, without much further thought as to the consequences, I impetuously fled Regenstein Library early in the afternoon, drove downtown, parked in the Grand Park underground, and, after walking back and forth in the rain for a half hour trying to work up my courage, I entered the 30 North Michigan Building—decisively pushing the revolving door—and rode up the elevator to Kieran's office.

It almost broke my heart to see him again. I wanted to cry when he opened the office door. Same old Kieran.

He was thin as ever, maybe thinner. He was not as short as he was in eighth grade, but àt most he was only three or four inches above my five-five. His sandy hair was flecked with gray. His gray eyes were as kind as ever. His fine, slender face had somehow become distinguished. The beard which always appeared in late afternoon had made its appearance. My rebel hands wanted to stroke that wonderful face and feel its fine, sharp hair.

In some vague and elusive way, he was a different Kieran—satisfied with himself now, at peace with his world, a man who had acquired wisdom.

More than anything else, Kieran Patrick O'Kerrigan looked like a priest, and, with my daughters, like a young priest working with teenagers whom he understood and liked, a low-key and much wiser version of that cute Father Brendan McNulty.

He was so gentle and considerate with me that I thought I might throw myself into his arms and tell him everything.

Anyway, I pretended to the self-possession he had always admired— or claimed to have admired.

My rebellious body almost betrayed me. It hurt terribly from what my husband had done to me, but its hormones began to work when I rolled up the sleeve of my dress for him to take my blood.

The worst moment was when I told him that I came to him for the test because I trusted him and he said that I must have changed my mind.

I realized at that moment that I *had* changed my mind. The reason

I had turned my back on Kieran so many years ago was false. How long had I known that?

I admitted to him that I had been wrong—not an easy acknowledgment for me to make. Did he realize that?

I left his office feeling that he knew everything there was to know about me—both about the girl who had rejected him and about the troubled woman who had come for his help.

PART II

KIERAN

"Donahue residence," said a very grown-up teenage voice—Megan Marie, I incorrectly presumed.

"Doctor O'Kerrigan with good news for Mrs. Donahue."

"Oh, hi, Doctor O'Kerrigan. This is Maeve. Mom's in her study working on her dissertation. You can call her on her private line." With that, Maeve rattled off the number.

"Her dissertation?"

"Right. Mommy is going to be a Doctor, too, in March. A Ph.D. doctor, the kind, like we say, that doesn't do any good for people. At the University, which means, like The University of Chicago when they say it. Isn't that totally excellent!"

"Totally, Maeve. . . . Will I be in terrible trouble if I call her on her personal phone?"

"Not with good news. She needs some."

"Thank you."

"Oh, hey, Doctor O'Kerrigan." Maeve caught me as I was about to hang up. "She may snap at you because she's distracted from her work when the phone rings, but don't pay any attention to that."

"Got it, Maeve."

What, I asked, while I dialed the number, did that wise little child mean by her comment that Mother needed some good news?

"Yes," said an impatient voice, as predicted.

"Doctor O'Kerrigan with good news for soon-to-be Doctor Donahue!"

"Kieran!"

"Maeve Anne said I shouldn't mind if you sounded distracted, because you were working hard on your dissertation."

"I'm sorry to have been abrupt . . ."

"She said you might snap, but you didn't, not quite."

"The little brat!" She laughed. "She knows me all too well. . . . You did say good news?"

"Absolutely."

"Thank God for that."

"Amen."

"You're sure?"

"I'm sure. You probably should repeat the tests in another month or two, but I think there's nothing much to worry about."

"I will . . . I suppose I overreacted."

"Mothers do that."

"I'm very grateful, Kieran . . . and I'm sorry I was so distracted when you called. I get so involved in this damn dissertation. . . ."

"I know what it's like, Kathleen. I write an article now and then and I resent interruption too."

"Thank you for interrupting with good news."

"I'm glad I could help. . . . Give my very best to Brien. I must take the two of you to dinner sometime soon. I seem to have missed the wedding celebration."

"That would be very nice."

It didn't sound like she thought it would be nice at all.

My heart jumped a couple of times.

"I'll be talking to you soon."

"Thanks again, Kieran."

End of conversation.

There was trouble in that home, no doubt about it. Maeve knew there was trouble. The false tone of voice with which Kathleen had reacted to my proposed belated wedding celebration suggested there was trouble.

Thin shreds of evidence, but when added to the HIV test . . .

I would not intervene to attack a reasonably happy marriage, I promised myself. But if the marriage were falling apart . . .

What if Kathleen were in serious danger of more brutalization? Or something even worse?

I must act like a grown-up and wait till there was more evidence of that. Right, Maggie?

But what if he killed her before I had more evidence? I shuddered at the image of Kathleen in a casket.

I would wait for a little while longer. In the meantime, fate or God or something or Someone had provided a chance for us to talk and neither of us had made anything of it.

I only hoped I hadn't blown yet another opportunity.

The day before I'd left New York for the long trip home—a journey of light-years in fact—my training analyst, seventy-two-year-old Doctor Franz Rosenblum, scribbled a name and a phone number on a piece of yellow note paper torn from his pad.

"Ya, you will see Margaret Mary Ward in Chicago, no? She will remind you of your grandmother, so?"

"Margaret Keenan?"

"Ya, you know her?"

"I've seen her at seminars. But she's not a physician as I remember."

"So?"

"Would the institute approve?"

"For her they make an exception, but they pretend they don't. They figure if Franz Alexander is in heaven, God will hide it from him. So you see her, yah?"

"If you say so."

"She is totally unorthodox. You think I break all the rules, no?"

"I guess."

"She is different from me. It bothers my conscience when I break rules, yah! She is Irish Catholic"—he rocked with his great belly laugh—"she has no conscience."

He was right. She was unorthodox. And she did remind me of my grandmother. Like that woman, God be good to her, she let me get away with nothing. And she wasn't about to make an exception where Kathleen was concerned. I had already told Maggie all about Kathleen. That day I filled her in on my suspicions with regard to Brien.

"Are you willing to admit that your concerns in this woman's problem are totally narcissistic?"

"Not totally."

"Mostly?"

"Partially."

Maggie is a pretty, well-groomed woman in her early sixties, with neatly coiffed gray hair, twinkling gray eyes, gray business suit. She is married to a retired federal judge and World War II flyer who writes novels and has a bunch of kids in various strange and not so strange professions running from oceanography to the priesthood.

"Essentially flawed?"

"I guess. Until I rid myself of the narcissism."

"Which you can do because you can do everything?"

"Naturally!"

"Time's up," she sniffed.

"Saved by the bell."

"I think not."

I struggled off the couch. "Next week?"

A good analyst has to see his training analyst often. If he doesn't he should start worrying about how much countertransference has claimed him.

"If you wish. . . . You are even thinner, Kieran, than you were last week! Don't you ever eat?"

"Now you really are my grandmother!"

"Nonsense. I think you deserve a real West Side malted milk. Have you ever been to Pedersen's?"

"I look forward to the first time."

Rosenblum was right. Maggie broke all the rules—without the slightest sign of guilt. In this respect, she was also like my grandmother.

So, on an unbearably sweet Indian summer morning, I sat with my training analyst in an ice cream parlor on Chicago Avenue in Oak Park, sipping a malted milk and admitting, in the name of reluctant honesty, that I knew of no South Side ice cream parlor that could match it.

"To the point, Doctor O'Kerrigan," she said, gently but persistently sipping at her straw. "I think it would facilitate our mutual concerns if you knew I was a battered wife."

"What!" I choked on my malt.

"Not Jerry, poor dear. No, I was married before him. Back during the war—our war—which was World War Two. Pregnant at seventeen. Sailor home on leave. Neither of us knew really what we were doing. The little girl died of what we now call crib death."

Tears formed in her eyes. "A few years short of a half century ago, and I still miss her, poor little tyke. . . . Anyway, my husband, God be good to him, was not much on impulse control. So I know what it's like."

"What happened to him?"

"I killed him. Note I don't say I murdered him, though it took me a long time to make that distinction. He was trying to throw me out of a second-story window in a navy petty officer's apartment complex. I pushed harder than he did."

"How old were you?"

"Just eighteen. . . . I often tell myself that the girl who did that was someone else, but my dreams won't permit this deception. . . . You wonder why I break the rules again?"

"I sure do."

"At some time it may be a matter of survival for your friend Kathleen that I see her. If it develops that there's conflict in continuing with you . . ."

"You'll drop me?"

"Of course."

"You think he's beating her."

She lifted her diminutive shoulders. "Probably not. Probably she hurt herself in some form of strenuous exercise to which women of her generation seem devoted. As I said before, he is probably not a bisexual. And if he is, the odds are that he is not a sadist. Yet some men do undergo terrifying temporary personality changes. I sniff the possibility of dangerous tensions, possibly murderous tensions. I presume you do too?"

"Possibility of poor impulse-control?"

"Precisely. Your little friend, for all her confidence and self-possession, may well be in over her head."

"You think she will come to me with these problems if she does have them?"

"Does the sun rise in the east each morning?"

"I understand."

"Don't try to treat her yourself."

"I know better than that."

"I certainly hope so."

I had several free hours between my session with Maggie and my meeting with Father Brendan McNulty. So I drove down Harlem to the Congress Expressway (as Chicago Irish Democrats call the Dwight Eisenhower Expressway) and out to the Morton Arboretum, beyond the Yorkville Mall. Since I have returned to Chicago I wander through it at least once every spring and autumn, to gaze at the wild flowers and flowering trees in April and the red and gold maple and oak leaves in October. Usually I try during this semiannual visit to figure out what life means—life in general and my own life in particular.

That day I thought again I'd like to live across the road from the Arboretum and savor the changing of the seasons in a (more or less) natural forest environment which, because it was private, was also safe and clean. A good place, it would be, to raise kids.

Only I had no kids and the Arboretum was only twenty-five minutes in non-rush hours from my office on Michigan and a few minutes less from the Medical Center.

I was, I decided as I strolled down a path under the cathedral-like trees in the "native woods," very good at what I did, partly because of first-rate training but mostly because my work depends on the same political skills which Kathleen and I used to celebrate. Unlike a lot of people, I had not lost them in college, medical school, residency, and analysis. I had won a national reputation because I was a glib and facile writer. I had put little effort into my success.

Yet I had turned forty and did not have a wife or family. I was not unhappy, but I was missing something too.

My life was probably more than half over and I had not accomplished much. As Woody Allen said in one of his films (I think it was Woody), by the time Mozart was my age he had already been dead for four years!

Both Maggie Ward Kennan and Franz Rosenblum insisted that I repressed much of my passion.

"Not just for women, Kieran," the former said, "but for life itself. You justify this repression because you've been hurt and badly several times. But you are not ready to admit that you wanted to get hurt so you could escape the demands of life."

How could I argue?

Well, Kathleen Leary Donahue might be a demand of life, I thought later that day in my office at the Medical Center, might she not?

I found myself humming:

"Kathleen Donahue, I'll tell you what I'll do . . ."

Then I stopped. Talk about narcissism! I had no right to hope that her marriage was falling apart. I ought to be ashamed at myself for wishing such suffering on people with whom I grew up and who were once my closest friends. I would no longer, I solemnly resolved, indulge in such narcissistic fantasies.

On the other hand . . . on the other hand, what?

On the other hand, her life might be in danger.

There was a knock at the door.

I stood up and opened it. "Come in, Mr. McNulty. Oh, I'm sorry—Father McNulty."

"Brendan!" He shoved out a strong hand and beamed happily.

I knew Brendan McNulty. I don't mean that I had met him before, but I knew his type. You run into him everywhere—your smooth-talking witty black Irishman with a mischievous smile, dancing eyes, a quick wit, and a very persuasive line. He might be an undertaker, a car salesman, a cop, a lawyer, a precinct captain, a gambler, a pimp—or even a priest.

I don't know whether any of them have become psychoanalysts yet. Heaven save the profession when they do. Once a Mick like that moves into the block, pretty soon the whole neighborhood changes.

"That's a Jack Yates behind you, isn't it?" he began. "Portrait of his brother Willie?"

"Right. My only real *objet d'art.*"

In my apartment at the John Hancock Center, the City of Chicago, outside my window, provided all the imagery I needed. At the Institute I tried to brighten up the office with Yates and posters from the Art Institute—I had left my New York posters in the apartment with Rebecca when I left. When I cut my losses, I do it decisively; and I've done it twice so far.

Without being asked, Brendan McNulty arranged himself on my chair.

"How can I help, Father McNulty?" I asked, partially distracted by the thought of what Willie Yates would have been like on the couch.

"Your friend James Leary, D.D. *honoris causa,* sent me." He sat in front of my desk and crossed his legs. "I'm engaged in a little adversarial law with the Catholic Bishop, a Corporation Sole, and he claims that I don't know anything about kinky sex and that you do. You can send him the bill."

"We won't worry about that, Father . . ."

"Brendan!"

"All right, Brendan. I owe James. When I decided to come back to the Church he was a big help."

He did not ask the usual Catholic question: "Why did you leave?" Rather he asked a much better one: "Why did you come back?"

"I found out that I had never left and couldn't leave if I wanted to and decided to make my peace with that fact. Once a Catholic—"

"Always a Catholic. The metaphors take possession of you. Best metaphors in the world. Not much good at anything else right now, but we still have the metaphors. . . . Yeah, James is a fine priest, hell of a fine priest. A bit too conservative, but better than most of them. You can't preach the Gospel without an institution, but when the institution becomes an end in itself, you lose the Gospel."

One of the reasons I would come to like Brendan McNulty in the days and weeks to come was that he would toss off dicta like that, pregnant with insight and wisdom, as though they were self-evident truths which we both knew well.

"What parish are you at, Brendan?"

"St. Praxides out in Beverly. The Bishop's nieces, Megie and Maevie, permit me to hang around their high club. High-powered political types. They should be running for the Senate."

"Law and teenagers?"

"Brendan McNulty"—he laughed—"all-purpose priest. . . . You know their mother? Kathleen?"

"We grew up together."

"Some dish, huh? When the Irishwomen start running for public office, the rest of us will all be finished. . . . Well, let's get down to business. First question: is homosexuality genetic or acquired?"

I sighed my best professorial sigh.

"The first thing you must learn, Brendan McNulty, is that no zero/ one model ever captures the complexities of human reality. I don't doubt that some homosexual orientations are acquired and some are genetic. In the real world there are probably many different kinds of sexual orientations toward one's own gender, many—perhaps most—

the result of a combination of heredity and environment. . . . Do I sound pedantic?"

"Yeah, but interesting. Go on."

"Moreover," I continued, forming my fingers into an arch under my chin as I usually do when I teach, "most of us are a combination of gay and straight. It's a continuum rather than a dichotomy, or more precisely perhaps a whole concatenation of continua. So some of us can have intense relationships with members of the same sex when we're growing up—in boarding school and in the military, for example—and still end up on the straight side of the continua."

"Can such a relationship fixate a person on the other side of the continua?"

"Tough question, Brendan. My best answer is 'maybe sometimes,' but I'll qualify that by saying that perhaps such a person was already inclined to stay at that end of the continua anyway and then add that the word 'continua' implies an overly simple model."

"We don't know much about human sexuality, huh?"

"We know more about the moons of Jupiter. We're at the phase astronomy was at when the Church went after Galileo for thinking the earth revolved around the sun. Our diagnoses are the equivalent of wetting our fingers and holding them in the wind."

"Can a person's sexual orientation to his own gender be changed?"

"The other way of phrasing that question is whether or not homosexuality can be cured. Sometimes it would appear that therapy will help a person who seems to be bisexual inch along the continuum so that his or her sexual activity is confined to members of the opposite sex. I don't think that necessarily means the person has really changed sexual 'preference.' Maybe there is only a strong-willed decision to limit activity."

A corner of my mind was thinking about Brien Donahue. I forced him from my mind. "How does the Church handle homosexuality these days?" I asked.

"As far as parish priests are concerned, we treat them just like straights—counsel them to stable relationships and leave the rest to God. . . . If they think they are free to receive the sacraments, who are we to say they can't? Even the Vatican is now willing to admit that sexual preference is not a matter of free choice."

"Do you preach against gay-bashing?"

"I sure do. I'm probably in a minority, but some of us tell our congregations that gays are entitled to the same dignity that straights are and that contempt for them is a grave sin."

"Are all priests so sympathetic to alternative sexual orientations?" I asked.

"Hardly all priests. But there are enough of us so that gays can find a sympathetic ear, much the way married couples can easily find priests who won't lecture them on contraception, the Church's official view notwithstanding." Then Brendan had a question for me.

"I gather you don't like the word 'preference.' "

"It isn't an accurate word, Brendan. Most of us don't have much of a choice about how we get our sexual kicks."

"Including paraphiles?"

"Where did you learn that word?"

"From your good friend Bishop James Leary, D.D."

"*Honoris Causa?*"

"Right!" He exploded in laughter, realizing perhaps that he had found in me a kindred spirit.

"No argument there. I understand you've got a paraphile case."

"Yep." He frowned. "A real winner."

"Tell me about it."

"Read this."

He handed over a police report, dated 1981. It was horrific—anal rape of two twelve-year-old boys in a Chicago suburb by a priest.

"Dear God in heaven, Brendan McNulty!"

"I don't think She liked it at all, Kieran O'Kerrigan. . . . You have cases like this often?"

"We get them here, sure. But never priests. What's happening to the Catholic Church?"

"Good question. Probably always have had cases like this. They were hushed up like this one was. Maybe more now because we've been ordaining all kinds of strange people. But the laity are not ready to have things hushed up these days. I know of at least two hundred child-abuse suits around the country against the Church and I wouldn't be surprised if there's not several hundred more that I don't know about. They keep popping up every day."

I nodded. "The statistics on abuse are staggering. At least twenty percent of the women in this country have been molested by someone in their family. I have a case of a three-year-old raped by her ten-year-old cousin."

"A great ugly secret, particularly where a man of the cloth is concerned. . . . But what about this guy? Is he curable?"

I tapped the police report with my finger. "The usual distinction we make is between pedophile and ephebophile, depending on whether the object of rape or seduction is a child or an adolescent. We say that maybe the latter can be treated. With the former we are much less hopeful. Some therapists these days use a drug called Depo-Provera, which is a form of chemical castration."

Brendan McNulty gulped. "Doesn't sound like much fun."

"It isn't. There's a good book by an M.D. named John Money called *Vandalized Love Maps*. The title of which tells the whole story. These men, and occasionally women, have had their love orientations profoundly screwed up, if you'll excuse the expression, usually because they have been victimized themselves in childhood. . . . As to your case"—I gestured at the report—"obviously I can't render a professional opinion without knowing more, but I would not be hopeful in my prognosis on the basis of this."

"Would you recommend that he be reassigned to a parish?"

"Absolutely not!" I almost shouted at him. "Never! Who would think of doing that?"

"The Catholic Bishop of Chicago, a Corporation Sole. Let me tell you about it, Kieran O'Kerrigan. This police report doesn't exist. It disappeared from the files. We have it only because the cop that made the report kept a copy. The cop was fired because he protested the inaction of his superiors, who were bribed, he says, by the local pastor. One of the kids was from a Methodist family. They were given four hundred thousand dollars, it is said, and a home in Arizona. The mother of the Catholic kid, a widow, got not one red cent. Needless to say, the kid was and is a mess."

"You have any other evidence?"

"A letter from the Monsignor who engineered the cover-up to the pastor in another parish with the same problem, commiserating with him on the agony of having a pedophile in the rectory and saying that he had one in his rectory, the same year as our client claims that he was assaulted and our cop claims there was a cover-up."

"How did you get the letter?"

"Legitimately, but don't ask. You don't want to know."

"Did they send the priest away?"

"Of course not. They do now, usually because they're afraid of litigation, but even then only for a few months. Then they reassign the priest to a parish if they can possibly get away with it—naturally without telling the pastor."

"Did they reassign this man?" I pointed at the police report.

"Sure, they reassigned him to the chancery, where he became a favorite of the nut case who was Cardinal then. He held an important role in the Church in Chicago until they finally sent him out to a parish. There were too many rumors about him being the head of a network of active gay priests in the Archdiocese with nationwide links."

"Were the rumors true?" I felt sick to my stomach.

"Everyone I know thinks they are. We ordained a lot of gays in the last twenty years because there is an acute shortage of priests. They decided out at the seminary that the issue was not sexual orientation but celibacy. Some of the gays, not all of them by any means, became active after ordination."

"What a mess!"

"The Church is in one of the great all-time messes in human history, but so what else is new? No one promised us a perfect Church." He shrugged as if naturally I knew that.

I did, but it had taken many years.

"So the case now?"

"This guy has assaulted and raped a fourth grader. The parents, who will not be intimidated or bought off by the Church, have sued; as a price for settlement, they demand that some sort of outside and independent review panel be established, a 'victims' advocacy board.' The Archdiocese's psychiatric consultants, doubtless acting in good faith, say he's not a pedophile, which perhaps by their standards he isn't. The Church takes the position that the kid's father did it. Half the priests in Chicago, in dubious good faith, will tell you that and add that the father is an alcoholic and a drug addict. That's what our friend James believes. He figures I don't know enough psychiatry, so he sends me to see you so you would tell me that he's right. Is he?"

I ignored the question. "What do they say about the previous case?"

"There's no record of it, so they deny that it happened. They'll try to discredit the cop who gave it to us, crucify him in deposition. They don't know about the letter I have. The priest, Gerry Greene, is suing the father of the kid for libel because he wrote a letter of complaint to the Cardinal. His lawyers, for whom the Church is paying, by the way, are threatening to sue the cop too. And they're giving the plaintiffs hell in their depositions—stonewalling, intimidating, ridiculing, eating up their money—"

"What!"

"I know, I know." He pushed his hands toward me in a calming gesture. "James, like most priests, is blinded by the will to believe that one of our own is innocent. So they are listening to our lawyers, who take an adversarial approach to everything. Good law, maybe, but lousy Gospel."

"James Leary buys this stuff?"

"He thinks he has the best lawyers in town—probably because they're the most expensive."

"They make a lot of money out of the litigation?"

"There are at least a dozen similar cases pending in Chicago alone. The Church is well known to be a cash cow for law firms."

I shut my eyes and leaned back against my chair.

"Brendan, that's terrible!"

"Don't blame James," Brendan said anxiously. "He's overworked and he was not trained to be the de facto CEO of a large corporation. He spends two hours with the lawyers once a month while they summarize things for him and then has lunch with them. That's maybe $6,000 billing, which he probably doesn't realize. Then he goes back and tells the Cardinal that everything is fine and they both can sleep at night."

"What about the police and the State's Attorney and the Department of Children and Family Services?"

"They did their routine investigations and concluded, as they do routinely, that there is not enough evidence to bring charges."

"Is there ever?"

"Funny you should ask. In the territory of the Archdiocese of Chicago, Cook and Lake counties, against a priest, never."

"Will this case ever come to trial?"

"They'll stall and intimidate as long as they can. I'm not sure about a trial. If the parents hold on long enough, there will be one and there'll be the devil to pay, literally perhaps."

"Does the Church usually buy off families?"

"It used to be for twenty thousand. Now that a lot of lawyers have become specialists in these kinds of cases, maybe a half million, a million a throw."

"Wow!"

"We want the Archdiocese to set up this independent board, which will be an alternative to litigation and take James and the Boss off the hook. Then we'd settle—but for a lot less. However, the Archdiocese is afraid to give up power and their lawyers are afraid to give up some of their income."

"What will happen?"

"God knows, Kieran. But it won't be good. The one I'm most worried about is James. There's a pattern in these cases all around the country. The good administrator tries to protect the Church and the priest, and do his best for the victim too, though that's not so important because he's concerned about the institution, not people. He gets inadequate legal advice and inadequate medical advice and, without realizing what is happening to him, he is swept up in a tangle of deceit and self-deception that destroys him."

"Poor James."

"Poor everyone."

"What do you want me to do?"

"Call James, tell him you want to know more about the case. If he is ready to listen to you, maybe you can talk him out of the disaster he's courting. There's no reason why you should, unless you care about the Church."

"I do. And about James. What kind of a guy is this Greene. A monster?"

"Probably. Doesn't look like it. Wimpy little guy. Pretty sick. You think he did it, and not the father?"

"Ten-thousand-to-one odds if everything you tell me is true. These guys are usually chronic repeaters. He's still in the parish?"

"Sure. The Church doesn't want a prominent and respected priest to be disgraced."

"More victims then?"

"Sure. . . . These men are victims too, Kieran. They were abused when they were children. If you want to blame anyone, blame the Church leadership and their lawyers and their psychiatrists that send them back into parishes."

"All with good intentions?"

"More or less. . . . Here's what I propose: I want you to meet the victim's family, eat dinner with them. Then have lunch with a gay priest who is celibate so you can see the world from his viewpoint. Then maybe you can go out and have a look at Gerry in his parish some Sunday morning. After that, if you think it proper, maybe you can talk to James."

"It's a deal. I owe him a favor."

"We have to do it soon. There's some urgency in all this."

"Oh?"

"If the Church doesn't set up that review board, there will be a trial no matter what James thinks, and it will produce scandal on the front pages of the papers for weeks. . . . There's another factor at work about which maybe I can tell you later. Believe me, Kieran, there's not much time."

"How much time?"

"A couple of weeks."

"That little?"

"The pot is boiling. It could spill over anytime—and you don't want to know why just now."

"All right, I'll follow your schedule; the sooner we get this stuff done the better."

He patted my shoulder in reassurance. "Don't let it get to you, Kieran. If God wanted a perfect Church, She would have turned it over to the Seraphim. Anyway, it's your Church and my Church as much as it is James's Church."

"And Gerry Greene's too."

He lifted an eyebrow. "His too . . . and most of all Megan Donahue's."

"If she's anything like her mother I'm sure she'd agree with that."

"She is and she would. Hey." He turned at the door. "Do you know why they bury lawyers thirty feet deep?"

"No, why do they bury lawyers thirty feet deep?"

"Because deep down they're nice people!"

"And do you know what they call ten thousand lawyers chained to the bottom of the sea?"

"What?" His blue eyes sparkled.

"A good beginning!"

"Great . . . allow me the last one. I heard this one from Megie Donahue. She collects them. You're in a room with Saddam Hussein and Hitler and a lawyer and you have two bullets in a gun. Whom do you shoot?"

"I don't know."

"The lawyer, twice. Make sure he's dead."

"You're wrong, Brendan McNulty. I'm the layman so I get the last joke. You know what they call a bus of thirty lawyers that plunges over a waterfall with two empty seats?"

"I'll bite, what do they call it?"

"A lost opportunity!"

"Remind me to hire a less-prejudiced shrink when I need one."

So Brendan McNulty, his geniality restored by the thought of Megan and her mother, left my office. I'd have to ask Megie and Maevie about him. I'm sure they thought he was prime time.

After I met the alleged victim and his parents and Brendan's gay priest, I would call James Leary and offer my opinion. I presumed the institutional pressures on him would be such that he wouldn't really hear what I said. The consequences of my being right would force him to engage in denial.

That would be fine with me. I didn't want to step into the sinkhole the Archdiocese had opened for itself.

So I was involved with the Learys and the Donahues again. Just like twenty years ago.

Well, not quite just like twenty years ago.

I began to hum.

"Kathleen Donahue, I really do love you . . ."

I cut short the song. Could romance still be possible in a world with so much sexual ugliness?

BRENDAN

So, I thought to myself, the good Doctor O'Kerrigan was once in love with the good Ms. Donahue, soon to be Doctor Donahue, *non honoris causa*.

Welcome to the club, good Doctor O'Kerrigan. Except I'd bet your feelings for her were more than a passing infatuation for a beautiful and intelligent woman.

What went wrong? Not that it was any of my business.

And how did her brother James fit into the picture? Also none of my business.

Was I mixed up in some kind of Greek tragedy? But Micks are comedians not tragedians. We go for happy endings. Like God does.

Was there something brewing among the four of them that was beginning to shudder like a volcano about to explode, a Mount Pinatubo on the South Side?

In my parish? Still, none of my business.

The hell it wasn't. This was my parish. I resolved to better watch the whole crowd carefully. Someone had to be around to take care of the kids if Mount Hoyne Avenue blew its top.

KIERAN

Despite all Brendan McNulty's disturbing revelations, I couldn't pry my thoughts from Kathleen. I remembered that fateful summer in the wake of all the indictments, the trial, and my poor father's conviction. Kathleen's solution to all that misery and pain was for us to get married. Fool that I was, I resisted just long enough for unlooked-for disaster to separate us once and for all—or so it had seemed until now.

I was accused of stealing money I had never touched—and of whose existence I was unaware—and I fled in angry humiliation, a deeply disturbed young man, as I would say of one of my patients who did the same thing today.

When Kathleen found out where I lived in New York—as I knew she would and in a way was hoping she would—she phoned me.

That was the critical moment.

"Kieran?"

"Yes," I had said, hardly able to believe that it was my Kathleen.

"What happened?"

"I ran away."

"Without telling me?"

"I have my own life to live."

"Did you take the money?"

"What do you think?"

"They say that if you hadn't taken it you wouldn't have run away."

"Do they?"

"If you tell me that you didn't take it, I'll believe you."

"I don't have to defend myself to you, Kathleen, not to you or anyone in your family."

With that, I hung up the phone.

She called me twice more and both times I hung up in fury. I took my anger out on my love and drove her away.

A few days later, regretting my error and feeling ashamed, I called her to apologize. James, his voice even and noncommittal, took the first message.

"Just tell her that I called. She has my number."

"All right, Kieran. I'll do that."

The second time their mother said that she would tell Kathleen that I called.

I wondered whether she would get either message.

But I never tried again.

Several times that first year in New York, disoriented basket-case that I was, I picked up the phone to call her. I even dialed the number a couple of times, always hanging up before the phone was answered.

LEARY

"You could at least have called and said you were coming." Kathleen, wearing jeans and a maroon University of Chicago sweatshirt, impatiently flicked off the switch on her computer.

I wanted desperately to help her. I loved her as much as I have ever loved a woman in my life, including my mother and poor Mary Anne. Yet we'd never been able to talk to one another without fighting.

She was sitting in the small third-floor room, little more than an attic, which she had turned into an "office"—library shelves, two desks, expensive stereo components, and even more expensive computer equipment. Some sort of trumpet music, baroque I suppose, was playing on the stereo.

"What's so important?"

"My dissertation. What else?"

"How is it coming?" I asked politely, knowing full well that she'd never finish it.

"Two-thirds done. I'll have it finished by Christmas and will graduate in March."

"Then what?"

"Then I'll be a trained historian, that's what."

"Will that earn you any money?"

"Go read Cardinal Newman, James. He wrote about knowledge being an end in itself. . . ." She shrugged. "I'll turn the dissertation into a book. Maybe it will be a bestseller. . . . So what do you want?"

"As you well know, it's about you and Brien."

"What about me and Brien?"

"You've got to find it in your heart to forgive him and begin again. For the children's welfare, if nothing else."

"The children and the campaign, you mean."

I winced. "He still loves you, Kathleen."

"More than he loves his gay lover?"

"What?"

"He didn't tell you that, huh? His gay lover who told me on the phone the details of my marital intimacies with Brien as well as the number of times they'd had sex since the last time Brien and I had it. Do you want to hear a full account?"

"I can't believe that!"

"You'd better believe it—because it's going on the public record in my divorce trial."

"It's not possible!"

"Isn't it? What if I have AIDS? Or your three nieces? Brien wouldn't get a test, so we had to."

"During the campaign?"

"Try to get the idea through your thick ecclesiastical skull. I care about my daughters' health and my own and right now nothing more."

"You're sure it was a man who called you?"

"And when I confronted him, your friend beat me and raped me and sodomized me!"

"I will not believe that!"

She pulled up her sweatshirt. Her upper body was a mass of welts and black-and-blue bruises. "You'd better believe this! Sorry to shock your celibate sensitivities, James." She pulled the sweatshirt back down. "My breasts are still too sore for me to wear a bra. And, James, he loved every second of it. The only kind of straight sex he enjoys is torturing a woman. He really loves that."

"My God!" I felt my breakfast rise in my stomach. I fought the urge to run into her bathroom and vomit.

If I had, she, being Kathleen, would have rushed in to comfort me. The barrier between us would collapse. I wanted to weep for her pain. I wanted to embrace her and promise that I wouldn't let it happen again. I fumbled for the words and the movements, almost had them, and then lost them just as she spoke again.

"He loves it so much that he'll do it to someone else before long. Then what?"

I had no answer for her.

"He's a very clever sadist. No marks on the face or arms."

"Did you see a doctor?"

"Afraid that it will leak to the media that your candidate is a wife-beater? No, I didn't see a doctor. I'm consuming Advil and gritting my teeth. But I've taken some Polaroid self-portraits in case I need evidence. Want to see them?"

"That won't be necessary."

How could Brien, my best friend, my more-than-brother, do this to my darling sister?

"So, brother, what do you think now?"

"I'm sure he still loves you," I stammered. "Perhaps you need a vacation together to put some romance back in your life."

"Romance!" She jumped from her chair and shook her fist at me. "What will it take for me to make it clear to you! He doesn't like women! He likes men! He's not interested in sex with me. Do you think it's normal to make love at our age a half-dozen times a year? When he's drunk? The rest of the time every initiative I make is ignored. I don't even exist as a sex object for my husband. I'm a social convenience to him, nothing more."

"You seemed to be happy before this happened."

I was groping for an opening through which I could penetrate the wall of rage she had built around herself. I was never a match for her contemptuous anger. If only she would calm down, I might be able to offer her the consolation that was in my heart.

"I fooled myself into thinking our life was normal. Then his boyfriend phoned me."

"Would it have made you feel better if it were another woman?" I asked.

For the first time since I'd come, she visibly softened. "I'd still feel violated. With another woman I could compete. I'm not saying I'd be tempted to, but I could." She paced back and forth by the window, which overlooked Ryan's Woods, the Forest Preserve across from their house. "How can I compete with a male lover? Tell me that?"

She collapsed back on the chair in front of her computer and began to cry. "I want him out of my life, can't you understand that? I want him out of my bed and out of my home and out of my life! Forever!"

"Might I suggest that you pause to think about what this will do to your children?"

"It will be difficult for them. Don't you think I know that? But I'm not going to risk life and limb just to keep the illusion of a happy family for them."

"Your Christian faith demands that you forgive him, Kathleen," I said sternly, now firmly back into the mask I always wore when she was in trouble.

She struggled to control her tears. "Damn it, James. I forgive him. I just want him out of my life."

"What do the children think of their father's living out in the coach house?" Unable to console or heal as I wanted to, I fell back on that skill at which I had some talent: searching desperately for some sort of compromise solution.

"They don't think anything about it. Maybe they figure he's out there working on campaign speeches. He's gone there before when he's needed a place to think or when I've sent him there to dry out after one of his binges. He doesn't have any time for them, James, and they don't have any time for him."

"The poor man needs help, Kathleen."

"Tell me about it." She dabbed at her eyes with a tissue. "I begged him for years to go into therapy, family therapy, any kind of therapy. And to join the AA. He's a drunk, you know, just like Dad. Only Dad was kind and funny when he was drunk. Brien is just the opposite. He goes crazy. The other times he's beaten me he's been drunk too."

"Other times?"

"This was the third time—and the last!"

I felt sick to my stomach again. We had all thought they were so well matched and that they would settle each other down. How wrong we'd been.

"What does he say to your suggestions about therapy?"

"That it's all right with him if I think I need it, but he doesn't need it and he's not a drunk. Or a gay. Or a wife-beater."

"Let me propose a temporary solution, Kathleen." I sighed.

"All right." She calmed down. "I'm listening."

Now we were playing out the last scene in the little dramas we had enacted all our lives.

"Under the circumstances I'm afraid that it would be best for Brien to remain in the coach house."

"Damn right."

"Please." I held up my hand. "Hear me out."

"I'm still listening."

"I will guarantee that he will have an HIV test, go into therapy, and accept some kind of substance-abuse treatment. You will postpone, for the present, any precipitous legal charges or actions. We'll see how things are in six months."

She watched me intently. "I told him that I would forgive him if he did those things. If you can talk him into getting help, that's fine. He still doesn't get back into the house or into my bed."

"Understood." I held up my hand again. "Understood."

"He gets elected to the Senate and he goes off to Washington and leaves us alone and then there's a nice quiet little divorce because of incompatibility of interests, no fuss, no muss, no scandal?"

"That's one possible outcome," I agreed.

Another was a change in Brien—and perhaps in Kathleen too—which would make a reconciliation possible.

She eyed me shrewdly, as our grandmother Maggie might have done, Red Hugh's mother.

"One more condition," she said. "Brien agrees to cooperate with an annulment—and you back that promise up with your own."

"An annulment! Kathleen! Those are difficult and they take time."

"Bullshit, James. Those priests down in your office give annulments to just about everyone who asks for one. They take about a year. You can speed the process up."

"There's never been a divorce in our family, Kathleen."

"There's about to be one—accept that condition or I'll call a lawyer tomorrow." She reached for a sheet of paper on one of her desks. "I've got a name and number right here."

"Why haven't you used it?"

"I figured you'd come around trying to save his balls, such as they are."

"Kathleen." I tried to remonstrate with her.

"Do you accept these conditions?" She rose from her chair again, ready, I feared, for another fit of rage.

"Of course." I raised my hand to placate her. "I'll insist on all those conditions."

"I want it in writing."

"From your *husband?*"

"Certainly not. I wouldn't trust anything he says or commits to on paper. I want it in writing from you."

"Very well." I sighed. "I'll send you a note from the Cathedral tonight."

I bowed my head in submission. Kathleen controlled all the leverage and she knew how to apply it.

"James," she said just as I was preparing to beat a retreat.

"Yes?" I turned toward her.

"What would you do if he killed me?"

"He's not going to kill you, Kathleen. Don't be absurd!"

"You saw something of what he did, James. A man can't do that kind of damage without risking a punch that is fatal. Can you deny that?"

"He won't kill you," I insisted. Meanwhile, I couldn't help but think: Dear God, what if he did!

"Won't he? He was awfully close this time, closer than he was the first two times. If I had resisted any longer, I think he would have killed me."

"Nonsense, Kathleen. Brien is not a murderer."

"Isn't he? Well, I guess we will just have to wait and see, won't we?"

"That's absurd," I said, but the worry had been planted.

I heard her sobbing again as I closed the door.

KATHLEEN

After James left my office, I dragged out the box I had found of Red Hugh's papers. I thought I might find in them some key data for the last part of my dissertation.

I was absolutely determined that no matter what else happened, I would win my final victory over The University of Chicago by spring. After two years I had worked up enough nerve to try the prelims—two days of solid writing, on my laptop computer, thank goodness. The questions were tough, challenging, devious, practically impossible.

I vomited for fifteen minutes after the first day.

I went home after the second day and cried myself to sleep. I knew I had failed miserably and would be asked to leave the University. I was sure I hadn't written a presentable answer to any one of the ten questions to which I had chosen to respond.

The grades don't come back quickly from such tests. Two faculty members grade each question. Neither knows the other's grade, and of course neither knows the student's name.

After a month of dutifully checking the committee bulletin board every morning, I gave up. They would never list the names of those that had passed.

Finally, a week or so after I had quit hounding the board, an assistant professor stopped me in the corridor. "Congratulations, Mrs. Donahue."

"Thank you." My heart started to beat rapidly. "For what?"

"You passed the prelim with honors. You were the only one."

I hugged him enthusiastically and raced down the corridor to the board. Sure enough, there was the official notice:

RESULTS OF
PRELIMINARY EXAMS
Pass with Honors—Kathleen Anne Leary Donahue.

No other names. I felt sorry for the others at first, then very happy for myself. I whispered a quick Hail Mary in gratitude.

There was a note in my box that I should call Mr. Mills, my adviser, for an appointment.

Dummy that I was, I thought he wanted to congratulate me.

That night my three kids danced around me in celebration.

"Mommy passed! Mommy passed! Mommy is a genius!"

I told Brien almost ecstatically, "I passed my prelims!"

"Does that mean you're finished over there?"

He wasn't being nasty. He simply didn't know any better. He was merely anticipating what James would say. In truth, however, he didn't want to know any better. On critical matters he had long since given up thinking for himself, especially when the subject was me, and substituted James's thoughts for his own.

It took Mr. Mills a week to squeeze in ten minutes to see me.

"I'm very sorry to have to tell you, Mrs., ah, Donahue"—he fussed with a small sheet of paper from which he pretended to be reading—"that this committee, after considerable deliberation, has decided not to admit you to candidacy for the doctoral program."

"What?"

"We recognize your enthusiasm and industry and, if I may say so,

respect both very much. You have many commendable talents as a
student. However, this committee administers a very special program
and feels that it must be very selective in choosing the students we
admit to candidacy. Admission to candidacy in this committee is not a
right, it is a privilege that we must preserve for a very few students and
so—"

"I passed the prelims with honors—"

"Mastery of test materials, in and of itself, does not establish that a
student has the intellectual maturity, the emotional strength, and the
proper balance of creativity and responsibility which are required of the
select few that we feel we can best serve with our program."

I will not cry, I told myself, absolutely not.

"We don't feel," he droned on, "that we would be being fair to you
if we gave you reason to think that you had the qualifications required
for one of our doctoral candidates. This committee feels that you would
simply not be happy with us."

"The committee feels that way, Mr. Mills, or you feel that way?" I
was being very calm, letting the head of steam build up slowly.

"If I may say so"—his face turned redder—"I speak for the whole
committee."

"I see. . . . What you're saying, Mr. Mills, is that you don't want an
Irish Catholic matron from Beverly with three kids in your program."

He began to stutter. "Young woman, we only accept first-rate minds
into this committee. Most of my students, you included, do not have
a first-rate mind. That last remark of yours merely illustrates my point."

"Irish Catholics can't have first-rate minds, right?"

"This conversation is over!" He stood up.

"Sit down, Mr. Mills—it's not over."

Surprisingly, he sat.

"The committee will reverse its decision. I have kept careful notes of
all our conversations (first lie) including your anti–Irish Catholic slurs;
moreover, your colleagues, not knowing the name of the student,
graded me with an honors pass; these two facts create grounds for filing
suit charging sexual and religious discrimination. I propose to file such
a suit (second lie). The lawyers which abound in my family would enjoy
enormously dragging you and the University into court (third lie).
Moreover, I am reasonably well known in this city; the University
would be seriously injured in its upcoming fund-raising drive if I en-

gaged in a public attack on it. I have every intention of doing so (fourth lie)."

I stood up and very calmly left his office.

"This committee," he shouted after me, "and this University will not be intimidated."

But I had scared the daylights out of him.

I cried all the way home.

If only, I told myself, there was someone to talk to. I thought of Kieran, who I had heard was back in Chicago.

Then I decided that was not a very good idea.

The next morning, after maybe two hours' sleep, I devised a better strategy than threatening litigation which never in a million years would I win.

I called a certain friend and said, "I need a personal favor."

"You got it."

"A certain phone call . . ."

I told him the details.

"Consider it done." He chuckled. "It'll be a pleasure."

"I owe you one."

"We still owe you a lot of them."

The following week I received a note informing me that the committee had accepted me as a doctoral candidate. It had assigned a woman Ugaritic (that's an ancient language) scholar to be my adviser.

If I was going to finish my dissertation on schedule (my schedule, that is) I had to tune out my problems with Brien—at least for several hours each day. Nor did I want to admit to myself that I had made a bad deal with my brother. At a minimum I should have insisted that Brien find himself an apartment somewhere else and turn over all the keys to our house to me.

I had thought of Kieran for weeks after Dad's death, remembering with a sad, aching pain, those wonderful nights on the beach under the stars, Kieran's lips pressing against mine, his fingers dancing over my body, his hands pressing my breasts, his laughter making me laugh.

I had thought of him, though very quickly, whenever I had driven by his old house at Grand Beach, now down the Lake from our own property.

And I thought of him now, now that the idiocy of my marriage to Brien had been so completely revealed. Not that I was about to go running into his arms. And despite the hard bargain I'd driven with James, I wasn't eager for a divorce. I worried about what it would mean for the children. And for me.

I wanted to decide about Brien and about Kieran—if there was anything left to decide—separately. I didn't want to use the fact of Brien's adultery as an excuse to seek solace in Kieran's arms.

University of Chicago degree or not, I am enough of an old-fashioned Catholic to have a horror of divorce. I have grounds for civil divorce and now that I know he's a switch hitter, grounds for a canonical annulment—an annulment to which he has agreed, according to James, whom I don't totally believe.

Yet . . .

And the "yet" shows that I am indeed a victim of the battered-wife syndrome.

I understand the theory behind annulments—our marriage was never mature enough to be a full-fledged sacrament and God knows that's true.

Yet . . .

We have shared a common life for eighteen years. We have three children. We are married for better or worse.

Still, I wondered about the wisdom of making that agreement with James. Clearly, Brien's candidacy was important to me too. Maybe I didn't deem it as precious as the rest of our families did. But were it not for that, I surely would have called a lawyer by then. And maybe Kieran too . . .

But second thoughts or no, I'd made an agreement. It was one I'd see through until after the election. The primary was only a few months away. There'd be a bit of a lull before the general election. Maybe I could obtain my quiet divorce then. Kieran could wait. After all, he'd waited this long.

I was quite sincerely frightened for—and by—Brien. Maybe I'd raised the possibility with James for negotiations' sake. But the chance of Brien's getting violent again could only increase as election pressures waxed. Was I being a fool to allow him to stay? There could still be a next time. And maybe next time he really would kill me.

LEARY

As I walked down the narrow, steep stairs to the bedroom floor and then to the first floor of their elaborate house—in which a full-time housekeeper and part-time maid were hard at work—I wondered if my sister realized how lucky she was.

Obviously, she was in a period of acute difficulty in her marriage. Just as obviously, her husband had acted like a beast. But could she not see that she was one of the most fortunate women in the world and that she was in great part responsible for Brien's bestial behavior?

I told myself with a heavy heart that she would never be able to see those truths. The best I could hope for was a delaying action in which I would put trust for long-term solutions in the hands of God.

As I descended to the lower level of the house, I heard a woman's voice singing a Latin Psalm, though it was certainly not Gregorian Chant. Rather, unless I was mistaken, it was a Mozart *Jubilate*.

Mary Brigid, obviously. Mozart was a long way from the Lerner and Lowe that her mother had sung at the same age.

I was met by an altogether different noise as I passed what was the family room when our parents had lived here. It was a loud banging noise. I pushed open the door. Maeve Anne, barefooted and dressed in white pajamas tied by a thick black belt, was kicking what seemed to be a punching bag, hung higher than her head.

"Good heavens, child, what are you doing?"

"Oh, hi, Uncle James. Practicing my Taekwondo. . . ." She bussed me on the cheek. "Do you want to see me break a two-by-four in half with my foot?"

"Good heavens!" I replied, repelled but fascinated.

"Be quiet for a minute," she said, arranging a board between two stools. "I have to concentrate to get myself into the proper attitude. It's like, you know, a matter of discipline and responsibility and harmony with the forces of life."

The room was littered with a wide variety of exercise equipment, all of it, I was sure, very expensive.

Forces of life indeed. Pure paganism.

"Ahgh!" she shouted without warning and kicked the board with her heel.

As predicted, it splintered into two fragments.

"My God!" I exclaimed in dismay.

"Cool, huh, Uncle James?"

"Did you hurt yourself?" I asked.

"Course not. I might have if I was not in control of the basic forces, but I wouldn't try to do it unless I was."

"What do your little friends think of this?" I asked, instantly regretting the adjective "little."

She smiled at it but did not take issue with me the way her mother probably would have.

"They think it's totally awesome, the boys especially. No boy will ever try to fool around with me when I don't want him to. Totally."

"And the girls?"

"Some of them want to take lessons. Mom is a beginner and so is Brigie. Once basketball season is over, Megie will start too. Won't we be like a really awesome group then?"

"I'm sure you will. . . . Does your mother use all this equipment?"

Maeve nodded. "That's why she's got such a great figure for a woman her age. She's not feeling well right now. But she says she'll be back at it next week. Awesome!"

"And your father?"

A mask descended on the child's face. "No, he usually works out at his club."

As I walked through the garden, dazzling with bronze and white and purple chrysanthemums (planted, no doubt, by an expensive gardener), I prepared myself for a very authoritative conversation with my brother-in-law.

He was in his "library" on the top floor of the old coach house, dressed in a white tennis warm-up suit, watching CNN and reading *From Beirut to Jerusalem*. Next to his easy chair I observed other books on the Mideast. He was holding a glass of what I took to be vodka and tonic in his hand.

"Hi, James." He placed the drink on the floor and stretched to shake hands with me. "Read this? It's damn good. Smart man."

"Yes, I've read it, Brien," I said heavily. "And, Brien, you have not told me the truth!"

"What do you mean?" He looked puzzled and a little hurt.

"You did not say that your lover was a man."

"I didn't say he was a woman either, did I? Drink, James?"

"Thank you, no. . . . You're a mess, Brien, I hope you realize that. You're a mess and you're in a mess."

"You talked to her?"

"Of course."

His shoulders slumped and he bowed his head.

"You got it right, James; I'm in a terrible mess. It's all my fault too." He rubbed his hand across his face. "You sure you don't want a drink?"

"No!"

"Excuse me while I sweeten mine up a little." To "sweeten" the drink meant to add a strong dose of vodka.

"How long has this been going on?"

"You mean with the guy?"

"Who else would I mean?"

Brien slumped back into his chair. "Not long. A year. Year and a half maybe."

"Was not your relationship with your wife satisfactory?"

"With Kathleen?"

"That's your wife's name, I believe."

"Yeah, well, I got no complaints about her in bed. I mean, she doesn't refuse me or anything like that."

"But you need a male lover?"

"I don't need one exactly." He sipped at his drink, a long sip. "It's just that the pressure builds up and it's like I'm out of control and then I find this guy and it all goes away for a while. I hate myself, believe me, James, I really hate myself. I'm not a swish, but I know I'm acting like a swish and it makes me ashamed. I finally decided to stop and that's when he called her and she ruined everything."

"There have been others?"

"A few here and there, you know what I mean. But nothing important. Even this one wasn't important. Not really. It's just something that happened. But I can't seem to explain that to Kathleen. I guess she doesn't want to listen, you know."

"So you batter her and assault her? You could have killed her."

"I know." He buried his face in his hands again and began to weep. "I know. I didn't want to do it. I hated the man who was doing those terrible things to the woman he loved. . . . I do love her, James, as God is my witness, I do love her. I'd do anything for her. I hated that terrible, laughing savage, but it wasn't me. It was a demon who got inside of me. I didn't do it. *He* did it."

"Brien, *you* did it."

"I know that." His tears turned to sobs. "I KNOW that. But I didn't want to do it. I hated doing it. I couldn't stop. It was just this terrible thing inside me. It was like I was in a dream watching something evil that someone else was doing."

"Yet you enjoy it?"

He stopped sobbing long enough to reach for his drink. "The demon inside me enjoyed it; he loved every second of it. He enjoys torturing women. I hated it. Dear God, I hated every terrible second of it! Can't you understand, James? I'm being torn apart!"

"Brien," I said solemnly, "you need help."

"I can lick it by myself, I know I can. I don't want any shrink messing around with my head."

"Brien, listen to me: if you want to avoid a scandal which will destroy your family, ruin your reputation, devastate the lives of your poor parents, and permanently end your political career and your marriage, you will go into therapy, join AA if the therapist thinks you should, and be tested for an HIV infection. Do you understand?"

"I don't want to." He was crying again.

"I know you don't, but you either do that or this monster inside you will be front-page news. Suppose Kathleen was injured severely and had to seek medical help at the Little Company of Mary emergency room? Do you want that to happen?"

"No, God no. . . . Is she going to get a divorce?"

"Not if you agree to the HIV test, therapy, and whatever alcohol treatment is prescribed. You have no choice."

He continued to weep.

I saw no point in mentioning the annulment just then. I would commit myself to that process in my letter to my sister. My promise would suffice.

"Do you understand, Brien?"

What had happened to the gifted, golden youth with whom I had spent so many happy summers at Long Beach, who had inspired so much hope in so many of us?

Somehow I had to save him, save him for the campaign, but also save him, even if it meant no campaign.

"Yes, James," he choked. "I understand. I suppose it can't hurt and maybe it'll help. I'm in terrible shape. . . . Can we keep it secret?"

"I believe we can, I have some useful contacts. . . ."

"What about Kieran?"

"Who?"

"Kieran O'Kerrigan—you remember him. I hear he's back in town. I always liked the guy and they say he's really good at headshrinking. One of the partners in the firm sees him."

I was astonished. How could Brien possibly believe that the man who had lost Kathleen to him, in a process about which Brien was not completely informed, would be a good therapist for his problems?

"I don't think he would be appropriate, Brien."

"Look, James, I'll agree to do everything you and my wife want, but you've got to agree to persuade Kieran to take care of me."

For the moment I was willing to compromise. "I'll see what I can do; he does owe me a favor."

As I drove through the Neighborhood, breathtakingly lovely in the soft and caressing autumn sunlight, I reflected again on the tragedy of our lives.

Where had we gone wrong? We had everything—money, talent, intelligence, promise, bright dreams, family background, quality education, everything. We had grown up in the sixties but were relatively untouched by its excesses. Nothing seemed to stand in the way of achievement and success. Now it was all coming apart. Why? What had happened to all our bright dreams?

As I emerged from Ryan's Woods and turned left on 87th Street, I was afraid that I knew the answer. It could well be all my fault.

I had to save them all—Brien, Kathleen, my three nieces, my mother, the Donahues, who were like Aunt and Uncle to me, the Cardinal, Gerry

Greene, Brendan McNulty, the whole Church in Chicago, which lately seemed dead in the water with a frozen hand on the tiller. Why I felt so responsible was irrelevant.

There was a message from the self-appointed Outfit envoy waiting for me at the Cathedral.

Another worry.

"This is Bishop Leary."

"Yeah, hey, Bishop, how goes it?"

"Just fine. Why did you call me?"

"You know that matter we discussed at the Ireland Fund Dinner?"

"What about it?"

"Well, you see, my friends are very nervous about this good friend of theirs who has a lot to lose if that letter ever comes out. Like his life, know what I mean?"

"I understand that."

"You said that you didn't think anyone had found the letter, right?"

"To my knowledge, no. I will keep an eye on the situation, however."

"Do you think you could promise me that you would do a little hunting for it, maybe ask your sister some gentle questions about it?"

If I didn't make the promise, there might be more trouble. "I don't see why not."

"Hey, Bishop," he crowed, "that's great news. My friends can stop worrying—know what I mean?"

"I'm glad to hear that."

In my room, for some unfathomable reason I remembered the scene at my father's grave.

I stood next to Tom Donahue in the rain at the graveside after the ceremony. Mom and Sheila had gone back to the car with Brien and Kathleen, the latter tight-lipped, dry-eyed, and preternaturally silent— as well as in the advanced stages of pregnancy.

Mom—Mae Lenihan—and Sheila O'Brien, friends since they were little girls, dated Hugh Leary and Tom Donahue when they were both attending Barat College in Lake Forest (taught by the Madames of the Sacred Heart, a name which always amused my father) and the young men were students at Loyola Law School. Tom was a decorated Navy pilot and Dad was a clerk in the County Treasurer's Office who had avoided service because, as he used to say, "My body's a physical wreck."

Tom was thoroughly acceptable to the O'Briens, even if he was from Beverly, where his father was a power in the 19th Ward Organization (of which it was said that along with Maine and Vermont, the 19th was the only place in the country to deliver a majority for Alf Landon against Franklin Roosevelt in 1936). He had attended Notre Dame before enlisting the V-5 pilots training program and had vigorous political ambitions.

There was, you see, a long-standing rivalry between the O'Briens and the Lenihans as to which family would produce a mayor of Chicago first. Both families had contempt for Tony Cermak (who was shot in 1933 in Florida by an assassin aiming at Roosevelt) and for his successor, Ed Kelly, who had become a millionaire while working for the sanitary district. Both assumed that families like ours had a right to run City Hall—certainly more of a right than did the Shanty Irish from Bridgeport (as they invariably called politicians from the 11th Ward). Grandpa Lenihan's hopes were smashed when both his sons were killed in the war.

One of the O'Brien boys had become a Jesuit (he left the priesthood twenty years ago to marry a former Madame of the Sacred Heart). Another was at St. Mary of the Lake at Mundelein, the Archdiocesan Seminary (and is now an embittered suburban pastor emeritus who will not speak to me because I am a "young radical"). The third son was not "interested in politics" or much of anything else, women included, and now lives in San Francisco, which suggests to me that he might be gay.

Hence, in the year after the end of the war, both families put their political hopes on sons-in-law. Tom Donahue had promise and political ambition. Hugh Leary had enormous talent but was too witty, too wild, and, worst of all, too comic to become a professional in politics—however much he reveled in playing the game at the fringes.

Tom was tall and erect, handsome and solemn, his silver hair glistening in the rain.

"Nice homily, Father James."

"Thanks, Uncle Tom."

"You're going back to Rome to finish your degree?"

"Another year."

"He was proud to have another lawyer in the family even if he didn't think much of canon law."

I laughed despite myself. "He didn't know about it and he didn't want to know about it yet I found a commentary on the Code by his bedside."

"You're what—thirty-one, right?"

"Just."

"Thirty-three years seems like a long time, doesn't it, Father? Yet, as I was looking at him in the casket last night, I couldn't believe that it had gone by so quickly. Same feisty little redhead that sat next to me the first day of law school and said, 'Fuck the law and fuck all the lawyers!' Now he's gone."

I nodded silently.

"Everything looked so good in those days. We had a hell of a lot of fun, we had two beautiful girls we loved and who loved us, we knew the country was expanding and there might not be another Depression. We were convinced that we'd have good lives. I guess we did. But somehow something went wrong. Now it's all over for him. We missed something, and I'll be damned if I know what it was. It went by too quickly for us to realize that something had slipped between our fingers."

"The sands of time," I said without much imagination.

"Not exactly."

"The drink was a terrible demon."

"Was it?" He turned to walk back to the other mourners waiting in the limousines. "I don't think it was, really. He proved at the end he could lick it anytime he wanted. But I don't know what it was. I think . . . I think he was never sure what he wanted to do with his life and died before he figured it out."

What would Red Hugh think of me now?

He'd probably be ashamed that I have become a stuffed shirt.

If my father were still alive, I wondered, what would he advise me to do with the evidence I had gathered that suggested that one of our lay staff had indeed taken kickbacks? Knowing him, he'd probably advise me to get rid of the guy as quietly as possible.

My thoughts turned again to Brien and Kathleen. I wondered if we really could make it through the election without scandal. At the rate things were going, that seemed highly unlikely.

Maybe I'd subconsciously wanted to forget it, but for whatever reason, by the next morning I had completely forgotten the promise I had made to the Outfit ambassador.

BRIEN

He called again today.

"You see what happens, Brien, when you're not a good boy?"

His voice is soft, insinuating, magical.

"You've ruined my marriage."

"I told you I would."

"I don't want to talk to you."

"But you will, Brien," he chuckled, "you will . . . and you know the price for getting back into the group. I want that price, Brien, I mean to have it."

"I will not give her to you."

"Yes, you will, Brien. You know that you will and I know that you will."

"You'll hurt her."

"A little bit, Brien. But it's only an initiation ritual, an introduction to a higher life. She'll always be grateful that you snatched her out of the dull mediocrity of ordinary life."

He was a demon, he was the demon that had made me beat my wife. I would not give in to him.

"The answer is no. It will always be no. You can't have her for your sick pleasure."

"It will be your pleasure too. Don't tell me that you are not already aroused at that thought."

"She'll talk about it and then I'll be finished."

"They never talk about it, Brien. They don't want to talk about it. They enjoy it too much."

"No!" I screamed and hung up on him.

I was shaking like a man with a terrible fever. I had fought him off this time. But he'd keep coming back. He had captured my body and he was trying to take possession of my soul.

Dear God, I prayed, protect me from him.

BRENDAN

"Now, Ms. O'Malley." Laura Taylor's expression appeared reasonable. Her voice sounded reasonable—a sure sign that she was about to indulge in another cheap shot. "How often do you chastise Jack?"

"Chastise?"

"Yes."

"What do you mean by chastise?"

"Punish . . . what else could I mean?"

"Perhaps once a month."

"How severely do you beat him?"

"Beat him!"

"Is that not how you punish him?"

"Certainly not!"

"Well, how do you punish him, then?"

Her colleagues were giggling again.

"Let the record show that counsels for the defendant are laughing again," Ron Long observed.

"Rather let it show that counsel for the plaintiff claims that they are laughing. . . . How *do* you chastise your son, Ms. O'Malley?"

So it went—the seemingly endless "discovery deposition" in a stuffy windowless room at the LaSalle National Bank Offices of Crawford, Keefe and Schultz, the Archdiocese's law firm.

"Ground him or forbid him to watch television or simply reprimand him."

"How often do you beat him?"

"We don't beat him."

"Ever?"

"No. Not ever."

"Even when he was a child?"

"We might have paddled his rear with one light blow when we found him playing with electrical sockets."

"You don't believe in bodily punishment of children?"

"No."

"Doesn't the Bible say spare the rod and spoil the child?"

"This is not an exam in biblical exegesis, Ms. Taylor," I said.

"Isn't it, *Father* McNulty?"

"I direct the witness not to answer the question," I said serenely.

"I will certify it, *Father* McNulty."

"Off the record," I said to the court reporter.

Ron Long was grinning. He had told me that the wraps were off in this session.

The court reporter took her fingers off the keys and pushed the pause button on her tape recorder.

"Stop acting like an asshole, Ms. Taylor," I said with my usual pleasant smile. "You know as well as I do that you'll never go before the judge with that question. Back on the record."

Laura Taylor turned crimson. "Nonetheless I will certify that question." I threw back my head and laughed. "Let the record show that Counselor McNulty laughed."

Our strategy now was to sustain Helen O'Malley through the final torments of her deposition. So we were counterattacking, more to fluster the Archdiocese's lawyers than anything else. Or rather I was deputed to do the counterattacking because, as Ron Long had said, "Beneath that charming exterior of yours, Brendan McNulty, there lurks a really mean SOB."

"Guilty as charged," I'd chortled.

"You are stating under oath that you never physically punish your son?" Ms. Taylor continued.

"That is correct."

"Don't you think that is rather remarkable?"

"I don't know," she replied.

"Well . . . if I'm not mistaken, you continued to work as a social worker through your son's infancy and early childhood, did you not?"

"I went back to work when he was two, yes."

"And his grandmother took care of him?"

"Yes, she lives with us."

"Do you think that was healthy for the little boy?"

"Yes, I do. He gets along fine with his grandmother."

"You believe then that it is possible to be a good mother and still pursue a professional career?"

"Yes, I do."

Clearly this was the theory that Crawford, Keefe was pursuing, insofar as they were burdened by anything like a theory. The O'Malleys had neglected and abused their son and were blaming what had happened to him on their parish priest and school principal. Their theory wouldn't stand a chance in a trial. But those arrogant lawyers were confident—mistakenly, I was firmly convinced—that the case would never come to trial.

"You never had any doubts about this conviction of yours?"

Helen hesitated. "I often wondered about it. I think most mothers do. I did not worry about Jack. He seemed a healthy and happy little boy. I worried about what I was missing."

"Doesn't that seem selfish?"

"Come on, Counselor," I interjected, "that's a moral judgment which has no place in this deposition. You heard Ms. O'Malley's response. Why don't you get on with the work at hand."

She glared at me. "Very well, Ms. O'Malley, let me put it this way. Do you have any guilty feelings about how you might have neglected your son?"

"I don't think I have neglected him."

"You believe that you've been a good mother in every respect?"

"I've tried to do my best. I don't think I've been perfect, but I've tried."

"Haven't you and your husband tried to compensate for your neglect by forcing Jack into all sorts of activities in which he did not want to participate?"

"Objection, Counselor," I interjected. "Ms. O'Malley has already said that she does not feel that she has neglected her son. You're twisting her words."

"I'll ask my questions without any advice from you, *Father* McNulty."

"Wrong, *Miss* Taylor! You'll ask them in accordance with accepted principles or you'll find yourself before the Supreme Court on charges of unethical behavior. Now restate that question or I'll terminate the deposition."

Ron Long smiled benignly. I was indeed one tough son of a bitch.

Laura Taylor hesitated. If the session was terminated by counsel for the plaintiff, it would simply prolong the pretrial activities—which was part of the Archdiocese's strategy. On the other hand, if we elected to play hardball and go to the media with an ethics charge, they might be in deep trouble.

We had no intention of doing that. Rather, we wanted to finish our depositions and go after their people—Gerry Greene, an associate pastor who confirmed the assault and then changed his story for the good of the Church, Martin Roder, James, and the Cardinal. Before we put the last two under oath, they would begin to talk settlement.

"Well, Ms. O'Malley." Laura Taylor ignored me. "Don't you admit that you forced Jack into swimming and karate lessons against his will?"

She sighed. "As I said before, at first he was not eager for these lessons. But he soon changed his mind. Now he enjoys them."

"Indeed? What evidence do you have of that?"

"He has set a free-style record for his swim club and won the karate championship for the Midwest."

That stopped them.

"Really!"

"Yes—really!"

"What earthly purpose can there be in a boy his age learning karate?"

The question was outrageous, but I let it go because I knew what the answer would be.

"He can defend himself the next time a priest tries to rape him."

KATHLEEN

As soon as James left, I found myself mulling over the past. I'd found out about the indictment a little before Christmas, 1972. My father assured me it wasn't a big deal, but the fact that Grandpa, Uncle Tom, and Mr. O'Kerrigan had been indicted seemed like a big deal to me. I was away at Boston College, a school I'd decided to attend largely through Kieran's encouragement. No one had thought to give me a call to let me know.

The first thing I did was call Kieran. He sounded worried, even though his father, like mine, had told him there was nothing to worry about. But, like me, Kieran was worried just the same. "My parents are such sweet and gentle folks," I remembered him saying. "The publicity is terribly hard on them. Their health isn't very good either—Dad's diabetes and Mom's heart, you know."

I hadn't known. Kieran hadn't told me.

"There hasn't been much publicity so far."

"Not yet. But even an article or two in the papers devastates them."

I'd always thought that Kieran and I were so close. But for the next two and a half years, he turned me off.

"Why won't you talk about it?" I demanded the following summer at the Lake as we lay on the beach, facedown on the sand.

"I don't want to talk about it, Kathleen."

"Talking helps."

"Some people, sometimes."

"You heal other people's hurts; why don't you let other people heal your hurts?"

He didn't reply. I began to rub his back gently. His muscles were tied into terrible knots. Under the pressure of my fingers they slowly relaxed.

"Thank you, Kathleen." He sounded like he was crying.

"Share it with me, Kieran, please." I leaned over him, my breasts touching his back.

To hell with what anyone who might see us would think.

"I can't," he seemed to sob.

"Why not?" I pressed against him, like I might, as I thought then, against a husband I was trying to tease into lovemaking.

"It hurts too much."

That's the way it went. Somehow I had lost the weird but nice little boy who had carried my books to school the first day of eighth grade at St. Prax's.

Dad called me with the verdict of the bench trial.

"Your grandfather and Tom Donahue were innocent on all counts!"

"And Mr. O'Kerrigan?"

There was silence for a moment on the other end of the line.

"Guilty on one count of conspiracy. . . . Don't worry, Katie, my sweet, he won't have to go to jail. And we'll get him off on appeal."

After I had talked to Mom and Grandpa and had hung up, I felt vaguely uneasy. If the fix was in, why hadn't it worked for Kieran's father? Might Dad and Grandpa have cut a deal with someone?

I shivered at the thought. I still do.

No one told me about his mother's death until after she was buried. Jenny Cahill called me at college a week after the funeral. "Kathleen." She sounded confused. "Why weren't you at Mrs. O'Kerrigan's funeral Mass?"

"What?"

"She died of a heart attack the week after Mr. O'Kerrigan was sentenced to three to six years in prison."

"What!"

"Didn't anyone tell you?"

"No . . . my family probably didn't think it important enough to merit a long-distance call," I said bitterly.

"Kieran?"

"He's probably busy being a saintly Christian martyr."

"Oh."

"He's an idiot."

"You still love him?"

"I think so."

"I'm sorry I didn't call you, but I thought sure they would . . . then I didn't see you at the wake or the funeral . . ."

"It's not your fault, Jen. I'll think about it and then phone himself."

I thought of it for all of five minutes.

"Kieran . . ." I burst into tears, forgetting my anger and feeling only his pain.

"Kathleen . . ." He was weeping too.

The two of us wept together across a thousand miles of telephone line for several minutes.

"I would have been there if I knew." I grabbed frantically for a tissue. "No one told me."

"I wanted to call you." He tried to bring his voice and emotions under control. "But I didn't want to bother you with my problems."

"Good God, Kieran." I started to lose my temper. "It's still a Christian work of mercy to bury the dead."

"She's buried now, Kathleen."

"I'm coming home this weekend."

"Please don't," he begged.

"I'm going to transfer to Loyola so I can be with you."

"They were crushed, Kathleen. They folded up like used dolls a kid might throw away. It's been terrible. . . ."

"Oh, Kieran." My tears flowed softly this time.

"I'm not all that tough either, not half as tough as you are."

"I'm not so sure about that, but I'll admit it *causa argumenti.*"

"Those Jesuits are corrupting you with all that Latin. . . . What I'm trying to say is that if I don't concentrate all my energies on keeping myself pulled together, I won't be able to help Dad."

"But I don't understand why I can't help you."

"When I look into those enormous blue eyes of yours, Kathleen, I break down. Even the tenderness in your voice on the telephone . . ."

"I could help."

"Maybe later. Not right now."

"Fair enough . . . on one condition."

"That is?"

"You call me whenever things get really bad so you can cry with me on the phone."

Silence.

"Deal?" I demanded.

"It's done."

He was always persuasive, was Kieran O'Kerrigan, my love. But he failed to hold up his part of the bargain. When his poor father died a few months later, I didn't hear about it from him.

I threw myself into his arms when he greeted me next to his father's casket. Or rather, to be precise about my behavior, I threw myself against him, hugged him with all the strength I possessed, and virtually forced him to put his arms around me.

We held on to each other, clinging passionately and sobbing together.

"They loved you so much, Kathleen," he wept. "They thought you were the nicest girl in the world."

"I loved them too," I said, my Irish talent for Blarney rising to the occasion, "especially because I thought their son was the nicest boy in the world!"

We laughed together as we cried together. Slowly and very gently he slipped out of my embrace.

"When the wake is over I'm taking you up to Red's for a dog and a Coke."

"And a malt?"

"Done."

Later in the vestibule, I said to my dad, on whose breath there was already the smell of far too much gin, "Well, what happened?"

"You heard that the First Circuit ordered a new trial the day he died? He died happy, I think."

"It doesn't do him much good."

"I know that, Katie. Good Lord in heaven, how I know it."

"The fix didn't work?"

He looked around nervously. "Don't use that word . . . a few things went wrong. I did my best, Katie dearest, I really did. Please believe me."

I thought for a moment. "I believe you, Dad. Of course I do. I just don't understand."

"Someday I'll explain, I promise that. Fair enough?"

"It's a deal."

But he never did explain.

For a little while that night, he was the old Kieran Patrick O'Kerrigan that I had loved so much in eighth grade. At first we listened to the Beatles on the juke box and argued about Buñuel's films. I said *The Discreet Charm of the Bourgeoisie* was his best, while Kieran argued for *Belle de Jour* because, as he said, Catherine Deneuve in white underwear was the most beautiful woman in the world—"except for you," he added. "And I've never seen you in white underwear, though the prospect is interesting."

We laughed together. Then our laughter faded away as we remembered our sorrows.

Then we stopped talking, alone with our griefs.

I took Kieran's hand in both of mine. "I know I'm right; you're afraid to share yourself with others."

"These have been four hard years, Kathleen," he said softly. "Give me a little time to get over them, just a little time and it will be all right."

"Promise?"

"Absolutely."

"It's a deal."

"Done," he said.

Then, a month later, Terry's death just about killed our family. Grandma's stroke two weeks after that buried it.

I can still remember my father's expression when he told me the tragic news. "Katie, we've lost another." Red Hugh clasped me in his arms.

"Not Terry?" I couldn't believe his words.

"Maybe God is punishing us." Dad clung to me. "I don't know . . ."

"God doesn't work that way," I insisted.

"So much death," Kieran said to me at the wake.

"We all have to die, Kieran."

"I know." He sighed. "Maybe Ter was lucky."

"Maybe." I didn't like the way he looked or spoke. He seemed like someone who had just got out of bed after a terrible spell of pneumonia.

"I don't think your family appreciated him any more than they appreciate you."

"He was the quiet one."

"And deep."

Of course Kieran would know that.

At Grandma's wake he merely hugged me.

The deaths delayed my plans to persuade Kieran to marry me. Maybe if there hadn't been so many deaths that summer, I would have had the energy and courage I needed to go after him more vigorously.

Nothing if not direct, I launched my campaign on the night of Lady's Day in Harvest, appropriately an old Celtic fertility festival with a Christian interpretation.

"Do you want me, Kieran?"

We had come home from a movie in Michigan City and were walking along the tiny strand of beach which had survived the high water and the winter storms of that time. It was a lovely night—no moon, jeweled sky, light breeze, dry and clear. A perfect night for seduction.

"What?" He sounded scared.

We had made an implicit pact, like many of the others which had marked our friendship for eight years, that we would not discuss the tragedies in both our families that terrible summer of 1972. We'd sit through the film, discuss it over coffee or a malt somewhere, ride back to the beach, his or mine, and go for a walk.

"I said, do you want to make love with me?"

"Kathleen!"

"You sound like James."

"You mean now?"

"If you want . . ." I drew a deep breath and dove. "Or after we're married."

"Married!"

"That's what people do when they've loved each other for eight years."

He stopped, turned toward me, and tried to examine my face in the starlight.

"You're serious?"

"Sure. Why not?"

"You are proposing marriage, are you not?"

I leaned my head against his shoulder. "I think that's what it's called."

"Men are supposed to do that."

"Silly custom. Women usually make the decision. I'm just being more candid than most of them."

"All right." He laughed again, a little less enthusiastically. "Do you mind if I take the other role in the scenario?"

"No."

"You've astonished me."

"I would hope so."

"Do you want an answer tonight?"

I laughed for the first time.

"Certainly not."

"When would you expect that we would be married—presuming that I'm intelligent enough to accept the best offer anyone is ever likely to make me?"

Now I was certain that I had won.

"Soon. Why delay?"

"I have to go to medical school."

"So what?"

"After I sell the house in Beverly and the one up here and pay the bills, I'll barely have enough money for tuition. I'll have to moonlight to stay alive."

"That's silly, Kieran O'Kerrigan, and you know it. I've got enough money to take care of both of us. If it bothers you to take money from your wife—which would be unspeakably stupid in these days—I can get a job teaching. Money is not a problem. The question is whether you want to marry me."

I pulled his hands up to my breasts and pressed them hard.

Pull out all the stops, right?

"I don't know that I'm ready for marriage, Kathleen." He sighed. "I mean, there's been so much trouble for the last four years, I need to pause for a deep breath."

"That's a reasonable idea," I said judiciously. "I'll give you a year to catch your breath."

He laughed again, in spite of himself. "You close in from all sides, don't you, Ms. Leary."

"When I want something. Or someone. You bet."

I released his hands. Now he leaned against my breasts.

"I'm a terrible fool, Kathleen Leary."

"No, you're not." I stroked his back, its muscles still stiff and twisted.

"Yes, I am. Since that first day on Hoyne Avenue I've dreamed that we'd share each other's life. Now the opportunity is offered me and I stumble and bumble and lose my Irish Blarney."

"You've had a rough time of it, Kieran."

The tension in his back responded to my ministrations, but oh, so slowly.

"Not as rough as you." He nuzzled his head against me. "I at least want to say that you are the most perfect woman I've ever known. I would always be happy with you."

"There'd never be a dull moment," I conceded.

Suddenly we both realized how funny it was. Laughing like maniacs, we dragged each other down to the beach and engaged in comic love play, more passionate but also more light-hearted than our earlier exercise. Neither of us, I reflected as we frolicked together, had much experience at this sort of thing, but it didn't matter. After marriage we'd soon be skilled lovers.

I suppose we might have made love that night if I had wanted to or had encouraged him to. Somehow it didn't seem right. Yet if we had, maybe I never would have lost him.

I slipped quietly into our "cottage" for fear James might be around and be waiting for me. However, he was either not there or asleep.

I told myself as I threw off my clothes and pulled on a thin T-shirt that I was completely happy. Kieran would marry me and marry me soon. He would take me away from the oppression of my family and I would bring joy and laughter back into his life.

But the next week he was gone—without ever saying a single word of goodbye.

"I have bad news, Katie, my sweet." Dad was already tuned—and Mom too; and it was only ten in the morning of a chilly, rainy Labor Day.

"Not another death!" I cried out.

"No." He would not look up from his gin and tonic. "Not that."

"What then?"

"It seems that Kieran is in trouble. . . ."

I had flown to New York on the Friday of the Labor Day Weekend to be a bridesmaid in the wedding of some friends. All through the Mass I had fantasied about my own wedding, which, I told myself, would certainly occur no later than the following Labor Day. I had returned to O'Hare late Sunday and, too tired to try to drive to Long Beach that night, had slept at our house on Hopkins Place.

Oblivious to the rain and the mists and thinking only of my Kieran, with whom I was dizzily in love, I drove up to the Dunes on Monday morning.

"What kind of trouble?"

"Well"—Dad squirmed in his chair and put his glass on the coffee table—"someone took the Calcutta money from Regan's house over in Grand Beach, you know, right next to the O'Kerrigan place. And Father Pat, Pat O'Connell, saw Kieran coming out of the house and the people in Grand Beach wanted to arrest Kieran, but your brother wrote a note for twenty-five thousand dollars to cover it so they didn't call the police which was pretty generous of James and no one—"

"He didn't take the money." I turned on my heel and dashed for the door of our house.

"No strength of character!" Mom shouted after me. Her voice was already slurred with drink. "Just like his father." My mother had never been a fan of Kieran's. No doubt she found his family pedigree unsuitable for her political ambitions, ambitions she could now see realized only through me and James.

I knew I had to see Kieran. I drove with reckless disregard for stop signs, other cars, and slippery streets over to Grand Beach, pulled up to the tiny, elegant O'Kerrigan house—a refurbished Sears portable from 1915—and pounded on the door.

No answer.

I ran around to the lawn in front of the house, paying no attention to the rain or the surging waters of the Lake, and peered in the front windows. There were no lights and no sign of life. I beat against the windows and the front door.

"Kieran," I shouted. "Kieran! Where are you?"

He did not reply. Then I realized I was behaving like a fool. My love's old battered blue T-Bird was not in front of the house. He was not home.

But where was he? And what had happened?

James would know, I decided, and hopped back in my Mercedes and raced over to Long Beach Country Club in search of James. He would know what was happening.

He was sitting in the bar, nursing a beer and talking to Brien Donahue and some guys with whom they had played basketball at Carmel. As soon as he saw me storm into the club, he excused himself and headed me off at the entrance to the bar.

"Let's go talk about it, Kathleen," he said tenderly.

His face was white and drawn, his forehead creased in a worried frown. He took my arm and led me into the small lounge overlooking the seventh tee.

"What happened?" I asked, tempted to tears by his gentleness.

"Kieran was accused of taking the money," James said softly as he settled me into a chair. "I covered the loss with a note before they could call the state police. He's gone away."

"Gone away!" I swore to myself that I would not break down. "Where has he gone?"

"To New York, I presume. To medical school and a new life. There's no future for him here and he knows it."

"He didn't take the money, James. I know he didn't."

My mind had gone out on strike. I couldn't think, couldn't decide, couldn't act.

"He says he didn't." James's face was contorted in agony. "I don't know what to think. If it were me and I were innocent I'd stay and fight them."

"He's been through so much," I pleaded.

"I understand, Kathleen. But so have we all. You or I wouldn't run away from the fight, would we?"

"It would depend. Are you sure he's gone?"

"I think so."

"He'll be back," I said with more confidence than I felt.

That night, as I was saying my night prayers, I begged God for help—help for me and help for Kieran.

The next week I learned from Cornell Medical School, in New York, where he was living. I called him three times and pleaded with him to deny that he had taken the money. He shouted at me angrily and hung up. In retrospect, I think I blew it. I should have told him that I loved him.

He'll call tomorrow, I told myself when he had hung up on me the second time. Kieran doesn't stay angry for long.

But Kieran didn't call the next day or the next week. I found a job teaching at a Catholic school in a black neighborhood and enrolled in Loyola's late-afternoon MA program. I don't think I ever formally decided not to pursue my Kieran O'Kerrigan, my weird, magical, wonderful love. Rather, I sort of drifted into my new post-college life, like a log floating down a quiet river.

After the first couple of weeks, I abandoned any serious thoughts about running after him I might have entertained.

And so, through a series of tragedies and one inexplicable mystery, I was forever parted from the great love of my life.

Kieran's back in town now, has been back for two years. Jenny Cahill Riley has met him a couple of times at medical gatherings with her husband, who is an ophthalmologist (and prescribes for me my contact lenses).

"Same old Kieran," she tells me. "Kind of weird, and real nice with that sweet smile of his. But he seems a lot stronger now. Like more powerful or something."

"Maybe more self-assured?"

"Yeah." She seems surprised that I know the right word. "That's it: a LOT more self-assured. Don says that he's really good at what he does."

"I'm sure he is."

"You'll bump into him someday, you know that, Kathleen."

"I suppose so."

"What will you say?"

"Hello, Kieran, nice to see you again—something like that."

Sometimes I thought I saw his face in a crowd or the back of his head at a concert or I imagined that I saw his back on Michigan Avenue near his office—oh, yes, I knew where his office was. But I was careful never to go near it unless there was another reason for going by. An adulteress I am not.

BRENDAN

Kieran O'Kerrigan, I decided at the O'Malley home, was something else altogether.

I had been watching him all day, careful to observe the way he dealt with John Creaghan over lunch, and, later in the day, with Kevin and Helen O'Malley. He was charming, deft, sensitive, a mixture of priest and healer with a diffident smile that would melt your heart.

John, ordained the year before me, was silent at first, inhibited in the presence of someone he did not know. A quiet, private man whose shyness seemed at odds with his square shoulders, closely cropped hair, and resolute expression. I'd wanted Kieran to meet him in order to gain the perspective of a celibate gay priest.

"I'm glad you have time to talk to me, Father," Kieran had said hesitantly. "I'm new at this business of being a consultant to the Chancery office, albeit an informal one."

"A tremendous amount of denial exists," John said. "There are several homosexuals in the Chancery itself who either refuse to acknowledge it or who are so repressed, they honestly don't realize it."

We were eating in a little Italian restaurant on Oakley, in the "Heart of Chicago" district. The pasta was incredible.

"It's always interested me"—John began to relax—"that the men who are most likely to be homosexual are the ones who make the decisions about the ordination of homosexual priests and then are appalled by their own decisions."

"What we'd call a complex in my profession."

John even grinned. "Exactly. Look, I've known since I was a kid that I was homosexual. I decided to be a priest and a celibate priest. Maybe it's a little harder for me, I don't know for sure. But I feel I bring a special sensitivity and concern to the priesthood that you wouldn't ordinarily find in straight priests."

"I'm sure that's true, Father." Kieran nodded sympathetically.

"Men like me aren't advocating a predominantly homosexual priesthood. But if homosexuals make up ten percent of the population at large, we think that the priesthood should be more reflective of that percentage, don't you agree?"

"Give or take a few percentage points." Kieran thoughtfully sipped his tumbler of red wine.

"But these idiots in charge ordain scores of men who are clearly the acting-out type. Then they wring their hands when this type of priest moves his male lover into an empty room in a rectory."

"They wring their hands but do nothing?"

"They don't have the courage to do anything. Martin Roder huffs and puffs but he's afraid to act—except against folks like Brenny, who works at law, and me."

"Against you too?"

"Roder thinks I spend too much of my free time in counseling gay men and women. Interferes with my parish responsibilities. He doesn't say anything about the parish responsibilities of the pastor who has a lover tucked away in the rectory."

"So they harass you and leave Gerry Greene's crowd alone?"

"You know about that bunch, do you? They're not into gay liberation, heaven knows. They're not gay activists. They're active gays, seeking their own pleasure and nothing else. Gerry, of course, is something special. He's off-the-wall goofy."

"So I understand."

"Martin Roder was so funny"—John pushed away his pasta dish—"he couldn't figure out whether I was gay or not and I wouldn't tell him. It's none of his business."

"No one's but your own."

"Right. And if I said I was gay, he would have backed off immediately. They have a double standard. They harass those who are not gay and leave the gays alone unless there is some public trouble, like an arrest. Then they cover that up and send them away for a couple of months."

Kieran nodded.

"They're harder on people like me than they are on sexually active gay priests, and they're harder on them than they are on flakes like Gerry. And they're hardest of all on straights who are caught in the sack with women."

"How would you explain this multiple standard?" Kieran had become a student at the foot of a master teacher.

"I'd chalk it up to stupidity and fear, mostly. Martin Roder is one of the dumbest men in the world. James Leary is a lot smarter, but he's hemmed in by past procedures and practices—and terrified of what he might find under any stone he's thinking about turning up. And there's more to it than that. Someone like me, or a straight who's in a love affair, is still vulnerable to the old appeals of clerical culture—the good of the laity, what other priests are saying, protecting the Church, obedience to the bishop, that sort of thing. Gays who are sexually active couldn't care less."

"Where will it all end, Father?"

"I care about the priesthood." John shook his head sadly. "I care deeply about it. Sometimes I think that there's only a few of us left who respect our vocations. Gerry Greene and Martin Roder are two of a kind, one a super-flake and the other a super-phony. They make the priesthood a mockery."

"What did you think?" I asked later when I picked up Kieran at the Hancock Center in my Chevy convertible.

"He's a good priest," Kieran replied as he tightened his seat belt. "And a grieving priest. Not because he's gay but because he sees the priesthood falling apart."

"He's maybe too easy on the straights who have taken lovers of one kind or another. They don't give a damn either."

"Should the Church abolish celibacy?"

"You know something, Kieran," I said, easing over to the right lane of Michigan Avenue to make the turn onto Ontario, "those guys wouldn't be faithful to their wives. Celibacy doesn't cause immaturity; and marriage doesn't cure it."

"Amen," he said fervently.

I wondered fleetingly about him and La Belle Kathleen who, at Mass that morning, had looked even more worried than usual, not that I'd share my observation with Kieran.

"Tell me about John and Jane Doe," he said, using the names which the plaintiffs, Kevin and Helen O'Malley, used in their suit to protect themselves and their son from publicity.

"What can I tell you? They're good, solid, parochial-school Catholics, more conservative than most. Their kid was repeatedly abused, physically and sexually, by Gerry. The Church wouldn't listen to their complaints. The nun who was supposed to 'arbitrate' their complaint told them at the beginning that 'Father' would never do anything like that."

"Even though he had a past record of abusing kids?"

"You got it. . . . Admittedly, Martin's 'procedures' were not in place then, but no one has tried to make them retroactive. Not a single person in the Church ever listened to them or tried to respond to them till I came along. They were put down by the Church, the police, the State's Attorney's office, the DCFS, even by other parishioners who know Gerry for what he is. So the O'Malleys moved up to Park Ridge, where they live now, and filed suit."

"And the Church has fought back?"

"Every inch of the way. Hardball adversarial law and whispering campaigns. The idea is that as the Does' resources diminish, they'll settle, if not for peanuts—which is what we used to give people—at least for a million or so."

"A million!"

"Routine payoff these days."

He paused to digest that as we sped up the Kennedy toward Park Ridge into the rapidly fading sunlight.

"Will the O'Malleys settle?"

"Nope."

"Sure?"

"Absolutely. But meanwhile the Archdiocese's lawyers tell James every time they see them that the O'Malleys will settle without their demand for the outside review panel being satisfied. These same jokers subject the family to harassing and humiliating depositions to wear them down. They turn witnesses, they intimidate priests who are willing to testify against Gerry, they threaten to indict John Doe for fraud. But the trial will be called at Christmastime and it will be dragged into court."

"What will happen then?"

"Hard to say. Depends on James mostly. He'll be furious at the lawyers for misleading him, but I suspect that he'll be readier than most to give up a little power to avoid an enormous public scandal. Can't say for sure, however. James can be pretty stubborn when he's convinced he's right."

"Tell me about it," he said with a sigh.

"I have three reasons for a sense of urgency, Kieran. I want to protect the Church from public disgrace and it's bumbling toward it, I want a review panel established so this sort of thing won't happen again, and I have a third even more powerful reason, which I can't tell you about just yet."

"It involves Greene?"

"It sure does."

I let him chew on that for the rest of the trip to Park Ridge.

Kieran's manner at the O'Malleys' house was utterly different from that which it had been at lunch, same diffident smile and quiet charm, but now he was a South Side Irishman with two of his own kind who were only a couple of years older than he was. He told stories about the "old days" and talked about friends and acquaintances. Any unease the O'Malleys might have felt about a stranger headshrinker at their supper table quickly vanished. We all relaxed and enjoyed our meal.

Jack, the lad who had been abused, was an adorable little boy whom it was impossible not to like. If only, I had often thought, the Cardinal or even James could meet the kid.

Kieran delighted him with a few simple magic tricks.

"How do you do it, Doctor O'Kerrigan?" He smiled happily. "Are you really a magician?"

"I am the Great O'Kerrigan the Magnificent." He deepened his voice. "Now pick a card, any card."

"You'll have to show me that one someday, Kieran," I said after the last trick.

"No way!" he said with a smile.

I wondered why a man who liked kids so much and was so good with them didn't have any of his own.

What had gone wrong between him and Kathleen back in 1972?

There had been no drinks before dinner and no wine with the meal. After supper we settled down in their parlor for a sip of Baileys.

"You'll note that we're heavy drinkers, Doctor O'Kerrigan," said Kevin O'Malley with heavy irony, "just as almost every priest in the Archdiocese will tell you."

"Why do you put up with it?" Kieran asked, now suddenly intense. "Why do you let them say and do terrible things to you, when you could collect a million or so and be done with them?"

"We don't have much extra money," Kevin began. "I'm an accountant and my wife is a nurse. We're comfortable, but we've run through all our savings and we're heavily in debt. We want our legal costs paid, but that's not what it's about."

"What is it about?"

"We're old-fashioned Catholics, Doctor," Helen explained. "We would like to be able to walk out on the Church, but we can't do it. We care about what happens to it."

"I see." He frowned. "Even after what they've done to you and your son?"

"He beat him repeatedly," Kevin continued. "So badly that his neck might be permanently damaged."

"Incredible!"

"We didn't believe it either. It took our son many months to work up the courage to tell us. Father Greene warned him that if he did tell us, Father, who as a priest had magical powers, would kill us all in our sleep."

Every time I heard the story I found myself not believing it. Yet there were the lie detector tests.

"Dear God!" Kieran exclaimed.

"He broke down and told us only when they demanded he bring in another boy and a little girl Father wanted to assault. We think he was very brave to risk his life, as he saw it, to save them."

"Indeed he was. . . . Anal intercourse?" Kieran asked casually.

"Attempted," Helen replied with equal casualness.

"We don't feel sorry for ourselves," her husband added. "Not most of the time anyway. We figure that it's our vocation, that God permitted this to happen to us so that we could turn the tide against sexual abuse in the Church. We'll fight it to the bitter end."

"And continue to be Catholics?"

They both laughed. "What else can we be? That's what we are, isn't it?"

"Sometimes we feel tired," Helen said, "very tired. But we're not going to turn away. We'll force the suit to trial and we'll win."

"We've got a break lately, as Father Brendan may have told you. A witness came forward on his own when he heard there were questions being asked. He says he saw Greene raping boys repeatedly in the school basement."

"Who is he?"

"A janitor, now kind of retired, who lived in the school basement. Still does. He said that it had always bothered him and he wanted to straighten it out before he died."

I noted that Brendan seemed less enthused about the new witness than Kevin O'Malley did.

"And what do you think of the men who did this to you?"

"You mean Father Greene?" Kevin shrugged. "He's a sickie. He's not responsible for what he does. Everyone seems to know that."

"No, I meant the Cardinal, Father Roder, Bishop Leary, the lawyers and psychiatrists who work for the Church."

"At Saint Theodore grammar school—back of the Yards, Doctor, in case you've forgotten—they told us that we should never judge the Church by what its leaders do."

"What good does it do to be angry at them?" Helen said. "They're not the Church, we're the Church. We're going to work to make it a better Church as long as God gives us life."

"And you gotta understand"—her husband poured a refill for Kieran's Baileys glass—"that I'm so much a conservative that I'd like to see the Mass back in Latin again."

"What do you think?" I asked Kieran as we pulled away from the house.

"Why won't James or the Cardinal meet with those nice people?"

"The lawyers tell James not to meet with them."

"Are the goddamn lawyers running the Catholic Church?" Kieran shouted furiously.

I hoped that no windows were open wide enough on that quiet street in Park Ridge to hear him.

"Yes," I said in answer to his question.

We drove downtown in silence. So Kieran O'Kerrigan had a temper. How very interesting. . . .

At the Ontario Street ramp he said, "The literature suggests that in his lifetime a pedophile may have as many as three hundred victims."

"So I'm told."

"Many of whom become victimizers themselves."

"Precisely."

"Figure that men like Gerry Greene have half a lifetime to go, more or less. That means there's a hundred fifty kids out there that he'll rape, given half a chance."

"You see why I want to put a stop to the Archdiocese's cover-up strategy?"

"I sure do."

"I've got another question, Kieran O'Kerrigan, top gun from out of town," I said as I drove him back to the Hancock Center.

"Question away."

"What do you know about Satanism?"

"You mean as a form of sexual abuse of children?"

"Yeah. Maybe the ultimate form of sexual abuse." My blood ran cold as it always did when I had to talk about this subject.

The Chicago skyline loomed ahead of us, a delicate lacework of lights against the dull night sky.

"There have been cases of apparent ritual murder in various parts of the country which the police think might have been the work of Satanic cults. I know that some clinicians have seen cases of multiple personality disorders—extreme disassociation—in which, under self-hypnosis, the patient describes himself as having been tortured in such rituals. I know that one hears rumors that such things happen in some affluent suburbs. According to the rumors, there are men who submit their daughters to such rituals. But I've never seen any proof of the rumors."

"You've treated such cases?"

"No. To tell the truth I want no part of them. The details can be quite grisly. In one case about which I read, the woman described how her father and his friends drugged her, stripped her, stretched her naked on a slab, celebrated a black Mass on her belly, violated her sexually, marked her with a knife and branded her and then went through the pretense of driving a big knife through her heart in a human sacrifice. There were scars on her body and brand marks."

We were both silent for a moment. Then Kieran continued. "The woman in the case I read told stories of babies killed in sacrifices and pieces of their hearts distributed in mockery of the Catholic Eucharist, of children penned in cages and forced to watch, of girls sacrificed because they resisted the demands of the cult leaders or performed rituals poorly, of women held captive to breed babies for sacrifices. She even pictured herself as a priestess who cut out babies' hearts and killed other girls who had failed the tests. She enacted some of these murders in hypnotic trance."

"Do you believe that such things actually happen?"

"Not really. The same charges were made against the early Christians, the medieval Jews, and the witches in the early years of the modern age. No arrest has ever been made, no conviction ever rendered by a court, no bodies of sacrificed babies ever found. The trouble is that people might read these stories and figure why not give it a try—just to see if it's as much fun as it sounds."

"You're a skeptic, then?"

"I think the woman in the article was ritualistically abused by her father and a group of other men and women. I'd bet on that. Her father committed incest with her often, telling her that he could do so because she was a child of Satan. I don't doubt that either. The victimizers had drugged her repeatedly, I'm pretty confident of that. The fantasies about ceremonies . . . about those I'm dubious. . . . But why are you interested in Satanism?"

"There's whiffs of it floating around at the edges of a couple of pedophile stories," I said casually.

"Horrible stuff."

I was relieved when Kieran didn't ask me anything more. I couldn't tell him all I knew. Not yet. It was more horrible than he could imagine.

LEARY

"I think you'll like this, Your Excellency." Ignatius Loyola Keefe handed
me a letter. "It should eliminate one of our minor problems."

Ignatius Keefe, senior counsel for the Archdiocese, is a tall and
handsome man with wavy silver hair and piercing blue eyes. We believe
that he is the best lawyer in Chicago for our purposes and is worth far
more than it costs to retain him. I find it a little hard to accept his
patrician style—hand-made shoes, razor-cut hair, fifteen-hundred-dollar
suits, an affected New England accent—because I know that his father
drove a sanitation truck for the city. But his style is his business, not
mine.

He certainly strode into the paneled grillroom of the Chicago Club
on Monroe and Michigan—the city's most prestigious club—like he
owned the place. The various employees, from the lobby to our table,
had fawned on him like he was someone very important. Which I guess
he was.

I opened the letter. It was addressed to Ronald Long.

Dear Mr. Long:

It has come to our attention that a certain Brendan McNulty is
acting for your firm in the matter of John and Jane Doe versus the
Catholic Bishop of Chicago a Corporation Sole. Be advised that Mr.
McNulty is in fact a Roman Catholic priest. Be further advised that
he is therefore an employee of the Catholic Bishop of Chicago, a
Corporation Sole. Finally, be advised that it is inappropriate that he
should be engaged in legal work against the Catholic Bishop of
Chicago, a Corporation Sole.

We ask that you remove Mr. McNulty from this case and cease all
contact with him until the matter is resolved. In the event that you
do not comply with this request we will take appropriate action to
vindicate the rights of the Catholic Bishop of Chicago, a Corporation
Sole.

We further direct that you cease and desist from all contact with employees of the Catholic Bishop of Chicago, a Corporation Sole, unless you have received written permission in each and every case from this office.

> Cordially Yours,
> Ignatius L. Keefe, Esq.

I handed the letter back to Keefe.

"That will fix McNulty." Martin Roder laughed. "They'll have to dump him. He has no right to get involved in these depositions."

"Strictly speaking, Iggy," I said, "he does not work for us. We don't pay his salary or his benefits."

"If he's a priest, he works for the Cardinal."

"You think the courts will buy that?"

"Sure they will." He waved his hand, on which three rings glittered. "Everyone knows that a priest works for the Church."

"If you think it's necessary . . ."

"It is. He's responsible for the O'Malleys persisting in the case. If we get him out of it, they'll collapse."

"I suppose so."

"He just wants to embarrass the Church," Martin said piously.

"I'm sure he's involved," Iggy continued, "in this matter of the engineer who claims to have seen Father Greene molesting boys years ago."

"That is troubling testimony."

"Not to worry." Iggy waved his rings again. "Ned Kelly has changed his story. Now he admits that O'Malley and Long paid him twenty thousand dollars to accuse Father Greene. There was not a word of truth in what he told them. He's given us an affidavit. We're going to ask for a criminal indictment of O'Malley and Long."

"That will end the whole affair," Martin crowed triumphantly.

"Witnesses have changed their stories in a couple of other cases against us, haven't they?"

"That's because the plaintiffs think the Church is a pushover." Iggy leaned toward me. "We'll show them that they can't push the Church around."

"That's why they'd spend twenty thousand dollars on a bribe?"

"Why not? They think they can make five million off us. What's twenty K in that context?"

"I suppose so."

"Your Excellency, if we cave in on one of these cases, all the vermin in Chicago will crawl out of the woodwork. They'll bankrupt the Church."

"If we don't do it first."

KATHLEEN

I sat on a Grant Park bench, eating popcorn and looking at the 30 North Michigan Building.

It was another incredible Indian summer day. I was wearing a light spring dress and carrying a sweater, just in case it turned cold before I drove back to the Neighborhood. Not much on under the dress. The popcorn, the park, the warm sunshine made me feel like a teenager again, carefree, reckless, buoyant.

I was fixated on the man up in that office on the 18th floor. Obsessed by him, enthralled by him. He would bring me pleasure and freedom and dignity and safety. My body yearned for him. I wanted a man who would desire me, lust after me, overwhelm me with his passion. Kieran was such a man. I could have him this afternoon.

If I had enough nerve to go after him.

I longed to see him and tell him the truth: the truth about Brien and the wreck of our marriage, the truth about how I felt. I was confident that Kieran could help me. For all that had happened, I still believed in his promise of long ago. But that didn't prevent me from losing my nerve at the elevator. Despite desire and need, I couldn't bring myself to confide in him. I hoped one day I would be able to make it to his door. I was beginning to understand that I needed his professional help as well.

Like the dutiful scholar that I had become, I'd researched the "battered wife syndrome" literature. In some ways I was not typical. The beatings had been rare. I had not become pliant and submissive.

Yet I still fit. My seventeen years of marriage had been filled with terror. I had learned to tread on eggshells without realizing that I was doing so, I had avoided arguments with him when he was drunk, and I'd never really confronted him with the anger I felt about our inadequate sexual life.

Part of me, deep down inside, had lived in fear for all those years. I had not noticed the fear or pretended not to notice it, but it was there and it had affected everything in our marriage.

"You never forget a beating," one woman had said in an article. "No matter how long it has been since the last one, you wait for the next one. You know it's coming."

I had realized all along that another one was coming. It finally did. There would be more unless I fled from him. In one of them, he would kill me, poor man, without intending it or knowing what he was doing.

Like the other women, I had talked to no one—not even a physician. I was ashamed, bewildered, humiliated, mortified that something like that could happen to me.

So I had lived in secret terror. For all my education and intelligence, I had cowered in the dark and waited for the next blow to come.

What were the chances that yet another blow, perhaps the final one, would come?

On the basis of the literature, the odds were overwhelming unless Brien went into intense therapy. Even then, the chances of a recurrence were considerable. Battering husbands were never cured; at best they learned to understand and control their impulses.

As the pressures built up in his senatorial race, Brien's deep anger would surge to the surface again.

My husband hit me for the first time when we had been married for four months.

I had been arguing with him about Chicago politics. He had come home late from a meeting of the 19th Ward Organization. His awkward weave up the stairs to our tiny bedroom on Prospect Avenue warned me that he had been drinking, probably a lot.

He told me with some conviction that he had found a group which was ready to push him for ward committeeman when the present incumbent, who was in poor health, resigned.

"Who are these people?" I demanded.

"Jim Lawless, Larry Ryan, Bert Nelson."

"Jerks," I said.

He frowned unhappily. "Why do you say that, Kathleen?"

"To begin with they're lightweights; and to end with the committee-man will be someone of whom the Mayor approves. He's not going to run the risk of the 19th turning rebellious again."

"Why does that rule me out?" He sounded angry, an emotion which he had rarely expressed against me thus far in our marriage.

"If you can talk the Mayor into supporting you, you might have a chance. Why don't you call him for an appointment? Even if he declines, you'll earn a lot of points for asking. Come back to run for something on another day."

"Why won't he support me this time?"

"Because the Daleys don't forget, that's why."

"Fuck the Daleys!"

That outburst was a warning that he'd been drinking more than I thought. Even in the privacy of bedrooms, in Chicago politics you didn't say something like that. Moreover, Brien rarely used obscene or scatological words and seemed genuinely shocked when I did, which, alas, was too often—and still is, with six little ears around the house picking up every word and every nuance.

"That doesn't solve the problem," I said, not unreasonably, I thought. "You're only going to make more trouble for yourself if you run without the Mayor's support and against his wishes."

"My mother says I could win."

"Your mother knows a lot about TV politics, but she doesn't know squat about ward politics."

That's when he hit me, a sharp slap across the face.

"My mother knows a lot more about politics than you do."

I hit him back. Naturally.

Then he slugged me, a solid punch to the stomach. I doubled over in pain, but still rammed his chest with my head.

It was a brief fight because he was so much stronger than I. He grabbed my arm, slapped me around, tore off my robe and gown, and forced me to make love with him.

The next morning he apologized abjectly, admitting that he was a drunken brute, promised never to hit me again, went out and brought me flowers and an emerald bracelet, and lavished me with apologies and concern.

"Please forgive me, Kathleen," he begged. "Don't stare at me with that stone face of yours. I'm sorry. I was drunk. I didn't know what I was doing. I'll never do it again. It was the booze, not me."

"*You* drank the booze."

"I'm off it. I promise that too. I'll never take another drink."

"That's what my father says."

"I'm different, you wait and see."

But he wasn't different. He stayed on the wagon for a month and then started drinking again.

I think everyone in both our families, with the exception of me and the possible exception of James and one of Brien's sisters, is an alcoholic.

I should have walked out on Brien that morning and threatened never to come back until he joined AA or saw a therapist or did both. But I was twenty-two and naive.

The real warning flag ought to have been how much he enjoyed raping me. He loved every harsh, brutal, degrading second of it. Ordinarily, sex was hard work for Brien, a duty and an obligation, not a joy. I was not so dumb eighteen years ago that I didn't notice the difference. But I didn't want to think about it, so I shoved the truth away.

Now I could look back with almost a laugh at my attempts to develop a mutually satisfying sexual relationship—not an easy task without a willing partner. After the doctor's lecture that was part of our pre-Cana conference, I'd decided to tackle the issue of sex straight-on.

"What do you want from me, Brien?" I asked him after that lecture.

"That you be a good wife and mother," he replied piously.

"I mean in bed."

His fair skin colored. "That will take care of itself."

"Don't you have any fantasies about what you would like to do with me?"

"There's a lot more to marriage than fantasy, Kathleen." He sounded just like my brother James, as he often did, even then.

"But fantasy is part of what holds husband and wife together, isn't it?"

"I suppose," he said, turning his head away from me.

"Do you imagine taking off my clothes?"

"Kathleen!"

"How would you enjoy it most—leaving my bra till second-to-last or removing it right away?"

He squirmed in the car as we turned off 95th Street.

"I don't think we should talk about that until after we're married."

Again the warning flag was up for someone who was open to seeing it. But I didn't want to see anything.

As it turned out, even after we were married, Brien did not much enjoy undressing me. Nor did we discuss our sex life. Ever.

Our wedding night at the Drake Hotel in Chicago and the subsequent days at Ashford Castle in County Mayo were a terrible disappointment. Brien was not brutal or insensitive or clumsy as so many grooms are supposed to be on their wedding night. Quite the contrary, he was gentle and tender, at least as gentle and tender as he could be, given the fact that he had to work very hard at sex.

"It'll be all right," he reassured me at O'Hare as we boarded the Aer Lingus plane for Shannon. "It takes time to adjust. Like they said at the pre-Cana conference. Besides, there's more important things in marriage than sex."

Sure there are, though without sex they're not likely to work all that well. But it's not an observation you expect from a young man who's just been married.

I was disappointed in what I took to be the failure of our honeymoon and wondered if there was something wrong with me—was I too forward?

Brien was not happy when I joined him in the shower at Ashford Castle.

"Kathleen! Didn't they tell us that we should respect each other's privacy!"

So they had. I never tried that ploy again. Thus rebuffed, I gave up on attempts of wantonness.

As I learned when I returned from Ireland by listening to the conversation of other young wives, our case was not all that untypical. Men, it seemed, were more frightened by sex than we were.

Maybe, I told myself, I was better off than most. Brien was at least a generous and considerate husband most of the time. It was not his fault that he was not that much interested in sex. I learned how to make the most, physically, out of our rare encounters. We did produce three children and we were partners in a joint venture, even if we weren't passionate lovers.

So eighteen years of marriage rushed by. I forgot about the second beating, though it was worse than the first. Actually, I never forgot about it. But until recently, I was confident that it would never happen again.

It had been an unbearable summer night at Grand Beach. Poor little Megie, then a year old, had a troubled tummy and had kept us awake for several nights. I was irritable and ill-tempered, angry at everything in general and nothing in particular.

Brien had gone over to Long Beach Country Club for a day of golf and dinner. He promised he'd be home early, not that I had demanded it.

Instead he arrived home at 2:30, roaring drunk, just as I had finally put a fitfully sleeping Megie to bed.

Naturally I blew up. I accused him of not caring about either me or his daughter. I should have known better. It has always been accusations about his mother or daughters that bring out the Mr. Hyde in my Dr. Jekyll husband.

He tore off my sleepshirt and administered a savage beating. He was so out of control, I was afraid that he might kill me and maybe Megie too. I soon stopped resisting and let him do what he wanted to me. When he was finished beating me, he raped me again, much more brutally than he had the first time. The assault sent him into a delirium of pleasure.

I should have realized then that beneath his smooth and gentle exterior Brien Donahue feared and hated women. I should have walked out then. I almost did. Instead, I acted like a classic case of the battered wife syndrome. I gave him another chance. He went to a therapist a couple of times—or said he did—and attended an AA meeting or two.

By the time it was clear he had no intention of pursuing either therapy or AA, I realized I was pregnant again, this time with Maeve. I could hardly contemplate divorce.

I didn't feel up to raising two children without a father. I gambled that the violence would never happen again.

Until recently it seemed like it was a reasonably good gamble.

BRENDAN

Ron Long was deposing the officer from the suburban police force to whom our clients had first complained about the abuse of their son. "Now, Lieutenant Klein, you are aware of the guidelines that the various relevant law-enforcement agencies—county, state, and your municipalities—have prepared for dealing with pedophile complaints."

The deposition was being held in our offices. Klein was a nervous witness and with good reason. His lawyer, who seemed in awe of the chic offices of Elias and McDermott, sat silently while Ron probed away.

"Yes, sir," he whispered. Steven Klein was a short, rotund man with receding blond hair and a fat, genial face. Under ordinary circumstances he would have been the perfect jolly youth-officer in an affluent suburb.

"I didn't hear him, Mr. Long," the court reporter protested.

"Would you please speak a little louder, Lieutenant."

"I said, 'Yes sir.' "

"Thank you, Lieutenant. You are also aware of the guidelines according to which the Department of Family Services works on these cases."

"Yes, sir."

"Let's review these guidelines."

Ron took him through the regulations in agonizing detail. He and Klein and Klein's lawyer quibbled about some of the particulars of the regulations. It was our turn to be time-consuming, but since we were moving toward a charge that the law-enforcement agencies had participated in a deliberate cover-up, it was not a waste of time.

Finally Ron said, "Well, I guess that pretty much covers the guidelines of the various agencies. And I would compliment you, Lieutenant, on your detailed knowledge of these regulations. But then child-abuse cases are one of your specialties, are they not?"

"One of my responsibilities as youth officer, sir."

"Indeed. . . . Now, can you tell me if any of these regulations were followed in your questioning of Richard Doe?"

"I beg your pardon?"

"Lieutenant, as you know, I have here the notes that were taken when Richard Doe was isolated in a room with you, an Assistant State's Attorney, and an official of the DCFS. It seems to me that you violated every single one of those regulations—no psychologist was present to ask the questions, the boy's parents were not permitted to watch and listen through a one-sided window, and the boy was verbally assaulted and battered as though he were on a witness stand being cross-examined by a hostile attorney. Can you explain why you violated virtually all the rules which you were bound to follow?"

He hesitated. "We had investigated the charges and we could find no confirmation."

"What do you mean by confirmation?"

"No other reports of such molestation." He loosened his tie and glanced appealingly at his lawyer.

"You mean no parents who were willing to respond to police questions?"

"That is correct."

"So this fact justified you using hardball interrogation techniques on a nine-year-old boy?"

"We wanted to see how he would act before a jury."

"That is the responsibility of the police or the State's Attorney at this stage of an investigation?"

"It depends on the case."

"I see. A guideline that is not recorded. . . . Tell me, Lieutenant, can you ever recall this extra guideline being involved in another case?"

"Uh, no . . . not really."

He loosened his tie again. Sweat was pouring down his face.

"Did anyone suggest why it might apply to this one?"

"Not exactly."

"Did you ask either the chief of police or the Assistant State's Attorney?"

"Ah, well . . . I did ask the Chief. And he said that I should do what I was told to do."

"Did he mention that this guideline might apply because the accused was a priest?"

"Well, not exactly. . . ."

"Did he mention the fact that the alleged victimizer was a priest?"

"Yeah, he did. He said it would be a terrible thing to ruin a priest's reputation."

"I see. . . . Lieutenant, do you know of any case in this county in which a priest has been brought to trial on such a charge?"

"No sir, I don't."

"Were there any attorneys for the Archdiocese present at the police station during the course of this phase of your investigation?"

"I . . ."

"Were there?"

"I believe there were, yes sir. They had the right to be there."

"Far be it from me to suggest that they did not. Were they in another part of the station during the interrogation of Richard Doe?"

"Yes, sir."

Bingo! Ron had bet that they were, though, as he had said, it would have been pretty stupid of them.

"Did you think their presence might have had something to do with the cover-up in which you engaged?"

"I object to that, Mr. Long." Klein's attorney woke up. "That's an improper question."

"Of course it is, Counselor. Let me rephrase that. Did you think their presence might have had something to do with the unusual features of the investigation?"

"Yes, sir—I did."

Klein seemed relieved that we had finally come to the heart of the matter.

"Let me see if I understand the facts to which you have testified, Lieutenant Klein. One: the procedure in the interrogation of Richard Doe was unique. Two: the issue of the alleged perpetrator being a priest was raised when you questioned the procedure and, three: attorneys for the Archdiocese were present in the police station during the examination of Richard Doe. Are those details factually correct?"

Klein closed his eyes and sighed. "Yes, sir . . . they are."

"I see. . . . Now, let me ask you a hypothetical question, Lieutenant. If you were visiting another jurisdiction and saw the events we have just described, as a professional law-enforcement officer might you in your professional capacity have had some questions about the possibility of a cover-up?"

"I couldn't be sure of that."

"Not sure, Lieutenant. Obviously. But the thought would have occurred to you."

"Yes, sir, it would."

Oh, boy. We were now talking punitive damages and possible criminal indictment for obstruction of justice. It might be hard to prove in this case, but when we were through questioning previous victims or their families we should show certainly a pattern of irresponsibility and perhaps a pattern of obstruction of justice.

"Does the priest conflict with the lawyer now, Brendan?" Ron folded himself into his "judge's" chair after the exhausted cop and his lawyer had left our floor of the IBM building.

"How so?"

"Would you want to see Bishop Leary indicted for obstruction of justice?"

"That won't happen, not in a million years."

"Iggy Keefe?"

"That wouldn't bother me. But it won't happen. When they see the pattern of our depositions, they'll back off."

"Don't bet on it, Brendan. Iggy is capricious. He works on instincts, not intelligence. He may not figure out where we're going until it's too late."

"Then let it happen."

"And the punitive damages—twenty, thirty, maybe a hundred million dollars? Open up all the Church's books and records for examination by our accountants? They could blunder into that, you know."

"Then let that happen too."

"You're pretty tough, aren't you, Brendan?" He favored me with his crooked grin.

"Damn it, Ron, the Archdiocese is oppressing its people—the union workers when it gives construction contracts to scab companies, the families of pedophile victims whom Iggy calls 'the enemy,' the parishioners whose churches and schools it arbitrarily closes. I don't think it will happen, but if it costs a hundred million dollars to stop it, then make them pay the hundred million!"

He rolled his eyes. "You would have done well in Florence under Savonarola."

"Or maybe in Wexford in 1798," I fired back.

His secretary interrupted our exhibition of historical trivia. "Mr. Keefe to see you, sir."

"Ignatius Loyola Keefe?" He cocked an eyebrow.

"Yes, sir." She grinned. "Should we sneak Father Brendan out the back door?"

"There isn't a back door. . . . Show Mr. Keefe in."

In his impeccable raincoat and with his razor-cut silver hair, Iggy Keefe looked the kind of distinguished journalist who might just possibly be the London bureau chief for *The New York Times*.

"Take your coat, Iggy?" Ron asked.

"No . . . I was just walking by for lunch and thought maybe I'd stop in and chew the fat with you for a few moments." Uninvited, he sat on the couch across from Ron's desk. "Nice to see you, Father Brendan. I ran into your sister and her husband at the Club the other night."

I didn't say a thing. I did, however, demand from God all kinds of points for not responding that I would have to warn Fiona to avoid bad companions.

"Always nice to have you drop by, Ignatius."

"Yeah, well, you know, I was thinking that we're all really on the same side in this case—we're all good Catholics, aren't we? And we might just as well settle it and get it over with. All of us have a lot better things to do with our time."

"We'd be interested in hearing your offer, Ignatius."

"Well." He went through the motions of calculating in his head. "We could be talking in the high six figures, you know. That's more than you'd ever get from a jury."

"We could get ten times that in punitive."

"If you could prove gross negligence—and I'm sure you wouldn't want to do that. . . . Well, maybe even low, and I mean very low, seven figures."

The attorney for the Archdiocese had casually walked into our offices and offered us a million dollars of the money of the Catholic people of Chicago.

"I gather on the street"—Ron did not blink an eye—"that a million or so is the standard price you people are prepared to pay for priestly amusements. Father Jim Crawford has already cost you two million for the two handicapped young women he's knocked up."

"You want more?" Keefe smiled genially. "Maybe I can get you a little more."

"Ignatius, how many times do I have to tell you that my clients are not primarily interested in money."

"We're all interested in money, Ronnie."

"They want to see this review board established so that men like Father Greene and Father Crawford are never reassigned to parishes and these cover-ups come to an end."

"Well." Keefe crossed his legs. "That has always seemed to me an interesting idea. Maybe we could learn something from considering that kind of an idea. I'll talk to Father Roder about it. Maybe we can work something out."

"That would be very nice, Ignatius."

"Don't you think so, Father Brendan?"

I chilled him with what Fiona calls my "old Irish monsignor" glare.

"Well." He stood up and jammed his hands in his pockets. "It seems like a good idea to me. I'll talk it over with Father Roder and the Bishop and maybe even the Cardinal and get back to you." He stretched out his hand. "Good to see you, Ron. Give my best to Tracy, will you?"

Ron shook hands with him. I continued to glare.

"What did all that mean?" I asked once Keefe had left.

"It didn't mean much of anything, I'm afraid. Just one of his instinctive moves, throwing up a smokescreen, tossing dust in our eyes, playing games with us."

"It's a little crazy, isn't it, Ron?"

"Crazy like a fox. He's trying to wear us down. If I had asked for two million, subject to consultation with our client, he would have proposed one-five and we would have a deal."

"He knew we wouldn't buy it."

"Yeah. But maybe we were growing tired of the game. Now he knows that we're not tired. Or maybe he knows. Maybe I'm attributing rational motives to behavior that is not altogether rational—not when you consider how much the Archdiocese has to lose if this suit ever comes to trial."

"Doesn't he know that?"

"If someone asked him that question over lunch, he'd laugh and say that no one has ever won a suit against the Archdiocese."

"Undefeated season, Ron?"

"Yep."

"So far."

BRIEN

He called again today. He still wants her. He promises more trouble for my life unless I give her to him. He's destroyed my marriage. Now he says he will destroy my political career. He can do it. He can do anything he wants. He has the demons on his side.

"We have the power of our lord and master, Brien," he said. "We always get what our lord and master wants. He wants her. You have no choice. You will deliver her over to us."

"No," I said feebly.

"We will destroy you and your family unless you yield to our lord and master. We have destroyed others. We always go unpunished because darkness is on our side."

"No," I repeated.

He laughed. "You'll see, Brien, you'll see."

I can't resist him much longer. I've pleaded with James to make an appointment with Kieran O'Kerrigan. Maybe he can help me resist the demons.

I couldn't tell James about the demons. He wouldn't believe me. Although he's a priest, he doesn't believe in demons.

I think he'll call Kieran. I hope he does.

I need a drink. One wouldn't hurt, would it?

KIERAN

"On the Rock Island Line, red hair like that could belong to only one woman."

I sat down next to her as the train pulled out of Union Station for its jolting ride from town to Beverly.

She smiled at me, not at all flustered. "We call it METRA now, Doctor O'Kerrigan."

She was reading printouts from microfiche. As we talked she gathered them together and slipped them into an expensive leather attaché case.

"The Rock Island Line," I said, "will always be the Rock Island Line."

Oblivious to the three or four other people on the car in the middle afternoon, we broke into the song "On the Rock Island Line."

> *I says the Rock Island Line is a mighty good road.*
> *I says the Rock Island Line is the road to ride.*
> *I says the Rock Island Line is a mighty good road.*
> *If you want to ride, you gotta ride it like you're flyin'*
> *Buy your ticket at the station on the Rock Island Line.*
>
> *Well, the train left Memphis at half pas' nine*
> *Well, it made it back to Little Rock at eight forty-nine*
>
> *Well, Jesus died to save me in all of my sin.*
> *Well-a, glory to God, we goin' to meet him again.*
>
> *I says the Rock Island Line is a mighty good road.*
> *I says the Rock Island Line is the road to ride.*
> *I says the Rock Island Line is a mighty good road.*
> *If you want to ride, you gotta ride it like you're flyin'*
> *Buy your ticket at the station on the Rock Island Line.*

The other folks applauded.

"You're crazy, Kieran Patrick O'Kerrigan." She laughed.

"Weird."

"But nice. What brings you to the Rock Island Line?" she asked.

Kathleen was wearing a light summer dress, green and red floral print with a large crimson belt, as was appropriate for the Indian-summer warmth. She was devastatingly beautiful.

"I'm having supper with Father McNulty at St. Prax's. He wants to show me some depositions from a case he's working on."

"The pedophile case?"

There were lines at her mouth and around her eyes. Despite her well-preserved and luxuriant body, my love was a matron who had passed her fortieth birthday. If anything, however, she was even more appealing than she had been decades ago. I wanted her with all my being.

"You know about the case?"

"Everyone knows about it," she said with a shrug. "The priests think it's a deep dark secret—as if we don't read *Time* or watch the nightly news."

There were no traces of discoloration on her arms. Had the bruises faded or was she wearing makeup or had I imagined it in the first place?

"And what do people think about it?"

"They figure the priests are guilty, of course. Why else would parents go through the agony of suing the Church?"

"Do you tell James this?"

"My brother? He couldn't care less what I think about the subject."

"Were those printouts for your dissertation?" I asked, changing the subject.

"From the old *Chicago Daily News*. That was a great newspaper. But tell me about yourself, Kieran Patrick O'Kerrigan. Besides being a famous doctor and still a little weird but very nice, what is happening in your life?" She averted my gaze, then looked me in the eye and posed another question before I could reply to her first. "You've never married, Kieran?"

I could only ever be totally honest with Kathleen. "I've lived with another doctor in New York for five years. We both intended that the relationship would end up in marriage, but it didn't work out."

"Why not?"

"Religion, I suppose. She was Jewish. I thought I was an atheist, but I found I was still an Irish Catholic."

"What else?" Kathleen was as persistent as usual. "You loved her?"

"Very much."

"Do you date?"

"Oh, sure." I laughed. "I haven't taken a vow of celibacy. I'll find the right woman someday soon."

"You're a practicing Catholic again?"

"Once a Catholic always a Catholic. . . . I sing in the choir at Old St. Patrick's."

"The Mayor's parish."

"That's right. I came back to the Church," I said, "when I returned to Chicago. Or maybe as James said, I finally admitted that I had never left it and couldn't if I wanted to."

"James? My brother?"

"I needed a priest to talk to. He was a big help."

"He's such a good priest. . . . You don't have any family left, do you, Kieran?"

"No, not really. Some distant cousins, but we were never very close."

"What do you do on holidays?"

I hesitated. "You'll think I'm really weird."

"I know that," Kathleen said with a laugh. "But nice too."

"I go off to New Melleray Abbey at Christmas and Easter—to pray with the monks."

"How wonderful! Are you going to become a priest?"

"No, Kathleen Anne, I'm not. I still want to marry and have a family."

"Are you happy, Kieran Patrick O'Kerrigan?"

"Yes," I said cautiously, not at all certain I was.

"Are you actively searching for a wife?"

There was no end to this woman's curiosity! "More or less—but carefully."

We continued to chat as the train pulled into 91st Street. I only wished I could be as bold as Kathleen. There was so much I longed to ask her, but I just couldn't bring myself to.

"I always loved this neighborhood in fall," I told her. "The trees are so beautiful. The best ones match your hair."

"We're having a bit of an Indian Summer. Could I make you a pot of tea before you go over to the rectory? Still no booze at my house."

We were standing at 91st and Hoyne, on the very spot where I had once taken her school books into my arms. "Brendan is expecting me. If I can have a rain check . . ."

"Of course. It's good to talk to you again, Kieran."

"It is good to talk to you again."

She was gone before I had a chance to change my mind. If I had accepted her invitation to tea, I would have demanded to know who had beaten her and why she had sought the AIDS test. And I might not have finished until I told her how much I still loved her. It was just as well I didn't accept, I tried to tell myself. Yet I couldn't shake the feeling that I'd blown yet another opportunity to declare my heart. Then again, I wasn't an adulterer and didn't hope to be.

Taking a deep breath, I rang the doorbell at the rectory. "Kathleen!" I exclaimed as she opened the door of the rectory.

"Hi, Doctor O'Kerrigan," said Maeve Donahue. "You're not the first one to think I'm my mother."

"I'm sorry, Maevie," I stuttered.

"Nothing to be sorry about. I'm flattered." She stepped aside to permit me to enter. "Everyone says that I look more like her than the other two, except that I'm quieter than she was at fourteen."

"She had her quiet moments, Maeve."

The girl, or rather young woman, nodded solemnly. "I think I'm more secure than she was at my age. She agrees."

"Then it must be so."

"Father Brendan said you should go right up to his room."

"Yes, ma'am."

I told myself as I went up the spiral staircase to the second floor of the rectory that I did not want to destroy that self-possessed young woman's family life. I was glad, I insisted mentally, that I had turned down Kathleen's casual invitation for a cup of tea.

"Did she startle you?" he asked when I entered his study.

"Only a bit," I said. "She does look like her mother—not that you'd have tied her mother down to a rectory job twenty years ago."

"In those days"—he sighed—"they didn't understand how important the gatekeepers were."

"Let's see those depositions."

I pored over them while we had a pre-dinner Jameson's, and through the meal, which Maeve brought in unobtrusively from the kitchen.

"You get extra for being a waitress?" I asked her.

"Father Brendan is negotiating with my union."

Oh yes, she was her mother's daughter.

The pastor of St. Prax's, it turned out, was on one of his many vacations. Brendan McNulty was, for all practical purposes, the pastor of the parish.

I finished the depositions about 8:30. In time to catch the 9:00 train back to the Loop.

"What do you think?"

"If anything could drive me out of the Church, these could."

"Pretty terrible, huh?"

"I can't figure out why James ran the risk of your showing me all this stuff."

"He thinks I'm wrong, Kieran. The will to believe again. He's convinced that when you see the evidence you'll agree with him and persuade me that he's right."

"And when that doesn't happen?"

"He'll be sorry that you're not as smart as he thought you were."

"Selective perception . . ."

"Something like that. . . . Take a look at this letter."

He showed me a letter from Ignatius L. Keefe to Ronald Long. It demanded that Brendan be removed from the case and that Long "cease and desist" from all contact with priests employed by the Catholic Bishop of Chicago, a Corporation Sole.

"How did Long answer?"

"He wrote Iggy Keefe that his demand was offensive and intolerable. It's a game, Kieran, the kind of games lawyers play all the time—at least Iggy's kind of lawyers. But the Church ought not to be playing it."

"That's exactly what I'll tell James."

"Lots of luck."

As I left the rectory, I stuck my head in the office to say goodnight to Maeve.

"Study that geometry, young woman," I told her.

She looked up from the textbook. "Barf city, Doctor O'Kerrigan. Do you need a ride over to the station?"

"It's a nice night. I think I'll walk. Say hello to your sisters."

"Yes, Doctor O'Kerrigan."

I walked by the house on Hoyne, though it was not on the direct route to the station. There was a light on behind the trees in a room up at the top of the house. Kathleen was working on her dissertation.

I stood there in the shaded darkness of a soft and windless night and longed for what I had lost.

It was a mistake, I told myself later as the train lumbered downtown, ever to accept Brendan's invitation to dinner.

KATHLEEN

I looked out the window of my office where I had been trying, with no success, to make some progress on my dissertation. Running into Kieran had been a blessing and a curse. I was thrilled, of course, for the chance to talk to him and ask some of the questions that had been troubling my mind. But I hadn't had the chance to tell Kieran how I was feeling. I still hadn't had the chance to confide in him the way I longed to. And being so close to him, close enough to touch, maybe even to caress, was exquisite torture.

The night was warm, almost hot. I had been working in my underwear, which is my favorite scholarly garb when I'm sure I will not be interrupted.

The neighborhood was utterly silent, no cars, no breeze, no shouts of kids. It was as if I was the only one alive in the whole parish.

I wondered if Kieran had gone home yet from the rectory. I would hear tomorrow from my daughter all about his visit. Unlike her older sister, Maeve would be concise and sparing in her details.

I rubbed my arms as if to stir up some energy in my body. The pain was returning. I knew I ought to take my final Advil for the day and go to bed.

Around the corner, out of sight in the coach house, my poor husband was probably sick with guilt and self-hatred and praying that God would make me forgive him.

If I had said three magic words to Kieran when I had invited him to tea, I know he would have come. "I need help." It's all I needed to say, yet somehow I hadn't been able to say it. I had never asked for help in my life. I never would. I had to solve all my problems by myself.

I wanted to cry for myself and for the little girl, still very much alive inside me, who had fallen in love with Kieran Patrick O'Kerrigan that first day on Hoyne Avenue as she walked to St. Praxides school.

The tears would not come.

LEARY

After lunch I made the call. I didn't want to talk to him but I knew I had little choice.

Earlier in the day, a call from Kathleen had interrupted my analysis of the income from the Cardinal's Annual Appeal, an attempt to dig us out of the financial mess that the last two Archbishops had created for us.

"I'm waiting, James."

"Kathleen, I'm terribly busy."

"So am I."

"Couldn't you call back tomorrow?"

"I warned you that I would file for divorce immediately if my beloved husband didn't (a) have an AIDS test, (b) check in with a psychiatrist, (c) join AA, and (d) agree on an annulment after the election. You tell me that he has accepted 'd.' I have no proof of the other three conditions."

"How can he prove these things?" I struggled to control my temper. "What kind of proof do you want?"

"I want the name of the psychiatrist, the location of the AA group, and the results of the test."

"He had the test, Kathleen. He told me that he did. He doesn't have AIDS."

"Fine. Then he has the written results. I want to see them."

"Can't you trust him in the slightest?"

"No."

"I'm very busy right now."

"I don't believe he had the test, James. So I'll give you two seventy-two hours to get a result into my hands. Otherwise my lawyers will file."

"Who is your lawyer?"

"If you think I'd tell you that, you're dumber than I think you are."

"Kathleen!"

"I'm sick of it all, James, particularly the way you manipulate him. Three days and I want the name of the psychiatrist, the location of the AA group, and the results of the AIDS test or you will have a major scandal on your hands."

She hung up.

I rubbed my hands across my face. I was dead tired and suffering from a fearsome headache. I needed a vacation, or at least a good night's sleep. There seemed to be no prospect for either.

Time was against us. It was now clear to me that Brien must get into therapy before the campaign began, not only to placate my sister but for his own good. It was only a couple of weeks before the planned announcement of his candidacy. Sheila would not budge from the first week in November. Nor could I explain to her that Brien needed therapy.

I would have to figure out a solution soon. The bombs were ticking all around us.

But for the moment I had to concentrate on Archdiocesan finance. No one seemed to understand that an Archdiocese can't file a Chapter 11 bankruptcy. Compared to that problem, my sister's complaints were minor. But I had to do something about them.

I called Brien at his office.

"Brien, do you have the results of that, ah, medical test you took the other day?"

Silence.

"Test?" he asked finally.

"You know—the blood test."

"Oh, *that* test."

"Yes. I'm sure the doctor gave you the result."

"Uh, yeah, he did. But I tore the paper up. I didn't want anyone finding it. I'd look bad if the media found out I had a test for . . . for that."

"You shouldn't have done that, Brien."

"Well, I did."

"Kathleen wants to see the results."

"She doesn't have a right to that," he said wearily. "I told her I was sorry and that I'd never do it again."

"I understand, Brien. I admit her demands are irrational. Still, she has some grounds for fear. Moreover, in her present frame of mind, it would be wise, I think, to humor her. You can't tell what she's likely to do."

"She wouldn't file for divorce, would she?"

"I hope not. But we'd better get her results of that test."

"I told you I threw it away."

"Then I'm afraid I'll have to ask you to have a second test or see if the doctor will give you a copy of the results of the first test. There's no choice if you want to avoid a scandal. Bring the results to me."

"All right." He sighed. "This doubles the risk of someone finding out."

"It's a certainty if she goes into court."

"Yeah. I'll have it done."

"You're going to AA?"

"Sure. It's a good group this time. I'm learning a lot. I like it."

"Where?"

"St. Ethelbert's over in Oak Lawn."

"And a therapist?"

"You were going to ask Kieran for me, remember?"

"I don't think that's advisable. I really don't."

"Why not?"

There is an innocence about Brien, despite his flaws, which is both appealing and maddening.

"He and Kathleen were once very close."

"That was a long time ago."

"People don't get over those kinds of things."

"Well, okay, but still we were always friends—wouldn't he want to help me?"

"I'm not sure he'd be able to be objective about your relations with Kathleen."

"I don't figure it, James. She's not the problem. It's all the pressures.

As long as I can cope with the pressures, there's no trouble with Kathleen."

"A therapist might think differently."

"I'd trust Kieran. Come on, James, I'm going crazy with the pressures now. In addition to everything else, the kids look at me like I'm a leper. All Kieran could do is say no. Ask him for me—what harm will it do?"

"All right, Brien, I'll give it a try."

I made a note to call Kieran and returned to the figures from the Appeal. I took my summary into the Cardinal's office.

The meeting was so discouraging that I would have forgotten about Kieran if I had not made the note.

"Doctor O'Kerrigan."

"James, Kieran."

"Hello, Bishop."

"I told you that didn't fly."

"Okay, James, just thought I'd try it."

"I hope you're straightening out that young priest of mine."

"He's a very gifted and intelligent young man, James."

"I know that. He could be a very dangerous bull in the china shop. I want him on my side. . . . But it's not about him that I'm calling, Kieran."

"Oh?"

"I, uh, I need a favor."

"You got it, James."

"No, not that kind. This is one you may not be able to do. I'm not picking up my marker, as the politicians might say. I would understand it if you say that you can't."

"Okay. What is it?"

"Brien Donahue, my brother-in-law, has been under enormous strain in the past few months. These political campaigns are hellish. They don't prove anything about a man's ability to hold public office, only about his ability to withstand constant media pressure."

I paused to give him a chance to comment.

"I understand, James."

His voice was guarded, like that of a lawyer.

"We think, Kathleen and Brien and I, that he would benefit from some counseling before he announces formally. But it's a delicate matter. You remember the Eagleton affair."

"Twenty years ago, James. The public is a lot better informed about therapy now than it was then."

"Yet one still wishes that it be given confidentially."

"I understand that. And I agree. I would be happy to recommend a couple of very able and very discreet people."

"That's not what I wanted to ask you, Kieran."

I hesitated, waiting for him to say something. He waited for me to continue.

"You see"—I tried not to stumble over the words—"Brien has always been very fond of you. He knows your reputation as one of the best in town. He also trusts completely your, ah, discretion. He wonders if you would consent to see him, perhaps only once or twice to get him started."

More silence.

"Kieran?"

"You know, James, that I was once in love with Kathleen?"

"I had rather thought it might have been something like that. But that was a long time ago. Besides, she need not be the subject of your conversation with Brien. The problem is not so much the marriage as the pressures of political life."

Again silence. I cursed the need to discuss life's most serious problems on the phone.

"The marriage relationship is crucial in any psychiatric interview. It would be impossible to avoid it."

"Have you seen Kathleen since you've returned?"

"I bumped into her once . . . very briefly."

"She's a wonderful woman and we all love her. She's a problem only in that her own immaturity puts more pressure on him."

"I couldn't even discuss that with him."

"He desperately wants your help, Kieran."

"I understand that. . . . I would violate my professional ethics if I did any more than refer him to someone else."

"After you see him?"

"Now."

"You're refusing to see him?"

"I'm sorry, James."

I put my hand over the phone and sighed. I had expected a refusal, but now what did I do about poor Brien?

"I understand completely. In fact, I told Brien you would probably have reservations about treating a lifelong friend. He was, however, insistent that I ask. Thank you for considering my request. Do stay in touch with me about Father McNulty."

I didn't mean to sound as stiff as I did.

"I'm sorry," he said again.

"I understand completely."

Later that day I called Doctor Michael Shanahan, one of the men who had been an excellent psychiatric consultant to the Archdiocese and in whose discretion I had complete confidence. He agreed to see Brien the following day.

Then I told Brien about the appointment I had made for him with Doctor Shanahan.

"I don't want to see a man I don't know," he muttered stubbornly. "This business is enough hell as it is without being forced to spill my guts to a complete stranger."

"He's not a complete stranger. I know him."

"But I don't."

"Psychiatry is almost always undergone with complete strangers, Brien. That's the way it works."

"Kieran turned me down?"

"He feels that professional ethics make it impossible to treat a friend. I think you'll find Doctor Shanahan very sympathetic. He'll probably give you a test in the first interview, nothing more than that."

"A *test?* What kind of a test?"

"Pencil and paper test."

"I don't like it."

"Brien, you have to do it. You don't want Kathleen to file for a divorce at this point in time, do you?"

"No," he said reluctantly.

"See Doctor Shanahan once as a personal favor to me and then we'll talk about it, all right?"

"If you say so, James."

Drained and depressed, I put the phone down. I didn't blame Brien. I would be reluctant to face a psychiatrist myself. Yet Doctor Shanahan and his colleagues had been a great help to us. Their tests had quickly and efficiently sorted out falsely accused priests from those who needed long-term help. Perhaps a simple personality test would tell us that

Brien needed only a period of rest and relaxation, a golf vacation somewhere in the South perhaps.

The Boss buzzed me. He was hoping, though he didn't say so, that I had taken care of the kickback mess so that it would never become public. His excuse for ringing me was that he wanted to discuss another anonymous letter about a young priest who was said to be too close to the young women in his parish.

As I went in to see him, I longed for the good old days when our worst personnel problems were heterosexual priests who seemed to enjoy women too much.

PART III

KIERAN

"Good afternoon, Doctor O'Kerrigan." The young woman, a very able junior colleague at ISPI, smiled tentatively at me. "I wonder if I might ask you for a favor."

We had met at the Coke machine in the office corridor. Jean Cummins was pretty, sweet, and wore a wedding ring—and a very large diamond. Like most of the junior staff she treated me with great respect.

"On one condition, Jean."

"Certainly, Doctor O'Kerrigan."

"That you call me by my Christian name."

She blushed. "Of course, Doctor . . . uh, Kieran . . . do I pronounce it right?"

"Close enough. He was the founder of Conmacnoise and had a dun cow. . . . But this is not the time for an Irish history lecture. What is the favor?"

"First of all, I want to thank you for the manuscript of your article on dissociation and symbols. I have one of those cases, you know."

"Really?"

"I think I've become a bit of an expert on it—not that I like the subject."

"Tell me about it."

"Young woman, well-educated, perfectly charming. Delightful. Victimized by her father and friends in a Satanic cult when she was a child."

I gulped. "Multiple personalities?"

"To some extent. A lot of imaginary friends inside."

"Not quite the classic case then, huh?"

"She tells me what happened and sometimes can't quite believe it herself."

"Do you believe it, Jean?"

"Absolutely. No one could make up that kind of evil experience. She wakes up in the morning and doesn't know whether it's going to be a good day or a day with demons."

"A lot of the ritual abuse of children by parents," I said judiciously, "involves drugs. Many of the memories are, in fact, recollections of drug-induced trances."

"Her parents used drugs all right, lots of them; but it's hard for me to believe that her memories are merely trances."

"Prognosis?"

"Not too bad. She's happily married and her husband is patient and sympathetic."

"Why are these victims so likely to develop multiple personalities?"

"I hypothesize that the reason is that they had to accept such bizarre garbage as kids—drinking animal blood, eating animal feces, participating in animal sacrifices, dismembering live animals, experiencing threats that they would become human sacrifices themselves—that they project these experiences into persons distinct from the self."

We sipped our respective Cokes.

"And your favor?"

"I wonder if . . . please feel free to say no . . . if you would consent to hypnotize her. There's a lot of muck that's blocking therapy. You're supposed to be very good at—-"

"I'll be happy to help in any way I can." In truth, I wouldn't be happy. As I had told Brendan, I was unconvinced by the Satanism cases and didn't like them. But I could not say no to such a promising colleague.

"Thank you ever so much, Doctor . . . er, Kieran."

Back in my office my thoughts turned to James's phone call and what it meant for Kathleen. Was she really living with a ticking bomb? Should I call her and ask her about Brien?

I had a bad habit of striking out with women. On a called third strike.

"So you think you can leave the goddamn Catholic Church behind you, huh? Without any lingering effects? You think you can do what James Joyce could not do?"

I was being skewered again on Doctor Rosenblum's couch. I had returned to see him some four years ago because of the unexpected crises in my relationship with Rebecca.

"I don't believe in God anymore."

"Yah. You write learned articles about symbols, but you don't believe in the power of symbols?"

"Symbols?"

"The dream we are discussing—you dream you are about to incorporate the Communion into your mouth and instead Jesus turns into the red-haired woman. That's not a symbol?"

"I can't control my images."

"Yah, precisely. Once a Catholic always a Catholic. They fill your heads with those gorgeous images when you're a child and you never get rid of them, no?"

"I hate the Catholic Church and all it stands for."

A few days later, Jean Cummins introduced me to the patient she wanted me to hypnotize.

"Peggy, this is Doctor O'Kerrigan. Doctor O'Kerrigan, this is my patient, Peggy, about whom I've spoken."

She was a tall, willowy blonde with a quick smile and a firm handshake. Not the kind you'd expect to have experienced horrors in her youth.

"I'm delighted to meet you, Doctor O'Kerrigan," she said. "And very grateful for your willingness to see me."

She seemed a mature woman, a good prospect for therapy. Jean was lucky. So, for that matter, was Peggy.

Jean Cummins had given me the scenario. While she herself used hypnotherapy to probe back into the layers of personalities or quasi-personalities inside of "Peggy," she wanted my confirmation that what she was picking up was authentic. If, as was unlikely, an "abreaction"—an acting out of some past horror—occurred, so much the better.

Peggy went into a deep trance quickly. She was therefore highly suggestible—and hence, perhaps, less able to sort out reality from fantasy.

In her relaxed state, Peggy was even more serene and lovely. I wondered if we should be stirring up dangerous memories.

"I want to talk to the one who protects Peggy from memories of what happened, when she was abused."

"Who are you?"

Peggy was replaced—that's the only way I can describe it—by a totally different woman. The new person was tough, hard, cynical, her posture frankly provocative, her facial expression suspicious.

"Who wants to know who I am? I'm the chief of intelligence. No one gets beyond here without my permission. So who are you?"

"I'm Doctor O'Kerrigan."

"What do you want?"

"I want to find out about the time Peggy thinks she murdered the baby."

"Yeah? Why?"

"I'm trying to help Doctor Cummins lead Peggy out of the troubles those deep memories cause her."

"Why should I trust you?"

"You trust Doctor Cummins, don't you?"

"Yeah. Mostly."

"Even if I wanted to do something which would hurt Peggy, which I don't, she wouldn't let me."

"I don't know about that."

"I'll leave whenever you tell me to."

"Promise?"

"I promise."

"I guess it's okay."

Classic dissociation phenomenon from the multiple-personality literature. But Peggy might have read the literature. Or perhaps she was unwittingly picking up signals from Jean.

"Mommy." A new personality had appeared, with the facial expression and voice of a pre-pubescent girl.

"Mommy, I don't want to take off my clothes and dance for all those people."

She twisted and turned in her chair as a girl that age might.

"I know if I do it well, they'll make me the head priestess. I still don't want to do it.

"I remember what they did to Marina when she didn't dance well. They cut out her heart. I'm afraid. Please take me home."

Then she—whoever she was—winced, as if she had been injected with a hypodermic needle. Her body relaxed as it might if a sedative had been injected.

Then she began to sing, or perhaps chant would be a better word, some strange rhythmic verses, something like Gregorian chant only far more sensual. She rose from the couch; her body began to sway in a lascivious dance—not the dance of a woman in her early thirties but of an early adolescent girl.

It was a bizarre, troubling, and extremely erotic dance—just as it might have been performed by a trained harlot who had been drugged.

Across the room I saw Jean Cummins sit up straight, clearly worried by what was happening. So, as a matter of fact, was I.

"Who are you?" I asked the dancer.

"I am Regina, the prime priestess. They all applaud me." It was a voice different from that of the child who had spoken with a mother, a monotonic, sensual, half-mad voice.

"What are you doing?"

"I am dancing for the family. They all admire and love me. The other children, the ones in the cages, envy me because they know I'm a good dancer. They know I won't die like Marina did. If I kill the baby right they will love me forever. I will be the best of them."

"So you want to kill the baby?"

"I must kill the baby. It is his will."

"Then what will happen?"

"They will all play with me."

"Do you like it when they play with you?"

"It brings me great pleasure."

"Always?"

"Sometimes it hurts."

"Ah."

"They're bringing the baby now. They're laying him on the altar. They're giving me the knife. He's a cute baby." The little girl returned. "I don't want to kill him."

She gripped her hands around an imaginary knife.

"I don't want to kill him. I don't want to . . . I must!"

She plunged her imaginary knife into an imaginary baby on my desk and with a quick turn of the blade pulled out an imaginary heart and sunk her teeth into it.

"Eat the flesh of the lord!" she cried and passed the imaginary heart to an invisible group of communicants. "Praise the lord Satan and praise his great priestess!"

Then she came out of the trance without my command, collapsed back on the couch and screamed, "I did kill him! I've always known I killed him! I murdered a precious little baby! That's why I can't have a baby of my own!"

She was fully conscious now. Jean wrapped her arms around her, motherlike, and permitted her to cry herself out.

"It wasn't your fault, Peggy." She repeated it like a mantra. "It wasn't your fault. They drugged you so you couldn't help yourself."

"I would have died rather than kill the baby," she sobbed.

"It wasn't you who killed him. It was those who drugged you and forced you to do it. It wasn't your fault."

Slowly, Peggy settled down and gained control of herself. "Will it be all right now, Jean?"

"It will be much better, Peg, much better. You know you're innocent."

"I guess that poor little girl was innocent. She didn't have any choice. So she wasn't to blame, was she?"

"Who was that poor little girl?"

"Me, I guess."

"So?"

"So I didn't have any choice," she said brightly. "I wasn't to blame. I shouldn't feel guilty."

"And?"

"And I can have a baby anytime I want."

"Absolutely."

I put her back into a trance and told her not to worry about what she had learned and not to let herself be troubled by bad dreams, because she wasn't guilty. With her classic abreaction reinforced by posthypnotic suggestion, she would survive the terrible experience she had endured in my office.

"Well?" Jean asked after we had sent Peggy home.

"Classic abreaction." I was badly shaken, but I ought not reveal it to a junior colleague—not any more than was already patent.

"Should I continue as I have?"

"I won't argue with success."

"She thinks she killed Marina too."

"Did she, Jean?"

"I'm never absolutely convinced. You did notice that she made an incision like a skilled surgeon?"

"I did indeed. Of course, she might have seen that in a film."

"That's certainly true."

"There's no doubt in my mind, Jean, that the young woman was drugged and ritually abused by her parents and by others. They surely did unspeakable things to her. She was made, at a minimum, to imagine terrible events. Whether all the events actually occurred"—I shrugged—"does not seem pertinent to her recovery."

"Sometimes she's not sure either."

"That's a sign of health. . . . The point is that your treatment does seem to clear her personality of guilt for what sometimes she thinks happened. I see no reason why you shouldn't continue the treatment as you have."

Jean sighed with relief. "I'm glad to hear you say that, Kieran."

"Is Peggy your only patient with this sort of problem?"

"Yes."

"At the risk of sounding authoritarian, no more, understand?"

She nodded her head. "You're right, Doctor, ah, Kieran. One is more than enough."

"You have a sympathetic training analyst?"

"The best—Maggie Keenan."

"I quite agree that she's the best. Again I will sound like I'm giving orders . . ."

"You're only saying it that way for emphasis, Kieran. It doesn't bother me."

"See her often until this case is terminated."

"I sure will. . . . Do you agree that these things must really happen?"

"What worries me most"—I evaded her question—"is that disturbed people read the books by people like Crowley and Huysmans, or even the psychiatric literature, get turned on by what they read, and give it a shot to see whether they like it."

I walked her to the door. "Keep up the good work, Jean," I told her. "Don't hesitate to consult with me."

I only hoped that should she need my aid in this troubling case, I'd be able to help.

KIERAN
1980

"So," my analyst said triumphantly. "You ran away from the woman because you were afraid of her."

I twisted uncomfortably on the smooth leather couch. St. Lawrence on the gridiron, I thought.

"In the circumstances, yes."

"You still plead that you went through a psychotic interlude at that time?"

"Not exactly."

"What, then?"

"A time of great confusion."

Franz Rosenblum didn't believe in "psychotic interludes." They were of the same order of unreality as "mental fugues" and "nervous breakdowns."

"She did call you after you came to New York?"

"Yes, several times."

"And you refused to talk to her."

"More or less. She accused me of actually taking the money . . . but when I called her back to apologize, she didn't return my call."

"How many times did you call her back?"

"Several."

"How many?"

"Twice. She never returned my calls."

"Why did you leave her?"

"Because I was angry . . . and because I lost my nerve."

"She frightened you?"

"Scared the hell out of me."

That dialogue occurred about eight years ago, in the early phase of my training analysis with Doctor Franz Rosenblum in his tacky office in the ground floor of a brownstone on West 67th Street in New York. I had finished my psychiatric residency at Beth Israel Hospital. I was already an assistant professor at Cornell, my medical alma mater, and my own private practice was flourishing. I had become everything I wanted to be when I left Chicago.

I even sang on the occasional weekend in an Irish bar—where there was considerable tolerant skepticism that I was an M.D. the rest of the week. My relationship with Rebecca was peaceful and physically satisfying and seemed to enjoy a promising future.

I entered training analysis because I wanted to be an analyst myself—or at least have the psychoanalytic credentials and the options which came with them.

By temperament I was an eclectic, still in that respect a Chicago political type with little preference for ideology. Yet I felt that there were cases in which analysis was the indicated method of therapy, especially if one used the self-hypnotic techniques which Erika Fromm had developed.

So that meant I had to undergo analysis with a training analyst.

And that meant that Franz—which I never dared call him—found the vast hole in my life: Chicago, Beverly, the Catholic Church, Kathleen.

It was painful to face the first two decades of life, yet it was also time to face them. I could not let the hangups of the past interfere with the treatment of my patients.

Or, as Franz forced me to admit, I did not want them to continue to interfere with my own personal happiness.

"Why did you run from a woman you claimed to love?"

I took a deep breath. I did not want to speak the truth, but why spend the time and money on analysis unless you are willing to face truth?

"I was angry, but there was more. I understand that I wanted to punish myself for failing my parents. If I could not protect Mom and Dad despite all my efforts, how could I protect such a fragile and sensual woman as Kathleen?"

"Ya, it is time for you to admit that."

That was the essence of it—an idealist's excuse for cowardice.

So, fool that I was, I ran away and left her totally unprotected. And thus punished her for what her family had done to me.

In some confused fashion I knew what I was doing even in 1972. Guilt for this terrible crime—in my religious days I would have called it a sin—had frozen part of my personality—what I would have called my soul.

Guilt. Guilt. Guilt.

I betrayed my love.

She could have come after me.

Nonsense. Not after I left her without a word. And shouted at her on the phone. And hung up on her.

I failed to protect her from her own family.

"A drunken cabin-hunter priest told them that I stole the money," I cried out, still feeling the pain of that terrible day.

"Go on."

"Isn't that enough?"

"Yah, I should reject three thousand years of Jewish tradition because of some stupid rabbis?"

Franz, it was said, never set foot inside a synagogue, but kept kosher and *maybe* believed in God. Maybe even in the "world-to-come."

"But you—ah, one can't go home again."

"Nonsense."

I shifted uncomfortably on the couch. "I can't make that decision irrevocably till I unpack the angers still inside of me."

"Now you talk like a good psychoanalyst."

"That neighborhood, that parish, that Church still have a fierce grip on me."

"That woman too."

He went far beyond the boundaries of orthodox practice when he said that. Boundaries don't worry Franz Rosenblum.

"Why won't they let me go?" I cried out.

"Because you don't want them to let you go," he replied somberly.

My past would not let me go.

I went through the motions of life and work and studied like a zombie. I used that metaphor advisedly. I was one of the living dead—a man who acted like he was alive, more or less, but whose emotions had been turned off to kill the pain.

I hated every moment of medical school. I disliked my teachers, my fellow students, the patients in the hospital, my neighbors in New York, the nasal whine of the New York accent, the dirt, the self-pity, the cruelty of the city.

Singing in the bar on the weekend and at Irish parties was all that saved the little bit of my mind that remained.

My success as a psychiatrist-in-training at Beth Israel was easy. My Jewish colleagues and supervisors were astonished at how quick and accurate my insights were and how smooth and effective were my responses.

"Doctor O'Kerrigan," said one elderly, bearded concentration camp survivor to me, "how old are you?"

"Twenty-eight, Doctor."

"I was twice your age before I could react to a patient the way you just did."

"Thank you, Doctor."

"You are a little uncanny, Doctor O'Kerrigan."

"If that's a compliment, I thank you again."

"It is a compliment, but how do you explain it? Have you suffered a lot in your life?"

"A little," I said cautiously. "Others have suffered much more."

"But how do you know so much about people?"

I knew the answer even then, but I had never spoken it. I might as well say it now and be done with it.

"South Side Chicago Irish political instincts."

"I see." He pondered the answer, then smiled benignly. "Your kind may drive my kind out of the profession."

I half suspected that he might be right. However, I responded, "Not without a fight."

"That's very funny." He howled with laughter. "Very funny indeed! I will tell the others! Not without a fight! Yes, but it will be a good fight, won't it?"

I was on a roll.

"I can't promise a clean fight."

He went off down the corridor, still shaking with laughter.

You don't want the Irish moving into your neighborhood, especially if they are South Side Chicago Irish from political families.

Two years ago I returned to Chicago. The generous and gracious offer at Illinois was not irresistible, but the city, I discovered when I returned for the interview that I had insisted was not to be taken seriously, turned out to be irresistible the first moment I saw it from the aging DC-9 as it lumbered toward Midway airport.

The city stretched out from the South Works to Lincoln Park like an irresistible invitation on a travel poster.

We flew over St. Prax's. I picked out the house I had lived in and, a few doors away, Kathleen's house.

That's when I told myself that if I came back I would reclaim my reputation and my woman.

Stupid vow.

They put me up at the Ritz Carlton on the Magnificent Mile. I hardly recognized the street or the city. Chicago was not the city I had grown up in, but a new and magical place. Not Beirut on the Lake but Camelot on the Lake. I was fascinated and addicted.

At a pasta dinner in a small Italian restaurant on South Oakley (a street which further south also ran through St. Prax's) in a neighborhood appropriately and poignantly called the Heart of Chicago, under the shadow of St. Paul's Church, after half a bottle of good Chianti (which I later blamed) I said to the Dean, "You've made me an offer I can't refuse."

By the time I had returned, another Daley was mayor of Chicago and seemed to be the same sort of effective mayor as his father had been, if not more effective. I met him at some kind of fund-raising reception.

"Kieran." He smiled enthusiastically. "You look just the same. Thank God you've come home!"

"I don't think I ever left, Your Honor." I stumbled over the words.

"What's this 'Your Honor' bit?" He pounded my elbow. "It's Rich. We grew up together at Grand Beach, didn't we?"

A bit of an exaggeration. He was nine, maybe ten years older than I was.

For one terrifying moment I thought he might ask me if I had seen Kathleen yet. Naturally he was too smart to do that.

Had he really recognized me? Or had he seen my name on a list? Or had he heard I was back in town and was on the lookout for me?

Who knows?

Where my not inconsiderable political skills ended, his just began.

Had he forgotten about the charges against me back in 1972?

Later than evening I cornered Matt McCarthy, a classmate of mine at Saint Ignatius and now a burly, red-faced internal medicine specialist at Little Company whose parents had owned a home at Grand Beach.

"The Mayor remembered me."

"The Mayor is dead, Kieran. You mean Rich?"

"I'm a new boy in town. . . . He talked about growing up together in Grand Beach. I hardly knew him then."

"Neither did I; but he talks about it with me all the time. He either remembers a lot more than I do or his research people have a file on everyone who ever lived in that village. . . . Now that you're back in town, you should think about buying a house up there. It's a grand place to raise kids."

"No kids to raise yet."

"Sorry, I forgot . . ."

"Just give me some time. . . . But how could I move back there after the scandal?"

He seemed puzzled. "Scandal? What scandal? I seem to remember something about your father, but he was exonerated, wasn't he?"

"The Calcutta money I was supposed to have taken."

"What Calcutta money?" His face screwed up in a baffled frown. "I don't remember any Calcutta money."

"From the Regan house."

He shook his head, "No, I don't . . . oh, you mean the time that drunken idiot Dave Regan, God be good to him, left it in the cupboard of his kitchen and told everyone who would listen where he had put it because, as he said, no one ever stole anything in Grand Beach? Gee, I'd forgot about it. It was so long ago. But how does that affect you?"

"Everyone thought I took the money."

"YOU! Kieran, if you weren't a psychiatrist I'd say you needed one. You, of all people! Why would anyone think it was you?"

"Father O'Connell said he saw me coming out of the house."

"O'Connell." He scowled more deeply, searching for images from two decades before. "I don't remember him at all. . . . Wait a minute. Yeah, Kieran, it does come back. A cabin hunter is what they called people like him. He would have said the sun came up in the west, sworn it on the Bible, if Dave Regan told him to. I remember it now. There were a few idiots in the village who wanted to call the State Police and have them arrest you. No one paid any attention to such nonsense."

"Oh."

"Long since forgotten, Kieran." He patted my shoulder. "Anyway you're a famous psychiatrist now. You appear on the 'Today' show and 'Larry King Live' and are quoted in *The New York Times*. We'd be delighted to have a celebrity in Grand Beach—another one that is." He jerked his head in the direction of the Mayor, a time-honored Chicago Irish political gesture.

Thus had time transformed poor Ulysses' departure for Troy. Or perhaps the voyager had remembered it wrong or misread the situation. Or all of the above.

Anyway, the Labor Day Weekend of 1972 was a fallen windmill at which, to change the myth slightly, Ulysses could not tilt even if he wanted to.

The Catholic Church was another windmill. But it refused to fight back.

"Monsignor James," I said to the Vicar General—he had not been named bishop yet—"I've been away from the Church for sixteen years, more or less, and it won't let me go. So I want the holy water and the collection envelopes back. I hear you still give them away free."

I had bought an apartment in the John Hancock Center when I came back and had begun to attend Mass—or the Eucharist as I learned it ought properly to be called—at the Cathedral. I switched to Old St. Patrick's at Adams and Desplaines because the homilies were better, the parish more vibrant, and it was close to the medical center.

I had not so much begun to believe in God again as to understand that I couldn't stop being a Catholic and I couldn't escape from God whether I believed in Him or not.

"Welcome home, Kieran." He jumped up from his chair and embraced me—most unexpected behavior from a Monsignor, especially James. "Those words are music to my tired old ears. Except I don't think you really ever left. And drop the title, it's out of fashion these days."

"I guess I didn't."

James was still tall and handsome, an *Esquire* model for a successful ecclesiastical bureaucrat. But his face was lined and his eyes tired. His fingers trembled frequently and I thought I saw an occasional slight twitch in his left cheek.

"Kieran, a good Catholic is mostly an agnostic. He doesn't believe in very much when push comes to shove. But the things he believes in, he believes in strongly."

"Like what?"

"God's love, which is stronger than death, Jesus who came to reveal God's love, the goodness of creation, which also reveals God's love, Sacraments, which tell us stories of God's love . . . things like that."

"That doesn't sound very orthodox, James."

He laughed nervously. "I wouldn't say it on the record, but it's true, Kieran. The only proper object of faith is God. We Catholics have a visible Church and a visible authority structure and we must take it seriously, but we ought not to confuse it with God."

So halfway through my sessions with James, who had become Bishop James while we were talking, I began to receive Communion every Sunday at Old St. Pat's. Then every day. And I joined their choir.

At the end of my brief reentry course—and I was the one who decided that I had taken enough of his time—I said, "Thanks, James, I owe you one."

The ultimate in gratitude for men like us.

"No, you don't, Kieran." He seemed disappointed that our conversations were over. "Let's try to get together anyhow in the months ahead. Maybe for lunch at the Chicago Club."

Kathleen never came up in our conversation. Neither her name nor the scandal at Grand Beach.

She was the last windmill at which I had to tilt.

I did drive out to the Neighborhood once, a silly and impulsive trip in my Mercedes convertible (itself a silly and impulsive indulgence). Nothing much had changed except that the trees were bigger and that there were some black faces in the crowds pouring out of St. Prax's.

I felt a lump in my throat as I passed the house and prayed for the repose of the souls of my parents, with apologies for having neglected my filial prayers for so long.

I had no intention of passing the old Leary house, into which, Jenny had told me, Brien and Kathleen had moved when her mother had bought a condo on North Lake Shore Drive.

But my Stuttgart-made car knew better.

I was startled to see a red-haired girl-child in front of the house.

Kathleen!

I was thirteen, going on fourteen, again, and it was 1964.

I swerved to avoid hitting a tree and woke out of my fantasy.

The Xerox copy must be a teenage daughter, Megie, I now presume. She was there, with her hands on her hips, viewing the passing parade, such as it was (only me) with curiosity and suspicion.

I searched for her in my rearview mirror. She was shaking her head in disapproval of my reckless driving.

Someone with a Mercedes convertible, her contempt seemed to say, ought to be a better driver.

I agree, kid.

I drove through Ryan's Woods and out on 87th Street as quickly as I could.

KATHLEEN

I had finished only five pages on my dissertation since encountering Kieran on the Rock Island. I was still humming "The Rock Island Line." My daughters complained about the tune until I taught it to them. Then they hummed it too.

I was in the grip of an adolescent crush on Kieran Patrick O'Kerrigan, an early-adolescent crush, indeed an eighth-grade crush. Or a premenopausal obsession. Images of making love with him were much more lascivious—and arousing—than any images I would have dared permit myself when I was a teen.

To distract myself I tried to think about my poor, sick, confused husband and worry about the divorce I knew would come. All I could imagine was Kieran after the divorce.

Then I tried to think about my poor brother. Brien was his closest friend. He was going to lose Brien one way or another. Poor dumb James, so generous as a priest and so insensitive in his personal relationships. I remembered the day he baptized Brigie. That took my mind off Kieran for an hour or so.

"Mary Bridget," James answered before I could. "After her two grandmothers and her aunt who is with God."

My husband said nothing. He never does when James intervenes. He would have said nothing if James had told me to climb up to the bell tower of the church and, with Brigie in my arms, jump.

"Isn't that sweet!" Mom smiled happily.

The priest looked at me quizzically. I did not bat an eye.

"How do you spell the second name?" The priest, just about my age, I think, looked embarrassed. "There's a number of different ways . . ."

"Like the parish," James said smoothly.

He knew about my promise to our dying father. He knew how Grandma Leary spelled her name, but he deliberately changed the name of my daughter on the day of her baptism so that my mother, who was already honored in Megan, would be pleased. He did it because that's what, according to his opinion, Mary Anne would have done. He did it because the family had spoiled me and produced a woman who was incapable of making a mature and sensitive decision.

You overrule kids when they do something irresponsible, don't you?

He would not, I almost told him, have treated a prostitute from St. Finian's the way he treated me.

To which he would have doubtless replied that they were more mature than I was.

"Her name is Brigie," Megan, then age four, and even at that age disinclined to hold her tongue, announced to the others. "That's what I call her."

"Hush, dear," I said.

"Well, that's what I DO call her."

So the water was poured on Mary Bridget Donahue without protest from her childish mother.

"Would you carry your granddaughter out to the car?" I asked Mom.

"Certainly." She smiled proudly as I handed the sleeping tyke over to her.

"Father Ready." I turned to the young priest who was putting away the baptismal oils.

"Yes, Mrs. Donahue."

"Kathleen."

"Jack."

"Fair enough. . . . Jack, give me that form."

"Yes, ma'am." He grinned.

I scratched out "Mary Bridget" and wrote the child's real name.

"I'm her mother," I said lightly. "Right, Jack?"

"No doubt about that." He grinned more broadly.

"I know her real name, right?"

"You bet."

"God will listen to me when I give the child a name, even if the water is not being poured."

"He'd better."

"Fine, we're agreed . . . and you don't have to tell anyone about this little exchange, as much as you'd like to rush back to the rectory and phone your classmates."

He laughed enthusiastically.

"Wouldn't dream of it."

So Brigie she is.

And I didn't make a scene.

For which I hope God gave me due credit and that up in heaven my father knew so he could join in what I fervently hope was God's laughter.

God wasn't laughing at me now, however. She must be angry at me because of my crush on Kieran. Obsession. Whatever. Or perhaps She had forgotten about me. I was all alone in my struggle. No one, not even God, would help me.

KIERAN

After the shattering hypnotic session with Peggy, I tried to return to my paper about dissociation and self-hypnotism in victims of sexual abuse, a paper I would have to revise in light of that experience.

Had it really happened? Had she really killed a baby? Were such rituals performed in reality as well as in drugged imaginations?

My answer, a marvelous academic cop-out, was that given the kinks of which human nature is capable and the literature on such rites, these rituals did not seem statistically improbable.

I would also keep an eye on Jean Cummins to make sure that this case did not drain her too much.

Brendan McNulty interrupted my musings by bounding into my office with only the most perfunctory knock.

"Here's the letter I told you about, Kieran," he said, nearly out of breath. "Look at this—see what I mean about cover-up?"

It was a letter apparently from one pastor to another, the former consoling the latter about a problem he was having with a pedophile priest.

It was only a few years ago that we were presented with the same problem that you are now facing with a child-abuse case. I know the anguish you and your people are suffering.

I know the sleepless nights you and your staff have experienced. I know the hesitation of answering the phone and the doorbell; the standing out in front of the church and greeting the people as they come to worship. The implicit accusations that come from people who do not understand and are so fast to criticize.

But let me again reassure you that for all the single inhumanities there are many who suffer with you during these days. They are not so vocal because they do not want to embarrass you and the good members of your staff by bringing it up to your face. But they are paying and suffering with you.

I tossed the note aside. "What a bunch of self-serving horseshit! Not a word of concern about the victims. Only self-pity."

"Yeah, except I think that if a classmate of yours was in trouble for surgical malpractice, you'd be sympathetic to his wife and family."

"The better parallel would be a psychiatrist who was fooling around with a patient . . . and yes, I guess I would feel sorry for the poor bastard and his family. Is Gerry Greene involved in this?"

"He was at St. Enda's then; the letter is addressed to his pastor. It's from the pastor of St. Theobald's. So it's evidence of two cover-ups. Incidentally, Gerry's pastor was forced to resign after the Archdiocese stonewalled and covered up the St. Enda case. They sent him off to Guest House—that's an alcoholic treatment center—though there's no evidence he drank too much." Brendan shook his head. He looked weary and discouraged. "It's discouraging. Your friend James and most of the priests of the Archdiocese blame the pastor for seeing a scandal where there wasn't one. The parents, they'll tell you, were drug addicts and alcoholics."

"But didn't the pastor pay off the local cops?"

"And sent the other family to New Mexico. But he tried to get rid of Gerry, you see. How can James be so blind?"

"It's easy, believe me, when you don't want to see the truth. . . . Did you find out any more about the family in New Mexico?"

"Yeah." He tossed another paper on my desk. "Our investigator filed this report. The Methodist kid who moved out there with his family has become a mess—drugs, delinquency, the works. We've advised him and his family that they have the right to sue, as does the kid here in Chicago."

"Will they?"

"I think so. And if they do, that will bring pressure on the Archdiocese to settle up with our clients for Greene's more recent amusements."

I read through the report. My stomach turned in disgust. I had to remind myself that Father Greene was a sick, troubled individual. But he ought not to be in a parish where he could do such things to young boys.

"Do you want me to talk to James about this stuff now?"

Brendan hesitated. "Let's wait a couple of days to see what more information I can find. James likes you, but I'm not sure he'll take you seriously once he realizes you don't see things his way. You're the top gun from out of town. But James is convinced that his consultants are the best there are—and his lawyers and his Vicar for the Clergy. They all tell him that there's no solid evidence against Gerry and that he's tested out as psychologically sound and that he's a victim of long-term persecution."

"How can the Archdiocese buy that line?"

"James and the Cardinal operate on the principle that the Archdiocese hires the best there is in professional help—law, medicine, accounting, management consultants, public relations. So if they have hired someone, no one is any better. They can't permit themselves to consider the possibility that they've been given bad advice about who is the best. When their consultants tell them that a harmless pastor, about whom people have complained, has a persecution complex and should be shipped off to an institution for a couple of months, off he goes."

"On the basis of personality tests?"

"Yep."

"That's professionally irresponsible. Why, that method's no better than witchcraft!"

"That's the Archdiocese of Chicago!"

"They send a priest to an institution because of personality tests and they leave Greene free because of another personality test? I can't believe it!"

"I know, Kieran. I wake up every morning and tell myself it can't be true. They're not malicious, only the prisoners of seeing the world the way they want to see it."

"Can anyone do anything to change these policies?"

"A couple of things might do it. A committee of wealthy contributors, major media coverage, a revolt among the clergy against the harm done to their reputation. But short of those kinds of pressure, they'll stand pat, believing what they want to believe despite all the evidence."

"And the chances of any of these events happening?"

"Poor. Except perhaps for a media blitz when the O'Malley case comes to trial. It's like banging your head against a stone wall. One family has cut off all their contributions to Catholic institutions. The Cardinal didn't budge an inch, which is to say James didn't budge an inch. They said the family was angry because they couldn't get an annulment for their son. In fact, they never tried."

"It sounds to me like a collective neurosis, systematic denial of all contrary evidence, seamless, impenetrable."

"There are such things?" Brendan's shoulders slumped in discouragement.

"You'd better believe it."

"There won't be any revolt among the priests, maybe because they are part of your collective neurosis too. As for the media, unless there is a public trial they can't ignore, the Archdiocese has pretty much intimidated them. They're scared stiff of a massive Catholic boycott. The Archdiocese's lawyers keep threatening that."

"They can't deliver."

"You know that and I know that and the news directors and the editors are pretty sure of that, but would you risk your career on 'pretty sure'? This is a Catholic town and the conventional wisdom as far as anyone can remember is that the Catholic Church is Teflon."

"The lay people know, don't they?"

"Of course they know, damn it. But ask any priest you bump into on the street and he'll say we have to keep these cases quiet because they'll shock the laity. But the laity know the score. Even the people out at St. Sixtus know about Gerry. But James and most other priests can't admit to themselves that the laity know . . . is that collective neurosis too?"

"You got it."

"Yeah . . . I don't know where it all will end—and they seem to have turned our key witness."

"The engineer?"

"They've submitted an affidavit in which he says that his previous one was false and that he gave it because Ron Long, our lead lawyer, and Kevin O'Malley paid him twenty thousand dollars."

"Did they?"

Brendan waved that possibility away with a sweep of his hand. "Certainly not! I think the pastor of the parish where the witness is working turned him around. There are obvious contradictions in his second affidavit. But they've asked the judge for a criminal prosecution of Ron and Kevin."

"Will they get it?"

"They think the judge is clean, but the Archdiocese's lawyers are capable of bringing all kinds of pressure to bear. There's a hearing in a couple of days. Do you want to come?"

"You'd better believe I do!"

"Great!"

He tossed a third sheet of paper on my desk.

"The FBI is involved now. They've picked up word that a big Satanist mass is about to go down in Chicago. This is a copy of the ritual they propose to use."

I glanced at it. It was disgusting, ugly, and obscene; a parody of the Mass with the belly of a virgin serving as an altar and then the ritual deflowering of the virgin by the chief Satanic priest and the rest of the male worshipers and then some sexual games with her by the female worshipers. I didn't believe that these things could possibly happen. Yet there were the descriptions of similar rituals by Huysmans in his book *Ici-Bas;* and in his later, devoutly Catholic days, he never repudiated them as false.

"Right out of Huysmans and Aleister Crowley."

"They're afraid if it goes down they'll have an epidemic on their hands. So they want to catch this crew in the act."

"That would be good work."

"They think there'll be a priest involved. The Black Mass bit is supposed to be much more effective if you have a real priest."

"You think it might be Greene?"

"I don't. Even Gerry is not that far off-the-wall. Besides, his kicks don't come from deflowering virgins. But the Feds think it might be him. They know his record. They don't have any proof on him yet. Not that they're telling me anyway."

"Why would Gerry be involved in something like that, Brendan? Gays make their own rituals, but nothing like what you describe."

"He's not really a gay, Kieran. More like a special kind of S-M. That's what the Feds think, anyway. I suspect they're right."

"Have you told James about this?"

"He'd laugh me right out of his office."

"He'd laugh the FBI out too?"

"Not if they came to him themselves, but they're as afraid of the Archdiocese as the TV stations. They're reported to have selected the victim already," Brendan added.

"What?"

"That's what the Feds tell me. They don't know who the victim is, but they think the organizers do. It's probably a child of one of the cult."

"I presume the Feds are using bugs?"

"Sure. That's why I don't want to tell James. He's quite capable of calling Gerry and warning him that the Feds are bugging his rectory."

"Would he really?"

"I keep telling you, Kieran, never underestimate the power of loyalty to the priesthood."

"What do you want me to do, Brendan?"

"Nothing for the moment. Keep listening. Come to the hearing. We still have a little time before Halloween, when this Black Mass is supposed to go down. James thinks you're mollifying me, so he'll leave me alone for a while. Later on, maybe in a few days even, when I've got together as much as I can, I'll go in with you and we can plead together that they settle this case, retire Gerry on a pension, and set up a lay review board."

"A board would take a lot of pressure off him."

"You're right, Kieran. Sometimes I think James likes the pressure."

He bounded out of his chair, visibly recharged by the conversation with me.

"See you soon, Brendan."

Then he really surprised me by posing an altogether different question. "You haven't run into Kathleen lately, have you?"

"Kathleen Donahue?"

He nodded.

"I've seen her," I said, wondering where this line of questioning was headed.

"She's been looking pretty grim lately."

"Isn't she working on a dissertation?"

"Different kind of grim."

"It's your territory, Brendan McNulty, not mine."

He grinned as we shook hands. "For the moment, yes."

What did he mean by that? I wondered when he had left. As I sank into my chair, I told myself that all he meant was that for the moment it was a priest's problem but it might become a psychiatrist's problem.

Some other psychiatrist, I told myself virtuously.

KATHLEEN

Kieran haunted my dreams when I was asleep and my imagination when I was awake.

Brien's November announcement of his candidacy was only two weeks away. He was still living in the coach house. The few times he was around the house, I kept a close watch on him. Any more violence toward me or so much as the hint of it and our deal, such as it was, was down the tubes. I also kept an eye out for signs of heavy drinking. I hated to think what effect his alcohol abuse might have on our children. If he created any kind of scene in front of them, I promised myself I would file for divorce the next day.

All day I struggled with only limited success at keeping my mind off Kieran and on the dissertation.

My dissertation was supposed to end with the death of Mayor Daley. I planned to add a brief epilogue about the surprising survival of Irish politicians in subsequent years and thus disprove the theory, repeated frequently in the literature, that the day of the Irish urban politician ended with the Mayor's death. My argument was that the Mayor was not the last of the old-fashioned bosses but the first of the new administrator-politicians.

The advantage of my theory was that it predicted what ultimately happened. Rich's election as Mayor after successfully billing himself as a skilled urban administrator.

If one read the articles on the late Mayor before the convention debacle in 1968, skilled municipal administration was the theme. It was just that the 1968 mess and his unusual diction on TV had projected a different national image.

My argument was revisionist, but, as my new adviser had said to me, "Revisionism is the way junior professors get tenure."

The task before me was to refute the popular thesis that the elder Daley's rise to power was the result of the death of his chief rival, Clarence Wagner.

My father, Red Hugh, had consistently argued that Daley would have beaten Wagner in the crucial vote of County Chairman in 1953 even if Wagner had been alive. The newspaper accounts of the time had described Wagner as the heavy favorite. But Dad had known the district better than the reporters.

"Poor Clarence would have collected only four votes against Dick Daley," he once told me.

"How do you know?" I remembered asking him.

"Dick himself told me. Now there's a man who does know how to count the votes."

For several days I had been systematically exploring the box of papers my father had left in my room before he went to the hospital to die. For ten years I had not been able to face the task of reading the remnants of a man I had loved so much despite all his failings.

My perusal had left me disappointed. Most of the papers were clippings about cases, correspondence with other lawyers, and an occasional memo to himself about cases which had been settled out of court. They might have been interesting notes at the time. Now they meant very little—though I would put them in an archive somewhere because I had learned that historians of my generation treasured the smallest details of the lives of ordinary people.

As I sifted through the remnants of my father's life, I grieved for him again. I would always miss him. He was the only blood relative I ever had who really understood me. Even on his deathbed, he'd been the one to console me. He was ashamed to be dying of what he was dying of.

"Cirrhosis of the liver—a drunk's disease."

"You beat the bottle, Daddy, you beat it all by yourself."

"With your mother's help . . . God, how much I let her down."

"She never wanted to trade you in."

"I know that . . . despite it all I think we were as much in love this last year as we were back in 1945 . . ." His voice trailed off.

"I should have left town, got away from her family."

"Would she have come with you?"

"Back in the days before you were born, she would have. . . . Mind you, I'm not blaming Jimmy or Maude. It was my fault."

"They were no help," I said.

"I would have been a drunk without them."

I wiped some of the sweat off his forehead.

"I've done a lot of things," he continued, "of which I'm ashamed."

"Haven't we all."

He lost consciousness for a couple of minutes.

"Katie," he whispered, opening his eyes again.

"Still here, Daddy."

"Kieran will be back someday."

"Perhaps."

"A hell of a kid."

"Yes."

He closed his eyes again.

"You should have married him."

"He didn't want to marry me, Daddy."

Another long pause.

"I've written you a letter, Katie. You'll find it someday soon. Figure out for yourself what you want to do with it."

"Yes, Daddy, I will."

But I never found that letter. Maybe he'd only thought about writing it. It wouldn't have been the first time my father's resolution fell shy of his aspirations.

In the years between his death and now, I've often wondered just what it was my father thought he'd written me.

I still hadn't gone completely through my father's things, but so far hadn't come across anything revelatory with respect to the 1954 contest for Democratic Committee Chairman or my father's phantom letter.

My thoughts had begun to drift back to Kieran when I caught sight of the corner of an envelope sticking out from the cardboard fold of the box's bottom. Sliding it out with trembling fingers, I saw that the envelope bore my name.

Before I had a chance to open it, my fax rang and began to whir as the transmission came through. The fax spat out a copy of the results of an HIV test for Brien T. Donahue. They were negative. I sighed with relief. If the viruses were not active in him, he could not have transmitted them to me or through some kind of chance contamination to the kids. So one big worry was eliminated.

The phone rang. It was James.

"You received my fax?" he asked.

"Yes."

"Does it satisfy you?"

"It proves that his extramarital activities haven't infected him yet."
My brother sighed.

"He says that they won't happen again."

"He promised twice that he wouldn't beat me again. Yet he has."

"Those promises were a long time ago, Kathleen. I think he means his promises this time. He has joined the AA group at St. Ethelbert's and is seeing Doctor Michael Shanahan. I hope those facts put your mind at rest."

"As long as he continues both, I won't file suit. That's what I promised you."

"Still no forgiveness in your heart, Kathleen? Still no mercy for the poor man? Still no concern for your children?"

With unerring instincts James had hit at my weaknesses.

"I'm still afraid that in one of his 'fits,' or whatever you might call them, he will kill me or one of the kids."

"That's most unlikely."

"You weren't there when he beat me the last time."

"Doctor Shanahan will prepare an excellent psychological profile. It will give us some hints about what kind of behavior, if any, is likely to recur."

"Doctor Shanahan wasn't there either."

"I'm aware of that."

"James, part of the arrangement is that he agrees to an annulment after the election. You guaranteed that. . . ."

"I know. I know. I do hope that time will change your mind. You surely will not want to deprive your children of their father when it comes down to that."

"I'll make that decision without any advice from you, James."

"You're being very stubborn, Kathleen."

"Call it what you want. My husband's current good behavior earns him a respite from divorce proceedings, nothing more."

As usual, James's arguments had strengthened my resolve in the opposite direction.

Yet despite the physical aches that I still suffered and despite my fear of a repetition, I dreaded the trauma of even a quiet divorce.

Either way I feared for the children. I did not want them torn apart by a conflict between me and Brien. At the same time, I didn't want to subject them to any future outbursts. I felt so trapped; whatever I did, there were bound to be damaging repercussions for the three people in the world I cared about most.

I carefully pried open the flap on the letter from Dad.

The phone rang again. Brien this time.

"Could I talk to you for a few minutes, Kathleen?" He sounded contrite.

"Go ahead."

"I mean face-to-face."

"Not in this house."

"You could come over here to the coach house."

"Do you think I'm out of my mind?"

"I haven't been drinking, I wouldn't hurt you, I promise."

"No. I'm not about to take any chances."

"In the yard? At the picnic table? It's important."

I thought about it. I should refuse. There was no point in giving him encouragement which would mislead him into thinking I would ever risk myself with him again.

"Five minutes."

I put on a sweater—it was a crisp, windy day: Indian summer replaced by real autumn—and went into the backyard. He was already sitting at the picnic table next to our rose garden when I got there. The plants were cut back in preparation for winter; a season had ended and so had a marriage.

"Well?" I wanted to get this over with quickly. My husband had lost weight. He looked tired and distracted. I could not help feeling sorry for him.

"So I saw Doctor Shanahan today." His eyes were blinking rapidly as we talked.

"That's part of our agreement."

"I know . . . but he talked to me for a couple of hours and gave me some tests. He's doing a psychological profile on me. He says that I'm going to be all right."

"After one session?"

"I'll have to see him again, of course, but he doesn't think I'm crazy or anything like that."

"You told him about your gay lover?"

He turned away from me. "I wish you wouldn't use that sort of language, Kathleen."

"Did you tell him?"

"Yes. He didn't think I was gay, however, not really."

"After the first session?"

"He said that was his preliminary evaluation."

"Did you tell him how infrequently we've had sex in our marriage?"

"No."

"Did he ask about that?"

"No."

"Then what kind of quack is he?"

"He's a fine doctor. James said so."

"Did you tell him you've beaten me three times in our marriage?"

"Twice, only twice, Kathleen."

"I'm the victim and I remember three times."

"All right, Kathleen." He stretched out his hands to placate me. "I don't want to argue about that."

"Did you tell him?"

"Not yet."

"Then what the hell is his psychological profile worth?"

"He's a good doctor . . . I mean, I thought that since he said I wasn't really crazy, you'd . . ." His blue eyes pleaded anxiously with me. "You'd, well, let me back in the house."

"No! Absolutely not!" I stood up. "Moreover, I tell you now and I will tell James that Doctor Shanahan sounds like a quack to me. If you don't tell him the whole story, then our deal is off."

"Kathleen," he entreated me, "you don't know what this is doing to me!"

"You might consider again what you did to me."

"What do you mean?"

"You beat me and raped me!"

"You're my wife."

"And that means you can abuse me? I don't think so, Brien."

He hung his head.

"Not counting that time, how often did we have sex in the last year?"

"Ten or fifteen times?"

"More like four or five. Either you tell him that and about your assault on me or I file suit."

"I can't talk about those things."

I took a deep breath. I had to be patient if I hoped to make any kind of impression. "Brien, if you honestly want help, you're going to have to open up to your doctor. He won't be able to help you unless you do." Brien looked so downcast and dejected, it was hard to tell if I was getting through to him. I wanted him to get the help he needed, but I was still afraid. There was no telling if even this kind of mild conversation might send him into a fury. Brien needed help, all right, but I wasn't necessarily the one who had to see he got it. I decided to conclude our little *tête-à-tête* before we got into another argument. "Brien, I've got to go now." He looked at me as if I'd cut him to the quick. "Kathleen . . ." he began.

But I was determined. I wasn't about to risk my safety again. "Take care, Brien," I told him and before he could say another word, I turned on my heels and headed back to the house. I felt the hot sting of tears in my eyes as my vision blurred. Some days it was so hard to believe this was really my life, that my marriage had come to this. Part of me felt like I should be waking from this nightmare. But another part of me understood that this was no bad dream, this was the way it was.

Against my better judgment, I glanced back toward the picnic table. Brien was still sitting there. His face was buried in his hands in an attitude of such genuine grief I was tempted to run back to him. But my survival instinct kept me at bay.

Back in the house, I tried to keep busy. I thought about going for a long run, but I felt there'd been something I'd been in the middle of before Brien's call. I was straightening my desk when I remembered: the letter from my father.

I searched through the papers on my desk, found the envelope, took out the letter and began to read.

LEARY

After I spoke with Kathleen, I paid little attention to our financial administrators as they tried to explain why the Cardinal's Appeal had failed.

Once more my sister and I had fallen into the roles we had played all our lives. I was stern and disapproving. She was angry and outrageous.

Would we ever be able to break out of those roles?

I wanted to help her. I wanted to protect her. I did not think she was in any great danger from Brien, but I could not be sure. My lifelong friend, the most important person in my life really, had indulged in behavior I would not have thought possible.

BRIEN

I needed that drink, Dear God, how I needed it. Only one. Or maybe two. I'm not a real alcoholic. I can hold my liquor except when I'm under all that stress.

He called again today. He's confident that I'm going to give her to the group. He talks as if I've already agreed. I hate him. I don't want to talk to him.

But he makes me talk to him. The things he describes in the ritual are disgusting.

Yet they fascinate me.

I'm not that depraved. I'm not totally depraved. I was fine till I met him. He's torn me apart. And the election.

How am I going to survive?

Maybe I should kill myself.

I wish I could talk to Kieran. He always seemed to like me.

KATHLEEN

The phone rang again.

"Yes?"

"Mom?"

"Megie, hon, sorry I snapped."

"Okay, Mom." She giggled. "We understand."

"How come you're home so early?"

"It's four-thirty, Mom. Your day slipped by pretty quickly, huh?"

"It always does when you're having fun, hon."

She laughed. "Can I come up and talk to you?"

"Sure." I folded the letter and replaced it in the envelope. "You could have knocked at the door."

"This is, like you know, kind of more professional, okay?"

"Absolutely. Come on up."

I met her at the door. We hugged each other with more than the normal enthusiasm.

"Would you like a cup of tea, Megan?"

"I'd love it."

"You don't mind a tea bag?" I plugged in my electric kettle.

"Mommy!" She was still dressed in her school clothes—suit and blouse instead of the required after-school dress of jeans and sweatshirt. She was businesslike and very grown up.

How quickly kids become young women.

"You're being professional, so I thought I would be too."

Once we had settled in, each with a cup of Bewley's Irish tea, she asked the opening blunt question.

"We're wondering if you and Daddy are going to get a divorce?"

"We?"

"I guess I'm kind of the official representative for the three of us. Like, we know that parents of other kids do get divorced and we're wondering if it will happen to us too."

Dear God, give me strength and wisdom—and honesty too.

"I don't know, dear. I really don't. If we do, it won't be for a while."

"Not till after the election?"

"That's right."

How perceptive they were. Big eyes and big ears.

"Uh-huh, we kind of thought that."

"There are a lot of things we have to work out before we make a decision."

"The other kids say their parents always say that."

"It wouldn't be good to hint to anyone else . . ."

"Oh, Mom, we'd never do that."

"Just touching base."

"I understand. . . . Well, what we want to say is that we hope there isn't a divorce . . . and if there is one, we would be very sad."

"I know, dear." I must not cry, I absolutely must be as "professional" as she is.

"But we wouldn't hold it against you."

No tears. Absolutely no tears.

"In marriage when something goes wrong, no one is innocent."

She considered me intently. "We knew you'd say that. Look, Mommy, we love Dad. We think he's kind of sweet, though he doesn't understand kids and we get on his nerves a lot . . ."

"And he loves you very much."

"But Daddy is awfully insensitive to you. He doesn't mean to be, but he is, just the same. Like, he doesn't respect your work at the University and says mean things about it."

"Not mean, dear. He just doesn't understand."

"He *should* understand, Mommy. And Uncle James is no help. We think he eggs Daddy on. You know?"

"We grew up in a different time, honey. Dad and Uncle James can't imagine why a mother of three kids who doesn't need the money would want to work on a dissertation."

"You didn't grow up in the middle ages, Mommy. I mean, that kind of attitude is barf city."

"I think so too."

She placed her teacup carefully on a coaster on my office coffee table.

"We're not taking sides."

"Don't ever do that."

"And we're not spacing out about it."

"It wouldn't help anyone if you did."

"We'll be out of here in a couple of years anyway."

Now I really wanted to cry.

"Well, not completely."

"And you have the rest of your life to live."

"I hope so."

"And we know that sometimes divorce is the only alternative. Even the Jesuits say so."

"Then it must be true!"

We laughed together.

"So you can count on our sympathy and support."

"I hope your father can too—if it comes to that."

"That's between him and us, isn't it, Mommy?"

A chilling reminder that they were adults, or almost adults, and they'd make up their own minds.

"It is, Megie. It truly is."

We hugged each other again. She slipped away, probably to report to her co-conspirators and then to cry in the privacy of her room.

I had my privacy already, so I cried for maybe ten minutes.

I'd been given a vote of confidence. But the ache in the children was already there. I had wanted to protect them from such aches and I had failed. I had tried my best, but it was not good enough.

Without paying much attention to what I was doing, I unfolded the letter from my father again and began to read in earnest.

HUGH

Katie, my sweet,

I've thought a long time about writing this letter to you. I want to tell you how much I love you and how sorry I am that I let you down so often.

As far back as I can remember, I have been both fascinated and frightened by those wide blue eyes of yours which see everything and understand every-thing—usually I think that they see too much and understand too much.

You know how much your mother and I love one another despite everything that has happened. I fell in love with her the first time Tom Donahue and I double-dated with her and your Aunt Sheila.

I never got over it and neither did she. When the world left us alone, we couldn't help ourselves. All the old passion came back. She put up with my drinking and I put up with her parents because we needed and desired and wanted each other so badly.

We both put up with too much as you know, but we meant well, for whatever that is worth. When it looked like maybe we could break away, then all the deaths came and it took years before we could work things out and I finally gave up the booze, this time, please God, forever.

Without her, I couldn't have done it. Without me, she couldn't have begun to draw the line where her mother and father were concerned. She did it so subtly that they never noticed. I'm sure you did.

I used to tell her that I didn't know why she loved me after all I had done to her. She'd say the same thing to me. I guess God designed physical passion to keep men and women together no matter what happens.

You've figured all that out. You've even figured that James, poor guy, who is so self-righteous about everything, was conceived out of wedlock, first time we tried it, I think. We were going to marry when we did anyway, so it didn't make that much difference. It would take the wind out of his sails if he knew, but I never had the heart to tell him and I'm glad you didn't either.

The old man was all right, pompous and vain and with a much higher opinion of himself and his antecedents and his political wisdom than he was entitled to. But on balance not bad. It was the old woman that made everything bad for everyone, kind of like Sheila has done to poor Tom and his family.

Well, you know all of these things without my telling you. But it helps to get them down on the record, so you'll understand a little better. I hope you'll forgive me for everything. I know you will. I know you have already. I know you will even forgive what's in this next letter. What you do with it is up to you. Maybe by now it's all irrelevant.

Except, I suppose, to Kieran. As I told you about him once, he's a great man and everyone will know that some day.

Not just a good man like his father, but a great man.

Anyway, I'm kind of looking forward to the surprises ahead of me. Maybe Himself will let me plead my own case. Or, if I'm to believe the priest to whom I confessed my sins, maybe He'll take the case himself and do a better defense job than I could do myself.

I love you, Katie. You and your mother are all that matters in my life. God protect you and care for you.

Goodbye,
Red Hugh

KATHLEEN

Red Hugh gave me more credit for understanding than I deserved. I had figured some of it out, but not all of it. It was the second letter which troubled me. With tears pouring down my cheeks, I read.

HUGH

I am writing this letter to record for anyone who wishes to know the fact that Joseph O'Kerrigan was completely innocent of the bribery and conspiracy charges brought against him by the State of Illinois. He acted in a perfectly legal and proper fashion and was convicted and sentenced because of the failure of a plot designed by James Lenihan and executed by me to protect James Lenihan and Thomas Donahue from conviction on the charges of which they were certainly guilty.

Joseph O'Kerrigan was also supposed to be acquitted, but something went wrong in the deal we had arranged. I was assured that his conviction would be reversed on appeal. Although I was not his lawyer during the trial, I took over his appeal and finally won a reversal and an order for a new trial, which was granted on the day he died, fortunately while he was still conscious enough to know that he had been exonerated.

I can say in my defense only that when the scheme I had engineered at Jim Lenihan's insistence went sour, there was nothing I could do about it—not without putting all of us in jeopardy and in the process not helping Joe O'Kerrigan in the slightest.

Anyone who is interested in the story can read the court records, which have never been sealed. It is evident that the judge who heard the case in the bench trial cleared the men who designed the conspiracy to win a contract by illegal means for their clients and that Joseph O'Kerrigan was nothing more than an innocent message bearer. He was poorly served by his lawyers and should have been freed even if the fix was not in.

However, the fix had gone sour because of an internal squabble in the Outfit, and the appellate judges, fearful of their own safety, leaned over backwards to avoid a reversal.

The whole problem would never have happened if Jim and my classmate and lifelong friend, Tom Donahue, had not been greedy. The rules were changing, even in the late nineteen-sixties.

Bribing state contract officers to get a fat fee from the companies who had won an overpriced bid was standard procedure for as long as anyone could remember. It was illegal, you see, but accepted practice. "Cost of doing business," the contractors would say.

Someone, we never did find out who, bleated to the press. A couple of two-bit hacks, who knew the rules and had played by the same rules themselves, saw a chance to win a prize. So they spread the story over the front page of their papers for a couple of days. A prosecutor who saw a chance to make a name for himself got an indictment.

"You're guilty as sin," I told Jim and Tom, "but they don't have much of a case against you."

"I don't want to take any chances," Jim Lenihan replied.

"We'll get a bench trial. I can talk the State's Attorney into that. No judge will convict you on the evidence."

You have to remember that was back in the days before the prosecutors began to use immunized witnesses, and juries routinely found public officials and their friends guilty regardless of the evidence. It was in the era when Governor William "Billy the Kid" Stratton was acquitted on evidence that was much stronger than that which later put Governor Otto Kerner in jail.

"No chances," Jim replied, wiping his bald head.

"What do you want me to do?"

"Fix it."

I figured that they were legally innocent if morally guilty and that a fix would only guarantee a fair outcome of the trial.

"How?"

"That's your problem. I don't want to know how you do it."

I didn't care much about what happened to him or Maude. But I did care about Tom, whom I figured he had corrupted, and especially about my wife, whose heart would be broken if her father went to jail—after all the other losses in our family. She was already drinking too much as it was.

So I said, "It will cost."

"I understand that."

In those days you could fix anything from a traffic ticket to a murder in the Cook County courts, criminal or civil. You still can for that matter, though it costs more money and is a lot riskier. Since there was so much money to be made by corrupting judges, the Outfit naturally took control of the operation, especially since it provided them with the techniques for protecting their own.

Outfit guys, dons or punks, were convicted in the County Courts only when the Outfit wanted them convicted.

The big cheese in fixing things was Anthony "Tony the Angel" Angelini. I put out the word that I wanted something taken care of. One of Tony's guys met me on the street corner at Clark and Van Buren on the dingy South Side of the Loop and said it would cost four big ones in cash. I had more sense than to argue with him.

Jim gave me the money and we paid them off. I figured that half of the money went to Tony and the other half to the judge.

I give the judge credit. He put up a good act, the crooked so and so.

Then I got a call from the Angel's guy. He wanted to see me on the Van Buren and Jackson corner. "Something has come up."

I figured they wanted more money and warned Jim.

But it wasn't more money they wanted.

"There's been some problems," the guy said to me out of the corner of his mouth, looking up and down the street all the time we talked. "Some of my friend's friends are upset about his being involved in this one."

"Huh?"

"They say we gotta give them one of the three."

"I thought we had a deal."

"So did my friend. They wanted Lenihan. My friend said he's paying the freight. They'll settle for O'Kerrigan."

"He's innocent."

"I understand. But that's not the point. I'm not asking you. I'm telling you. He'll walk on appeal, first thing. That's the best my friend can do."

I said what you say in conversations like that. "I understand."

You don't ask for a refund either.

I don't know what happened. The word I heard later is that some of the

Big Guys, a lot bigger than Tony the Angel, were very worried about it. They had told him before our case came up not to mess in political cases anymore. Tony broke the rules too. He could have ended up in the trunk of a car with a hole in his head. He did what he could, like his guy said.

They told Tony the Angel to stay away from the courts and warned him if the facts of the case ever came out he was dead. Tony the Angel was pretty big, so the guys that warned him must have been the really Big Guys. They mean what they say. The Angel is even bigger now, but he'll never be on top, so he's probably afraid that this story will be told someday.

The word went out after the trial that the fix was no longer in. So the appellate court backed off and Joe had to do time. Meantime his wife died and he got sick. I got him a new trial, honestly this time, on a second appeal. If he had lived another day he would have walked. The case would have been thrown out and he would be a free man—and ruled innocent by the courts of the State of Illinois.

I was a little too late.

That's about the size of it. There's a lot of reasons not to go public with the story as long as Jim and Tom and the Angel are still alive. Publicity can't bring the O'Kerrigans back to life. What is done is done. But I want to die with the knowledge that at least in this letter the record is set straight.

KIERAN

"I've got to talk to you, Kieran. It's not about the HIV test or anything like that."

"Certainly, Kathleen."

"I knew you were over at ISPI as well as in the Loop, so I'm calling you there. I hope you don't mind."

"Not at all. I'm looking at some of my research data and finding no pattern in them."

"Are you free for lunch on Monday?"

"I can be, yes."

"Are you so old-fashioned that I can't buy lunch for you?"

"Certainly not!"

"There's a nice Thai restaurant on 55th Street, near the University, east of the IC tracks."

"*Your* University?"

She laughed uneasily. "That's right."

"I'll be there."

"Noon?"

"Twelve-thirty all right?"

"Fine. . . . It's about your father."

She said it in such a way that I knew we were not to talk about it on the phone.

"I'll see you then."

As soon as I hung up, the phone rang for the second time.

And it was not over yet.

"Kieran? James again. Sorry to bother you."

"Not at all, James."

"I should have asked you about this when I spoke to you earlier in the week. Could you recommend someone that Brien might see about his, ah, stress problems? I thought of some of our consultants, but decided that might put them at a disadvantage because of my position."

"Sure, I'd be happy to give you a couple of names. Both of them are very, very discreet."

I recommended a man and a woman who were not associated with either ISPI or the Institute.

After he had hung up, I wondered why he had turned away from his Church consultants. It seemed to me that they would have been only too happy to give him the information he wanted—a verdict that all Brien needed was a vacation.

KATHLEEN

I went to Mass on Saturday afternoon. That cute Father McNulty gave a wonderful homily.

"You're looking tired, Professor," he said to me in the back of the church after the Mass.

"Three teenagers and a dissertation," I replied.

He smiled and nodded as if he understood.

And as if he didn't believe me.

Father McNulty was cute and good with the kids. But he saw too many things. "He reads your soul," a woman my age had whispered to me at a parish function. "He sees everything."

I didn't want this cute young priest reading my soul.

Brien was downstate for the weekend, giving speeches—the pre-campaign campaign.

I drove home from Mass, parked the car, and poked around in the trash can outside his coach house. No sign of a bottle.

He might, however, have taken it with him.

On Sunday morning I slept in, luxuriating for a long time in that blessed state between sleep and wakefulness when you can give free rein to your fantasies without being responsible for them.

I imagined myself a total gift for Kieran. He could, I told him, do anything he wanted to me.

A cold shower drove those images away, at least for the moment.

I could hardly wait until lunch on Monday, not that I intended to see any of my fantasies realized. It would be good enough just to be with him, or so I told myself. It would be good enough just to lay eyes on him and be in his company. At least that's how I tried to put it to myself.

KIERAN

Sunday morning, the sky gray and the air smelling of rain, I drove out to Forest Mount, an older suburb with wide lawns and big trees, to attend Mass at St. Sixtus parish and get a look at Father Gerry Greene, the pastor.

A younger priest said the Mass and preached a more than adequate sermon. The liturgy was performed with grace and the choir was pretty good for a suburban parish.

I prayed for wisdom and restraint at my lunch on the morrow with Kathleen. I would not ask about her marriage or even mention the AIDS test, not unless she brought either subject up.

If there were to be any departure from professional virtue, I resolved in the presence of the Lord, she would have to begin it.

After the Mass on the walk in front of the church, a small, thin priest with receding sandy hair and an apologetic smile was shaking hands and chatting with parishioners. He looked like neither a villain nor a monster—surely not a man who would be involved in Satanic rituals.

I strolled over and introduced myself to him.

"Kieran O'Kerrigan, Father."

"Welcome to Saint Sixtus, Mr. O'Kerrigan. I'm Father Greene."

"You're the pastor here, Father?"

"That's right." He smiled blandly. "It's not the job it used to be, but I like it."

He was faintly charming. The combination of a smooth and persuasive voice and meek manner somehow made him attractive in a low-key fashion. He certainly did not seem demonic.

"It's an interesting time to be a Catholic, isn't it," I said cautiously.

"It is that. . . . Are you new in the parish, Mr. O'Kerrigan?"

"I'm just looking around for a suburb into which I might move."

Even his eyes, vague and a little dull, gave no hint of evil, not even of unease. In my office, I would not have thought such a man to be deeply troubled.

"You'd certainly be welcome here. . . . Oh, good morning, Mrs. Carey. . . . How is your mother-in-law doing?"

Gently dismissed, I slipped away and tried to collect my impressions. Father Greene certainly seemed harmless enough. Did he radiate a subtle but perhaps dangerous subliminal magnetism? Or was that my imagination?

"Good morning, Doctor O'Kerrigan," a man spoke at my elbow. "What brings you to the suburbs?"

"Ted!" I glanced over at the man and recognized a colleague from the internal medicine department at the University. "I didn't know you lived out here."

"Thinking of moving out?" We shook hands. "Or investigating our pastor?"

"Is that him over there?"

"It is indeed. . . . He seems to have a predilection for young men, in case you didn't know already—ephebophile, I think you folks would call him. Other priests tell me that he was that way even in the seminary. Propositioned his own classmates."

"And they ordained him?"

"These days they take anyone who can walk, so long as he has male sex organs. . . . It works out; Gerry has his own house separate from the rectory, that place over there three doors down from the rectory. One sees a lot of kids in their late teens drifting in and out."

"From the parish?"

"No. He's careful about that. And the women on the staff never leave him alone in the rectory when any male teenage parishioners are afoot."

"You don't seem to mind very much."

"We kind of got used to it." He shrugged his shoulders. "So long as he leaves kids from the parish alone and doesn't interfere with the good work the parish staff is doing, we're willing to put up with him. It's a better parish now than it was under his predecessor, who was straight but conservative, authoritarian, and a drunk. Gerry doesn't care what we do in the parish so long as we leave him alone."

"A remarkably tolerant approach."

"What can I tell you!" He laughed. "The Catholic laity have learned to adjust and count their blessings."

I accepted his invitation to come back to his house and meet his wife and teenage kids and have a cup of tea. They were a cheerful, apparently happy family and made me regret my Irish bachelor status all the more.

The discussions of Father Gerry were remarkably candid.

"Oh," said a teenage girl about Maeve's age, "he's a bisexual. Everyone knows that."

"No, he's not," her brother, a year or two older, replied. "He's strictly gay and he likes handsome boys."

"That lets you out." His sister nudged him with an elbow.

"He used to pass out six-packs of beer to kids going on dates," my colleague's wife said calmly as she refilled my teacup. "We put a stop to that."

"There's a network of such priests," Ted continued. "They play poker at his house every other week and go to the same cottage in the summer. The rest of the clergy seem to know about them. To be fair, I don't know that any of the others in his group are addicted to young men."

"Partner of preference," his wife said dryly.

So, as Ted had remarked in front of church after Mass, the laity adjust and count their blessings. They were more candid than their parents and grandparents would have been about an alcoholic pastor—"Poor Father is sick again this morning!"

Instead of covering up for an alcoholic pastor, they joked about an ephebophile pastor—as long as he left them and their kids alone.

James would have a hard time believing such a reaction. So did I, come to think of it. A lot of things had changed while I was on hiatus from my tradition.

After my second cup of tea and third sweet roll, I left my colleague's house with a promise to return some night for dinner—his wife had the look in her eye of a woman who loved to make matches.

That kind of attention I didn't need right now.

I drove by the pastor's home, a couple of doors down the street from the rectory—a medium-sized two-story wooden home, built before 1920, not very different from any of the other homes on the block. An unlikely site for a Satanic ritual.

On the drive back to Chicago I thought about Gerry Greene. Did he believe in anything? Was he a complete hypocrite? Or had he compartmentalized his life, a predator in one role, a tolerant parish priest in another? Had he been a victim himself as a child? Was he trapped by powerful energies he could not control and did not understand? Or was he a sociopath, one of those ultimately unreadable personalities that are utterly opaque to us psychiatrists?

Incredibly clever he must be—and in that respect like a sociopath—to remain a priest, and indeed a respected priest as far as James was concerned, despite his well-known sexual activities and proclivities. Presumably the Chancery Office saw only what it wanted to see and wanted to see only what it could cope with.

But for the next twenty-four hours, that problem would go on the back burner while I prepared my emotions for lunch with my first love.

That night, after I had come up from the swimming pool, I received an odd phone call at my apartment.

"Doctor O'Kerrigan."

Silence.

"Hello."

"Some of my friends were wondering"—a thick, gravelly voice—"whether you're going to leave the past alone."

"What the hell!"

"You've left it alone since you came back, but my friends are nervous."

"What have I left alone?"

"You know."

"I don't know."

"Like we say, so long as you are a good boy and don't poke around any dark corners, no one's gonna get hurt. See?"

"What dark corners?"

"But if you do snoop too much, some people might get hurt. And you might just get dead."

"Who are you?"

"Let's just say"—he giggled—"that I'm a heavenly voice."

He hung up.

Was someone warning me to stay away from Kathleen? That was hardly likely. She almost certainly would tell no one about our rendezvous before it happened.

What kind of past was I supposed to avoid?

LEARY

The weather was appropriate for my mood, I told myself as I waited for Brien, who had flown in early in the morning from his downstate talks to get in a round of golf, in the dining room of the Club that dark Sunday morning. The low clouds, so close that it seemed I could reach up and touch them, raced across the fairways and sprinkled raindrops on the golfers whose colorful clothes glowed in contrast to the dark background and the nearly leafless trees.

A scene from an early technicolor film—a setting for a murder perhaps.

I shivered.

Where would it all end? I wondered. The Archdiocese and my family were both threatened with storm warnings. Neither seemed to care what would happen. It was my job to save both, without help from anyone else. How much longer could I take the stress? How soon would it be before I ended up in some psychiatrist's office? Or in a hospital someplace far from Chicago?

That one over there? Oh, he's an auxiliary bishop. Cracked up under the strain, you know. Quite harmless now. Doesn't talk much, just mumbles to himself.

Doctor Shanahan had called on Friday with the results of his "profile" of Brien. As usual he was enthusiastic and cheerful.

"I understand that I may share my findings about your brother with you, Bishop."

"Yes . . . I'm advising him about the, ah, spiritual aspects of the stress in his life."

"Well, I have good news for you. He's basically a healthy person with strong positive traits in his personality."

"I see."

"You're quite correct about the stress. I think that accounts for his temporary regression to adolescent sexual patterns. If we can remove the stress, I think that problem will take care of itself."

"That's good news."

"Yes, I think it is too. He probably needs a vacation, a month or so away from everything but golf before he announces his candidacy."

"His relationship with his wife?"

"He tests out as having normal attachments to, and affection for her."

"No trace of any violence between them?"

"Good heavens, no!"

It was indeed good news, the kind of news I had heard often from him about allegedly troubled priests.

Only this time I didn't believe the good news. Quite apart from the possibly exaggerated stories Kathleen had told me, I had seen the bruises on her body. Brien needed more than a vacation.

Moreover, he needed more than Doctor Shanahan. The man was doubtless sincere, but in this case he had not examined his patient closely enough.

He had come recommended to us as the best in his profession. We hire only the best at the Archdiocese because we believe that in the long run the purchase of quality services is the least expensive strategy.

Perhaps he and his staff were overworked.

Or perhaps there was a subtle conflict of interest in his treating the brother-in-law of a major client for whom he consulted. Kieran had hinted as much.

"Why are you looking so gloomy, James?" Brien, exuberant and colorful in a green sweater and white slacks, ambled into the dining room. "And do you have to wear that Roman collar in here? It's depressing on a Sunday morning!"

"Sit down, Brien."

"Wait till I get me some brunch. It's almost as good here now as it used to be. You want something more than coffee?"

"I've already eaten breakfast."

"So have I, but I shot two over par this morning. You know what that does to my appetite."

He came back with waffles, eggs benedict, bacon and sausages.

"Great food, James. Really great." He waved off a waiter with a champagne bottle. "No thanks, not this morning. . . . See what a good boy I am, James. God, I feel great today. I should forget about politics and law and play golf every day."

"That might not be a bad idea."

"You know I can't do that." His exuberance began to fade. "I have to announce in a couple of weeks."

"You could go away for a week."

"Yeah, that might be a good idea. Get the cobwebs out of my head. Maybe Kathleen would come along—Pebble Beach maybe."

"I don't think she's in the frame of mind for such a trip quite yet."

"I guess so. Shame though. Well, I'll see what I can work out. Maybe week after next."

"I want you to see another doctor before you go."

"What's wrong with Doctor Shanahan?" He put down his fork and his lip curled up petulantly. "I was getting along fine with him."

"There's nothing wrong with Doctor Shanahan, Brien. But you need someone who has the time to treat you in greater depth. We don't want a recurrence of these problems during the campaign or after you're elected."

"What problems?" He stuffed half a sausage into his mouth.

"I'll be blunt, Brien. You've had a homosexual lover. You beat your wife. Either or both of these are serious problems. Either or both could ruin your political career. And your marriage."

"I won't do them again."

"I fervently hope not. But the point is, you've done them before. Your wife, however immature she might sometimes be, is angry and, I would add, not without reason. Unless you take steps to avoid a recurrence of the problems, steps she deems credible, she may well sue for divorce and bring both of these issues to the media. I don't have to tell you what that would mean."

He pushed away his plate. "I didn't mean to hurt her," he said sadly.

"I understand that. But you did, several times, I gather."

He nodded in agreement. "But the other times were long ago. . . . Is she the one who insists that I see some deep kind of shrink?"

"Not unreasonably, Brien, given the circumstances. On this issue I can only agree with her."

"I saw Doctor Shanahan."

"You need more sustained treatment than he and his staff can provide. For your own good, Brien. And your family. And your career."

"I'm afraid."

I sighed. Yes of course he was afraid. I didn't blame him.

"And if my mother finds out, she'll be furious. I can't tell her about this stuff."

"If there's a divorce suit, she'll read about it in the papers."

"Yeah, that's true."

"It has to be, Brien. Here's a name and a number. Call the doctor and make an appointment. He's been advised that it's a highly confidential matter. You can trust him. See him this week and then take your vacation next week. All right?"

"If you say so, James. . . . Will you be checking up on me to see if I made the appointment?"

"I have no choice, Brien."

"Yeah." He folded the paper I had given him and put it in his wallet. "I suppose that's true."

I pride myself on my realism. I realized as I drove back to the Cathedral that there was little hope for a cure. The most we could expect was that Brien would learn to live with his impulses. Even that did not seem too likely.

I felt great sadness for him and wondered why God would permit so much trouble to happen to one man.

Perhaps Kathleen should seek a divorce. I could understand it if she did, though it would be a terrible family humiliation.

KATHLEEN

I dressed very carefully for my lunch with Kieran. I wanted to appear competent and professional. I didn't intend to betray any of the lurid fantasies I'd entertained. So I wore a navy-blue skirt, a light-blue blouse, only the top button open, and a dark-blue cardigan sweater, no makeup and only a touch of scent. I was determined to be the matron turned student and nothing more.

If I labored to create the image of a woman who was not trying to make an erotic impression, I did so with beating heart, nervous fingers, and an exhilaration I'd not felt in years.

I've got to control myself, I insisted, this is an important matter about his father. I will not tell him about Brien and me. Not today. I'll have to see what he says today before I even think of that.

My fingers continued to tremble as I turned over the ignition key in my Mercedes.

KIERAN

Brien was waiting at my office on Michigan Avenue at 7:30 Monday morning.

My appointments begin at 8:00. I usually try to arrive a half hour early to look over my notes and put myself in that special state of consciousness that I believe a good psychoanalyst must enter when he is treating patients.

"Hi, Kieran." Brien was leaning against the door and smiling broadly. "It's been a long time."

He stuck out his big hand in a gesture of friendship.

"It has, Brien." I shook hands cordially, trying to pretend that I did not know what I knew and had not surmised what I had surmised.

"Can I come in and talk to you for a few minutes?"

I glanced at my watch. "I have a patient coming in at eight."

"It'll only take a few minutes. I thought about calling you, but you know the Irish political rules." He grinned. "Always see the man face-to-face and on his turf."

"I seem to remember the rule."

I unlocked the door, stood back to let him enter, and then led him into the inner office. Outside my window, fog obscured the Lake in the distance and even Grant Park across the street.

He glanced around. "Kind of small, isn't it?"

"Small but comfortable. Anything more elaborate distracts the patient."

"Yeah, well . . ." He slumped into the chair across from my desk and immediately changed from a genial politician to an emotional wreck. "I guess I'm a potential patient. I'm a wreck, Kieran. I haven't admitted that yet to anyone. But I know it's true. I'm a mess. I don't deserve to be alive. I need help—lots of it. I wondered if you would help me. Please!" He was weeping by the time he'd issued his plea.

I stood up, put my arm around his shoulder in support, and let him cry himself out.

"Thanks, Kieran," he sniffled. "I'm ashamed of myself for bawling."

"You shouldn't be, Brien." I went back to my chair. "Emotional release is always helpful. Most men couldn't do that."

"I've never bawled like that before, not since we were kids."

"A long time ago."

"So." He wiped his face with the clean handkerchief he had carried in his breast pocket. "Can you help me?"

"I can recommend someone, Brien," I said firmly, "but I can't do it myself. I'd make a mess out of it."

"They say you're one of the best there is."

"I probably don't deserve the compliment. However, one of the rules of my business is you don't treat your family or friends. The links get too tricky and confusing."

"We haven't seen each other in a long time."

"I know that, but we were also very close for a long time."

Not exactly true, but true enough for the situation.

"Those were great days, weren't they?" He smiled wanly. "Too bad they ever had to end, huh?"

"Indeed. . . . What do they say in your profession about a lawyer who handles his own case?"

"That he's a fool."

"Same principle here. It's kind of my case, you see, because of my past ties with you. My emotions are involved as well as yours."

Dear God, help me to continue to say the right things.

"Yeah, I guess I understand. I've got the name of another doctor. I'm afraid of facing a stranger."

"The rules of our game say that it has to be a stranger, not a friend. Strangers can help you in this context. Friends can't."

"If you say so. . . . I kind of see what you mean. And you were pretty close to Kathleen, too."

"At one time, yes."

"She would have been better off if she had married you."

I tried to chuckle. "Come on, Brien. I very much doubt it. I'm your chronic Irish bachelor type."

"I'm going to lose her, Kieran. When this is over I'm going to lose her. Maybe it's better that way, but I'll miss her. I really do love her, but I haven't been a very good husband. I guess I never will be."

"I don't think we ought to be talking about that, Brien."

He stood up. "You're right, Kieran." The genial pol returned. "You used to be right all the time. Thanks for listening to me and giving me the courage to do what I should do."

"Glad to help." I shook hands again, firmly as before.

When he had left my office, I leaned against the wall, tried to recover my breath, and reviewed the conversation. I had done pretty well until he had mentioned Kathleen. I waited one exchange too long to shut off discussion of her, so I had heard something I should not have heard and did not want to hear—not as a professional therapist anyway.

I would have to keep that particular tidbit out of my mind when I saw his wife at lunch. I didn't want to know about it, I told myself. But that wasn't true. As a therapist I didn't want to know about it. As a lover I surely did.

But I would not use my knowledge. Brien and Kathleen would have to work out their problems themselves. Afterwards, and only afterwards, would I permit myself to be involved.

With that piety firmly planted in my consciousness, I concentrated on my four patients for the rest of the morning.

Only when I boarded the South Shore in the terminal under Michigan Avenue next to my office did I permit myself an estimate of the prognosis for Brien Donahue.

Poor, at best. Most likely much worse than that.

KATHLEEN

Kieran was waiting for me in the Thai restaurant.

"I'm not late, am I?" I glanced at my watch. Twelve twenty-seven. I had planned to be waiting for him, but a parking place had been more difficult to find than usual.

"I'm early," he said. "An old habit you might remember. And there was a South Shore train waiting for me at Randolph Street. Here, let me help you with your coat."

"Thank you."

I was nervous and clumsy and made a mess of letting him take my coat off. I winced in pain as my arm twisted against a bruised rib. Damn—I had done that in his office and he hadn't noticed it.

"Something wrong, Kathleen?"

"Bruised a rib doing that silly Taekwondo thing with Maeve," I lied. "I'm too old for that kind of craziness."

I was covering up the truth, just as the articles said a battered wife would.

"If you will accept just one plain and simple compliment, you don't look too old. Quite the contrary, you are lovelier than ever."

"Thank you, Kieran." I felt my face flame. "You were always good at compliments."

He ushered me to a table, in an alcove at the corner of the restaurant where no one could see us except the cheerfully grinning young waitress when she took our orders or brought us food.

"Do you like Thai food?" I asked.

"I'm afraid I've never eaten it."

"Don't they have it in New York?"

"They have everything in New York. But I guess I became addicted to Chinese food when I was there."

"This is different. I bet you'll like it."

"You'll have to order for me."

"I'll be happy to."

I told the waitress we wanted my-tai pork and pad Thai with extra noodles and rice, and a large pot of tea.

She giggled happily as she always did when she was finished taking an order.

Out of the corner of my eye, I saw Kieran watching me with quiet amusement. Evaluating me, but not quite undressing me. Perhaps liking what he saw.

"Still Ms. Take Charge, huh?"

"You don't object, I hope?"

"Did I ever?"

"Not that I can remember."

"How are the kids?" he asked.

"Wonderful! Do I beam with pride, Kieran? Forgive me if I do. I really am very proud of them. Maybe I shouldn't be. . . ."

"That's barf city." He laughed. "Of course you should be proud, they're like totally neat,' right? Outstanding! Really excellent!"

"You've got it down perfectly. I bet you're great at counseling kids."

"I try." He became sober. "By the time I get them, they're not always in very good shape. . . . And how's your mother?"

I felt guilty as I always do when Mom is mentioned.

"I guess I'm not a very good daughter anymore, Kieran. I call her every day and try to stop by her apartment on East Lake Shore Drive—you know, down the street from the Drake, right by the turn—every week or two. But she's not part of my life. I forget her most of the time."

"Oh?" Nice, nondirective psychiatric reply.

"She drinks. I mean all the time. She's never really blotto, but she's never really sober either, not even at nine in the morning. It kills the pain, I guess."

"Life has been too much for her. But I bet she likes the kids."

"That's the problem, Kieran. She picks at them constantly. Can't stand them. Complains to me about them every time I talk to her. Tells me that I'm spoiling the three of them—"

"Like they spoiled you?"

"That's the message. It's not her, not really. Left to herself she would adore them. But my in-laws, and James too, to tell the truth, are always on her about the kids."

"As they were about you?"

"Exactly. . . . So we talk but we never say much. I always become defensive and argue about the kids, though I know it's a waste of time."

"But you're punished by the argument?"

I sighed. "I guess that's what it is all about. I tell her that I won't talk about them anymore, but of course I do."

I was being absorbed by his kindly eyes and his sympathetic smile. It was time to change the subject. Business first. Pleasure, such as it might be, later.

My carefully thought-out strategy said that we ought not to spend much time on ice-breaking. Rather, I would give him the letters as soon as we ordered our food and devote the first part of our lunch to discussing them. Only after we had a chance to size each other up could we talk about our lives since he had left for New York—and only in the most general terms.

"I was searching in Dad's papers for some notes he might have kept about the Democratic leadership battle in the early nineteen fifties . . ."

"When Daley *père* was elected?"

"Right. . . . Your memory hasn't changed, Kieran."

"I haven't changed."

"About that I'm not so sure. . . . Anyway, I came across this envelope. There were two letters, one to me and one more general. This is the first."

I handed it across the table to him, a table so small that our heads were only a few inches apart when we leaned forward. Which both of us did.

His eyes seemed kinder than ever.

The waitress brought the my-tai and the tea.

He read the letter and gave it back to me. I put it in the envelope.

"That's a very moving letter, Kathleen. It must be a great consolation to you. How long has he been dead?"

"Twelve years."

"In a way it's a good thing that you didn't find it right away. It means more now than it would have then."

Same old Kieran, reading my inner thoughts like they were written on my face.

"I'm afraid that he had a higher opinion of my insights than I deserved."

"Perhaps, perhaps not. But that's hardly the point, is it? He loved you and your mother even to the end. Especially at the end."

"Yes," I said, forbidding tears. "He certainly did. . . . Now here's the reason why I phoned you on Friday. I suppose there's nothing to be done now, but I wanted you to see his second letter."

He read the document carefully with no change of facial expression. Then he read it a second time. He folded it up and tried to give it back to me.

"It's yours, Kieran. You should have the original. I've made a copy."

He folded the letter and put it in the inside pocket of his jacket. I could not read his face.

The pad Thai was brought to our table.

"I suppose I always suspected something like that."

"Are you angry?"

"At the dead?"

"My father-in-law is still alive."

"Poor guy was an innocent bystander. All his life. My parents are dead, your father is dead, so is your grandfather. Tony the Angel is dead."

"No, he's not. He's a very faded power over in the First Ward."

"Yeah, I guess I'm angry," he said. "But it's an old anger from twenty years ago. I'll experience it for the last time and put it to rest."

"Sounds like a shrink talking!"

"That's what I do for a living, Kathleen. Sometimes I even practice what I preach."

"Do you go to a shrink?"

"I sure do. We call them training analysts. They keep us sane, more or less."

"You'll discuss this with him, I bet."

"I sure will. Her, by the way."

"Her!"

"Yep! Very able woman."

"Attractive?"

"You bet." He grinned impishly. "Early sixties but still very appealing."

"How interesting," I said.

I didn't want to know about his training analyst. No way.

What was her name? I wondered.

"I appreciate this very much, Kathleen." He patted the pocket where he had put the letter. "You did exactly the right thing by calling me and giving it to me."

"You'll go public with it?"

"Why?"

"To clear your father."

"His conviction was thrown out. Why embarrass anyone today? Especially your father-in-law and Brien, who I hear is running for the Senate. You know me better than to think I'd be into revenge, don't you?"

"I thought you would say that. It's your call, however."

"I've made it. The case is closed. This goes into my archives."

"I think it's the right call."

"Thanks. Now, let's have at this pad Thai and hear about your dissertation."

"Never say that to a graduate student unless you want her to talk about it for the rest of a meal."

"That's just what I want."

So I told him at great length and in rich detail about my study. He had the courtesy to seem interested and the sense to ask the right questions. And the good taste to enjoy me.

"Do you agree with my theory?" I asked him finally.

"Do I have any choice?"

"Some, but not much."

"You sound very persuasive. I can hardly wait to read the book. And of course you're right. People like you and me have known that all along. It will be interesting to see how the scholars at *the* University react."

As the waitress removed our plates, she accidentally bumped my shoulder while maneuvering in the cramped space between my chair and the wall. Pins and needles of pain raced through my body.

"What's wrong, Kathleen?" he asked.

"Taekwondo bump," I said, lying again.

"I'm not sure I believe that."

With a quick and fluid movement, he brushed open two buttons of my blouse and forced my sweater, blouse, and bra strap off my shoulder.

I shut my eyes in humiliation.

With an equally fluid movement he put me back together again. The whole interlude, which seemed to endure for several lifetimes, could not have taken more than fifteen seconds.

"You had no right to do that, Kieran."

"Who says I didn't?"

"I do." My eyes remained closed.

"I say that I did."

"You have changed." I opened my eyes, feeling for the first time how hot my face had become.

"How?"

"You're stronger than before, more determined, more demanding."

"No less gentle, I hope."

"Not at all," I replied, feeling all my carefully constructed defenses slip away. "Not a bit less gentle."

KIERAN

"Tell me about it," I demanded.

"You have no right to know," she insisted, her face still red, her eyes still glued on her teacup.

"I won't debate that with you."

"It's none of your business." She sat up, stiff and straight, and tried to stare me down.

"Have you seen a doctor about your injuries?"

"No. I'm getting better. It doesn't hurt as much as it used to."

"See a doctor. Today."

"You're not my shrink. You have no right to give me orders."

"If I were your shrink, I wouldn't give you orders. We don't do that kind of thing."

"Then who do you think you are?" Her eyes blazed furiously, her lips tightened.

"The weird boy who carried your books the first day at St. Praxides."

That did her in, as I knew it would.

"I'm sorry, Kieran." Her shoulders seemed to cave in. "That was a very bitchy reaction. . . . Actually he was a nice little boy, not weird at all. And not little anymore either."

We smiled shyly at one another. My throat was dry again. I still loved her as much as I had that first day.

"Tell me what happened."

"I don't want to . . ." She breathed deeply. "Yes, I do. I haven't talked to anyone . . ."

She was fighting off tears.

I remained silent and hoped that I was radiating reassurance.

"I don't have to tell you. You know what happened. Or at least you can guess."

"So it will be easy to tell me."

She stared at me dubiously.

"I'm afraid to, ashamed, embarrassed."

"Don't be afraid of me, Kathleen. I'll cherish your confidence. You have to talk about it."

"You're right." She nodded decisively. "Brien is a bisexual. Maybe gay. Probably gay. His male lover told me all about it on the phone. I confronted Brien with the truth. He was drunk. He beat me. He apologized the next day. That's the whole story."

"Has this happened often?"

"Only once in the last fifteen years."

"Before that?"

"Twice. In the first two years of marriage."

"Once after the marriage and once after Megan was born?"

"How did you know that?"

"He was trying to adjust to the requirements first of marriage, then of parenthood. Now, I presume the burdens of running for office are too much for him. . . . Should he be in politics?"

"No." She had regained her self-possession and her intelligence. "He's good at corporate law and civic activities. If he could limit himself to that and playing golf every day, I think he'd be a happy man."

"His parents are forcing him into the race?"

"And James. And the expectations of a lifetime."

"Have you seen a lawyer . . . sorry to sound like a prosecuting attorney."

"A nice prosecuting attorney, not at all weird either. . . . Not yet. I threw him out of the house, made him live in the coach house. Then I made a deal with James. If Brien joins AA, finds a therapist, and promises me an annulment, I won't file for divorce until after the election."

In Chicago political families, always deals.

"He'll do it again, Kathleen. He's deeply disturbed, I'm sure, maybe suicidal, but give him a chance and he'll do it again."

"I thought he'd kill me this last time. . . . He . . . he raped and sodomized me too."

I clenched my fists under the table. For all my psychiatric wisdom and restraint I wanted briefly to kill her husband.

"He's dangerous, Kathleen. He doesn't mean to be, but he is. It's not because he's bisexual. Most men like that are no more dangerous than anyone else, maybe less dangerous. Poor Brien has a special kink."

"Isn't there any hope for him?"

"Do you think he will face and accept his own homosexuality?"

She shook her head. "Maybe he will, but it's not very likely."

I refilled both our teacups. "Might he withdraw from political life and return to his law practice?"

She hesitated, then shook her head.

"Think he'll stick with AA and therapy?"

"I don't think so."

"You should see a lawyer and a doctor and a therapist."

"File suit?"

"Line it all up so you're ready. And don't let him back into the house."

"Are you saying I should break the deal?"

I squirmed on the hard chair. "I'm saying that he won't keep his part of it—or James's part. He wants to, I suspect, after a fashion. But he can't do it."

An expression of great sadness spread over her face. "Are you saying, Kieran, that there is no hope for my marriage?"

"I don't see it, Kathleen. With help some men like him can adjust their sexual preferences, or at least their sexual behavior, to stay in relatively amicable marriages. Brien might want to do that. He may be telling himself that he wants to do that. But it's probably too late."

"I won't say I love him." She turned her head away. "But he was often very sweet and I am fond of him. I'm a Christian; I believe in forgiving even as I have been forgiven. I want to help him if I can. I worry about the effect of divorce on the kids. And it will break our parents' hearts."

A nice, neat summary of a typical argument from a battered wife, wrongheaded but not totally so until you considered the context.

"And you're afraid to make the decisive break?"

"Ph.D. candidate"—she looked at me, her eyes glistening—"and still acting like a dumb battered wife, huh?"

"All your motives are sound and valid, Kathleen, but it's too late. The impact will be far worse on your children and your mother and his parents if this happens again."

"If?"

I hesitated for the first time in our rapid-fire conversation. Had I said anything I would not have said to another woman in similar circumstances, one with whom I had not been in love for almost thirty years?

"Human behavior is never completely predictable, Kathleen. The odds are overwhelming that the right word is not 'if' but 'when.' Brien needs help desperately. You have to understand that you can't help him. Now you can only protect yourself."

"And my kids?"

"And your kids."

"I guess I suspected that." She nodded solemnly. "It's hard . . ."

"I understand."

"When he's stressed out and drunk, it all pours out of him."

"What?"

"His hatred for women, his mother especially. But all of us. Hatred and fear."

"A very insightful analysis, Kathleen. Again, gay men and bisexual men don't necessarily hate women. Brien has a special twist in his soul."

"I feel sorry for him."

"So do I. He's been dealt a bad hand."

"If I could help him . . ."

"Do you think he's likely to exorcise his hatred and fear?"

"Not without a lot of help from a professional over a long time. And for that help he's not a good candidate. That's what you think, isn't it?"

I realized that I was about to pass sentence.

"Yes, Kathleen. That's what I think."

She glanced at her watch. "I have an appointment with my adviser."

"Did you come in a car? I'll walk with you."

"Are you taking charge of my life, Kieran?"

"I bet it's that Mercedes convertible over there, right? . . . I knew it! Yes, to your question, I am indeed taking charge of your life. Just as I took charge of your schoolbooks a quarter century ago. And your raincoat a few moments ago. This time I won't run out on you."

"You didn't run out on me, Kieran."

"The hell I didn't."

I had been unfaithful to her and to my promise for eighteen years. If I had not run, neither she nor Brien would be in the trouble they were in. That was not a neurotic assumption of guilt, it was simple truth.

"You had reason to run."

"Not enough."

"I forgive you."

Full absolution and a plenary indulgence, as we used to call it, in three words.

"Thank you."

We smiled and shook hands. I helped her into the car, admiring her thigh as it was momentarily exposed as she slid in.

"I will call you tomorrow."

"I will be waiting for the call."

"See a doctor."

"Tomorrow."

"This afternoon."

"OK."

Kathleen was no longer a pretty and frightened little girl walking down Hoyne Avenue. She was a threatened and perennially beautiful woman. I wanted her, all of her, everything that she was, mind and body, heart and soul. I meant to have her. She was mine by rights and always had been. I would wipe away her tears and bring joy back to her life.

I would not abuse her trust. She had to work through her problems first, I could wait.

But not indefinitely.

Brien?

He had lost already. He had probably never had a chance, poor man. Now it was too late. I would not defeat him in a contest for this delicious woman. He had already defeated himself.

It was all straightened out in my head when I stepped off the South
Shore at Randolph Street and walked through the underpass.

Then I made what would turn out to be a serious mistake: I strolled
over to the Daley Center to hunt for the records of my father's trial.

KATHLEEN

"Bruises." Doctor Dorothy Halder pointed at the X ray with the head
of a ball-point pen. "But nothing broken. You were lucky."

I was in one of the outpatient rooms at Little Company of Mary
Hospital, feeling naked and powerless in a hospital gown after a thorough examination and numerous blunt questions.

"I guess I was."

Dorothy was younger than I; her oldest was in Brigie's class at St.
Prax's. She had responded promptly to my call for help.

"You should have come much earlier, Kathleen. Your injuries could
easily have been more serious. You might have died from internal
hemorrhages."

"I know that."

"This kind of violence ought to be reported to the police."

"I understand."

"Forgive me for probing"—she kept her voice objective and dispassionate—"and tell me to butt out if you want . . ."

"Twice before, fifteen years ago. He's in therapy now. And banished
to the coach house."

"He could have killed you, Kathleen. Do you understand that? These
injuries"—she gestured in the general direction of my poor, aching
body—"are the work of a man out of control."

"I thought he might kill me."

"He is likely to try again."

She was even blunter than Kieran had been.

"I'm taking every precaution."

"If I can be any help, please call me." There was a plea in her eyes. She liked me and wanted to help me.

"I certainly will, Dot. I've read about the battered wife syndrome. I don't intend to be imprisoned by it."

She nodded although she didn't look convinced. "You can put your clothes on now. I'll write out a prescription for some painkiller, something stronger than Advil but not habit forming. You *will* take it, you understand? No Irish martyr syndrome."

"No way."

After she had left the room, I put aside the gown and shivered. These rooms were always so cold.

As I dressed I realized that I was in love again. Still. Whatever. I had entrusted my life to Kieran. And forgiven him. No act of contrition, no purpose of amendment, no penance to be performed. I had wiped out his fall from grace with a wave of my hand.

He had taken possession of me. Without touching me, save for two quick handshakes and a brush against my breast, he had captured me and taken charge of my life. He had promised, in effect, to heal me and make me happy again.

How I wanted him.

The sooner the better. Even black and blue and hurting, I loved him so much that I had almost thrown myself into his arms out there on 55th under the dark skies with the Lake pounding wildly at the end of the street.

The touch of his fingers when he pulled back my blouse had sent an electric shock through my body which was still coursing back and forth between my brain and the rest of me.

It was not the chill of the examination room which made my nipples hard.

Later Brien phoned me in my office while I was sorting the notes from my conversation with my adviser—a very positive conversation.

"I, uh, have an appointment tomorrow with a first-rate psychiatrist, Kathleen. Doctor Beauregard. Someone a lot more thorough than Doctor Shanahan. I talked to him on the phone and he sounded very good. I think it will work out fine."

"I'm happy to hear that, Brien."

"I already have a second appointment lined up for Thursday. Then I'm going off to Naples, Florida, for a week of golf, kind of clear out my head, know what I mean?"

"That's a good idea. You've been under a lot of tension lately."

"And I'll keep on with the shrink when I come back. . . . I really feel very good about it all now."

"Wonderful!"

"There's no chance of you coming along with me for a few days, is there? Kind of a second honeymoon, know what I mean?"

The first one had been bad enough.

"Not this time, Brien."

That was not enough. I was not being as honest as I should be.

"Mind if I ask why?"

"I'm still afraid of you."

"Yeah, I understand. I guess you have pretty good reason to feel that way. I'll talk to you before I leave."

I had to be honest. I had permitted no illusions. Yet I had hurt him. My conscience rebelled. *He's your husband, you can't hurt him that way. You're his wife. You're the mother of his children.* And I had to protect them. That's where my responsibilities lay. Brien would have to rely on his therapist's help—and God's.

Before I could squelch the thought, I wondered if He would approve of my loving Kieran the way I did. As quickly, I answered my own question: If He didn't approve, why did He send Kieran back to me?

I couldn't come up with an answer to that.

BRENDAN

"I can't believe what I'm hearing and seeing," Kieran O'Kerrigan, top-gun shrink, whispered in my ear.

"It's typical," I whispered back.

Mitzi Collins, a lawyer for the Archdiocese, was leading Ned Kelly through a recitation of how Ron Long and Kevin O'Malley had persuaded him to sign an affidavit incriminating Gerry Greene in yet another case of pedophilia. For which they paid him twenty thousand dollars in cash. I was there in lay garb, but my good friend Martin Roder was sitting up in front in all his clerical excellence.

"And you called Father Greene and told him what you had done?"

"That's right," Ned gasped. "I was sorry I did it almost as soon as I signed the paper. But they made me do it."

Ned was a little old man on the wrong side of seventy, a couple of front teeth missing, a red nose, shabby clothes, and the bemused state of the chronic drinker of a bottle of rye a day.

"I see. Now, Mr. Kelly, did they tell you what to say?"

"Yes, ma'am, they did."

"You rehearsed it over and over again with them?"

"Yes, ma'am."

Ron didn't object because he wanted this description, taken from Kelly's second affidavit, on the record. Then he would spring his trap.

"Did they stop the tape and make you repeat words so you got it just right?"

"Yes, ma'am."

"How often?"

"Many times."

"How many times?"

"Twenty, thirty anyway."

"When Father Greene was at St. Retram's did you ever see him molest any boy?"

"No, ma'am."

"Not once?"

"Not once. Father Gerry, he was a good priest."

"When did you first hear of this charge against him?"

"When the private detective that said he worked for Mr. Long asked me about whether I had seen anything. He said there might be a lot of money in it. I needed the money real bad, ma'am."

Gerry Greene had learned of the first affidavit and then leaned on Ned to change his story. Persuasive fellow, our Gerry. Then Ned called Martin Roder and told him what Gerry had told him to say.

Neither Martin nor the best lawyers in town—because the most expensive—had bothered to take too close a look at his testimony.

Probably because their only intent was to harass the O'Malleys with a new charge and appear to be weakening their case.

"Your witness, Counselor," she sneered at Ron.

"Thank you, Ms. Collins." Ron unfolded his six feet five inches of former Marquette basketball star from the bench and bowed ceremoniously to her. "Now, Mr. Kelly, might I ask what you did with the money that Mr. O'Malley gave you?"

"Did with it?"

"Did you give it back to him?"

"Uh, well, yes I did."

"Did you ask for a receipt?"

"Objection."

"Overruled," said Judge Tim Clarke.

"Uh, no, I didn't."

"Didn't Father Roder or anyone who works for the Archdiocese suggest that you do so?"

"Well . . ." He looked at Mitzi.

"Objection."

"On what grounds, Counselor?"

"Mr. Kelly is not on trial."

"It's not a trial, Your Honor," Ron said smoothly. "It's a hearing for the court to determine which affidavit of the defendant should be believed before ordering a criminal investigation. By his own admission, Mr. Kelly has perjured himself at least once."

Tim Clarke rubbed his shiny black head and beamed. "I quite agree, Mr. Long. Witness will answer the question."

Tim was a shrewd old pro. He knew fakery when he saw it. And as a black Baptist he was not about to give the Archdiocese any breaks like an Irish Catholic judge might.

"I don't remember, Judge."

"You don't remember whether anyone told you to get a receipt?"

"No, Judge, I don't."

Ron Long shook his head in dismay. "In what bank had you deposited the money?"

"Bank?"

"Didn't you put it in a bank?"

"Uh, I didn't think of that."

"What did you do with it?"

"Well . . ." He searched desperately for an answer. "I put it in a box under my bed."

"Weren't you afraid someone might steal it?"

"Yeah, sure I was."

"But you didn't put it in a safe deposit box?"

"I never thought of that."

Kieran whispered to me. "Why didn't they give him ten thousand to put in the bank and then take it out?"

"You'd make a great crooked lawyer," I whispered back.

"I see," Ron droned on. "I would have thought given the crime rate in the St. Retram neighborhood that you would have been more concerned. . . . Well, so we have only your word that the money was given to you and that then you gave it back? No records of any kind?"

Mitzi tried again. "Objection, Your Honor, he's already indicated those facts."

"I just want them to be on the record. Will you stipulate them, Counselor?"

"Of course not," she huffed.

"Answer the question, Mr. Kelly."

"No, I haven't any records. But I'm telling the truth."

The poor old man was on the verge of tears—not that the Archdiocese cared.

"The issue, Mr. Kelly," Ron said smoothly, "is which time you were telling the truth. Now, Mr. Kelly," Ron said, closing in for the kill, "you've told us in court what you said in your sworn affidavit—that they made you repeat your words many times when they tape-recorded your statement."

"That's right. They really worked on me."

"They kept putting new tapes into the machine every time—you said twenty or thirty times."

"Of course not." The old man's reedy voice rose. "They didn't have to do that."

I'm no fool, he was telling us.

Alas, he was; and we would demonstrate him to be one.

"How many tapes did they use, do you recall?"

"Sure, I recall," he snarled. "Only one. They kept spinning it backward and starting it again."

"Rewinding it, you mean?"

"That's what I said, isn't it?"

"Your Honor, I would like to submit this analysis from the Illinois State Police crime lab of the tape on which Mr. Kelly's deposition was recorded."

"Any objection, Ms. Collins?"

Mitzi shrugged. "I don't care, Your Honor."

She should have cared, but she'd grown lazy on her three-hundred-dollar-an-hour charge against the greatest cash cow in Cook County.

"Mr. Kelly"—Ron resumed his questions—"would it surprise you to learn that the State Police say that the tape which recorded your statement was brand new?"

"I didn't know that, but what difference does it make?"

"They state that the recording was an original, not a copy, and that there were no corrections made in it."

"Yeah? Well, they're wrong!" He glanced at Martin Roder, who looked away. "I'm telling the truth."

The poor man wanted to flee from the courtroom.

"I suggest, Your Honor, that we know which statement to believe."

"Perjury is a very serious matter, Mr. Kelly." Tim Clarke looked solemn, like an angel perhaps on Judgment Day. "Are you sure of your testimony?"

"They copied it from another tape, Your Honor," the old man sobbed.

He should have changed his testimony and claimed that he was confused. Later, perhaps, coached by his lawyers, he would do that. But by then it would be too late.

"The crime lab would disagree with you, Mr. Kelly. No further questions."

"Come on, Kieran, let's sell this cheap hotel—and no questions till we're outside of it. There are ears everywhere."

Outside in the light rain which was falling on the Richard J. Daley Civic Center Plaza, I lifted my umbrella over Kieran.

"That poor man," he said.

"The response does you credit, Kieran. He was used in there and destroyed. They don't care. They'll demand a criminal investigation. Tim will order it. Depending on whether the fix is in—and I doubt it this time—nothing will happen or there'll be an indictment against Ron and Kevin."

"I know about those kinds of things," he said mysteriously.

"In which case the Archdiocese will agree to work for quashing the charges if the suit is dropped."

"They wouldn't be convicted, would they?"

"Not very likely. Not with that witness and that court record. But it would be a case that would hang fire for a while, cost the O'Malleys more money and more heartache. You beat people down long enough and they quit."

"But what if the fix isn't in? Will Ned Kelly be tried?"

"Are you kidding? Why would the People of the State of Illinois want to go after that poor old man? You see, for the Archdiocese it's a no-lose situation. In both outcomes they stretch things out, delay, pressure, eat up money. Why not do it?"

"Deliberately suborn perjury?"

We walked across the plaza and toward the University Club, where I had promised to buy him lunch.

"No, not exactly. Just play hardball law when they have a chance to. They didn't know whether Ned was telling the truth or not. They might have had their suspicions, but they didn't push too hard. Didn't push at all. They saw another chance to go after Kevin O'Malley and they did just that."

"Monsters."

"They'd say good adversarial lawyers. They're not—as they themselves quite properly would contend—interested in justice or truth. They're committed only to pursuing their clients' best interests."

"Who turned Ned Kelly?"

"Let me give you a scenario which probably fits the data pretty well. Mitzi sees the affidavit. She calls Gerry Greene and asks him if he knows the present pastor at St. Retram. He happens to be a classmate of Gerry—and Bishop Leary as a matter of fact. Gerry calls the good priest and learns that indeed Ned Kelly is still hanging around there, living in the school basement and puttering around with the decaying parish plant. Together, they hint that if he doesn't change his story, he'll be put out on the street."

"Will Ned change his story again?"

"Probably not. What difference would it make now?"

"You could file charges against the priests and the lawyers?"

"That would only delay the trial a little longer. We want to get to trial, you see. Then maybe we'll get a settlement."

"But Kelly's use as a witness is spoiled?"

"Yep, but he was frosting on the cake. I figured something like this would happen. They've turned witnesses in other cases."

"James?"

"He trusts his lawyers and he trusts his fellow priests. What else can you do if you're him?"

"Listen to you."

We were nearing the entrance of the Club.

"Fat chance. Martin Roder has told him I'm a selfish priest. There's also a rumor around among the clergy that the reason I'm obsessed— their word—about pedophilia is that I was molested by my father. Needless to say, it's not true."

"That's sick, Brendan."

"Yeah, but on this subject the clergy are sick. . . . I don't think James believes it."

"Does he trust Martin Roder?"

"Not entirely," I said after a moment's pause. "I think he'd like to have him out of there, but it's not high on his agenda. . . . Let's not talk about it inside the Club, huh?"

"One more question." He grabbed the arm of my raincoat. "Will the lawyers recommend settlement at the last minute if the O'Malleys don't back down?"

"I think so, Kieran. I think so. They'll keep collecting their charges no matter what happens. James will be happy to take their good advice. Maybe."

"Maybe?"

"James is the wild card in all of this. The attorneys don't figure him right. If he thinks the Church has a good case, he might just say to hell with the settlement, let's fight it out."

"Really?"

"He might figure that he can't keep giving away million-dollar settlements and that just this once he has to fight. Like they did up in St. Paul."

"What happened there?"

"Tons of media coverage. And a three-million-dollar settlement."

"Pretty soon now," Kieran said softly, "I'm going to have a long talk with my old friend James."

KIERAN

"So," said Maggie Ward, "you're proud of your professionalism in responding to Kathleen."

"Proud?"

"You kept your emotions out of your advice, did you not? Isn't that what a good adviser does in such situations?"

"Isn't it?"

"But what about the lover?"

"Lover?"

"As I understand it, you love the woman."

"That's right."

"They are different roles?"

"Not completely."

"It is impossible, I presume, that in leaning over backwards to be the fair and objective adviser, you will fail as a lover?"

"I thought the love was an impossible fantasy."

Had she not said the same thing the last time I had been on her couch in the office building on Harlem Avenue?

"It turns out that you were wrong in that evaluation."

I was wrong?

"I don't want to become involved in breaking up a marriage."

"The marriage, should it have ever been that, is already broken up."

"I can't say that."

"You will make love with her, naturally. Sooner rather than later."

"I don't know that."

"You think your passions and her needs are such that you will have a choice?"

"I do."

"I don't. Will it be adultery?"

Good question.

"Fornication, maybe."

"Only men and women under thirty are capable of that sin."

An interesting moral theory. One, I suspected, that would be thoroughly unacceptable to the Vatican.

"I don't think it will happen and I don't think that when it does it will be adultery."

"Nicely put, with an Irish flair for the deliberately self-revealing contradiction."

"You think I'm too emotionally involved with Kathleen to be a good adviser for her."

"Rather the opposite."

"I don't understand."

"That is the problem. The boy who carried her books would have understood."

"The opposite," I mused, twisting on the couch. "That would mean that I'm trying too hard to be an objective adviser and forgetting the obligations of a lover?"

"You have assumed responsibility for the woman in a far from objective way."

"That's wrong?"

"Did I say that?"

"No."

"You want her, you intend to have her—and doubtless on a permanent basis. You intend to take her away from a man who is brutalizing her. You will drag her into bed with you unless she drags you first, which I suspect will be more likely. And you are trying to be sure that you will be objective? Come on, Kieran."

"I guess."

"If you persist in your Quixote-like quest for professional objectivity, you may well fail her because of defect rather than excess. You probably have already done so."

"I see."

And I did.

"You are trying to please your mother and your grandparents, not your father. Perhaps you haven't made any mistakes yet because your professionalism has not yet interfered with your instincts as a lover. You do not want to take the risk that it will."

"You're giving me a hunting license, Maggie Ward."

"Since you propose to hunt, you might as well have a license. . . . You have not made a psychiatric referral yet?"

"Physician first, lawyer second, shrink third."

"You must understand, and I trust that you do, that the worst of the many faults of Irishwomen is their seemingly incorrigible propensity to appear stronger than they are."

"So I am told."

It was another totally unorthodox session, I reflected as I drove back to the Medical Center via the Congress Expressway, one that I would never have attempted with one of my own patients.

Yet the heart of the session was pure Freudian orthodoxy. I had been on the verge of transferring internalized paradigms from my past to a present relationship.

When I was as good as Maggie Ward, if I ever was, I could afford to be as heterodox.

I was now free to follow my instincts, a doctor of the soul indeed but also a lover. Objectivity does not suffice when the beloved is in deep trouble.

So I was anything but objective when I called her from my office at the University.

"Kathleen Donahue."

"You don't sound like an interrupted scholar this morning, my dear."

"Kieran!"

Dear God, she sounded happy to hear my voice.

"You have any extra books I can carry?"

"Not this morning—and no ribs that need to be taped either."

"You saw a physician?"

"Naturally. I was told to, wasn't I?"

"Who?"

"You mean 'whom' presumably. I saw Dot Halder. She was very thorough. Do you know her?"

"I may have met her. Attractive blonde?"

"Attractive and well married."

"Blondes are not my weakness. . . . What did she say?"

"What would you expect her to say? That I was a fool for not coming in earlier, that I should make out a police report, that I was lucky to be alive and relatively unhurt this time, that I should seek 'counseling,' and that I should take my anti-inflammatory medicine and not play Irish matron martyr . . . is that satisfactory, Doctor?"

Despite the grim recital, she continued to sound happy, almost carefree.

"For the moment. The next step is a lawyer."

She hesitated in her reply. "I'm not sure . . ."

"Look, divorce is not a political obstacle anymore, not if it is a quiet divorce—which it can be unless he's dumb enough to fight it."

"But he has always projected the image of a man concerned about family life because he has such a fine family himself."

"A quiet divorce will do less harm to his campaign than a noisy wife-battering scandal."

"That's true . . . I made a deal."

"I know that. He won't live up to it. He can't. You should not hate him, Kathleen; and I know you don't. But you should fear him. He's dangerous."

"Yes . . ."

"Get your ducks lined up with a good attorney, one that is on the fringes of politics and can keep his mouth shut, not a professional divorce attorney, so that you can act quickly when you have to."

I did not want to push her too hard. Not yet.

"Brien has two appointments this week with Doctor Beauregard. Is he any good?"

"The best." He was one of the psychiatrists I'd recommended to James.

"Then he's going away for a week to play golf and relax."

"That's wise . . . don't let him in the house."

"Oh, I won't."

"And make an appointment with a lawyer. Now. Today. Tell him the whole truth. Do you have anyone in mind?"

"Yes. Someone who fits your description perfectly."

"Fine. Call him—or her—today."

"Yes, Doctor."

"I don't usually order women, Kathleen."

"I know that. But when you do it you do it very nicely. Firmly but nicely. Just now in my life I appreciate those kinds of orders."

If we had been together I would have taken her into my arms.

"They'll keep coming."

"I'm very grateful to you, Kieran. I realize only now what a dead end I had come to. I needed to talk to someone."

"I'm glad I was there to listen and help. I won't run away this time."

"I've already forgiven that, Kieran. Besides, maybe I should have run after you."

"I doubt it."

"I want to be forgiven too—for my fall from grace."

"Dear God, of course I forgive you for whatever needs to be forgiven. But I do have one last question about the past before it is buried completely, okay?"

"Whatever you want."

"After I shouted at you and hung up, I called back a couple of times and left messages. Did you get them?"

She did not respond for a moment.

"No, Kieran, I did not."

"I kind of thought that. . . . Well, it's all buried now."

"I'm so glad that it is."

But actually, not all was quite buried.

I almost said, "I love you." I didn't. Perhaps I should have. At the time, I told myself there would be plenty of opportunities later.

KATHLEEN

The two self-revelations—emotional and spiritual to Kieran, physical to Dot Halder—had exhausted me. For the first time since the night before the Ireland Fund Dance, I slept well. I woke up in the morning feeling exhilarated, a feeling which was matched by the clean, crisp autumn sunshine. Somehow my world would improve. My life was about to begin again. With Kieran? I wondered.

Taking Kieran's advice, I called Phil Carver, an attorney from Palos who was a partner in a small but respected law firm downtown. I made an appointment for that afternoon. I knew Phil from Rich's last campaign. He was smart, sensitive, and discreet.

"An emergency, Kathleen?"

"In a manner of speaking."

"I'll be looking forward to seeing you."

When we met, I summarized my story tersely for Phil, a tall, thin, gray-haired man in his late forties, with kind gray eyes and a quick smile.

He wasn't smiling when I was finished.

"Good God, Kathleen."

"At least I have the sense to find myself a lawyer."

"How do you want to proceed?"

"My current agreement with poor Brien is that I will hold off filing for a divorce until after the election."

"Primary or general?"

"General. He is unlikely to have any primary opposition. Or at least that's the way he interprets signals from the Mayor."

"That's more than a year from now."

"It is indeed."

"Do you think he can keep his end of the agreement until then?"

I sighed. "I'm not sure. I have been advised by a therapist friend that he is unlikely to do so. Not because he doesn't want to—he surely does. But because he won't be able to do so."

"That puts you at grave risk, doesn't it?"

"I assume that it puts me at some risk. I'm in no danger until he starts to drink again. When that happens I take my daughters and go into hiding."

"At that point you want me to file the divorce papers?"

"Exactly."

"There is a danger point between the first drink and your escape, is there not?"

"I think he'll break the agreement before he starts drinking. If he misses an AA meeting or a therapist's appointment, I move out, kids in tow."

He nodded. "I don't like it, but I understand your decision. I assume that he will not under the circumstances contest the divorce."

I'd thought about that. "I assume so too, but there is a kind of craziness in his family and mine. His mother and my brother will probably get involved. Heaven only knows what they might try."

"Politically it would be suicidal."

"They're not too smart politically, although they think they are. I can imagine their convincing themselves that to contest a divorce and demand custody of the children against a feminist from The University of Chicago could turn out to be a political asset."

"That would be mad!"

"I never said they were sane."

"Do you think that might really happen?"

"It's unlikely, Phil. But not impossible."

"If they did try to obtain custody of the children, you'd be ready to charge physical abuse?"

Without any hesitation I said, "I sure would. My physician is prepared to testify on my behalf. She has already told me so."

He made some notes on his desk pad. "I don't think that we'll have any trouble with preparing a petition. I'll check with some of my colleagues here who know more about it than I do—on a John and Jane Doe basis."

"I'd appreciate that, Phil. I don't hate him. I feel sorry for him. I don't want to ruin his political chances."

"He's likely to ruin them himself, isn't he?"

"Probably."

"Will our mutual friend really support him?"

That indirect reference to Rich showed how deep Phil Carver's roots went in Chicago politics.

"I'm not sure, to tell the truth. If Danny Rostenkowski doesn't run again . . ."

"God forbid," Phil murmured.

"I hope She does. If Danny retires, Chicago will be short of clout in Washington. Rich might want a senator that cares about Chicago and knows how a legislature works and has a good chance of beating a Republican in what looks like it will be a Republican year. I'm not sure that's Brien."

"You don't want to be blamed if Brien is dumped?"

"I suppose I will be anyway, regardless. I don't want to really hurt his chances unless he forces me to."

"I understand. . . . Now, what would you want in the way of settlement?"

"I have income of my own from trust funds my father and grandfather set up. I want generous support for the education of the three girls, and the two homes, Beverly and Grand Beach. That's all."

"Nothing for yourself?"

"No. I have enough. Maybe I'll earn something from my Ph.D., though there's not a big market for historians just now."

"Or you could run for office?"

"I'm not the type, Phil."

He smiled gently. "I think my colleagues who specialize in these matters would hardly permit such a suit. It's not generosity you've just described, it's foolhardiness. In lieu of all other claims, I think they would urge us to seek a lump-sum payment, a substantial one at that. There could be medical expenses, your children might need help in purchasing homes, you might have investment opportunities, you might want to contribute to charities."

"I don't know . . ."

"A half-million would not hurt him, would it?"

"He earns that much in a year."

"In an investment account, that would be a nice sum for the proverbial rainy day."

"I'll think about it, Phil. I don't want a dogfight and I don't want to blackmail him or even seem to blackmail him."

"I fully understand."

I walked back to Union Station knowing I'd done the sensible thing, something I should have done long before. But somehow I only felt as raw and exposed as I had after my visit to Dot Halder's.

KIERAN

"They're talking human sacrifice," Brendan McNulty told me, his face an unsmiling mask. "There's some big deal Archpriest of the Satanism Cult coming in from San Diego. He's demanding a real sacrifice to placate their boss."

"You're kidding!"

"That's what the Feds are telling me."

"Why are they telling you?"

"You don't want to know."

"When is it going to happen?"

"Halloween, when else? Do you believe this stuff now, Kieran?"

"I'm inclined to believe it, Brendan. Less because of the Feds than because of a patient I saw recently."

"Yeah, I'm convinced now too."

"What are the Feds going to do?"

"Wait till it's about to go down and pick up the whole crowd."

"With the victim staked out on the slab?"

"You got it! The FBI to the rescue—lots of good PR for the Bureau. Make old man Hoover proud if he were still around."

"And imitators all around the country!"

"The Feds say that they'll sock this crowd so hard that it will scare other crazies for a long time. Judges and juries are not likely to go easy on people that try to cut up little children."

"I assume they have someone inside carrying a wire?"

"I didn't hear that question."

It was easy enough to guess that the Feds did not want a Catholic priest among the crazies they brought in. So they wanted Brendan to lean on the Cardinal to do something about Gerry Greene.

"I hope they don't cut it too close."

"The Bureau would look real bad if some young woman is violated and stabbed to death before they show up." Brendan folded his arms. "By tradition, the victim has to be a virgin, you see."

"And a victim has already been chosen?"

"So I gather."

"I hope they're watching her."

"I think we have to assume that they are."

"Do you know who she is?"

"No."

If he had said, "Don't ask," it would have meant he knew. So he didn't know.

"How does this affect us?"

"I absolutely can't tell James what the Feds have told me. He wouldn't believe it anyway and, as I said before, he might even tip off Gerry. But if he'll settle this case and set up a lay review board, as our clients demand, Gerry will become a liability—even if there is no admission of guilt. I could make a pitch that he ought to send Gerry away for a thorough evaluation."

"Is James likely to buy that?"

"I doubt it."

"Do you want me to go in with you?"

"Would you?"

"Sure. Do you think it will help?"

"It will make him think twice, maybe not much else."

"So the Feds may haul in Gerry Greene anyway. . . . that's exactly what the Church needs."

"Only nine percent of the Archdiocese contributed to the Cardinal's Appeal Collection last week. How can you worry about Satan and the violation of virgins when you have that on your mind?"

"What about the John Doe case?" I asked.

"They're leaning on the State's Attorney to go to a grand jury for an indictment against Kevin and Ron. Martin Roder is walking around like they've made him vicar of heaven. He says that when they get their indictment, the Cardinal will have to order me to abandon my selfish pursuit of law."

"Will they get the indictment?"

"Not on the evidence. On clout? I don't think so."

"James approves of this?"

"James approves of whatever his expensive lawyers tell him to approve."

"We'll have a hard time talking him out of it?"

"You bet. . . . By the way." Brendan stood up. "I saw herself this morning."

"Herself?" I echoed, though I knew damn well whom he meant.

"Megie Donahue's mother."

"Oh, her."

"Yeah. She seemed a lot better. I was kind of worried about her."

"I'd be inclined to the professional observation that you have a mild fixation on that woman."

"Who wouldn't? You know her husband, I suppose?"

"Sure. We all grew up at the same time. She lost two brothers and a sister when she was young."

"What kind of guy is he?"

"Brien? Nice fellow. Smart, charming, maybe not too deep. That was a long time ago. Why do you ask?"

"He's running for the Senate, you know."

"So I've heard. Going to announce first week in November."

"He doesn't have it, Kieran. Almost, but not quite. If he runs, Kathleen will have to take up the slack."

"That figures."

"I don't like it." The young priest's thick eyebrows contracted. "There's something wrong there."

"Is it your problem?"

He glanced at me. "The kids are. They are really fine young women, each in her own way. Transparent as they come. There's something eating at them."

"Why not ask them?"

"I will eventually. Maybe. My instincts say now is not the time."

"Follow your instincts."

"Yeah."

Late in the day, when I was packing up to ride the L back to my apartment at the Hancock Center—a safe enough ride if you did it by daylight—my colleague Jean knocked on my office door.

"You're very interested in this Satanism business now, aren't you, Kieran?"

"Very."

"I thought I might mention that my client is very frightened."

"Really! Why?"

"They've been calling her. Voices from the past."

"Internal or external voices?"

"External, I think."

"What do they want?"

"There's going to be some sort of ceremony which she must attend—or that's what she says she thinks they want."

"I see. What's she going to do?"

"She's paralyzed."

"Could she go to the police?"

"She thinks they wouldn't believe her."

"Maybe she could try the FBI."

"Why would they be interested?"

"Abuse of interstate phone lines? Something like that."

"I'll suggest it to her."

She turned to leave.

"Jean . . ."

"Yes, Kieran?"

"Insist."

She looked at me intently.

"All right, I'll insist."

"And keep me informed."

I looked up the phone number of St. Praxides. It hadn't changed.

"St. Praxides Rectory."

"This is Doctor O'Kerrigan calling for Father McNulty."

"Oh, hi, Doctor O'Kerrigan, this is Megie."

"Megan, how are you?"

"We won again last night, Doctor O'Kerrigan."

"And you got nine points?"

"You look at the box scores?"

"I have to cheer for the old alma mater, don't I?"

"Maeve and I found your picture on the wall. You looked awfully young when you were young, Doctor O'Kerrigan!"

"I was a weird little boy, Megan."

"My mother says you were a nice little boy."

"She has a poor memory. . . . Is the young priest in?"

"You mean the acting pastor? Isn't that totally cool! The pastor is away on another one of his vacations, and Father Brendan is running everything. Outstanding!"

"Maybe I'll join the parish . . . is he in?"

"Just a minute . . . Father Brendan," she yelled. "Doctor O'Kerrigan wants to talk to you!"

"Brendan here."

"Brendan, a young woman named Peggy—I don't know her last name—and I cannot tell you how I know about her—may in the next couple of days try to tell someone at the Bureau about calls from the cult. The right people should see her, they should take what she says very seriously, and they should protect her. Got it?"

"Got it," he replied. "By the way, we see James Thursday afternoon at four-thirty. Earliest I could get us in."

"I'll be there."

KATHLEEN

"Yes, Kieran," I said, pretending to the tone of a long-suffering old mother speaking to a wayward son, "I saw a lawyer yesterday."

"You did, really?"

"I said that I did," I snapped impatiently.

"Sorry if I sounded skeptical. I can't get over someone following my advice so precisely."

I tried to relax. "I don't know whether I'm coming or going, Kieran. I have to listen to someone. I thought I was such a self-reliant and independent woman. Now that I've talked to you and to Dot and to Phil Carver, I find that I'm hollow."

"It's an emotional release, Kathleen. You'll be all right."

"I'm glad I've found someone who will tell me what to do."

"Offer guidelines."

I couldn't help a burst of laughter. "You and the Vatican!"

"Mine don't carry any obligation."

"Neither do theirs anymore."

"How did it go with the lawyer?"

"Rotten . . . I mean he was very nice and will take charge. But he wants me to forget about the election and just file suit. But I can't do that. Not yet."

"If I were you I'd think very seriously about it."

"I will, Kieran. I really will . . . and he wants me to ask for a lump sum of at least a half-million from our joint property. It seems so . . . so mercenary. What do you think?"

He didn't say anything for a moment.

"If your instincts say don't do it, then don't do it."

"Good! I won't. I mean, he has to offer me what he thinks is sound legal advice, but I have to decide, right?"

"Right."

"I hear you talked to Megan last night. She was all excited. I didn't know you knew Father Brendan."

"He and I are working on something together for the Archdiocese."

"Oh. Wonderful priest."

"The best . . . how's Brien?"

"He called to tell me that he's seeing Doctor Beauregard again on Thursday. He said the first meeting was very difficult but that he felt good about it. . . . Is there any chance for him at all, Kieran? I feel so sorry for him . . . and, I guess, I kind of love him, too."

"It would be strange if you didn't kind of love him. You have shared the same house and the same life and the same children for a long time. I hate to admit it, Kathleen, but I'd like to see you again. Maybe early next week?"

"Fine. That would be wonderful."

"My treat this time."

"Big expensive lunch?"

"What else?"

So I was smiling and happy when our conversation ended.

I forgot to tell him that I had the strange sensation that someone was following me.

BRENDAN

"How many pedophile cases have you dealt with during your term as Vicar for the Clergy, Father Roder?" Ron Long asked gently.

Martin twisted in his seat. Laura Taylor, who had interrupted after almost every question, remained silent.

"Perhaps ten . . . but most of the accusers weren't credible enough—"

Ron cut him off. *"Perhaps?"*

"Let me see." He appeared to count. "Well, all in all, twelve."

"I see. And how many were there in the ten years before your appointment?"

"I believe that there were about the same number—not all that many when you consider there are over a thousand priests in Chicago."

"It's not a serious problem, then, in your judgment?"

"It's serious—but there are only a few cases."

"One case would be serious, wouldn't it? Especially if your child was the victim?"

"Yes, I suppose it would."

"Now, how many of the twelve cases you've dealt with were repeat offenders?"

"Repeat offenders?"

"Men who had been charged before with raping young men or young women."

"Uh . . . a couple."

"Please be more specific, Father."

"Four of them, I believe."

"Now, Father Roder, how many of the priests who were charged during your years in office did you send away for psychiatric help?"

"Most of them."

"How many?"

"Maybe nine or ten."

"And how many of these did you send back to parish work after they were released from the institutions to which you sent them?"

"We sent them back only when we were advised that it was reasonably safe to do so by the institution and by our psychiatric consultants."

"I understand. I repeat my question. How many did you send back?"

"All but one or two."

"Isn't it true that one of them who was charged with raping a handicapped girl is now facing another similar charge?"

"I object," Laura cut in. "That's irrelevant to this case."

"No, Counselor, it is not. It establishes a pattern of irresponsibility on the part of the Archdiocese. I'll certify that one for the judge. . . . Now, let me get this straight, Father Roder. You're telling me that at least ten priests charged with sexual abuse, most of them abuse of boys or young men, are currently working in parishes in Chicago?"

"Uh, well—yes."

"Where they will be able to find more victims to rape?"

"I object to that question."

As Ms. Taylor and Ron bickered and Martin looked pained and confused, I pondered the effect of his deposition if we should leak it to the media.

LEARY

"I would not dream of questioning the advice of your consultants, James—" Kieran was speaking cautiously.

"I should hope not, Kieran," I cut in. "They're the best there is. The Archdiocese hires only the best."

"Indeed. I hope it is understood that I am not seeking to replace them, and that I feel I have an ethical obligation not even to appear to call their work into question."

"I think I understand that."

"So it is in the context of that understanding that I offer my opinions—but only because you sent Father McNulty here to discuss this matter with me."

"Of course."

I strove to control my anger at Kieran. It had nothing to do with the conversation in which we were engaged. I was upset with him and upset with psychologists and psychiatrists and psychoanalysts and every other kind of witch doctor who tried to probe the mysteries of the human soul.

Outside a beautiful Indian summer had returned. I wanted desperately to walk into the gentle warmth for just a few minutes. Down to the Lake and back. All day I had tried to find the time. At one point I'd made it as far as the door of my office, but the Boss buzzed me before I could slip outside.

This conversation with Kieran and Brendan, a conversation that would infuriate our lawyers if they knew of it, had destroyed my final hope for a couple of moments of peaceful and quiet prayer at the side of the Lake.

I was beginning to get fed up with this alleged abuse case. After all, I had far more serious responsibilities to worry about. Rome was harassing the American bishops again about "too much" consultation with women. But, instead of devoting my time to fending off a Roman document which would be interpreted by the media as another attack on the equality of women, I was stuck listening once again to a psychological commentary on poor Gerry Greene.

Gerry and I had been classmates in the seminary. If he had propositioned other seminarians at the time, I surely would have known about it. I didn't remember him as an impressive intellect, but his record as a pastoral administrator was excellent. Probably he'd been over his head when he'd held a rather responsible position in the Archdiocese at the disastrous end of the last administration. But he was utterly harmless, a good priest assaulted by calumny for many years.

Brien had called me from the airport on his way to Naples just before Kieran and Brendan McNulty's appointment.

"How did it go with Doctor Beauregard?"

"Rough, James, really rough. But good too. I like him. I think he'll be a big help to me, but it's not going to be easy."

"Well, we never thought it would. Try to relax and have a good time down in Florida."

"Yeah. I wish Kathleen would come, but that damn dissertation of hers takes all her time."

"It's probably better to be alone this time."

"I suppose so. . . . James, do you think I'm gay?"

"Of course not," I exclaimed. "Whatever gave you that idea? Not this Doctor Beauregard?"

"He said I would have to admit eventually that I was a bisexual and mostly gay. To admit that would take a lot of the pressure off me."

"Admit it publicly?" I shouted into the phone.

"No, to myself."

"That's absurd."

"I've got to think about it. He also says I hate women."

"You hate women!"

"Hate them, fear them, resent them. He says that's not the same as being bisexual, but in me they kind of come together."

"Those are the craziest things I've ever heard!"

"I've got to think about it. You know, when I—well—when I hit Kathleen those few times I did, I must really have hated her."

"You were under stress, Brien, and she provoked you. That doesn't justify what you did—but it doesn't follow that you hate women."

"I think maybe some of the time I do. Well, anyway, I'll be thinking of you when I swing the clubs."

"Break par!"

"You bet! Every day!"

As I hung up the phone I realized that I would have to end his visits to Doctor Beauregard when he came back. Brien is a strong and vigorous man, I reflected, but he is easily led by someone who he thinks is smarter than he is. With the campaign coming on we did not need a doctor who filled Brien's head with such absurd notions.

It seemed that all my life I had taken care of Brien. It had never been a burden before. But I never had the other responsibilities that I had now.

Kieran had doubtless meant well in his recommendations, but we simply could not tolerate Doctor Beauregard. Kieran ought to have known that.

"Within the context we have established," Kieran was saying, "I have a number of observations to make."

Kieran smiled. "My first observation is that it is not seemly for the Church to play hardball corporate law against its own people, especially when they have been—or appear to have been—victimized by priests."

"Please, Kieran," I interrupted him. "I can't discuss legal aspects of the case in the absence of our attorneys. They would be most unhappy with this conversation if they knew it was taking place."

"I am not talking specific cases, James," Kieran replied. "And, if I may say so, you brought me into these matters by sending Father McNulty to see me. I speak as both a psychiatrist and a Catholic layman. Your legalistic approach does harm to the morale of laity far beyond a specific case. They are embarrassed. Frankly, I am embarrassed by the Church's behavior. Charges have been made and not responded to that the Archdiocese's attorneys turn witnesses and even suborn perjury. There are no responses to these charges."

"On the advice of counsel we do not respond to such charges."

"You cannot afford not to respond. You are doing grave harm to the faithful when you permit legal concerns to override all else."

"The Church," I said stiffly, "is a corporation. It must protect its corporate interests."

"At risk of widespread offense among the faithful? I think not, James. I think not. It's the faithfuls' contributions which ultimately pay the corporation's expenses."

Kieran was not backing down. He would deliver his tirade whether I liked it or not. He was no longer the meek little boy who had trailed along after us on the beach and never did learn how to water-ski. I had to admire his strength of character, as much as I disagreed with both the substance and the appropriateness of his remarks.

I noted that Brendan was listening with wide eyes. Although he must have known Kieran's thoughts, clearly he had not anticipated the force with which they were delivered.

"Secondly, I have no doubt that Father Greene did well on the various tests which were administered to him. I would add, however, that, given the nature of the charges against him and the number of times these charges have been made, a limited testing by the Archdiocese's paid consultants is not an adequate response. Father Greene should be observed at great length by some institution which is not retained by the Archdiocese. I don't think your tests will have any impact on a jury, nor will your consultants be taken seriously."

"I disagree," I said. "We have the best legal minds in Chicago on our team."

"The hell you do," Brendan said. "They're giving you terrible advice."

"I've done some consulting on psychiatric-legal matters, James." Kieran plowed ahead. "I can only tell you that Brendan is right. Should, God forbid, this ugly case come to trial, the Archdiocese will lose. Your strategy—successful in the past—of stonewalling and intimidating the parents of the victims into a small settlement will no longer work."

"They do not have a case against us," I insisted. "No jury will find a priest, especially a good priest like Gerry Greene, guilty of such a horrible crime on the basis of the testimony of a disturbed child."

"Finally," Kieran continued, "the plaintiff's request than an outside review panel be established to judge these matters, and especially whether a priest should be reassigned as Father Greene has been reassigned repeatedly, makes excellent psychiatric sense. Moreover, it would lift the burden under which the Archdiocese now labors. You would no longer be forced to worry about both the victim and the victimizer."

"I know all about that idea," I said, sighing wearily. "It has some appeal, I will admit. Candidly, I would be the happiest priest in America if I didn't have to worry about these matters. But there are legal problems. A decision by such a board might be used against us in litigation—"

"That's not necessarily true, James," Brendan intervened.

"I will simply say, Brendan, that lawyers more experienced than you say it is true. Moreover, we cannot give up the right and duty to protect our priests. The Cardinal cannot permit Father Greene's fate to be entrusted to a board over which we have no control."

"Unless you establish the board, this case will come to trial, James," Brendan went on. "Despite the machinations of your lawyers. And you will lose. And you will lose on appeal. You will end up with a huge financial loss and a public scandal. There will be more suits. I know of two others which will be filed within the next couple of weeks. There will be more legal fees and more settlements. You are being misled— unintentionally, I'm sure—by your counsel and your psychiatric consultants and you will pay for it."

"Are you accusing them of malfeasance?"

"No," he replied, "only of giving bad advice—which they doubtless believe, in good faith, is good advice."

"They are the best available resources; we will continue to take their advice in preference to yours." Something would have to be done about this Brendan McNulty.

"I warn you, James." Kieran returned to the conversation. "That priests who are guilty of pedophilia ought never be reassigned to parish work. Cures don't happen."

"Our best information is that the problem is like alcoholism. It can be controlled, particularly through group therapy."

"Bullshit," said Brendan. "That is pure and simple bullshit, James."

"I beg your pardon?"

"The alcoholic harms only himself and his family. The pedophile is a threat to the lives of hundreds of children. The Church's presumption must be in favor of the latter."

"I can't disagree with that. But I think we should give everyone a second chance. We're all sinners."

"Sin isn't the issue, James," he said solemnly. "The issue is a personality twist that is terribly dangerous. I have visited Forest Mount"— Kieran ignored the interruption—"and talked to people in the parish.

They believe that Father Greene is sexually active with young men. They speak of it openly. The young people joke about it. Such rumors demand more attention than a day or two of interviews and personality tests."

"That is why I cannot give up control of the lives of priests to outsiders," I shouted. "I cannot permit their fates to be decided by rumor and innuendo. I will not permit it. I trust that my position is clear?"

"If the rumors are true, they will never be proved through the efforts of consultants hired by the Archdiocese."

"You're questioning their integrity?" I shouted.

"Not in the least, James. Try for a moment to admit that integrity and credibility are not quite the same thing. The first question that is asked about a report clearing a priest is whether those who make the report work for the Church. If they do, they will not be considered impartial. That's the nub of your problem."

"I see your point, Kieran, and I value your recommendation. As I said before, the idea of an outside group which assumes responsibility, subject to our review, of course, has its appeal. If men as balanced and as Catholic as you are troubled by these cases, then clearly the Archdiocese must take some action to restore their confidence in the Church, your confidence in the Church."

I thought that was a gracious conclusion to the conversation. Moreover, having said it, I recognized its truth. If Kieran O'Kerrigan doubted us, we had a very serious problem. But I could not sacrifice a priest, someone who had dedicated his life to the Church, simply to alleviate this kind of doubt.

Kieran realized that my summary was a dismissal.

"I owe you a lot, James," he said, closing his notebook. "I sympathize with your problem. Yet when I hear teenagers joke about a priest's sexual activities, I have grave fears for the future of the priesthood and the Church."

I shook hands with him. "The priesthood will survive, Kieran. So will the Church. The parishioners of St. Praxides would not, I think, make such complaints."

Kieran started to say something, then hesitated, shrugging his shoulders, and said only, "Thank you for listening, James."

After they had left, I paused for a few moments to consider the conversation. There was nothing new in it. I had heard it all before. The difference was that now Kieran's prestige supported the critique of our policies.

If I were to be prudent and responsible, I ought to take his observations seriously. I would therefore think about what he had said. But I doubted Kieran's opinions would cause me to advise the Cardinal to reject the advice of our lawyers and our psychiatric consultants.

I was late that night for the weekly dinner with my mother and the Donahues at the Donahue apartment on East Lake Shore Drive.

My mother and Brien's parents are handsome, elegant people who wear their years with grace and do not complain about the tragedies which they have suffered.

Unfortunately, some of their serenity is purchased by drinking more than they should. They are not alcoholics, but they do drink too much.

When I arrived that night, I found them particularly giddy, especially my mother.

"Why doesn't Kathleen ever come to our dinners?" She laughed. "Doesn't she like us anymore?"

"She has three children to take care of," I replied, thinking to myself that Kathleen's failure to visit her mother was one more proof of her irresponsibility. She acted as if Mother did not exist.

"Brien sounded troubled," Sheila Donahue commented between sips of her martini. "He called from the airport. I think she should have gone with him. He needs support from her as he prepares for the campaign."

Brien had called me from the airport too. Based on our conversation, I was beginning to wonder about the wisdom of relying on Kieran's advice in that matter as well. Dr. Beauregard seemed to be of the opinion that Brien was bisexual at a minimum. More likely, he felt, Brien was gay. Of course I knew better than to tell the Donahues or my mother what was really going on between Kathleen and Brien.

"Kathleen's busy with her dissertation, I suppose," said Tom Donahue. He shook his handsome head in disapproval without disturbing his neatly trimmed white hair. "I never could understand why Brien tolerates that."

"She's spoiled," his wife agreed with him. "Even her own mother says so, don't you, Mae?"

"She's never had concern for anyone but herself," Mother said, hiccuping discreetly.

"Brien will win without her help, of course," Sheila insisted. "But she does increase the pressures on the poor boy."

"There were rumors at the office today," said Tom. "There might be another candidate in the primary: Neil Clifford from River Forest. Blue-ribbon candidate, they call him."

"The Cliffords are trash," Sheila insisted. "Brien is the blue-ribbon candidate."

Neil Clifford was at least a decade older than Brien. He was a wealthy businessman who had always been part of the Party Organization. He was smart, articulate, and photogenic. He would be a formidable foe.

"He wouldn't run . . ." Tom tilted his glass in my direction. "Another drink, Bishop . . . no? . . . he wouldn't run unless the Daleys told him it was all right."

"The Daleys need Brien," his wife insisted. "They wouldn't dare put up another candidate."

"If there is a primary contest," I said, "the Mayor will be officially neutral. A lot depends on what unofficial word he sends to the ward committeemen. Maybe he won't send any."

"We don't know that there's going to be a primary." Sheila signaled the maid that we were ready for dinner. "So let's enjoy our meal and not worry about it. If there is an organization candidate, Brien can always run as a reformer."

The rest of the night's conversation we devoted to praise and strategizing for Brien, punctuated by occasional snips at Neil Clifford. The praise grew more extravagant and the snips more vitriolic as greater amounts of alcohol were consumed.

As I walked back to the Cathedral from East Lake Shore Drive, I considered the prospect of a Clifford candidacy.

Neil Clifford would run only if the Daleys had decided they did not want Brien. That could mean there would be other candidates—someone from downstate and perhaps a black. We might still win, but it would be a bitter fight and weaken us in the general election.

In his present troubled condition, such a contest might be too much for Brien to bear. Would he return to his extramarital amusements, especially since his doctor was suggesting to him that he might actually be homosexual?

We would have to get rid of Doctor Beauregard as quickly as

possible. I walked home that night in the rapidly falling darkness, more depressed than I had ever been.

There was a message marked "Urgent" waiting for me inside the rectory. It was from the ambassador from the Mob. Again. I decided he could wait until the morning. But he called back that night just as I was going to bed.

"I'm sorry to disturb you, Bishop," said the young man at the switchboard, "but he says it's most important."

"That's all right."

"Bishop Leary," said the voice on the line, "I'm really sorry. I hope I didn't wake you up?"

"I'm wide awake."

"Good. Hey, you remember our conversation at the Ireland Fund Dinner?"

"Vaguely."

"One of the friends of my friends is upset. I don't quite know why. But he wants me to give you a message."

"Oh?"

"Yeah. He says he's going to send a warning. There'll be only one. Got it?"

"What kind of warning?" I asked. "What do you mean?"

"Sorry, Bishop. I can only tell you what I know. But knowing my friend, I don't think you'll have to wait for that warning for long."

KIERAN

I rolled over in my bed. I'd been dreaming. About what?

About Kathleen, naturally.

I looked at the clock. 1:00 A.M. Why was the alarm ringing at this hour? But it wasn't the alarm. It was the phone.

I groped across the room in the dark and picked it up.

"It took you long enough to answer, punk."

"Who is this?"

"A voice from heaven, from an angel, get it? You're messing around in things that don't concern you. You'll get one warning and that's all, get it?"

"What do you mean?"

He hung up.

An angel? Maybe a fallen angel. A warning from the Satanists. They were getting bold.

I thought I might have a word with the FBI the next day.

BRIEN

Geez, I wish I could live this way all my life. Thirty-six holes a day, a good swim in the pool or the Gulf if the waves are all right, a big dinner, and then a good night's sleep.

All the stress is gone. I don't need a drink. The thought of a drink makes me a little sick.

Why can't I live this way all the time?

I'll ask Doctor Beauregard that when I get back.

If only I didn't have to get back to Chicago to campaign. This lousy Senate race. I never really wanted to run in the first place. If only I didn't have to. Come to think of it, who says I do?

KATHLEEN

I came to a full stop at 87th and Pleasant. There is a terrible record of serious accidents at that corner, right on the edge of Ryan's Woods. I'm careful to warn Megan about it too.

There was no traffic in either direction, only a large gray van in the parking lot across the street, with its turn signal pointing west. I was going east, so I turned right onto 87th Street.

Out of the corner of my eye I saw the van, its turn signal off, coming straight at me. There was a terrible crunch as he hit the front of my car and sent it spinning back into Ryan's Woods.

Dazzling red and green lights exploded in my head. Then they all went out.

PART IV

KIERAN

There were eight messages on my answering machine after the last patient left—four from Bishop James Leary's office, each more insistent that the last, two from Brendan McNulty, and two from a Doctor Dorothy Halder.

With terror gripping at my throat, I punched James's number. Before the phone rang, James himself had stormed into my office, his face twisted into a look of almost demented rage.

"Don't you answer your phone calls, Kieran, no matter how important they are?"

"Not when I'm with a patient, James. When I'm with them they are the most important people in the world. God would have to wait."

He paced up and down, fury radiating from his tense body. "What the hell are you trying to do to us?"

"To whom?"

"To my family—to Kathleen."

"To Kathleen?" I clenched my fists.

"She's lucky they didn't kill her. What the hell are you two up to? I expect her to be irresponsible, but I am astonished at you!"

"James, calm down, and talk to me in a rational fashion. First of all, what has happened to Kathleen?"

"They crashed into her car at 87th and Pleasant, sent her to the hospital and wrecked the car." He gasped for breath. "She's not seriously hurt. They're letting her go home this afternoon."

"Thank God for that. Now, who are 'they'?"

"The Mob—who else?'

"The Mob?"

"The Outfit! The Syndicate! Whatever you want to call them!"

"Why?"

"You tell me why!" he shouted. "Are you fooling around with the past? Why can't you and Kathleen let the dead bury the dead!"

"I have no intention of doing anything besides that, James. Who thinks otherwise?"

"I don't know who. There's a man who brings messages back and forth between the Mob and the Church. We don't want the messages, but they come regardless. He has been warning me for years that they are afraid for some reason of a letter that my father might have written. Apparently Kathleen has found the letter and shown it to you and you have talked about it. This messenger called me last night and said there would be a warning, one warning. Then he called me after the accident this morning and said that it was the last warning. Unless the letter was turned over to them soon, they would kill her the next time."

Tony the Angel must want the letter badly. The Outfit did not normally threaten women. He must figure his life was in danger. Even today.

"I told no one, James. I merely obtained the records of my father's case from the court. I guess they have spies everywhere."

"You ought to know better than to take a risk like that."

"Are you aware of the contents of the letter, James?"

"Certainly not. Well . . . not in any detail. I didn't know of its existence until I began to receive these warnings."

"And do you know what happened in my father's trial?"

"No . . . Again, not in any detail. I had no suspicions at all until these threats began."

"The trial was fixed. My father was a sacrificial victim, offered up by your father and grandfather and Tom Donahue."

"I deplore that, Kieran. But that was long ago."

"Was it?"

"Wasn't it?"

"Perhaps. In any case, I have no intention of doing anything with the letter."

"Then I'll call my contact and tell him you'll give it back."

"Call him now. Here. I'll talk to him."

He looked at me dubiously. "They're dangerous men, Kieran."

"So I'm told." I pointed at the phone. "Call him."

"He might not be in."

"He's in all right. Waiting for your call."

James punched the numbers into my phone. "I have Doctor O'Kerrigan here."

I took the phone. "I want a sit-down with the Angel."

"What?"

"You heard me."

"Why?"

"You know why."

"You just don't demand a sit-down with the Angel."

"I just did."

"Why should he sit down with you?"

"He's got a problem with me and I have a problem with him. I think we can solve that problem by respecting one another."

"Yeah, that seems like a good idea. I'll call you back."

"I'll be waiting."

I gave him my number.

"What do you intend to do?" James demanded.

"Sit down with this guy and straighten him out."

"This isn't the Godfather movie, Kieran."

"Yeah, it is, James, oddly enough. I've dealt with these people before. It turns out that they have developed a self-image from watching the movies. They try to act like Robert De Niro or Marlon Brando or Al Pacino. If you act the same way, they think you're a man of respect. I'll take care of this little problem the Angel and I have."

"The Angel?"

"You don't want to know his real name."

I wasn't just going to give him the letter. Nor did I intend to let him touch Kathleen ever again.

"Are you sure you know what you're doing, Kieran?"

"Trust me, James."

"Kathleen . . ."

"They won't come near her ever again. Trust me."

The phone rang.

"Yeah?" I was not yet completely in the role.

"You know where Melrose Park is?"

"Yeah, I know where Melrose Park is." More or less.

"Mr. Angelini says he eats lunch there every day at this little restaurant on North Avenue, the Pergola, a block east of 25th Avenue, south side of the street. You come there Tuesday, one o'clock, and he has this sit-down with you. Got it?"

"One-thirty?"

"How come?"

"I got patients. Tell him I'm sure that he understands my professional responsibilities."

James watched me with astonishment.

"I'll call you right back."

"You have to pretend to be as tough as they pretend to be tough," I told James.

"They're dangerous men, Kieran."

"Only because they're scared stiff. Hurting the wife of a possibly future United States Senator is a crazy risk. They're not sure what I'll do. Suppose I go to the police instead of this sit-down? He'll be happy to talk on my time."

The phone rang.

"Mr. Angelini says he understands about professional responsibilities. One-thirty is fine."

"Yeah," I said and hung up.

I winked at James. "He understands about professional responsibilities. One-thirty is fine."

"You're taking a big risk, Kieran." James was now thoroughly mollified. And just a little impressed. He must have forgotten that I was an actor in those plays with his sister so long ago.

"No, I'm not. Not at all."

"Why are you so sure?"

"You don't want to know. Don't worry about Kathleen. She'll be safe from now on."

"I don't want anything to happen to her." His voice choked.

So he loved her after all.

"Nothing will happen to her, James." I could not resist the final words. "Trust me."

After I got him out of my office, I called Little Company of Mary and asked them to page Doctor Halder.

"Dorothy Halder," she said crisply.

"Kieran O'Kerrigan."

"Good afternoon, Doctor O'Kerrigan."

"Kieran."

"Dot."

"How's our mutual friend?"

"Our mutual friend is all right. Bump on the head, a few bruises. Nothing more. She's lucky."

"Always has been."

"I've sent her home with a sedative. Those three adorable children are having a great time playing nursemaids."

"That won't last the weekend."

She laughed. "You must have a lot of teenage patients. . . . It will last for the day, which will be enough. Kathleen wanted me to assure you that she was all right. Am I correct in assuming you know about the other problems?"

"Yes."

"She needs psychotherapy."

"Not from me."

"Regardless."

"You push gently and I'll do the same."

"Fair enough."

I phoned a florist in the neighborhood and ordered a dozen roses from "K.O'K."

Then I called the Acting Pastor of St. Praxides. I was put through to him immediately, this time by a housekeeper.

"You heard?"

"Yes."

"She wanted you to know that she was all right."

It was an observation that was also a question, not quite an accusation.

"I talked to Dot Halder."

"Kieran, I don't like it."

"Oh?"

"If you saw the Mercedes, it was no accident. The cops didn't think so either."

"Hit-and-run, I assume?"

"Yeah. It looked like it was deliberate."

"So?"

"I'm wondering if our friends are involved."

For a moment the existence of different groups of "friends" confused me.

"Not those friends."

"You sure?"

"I'm sure. . . . Why would you think so?"

"No reason in particular." He paused. "Maybe I'm spooked by the whole creepy business."

"I know what you mean."

"I hope she isn't in any danger."

"I'll take care of it, Brendan. Don't worry."

An unasked question hung in the air. I was not about to answer it. Let Brendan imagine what he wanted.

After I had ended on this ambiguous note my conversation with the Acting Pastor of St. Praxides, I left my office to engage in a few precautions for my sit-down the following week with Tony the Angel. Heaven forgive me, but I was looking forward to the encounter.

Mess with my woman, would he?

KATHLEEN

The roses from Kieran on Friday afternoon and his phone calls Saturday and Sunday were the only bright spots in a dismal weekend. I hurt all over again and I was lethargic from the medicine Dot Halder had given me. The last thing I needed was my mother and Sheila Donahue in my house, come to take care of me and "the children."

First of all I had to insist that we were not to disturb Brien's vacation in Florida. It was only with great difficulty that I talked them out of calling him instantly and summoning him home.

My decisive argument was that Brien needed undisturbed rest to prepare for the campaign. They decided that was true because the primary might be arduous. Neil Clifford, "nothing but trash," was reported to be considering a primary race—with the reported support of "your friend Richie Daley."

No one who liked him called him "Richie." To his friends, he was Rich.

Nonetheless, they were probably right. Neil Clifford would not have run without some kind of informal and probably implicit approval from the Mayor. It didn't mean that Rich would endorse him. He wouldn't endorse anyone until a Democrat was nominated. Why should he? But he was not about to protect Brien either.

My mother and mother-in-law had come over, but as usual they were more trouble than help. They made such a habit of poking their noses in every corner of my house, taking over everything they felt was awry. Even worse, they chided my girls on everything from their dress to the way they kept their rooms. I'd have to say my girls took their criticism better than I.

"Who is this K.O.K.? Who sent these tacky roses?" my mother asked.

"A friend," I said.

"It's Doctor O'Kerrigan," Megan explained. "He's a friend of Father McNulty."

"*Doctor* O'Kerrigan?" Sheila demanded. "Who's he?"

"He went to school with me. I guess Dot Halder, my physician, told him about my accident."

"I remember him." Mom nodded vaguely. "He was a strange little boy."

"I think he's neat." Megan would not be waved out of the conversation. "He reads the Saint Ignatius box scores to see how many points I score. Which is more than *some* people do."

"Basketball is not a ladylike sport. . . . Do you really have a female physician, Kathleen?"

"Yes."

"I would never trust my health to another woman."

"These roses are really tacky."

When the phone rang, I practically had to yank it away from Sheila's hand.

"How's the patient?" It was Kieran.

"She's doing fine, really. My mother and mother-in-law are here helping me out."

"Isn't that wonderful? I tried the line in your office. There was no answer."

"Oh, I might go up and take a rest in five minutes or so, but otherwise I feel all right."

"I understand."

I pleaded a splitting headache and retreated to my office. The kids, I figured, knew how to take care of themselves.

He gave me exactly five minutes.

"Hi."

"Oh, Kieran." I promptly burst into tears. "It's so horrible!"

"I bet they get along great with the kids, huh? Really like totally barf city?"

"It's a gross-out." I giggled in spite of myself.

"So how are you? Really."

"Terrible and all right, Kieran. I have a miserable headache and I'm angry at my mother and Sheila and the idiots who banged into me, but otherwise I feel all right."

"Your mother and Sheila only want to help, Kathleen."

"Don't give me that bullshit!" I shouted. "They don't want to help, they want to pry and poke and criticize and push my patience to the absolute limit so I will blow up at them and they can go home and say, 'See, I told you she was spoiled and ungrateful, didn't I?' "

" 'And she has absolutely spoiled brats for kids, too.' "

"Stop laughing at me, Kieran. And thank you for the flowers, which are beautiful. That was so sweet of you."

"I'm glad you like them. They . . . represent my concern and my affection."

"Thanks. I need both just now."

"I'll call you tomorrow."

I took some more medicine and slept till evening. I was awakened by the sound of a basketball thumping against the house. I peeked out the window. Meg and Beth Reilly were playing "horse" with two darling boys from their class. The boys seemed to be losing.

As I watched, Megie sank a jump shot from beyond the "three-point" line they had painted on the driveway. She and Beth squealed with delight. I wished for a moment that I could dash down and show her that I could match that shot, but not today.

I could imagine the first words I would hear when I went back into the maelstrom. It was "unladylike" for my daughter to play basketball with boys, especially such "unrefined boys."

But I outlasted them. I didn't lose my temper, not Saturday, nor Sunday till they went home at 4:30, sulking perhaps because I wasn't grateful enough and thoroughly shocked at my daughters, but unable to complain that I had shouted at them.

Kieran called Sunday evening to see how I was. He listened sympathetically when I filled him in on the rest of my mother's and mother-in-law's visit. Then I decided to change the subject. "What did you do this weekend?" I asked.

"Worked on a paper, finished it mostly."

"I didn't do a lick of work on my dissertation. I'll fall behind schedule if I don't get back to it this week."

"I know the feeling."

"Do you ever get lonely, Kieran?"

"A typical Irish bachelor get lonely?"

"You're not a typical Irish bachelor."

"Maybe not. . . . Yes, I'm lonely sometimes. I've learned to live with it."

"There are worse fates than being alone."

"I'm sure there are."

When Brien called right after Kieran and we had bid each other an ambiguous goodbye, my feelings of guilt increased.

"Hitting it really well, Kathleen. Broke par three times. Play thirty-six holes a day, fifty-four one day."

"Sounds like fun."

"Really great . . . only thing missing is you. I sure wish you could come down. Can you get away for a couple of days anyway?"

He meant it.

Why did he want me? Certainly not for lovemaking, though he'd probably try to do that just for the record. Probably to show me off.

"It wouldn't be a good idea, Brien."

"I suppose not. . . . How are things in Chicago?"

"Indian summer . . ."

"Politics?"

"Pretty quiet for the moment."

There was no reason to tell him about Neil Clifford now. Besides, it was just a rumor.

"Yeah, well, it's great down here. I'll give you a ring later on . . ."

"One more thing. A hit-and-run driver piled into the Mercedes. A lot of damage . . ."

"Gee, that's a shame. Have it fixed. The insurance company will take care of it."

"We're already getting estimates."

"Great. Well, I'll talk to you."

"Goodbye, Brien."

Not a word about whether I had been hurt. He could not have cared less.

No, that wasn't fair. If I had told him I had been taken to Little Company, he would have asked how I was and would have thought it "great" that I wasn't badly injured.

In spite of myself, I wondered if he was fooling around down in Florida. I couldn't help but feel that he probably was.

My sleep that night, though drug induced, was restless. The nightmares were vague and terrible. I woke up in the morning even more exhausted than I had been the day before.

No more drugs, I told myself, only the anti-inflammatories from now on.

After I sent the girls off to school I thought about going to Mass, but decided that I just wasn't up to the walk down to St. Prax's.

So I went back to my office, put on jeans and a T-shirt, and turned on the computer.

I stared at the text of my dissertation for a couple of minutes. Actually I was way ahead of schedule. Even with delays I'd be finished by Christmas.

I turned the computer off. I wasn't in a mood for work today.

I pulled off the shirt and jeans and, wearing nothing but my bra and panties, collapsed on the couch in my office and dozed off.

I was awakened by a persistent doorbell.

Woozily, I rolled off the couch and staggered to the small window and peaked out. Another Mercedes, and . . . Kieran!

I grabbed a thin cotton robe and rushed down the stairs.

By the time I got to the door, he was walking back to his car.

"Kieran," I yelled, clutching my robe. "Come back!"

He turned and smiled, that funny little smile from eighth grade, and walked toward me.

Once he was inside, I closed the door.

"I was sleeping," I explained. "I barely heard the bell."

He touched my chin. "Sorry to interrupt your dreams. I thought I'd stop in to see how you were doing."

I let my robe fall open and threw myself into his arms.

KIERAN

My last appointment had ended at ten. I didn't have to be at the Medical Center till four. I sighed and opened the folder in which my draft manuscript waited for me. I worked on it for a few minutes and then closed the folder.

I was thinking about driving out to Beverly and visiting Kathleen. Part of me said I just wanted to check in on her. Another part of me wanted to claim her as mine.

Still not completely sure of my mission, I paused in front of her house. Brien was away, the kids were at school. There was no sign of anyone in the house.

I rang the doorbell several times, to no avail. There was no answer. Then I leaned on it.

Still no answer. I turned to walk back to my car.

That's when I heard her call my name. I turned around. Red hair falling to her shoulders, a robe clutched at her waist, she was calling to me. "Kieran, come back!"

It was both an invitation from the present and a cry from the past.

I went to her so quickly, I have no memory of walking down the sidewalk. Inside the door, she threw herself into my arms and wept for joy.

"I've always loved you, Kieran. I always will."

"And I've always loved you, Kathleen. I'll never stop loving you." I held her close, just as I'd longed to do for so many years. "I promised once that I would always take care of you. That promise is operative again."

"I know." She sighed.

She was wearing a plain white bra and panties. I fumbled with the hook and pushed away her bra. I kissed her breasts gently. Then I tugged the panties loose from her hips and let them fall to her ankles.

"Kieran," she murmured, head against my chest. "Oh, Kieran."

She seemed anxious, yet overcome by the same desire—so long deferred—that I felt.

Suddenly she pulled back from me, covered herself with her arms, and turned away. "Oh, Kieran, I'm so afraid. You matter so much to me. I . . ."

I took her hands in mine and pulled her closer.

I was relieved to feel her relax as I kissed her neck, then lips.

She led me to a sofa on the sun porch.

She was more beautiful than in my most erotic dreams of her, round breasts, slim waist, smooth curving hips, trim thighs, and slender legs.

"I've waited a long time, Kathleen."

"So have I . . ."

My beloved seemed astonishingly inexperienced, but she was eager to learn and to please. She gave herself to me as completely and as trustingly as any woman could give herself to a man for the first time.

I took pains to be gentle. The bruises—from Brien and the "accident"—were still evident on her skin.

I was as gentle as a thoroughly aroused male can be, careful not to hurt her bruises and bumps, cautious with her delicate regions, nurturing in my demands. I caressed her and played with her and fondled her and kissed her until, gradually abandoning all restraint, she opened herself up and capitulated completely.

When we finally rode together on waves of ecstasy, it was better than even my wildest dreams.

KATHLEEN

"You're looking a lot better, Mom," Maeve informed me when she came home from St. Ignatius. "I can tell. Ready for some Taekwondo now?"

"Give me another week, till all the bruises are gone."

"I haven't seen you look so happy in ages."

"Afternoon naps will do it every time."

"Yeah, well, I suppose that's true when you get older."

I swung at her.

She chortled and scampered away.

I would not be able to fool them for long. The kids and I had always been close. I tried to be the sympathetic big sister. While I couldn't always carry off the part—I was still "MOTHER" some of the time—I was pretty good at it. One of the results was that they were as sensitive to my emotions as I was to theirs. That was dangerous, I had realized, after my last go-round with Brien, but it was too late now to do anything about it.

However, if I was dizzily in love, they'd sense it, and soon, no matter how hard I tried to cover it up. And then what? What about Brien? And our families? And the election?

Kieran and I would have to cool it for a time. There was no other choice in the real world.

Only that afternoon I didn't want to live in the real world. I was too happy in my own world of romantic love. Tomorrow I would be a realist: practical, competent Kathleen, the street-smart Chicago pol.

Tomorrow would be soon enough for that. Today I would revel in the experience that I was worth loving and had been loved.

KIERAN

"Sit down, Doctor O'Kerrigan," Tony the Angel said with a generous wave of his hand. "Eat some pasta. It's great . . . Joey, get Doctor O'Kerrigan some wine to go with his pasta, the best in the house!"

"Thanks, Mr. Angelini, don't mind if I do. Hey, this *is* great pasta."

The Pergola was a dark restaurant which smelled of Parmesan cheese and red peppers. We were seated in an éven darker alcove at the far corner—Tony the Angel, a little round old man with thick glasses, a benign smile, and the parchment skin which suggested inoperable cancer, kind of a beardless, dying Italian Santa Claus. On either side of him two aging thugs, "Joey" and "Alfie."

I ate the pasta at a leisurely pace and talked with "Mr. Angelini" about the Cubs and the Sox (we were both Cub fans, a happy omen), the Bears and the Bulls.

"Them Detroit Pistons are thugs," he insisted. "They belong in jail. They give a bad example to kids all over the country, know what I mean?"

I admitted that I did.

Finally, I had finished my pasta and drained my wineglass ("the best" was pretty bad), and wiped the remnants of the pasta off my face and chin.

"I'm glad, Mr. Angelini, that you could find the time to see me. You've got a problem and I've got a problem and I believe that we can solve that problem in a mutually satisfactory fashion."

"I'm glad to hear that, Doctor O'Kerrigan. We're all glad, aren't we, boys?"

Joey and Alfie nodded in solemn agreement, two chaplains to an aging Cardinal.

"First of all, I have another problem. Now, I've treated you with respect all along, haven't I, Mr. Angelini?"

My hands were sweaty. This role was a little more scary than any I'd played before.

"You have, Doctor. I'm happy to say that you have. I always like a man who does business respectfully."

"Yeah, well, see, I have this problem. You haven't treated me respectfully."

He looked genuinely puzzled. "What have I done wrong?" He spread his hands in bafflement.

"You have a problem with me? All right, you call me. You say, Doctor O'Kerrigan, I think we have a problem. Lets talk about it. Maybe you can come out to this great pasta place I know about and we work it out. Fine. We take care of it as men who respect one another. So what do you do? You send me a couple of incoherent warnings, wake me out of a sound sleep with one of them, and then you stage this clumsy accident. Against a woman, Mr. Angelini. That's not classy. I hate to say it and it doesn't lessen my respect for you, but it's not classy."

His little brown eyes hardened.

"You're either a brave man, Doctor O'Kerrigan, or a foolish one. Maybe both."

"Hey, that's what I mean. In my world I'm a big man. In your world, you're a big man. Fine. We should understand one another. Right? We should treat each other with respect, right? You're no dummy, Mr. Angelini, you've been around too long to be a dummy. I'm no dummy either, right?"

"Yeah."

"Would I come out here without putting a copy of that letter somewhere in case something, God forbid, happens to me?"

He looked at me suspiciously. The guy was not very good with his lines. My knees felt a little weak.

"Copy?"

"Sure." I pulled out Red Hugh's original. "I brought the original along."

Joey pulled it out of my hands.

"Mr. Angelini," I protested in an offended tone of voice, "is this the way we have sit-downs these days? No trust, no respect."

"Give it back to him, Joey."

"But, boss . . ."

"I said, give it back."

Joey complied rapidly. I tossed the letter aside on the table, near a wine spot.

I breathed a little easier. This was beginning to go according to my script.

"So, God forbid, we ever have a problem again, you call me direct, right?"

The Angel nodded his head. "If I had known the kind of man I was dealing with, I would have done it this time. You can't trust people anymore, Doctor. Let me tell you, it's hard to do business these days. They bug your restaurants, they bribe your friends, sometimes they even corrupt your family, know what I mean?"

"I understand. But men like you and me, we deal straight with one another, right?"

"You got it."

"Now, about that accident . . ."

"She wasn't going to get hurt. The guys that did it were pros. Mind you, I wouldn't do it now since I know the kind of man you are."

It was all monumental bullshit, but when in Rome . . .

"They weren't pros, Mr. Angelini. The cops don't think it was an accident."

"No?" He shifted uneasily.

"No worry. She doesn't know why it happened and no one is telling. I just want to make sure that it doesn't happen again."

"You have my solemn word."

Which along with a buck and a quarter would get me a ride on Rich's subway.

"Great. . . . Now, let's take care of this other little matter. . . . You've read this?"

I gestured toward the letter.

"No."

"Go ahead, read it."

He picked it up and read it, his face an expressionless mask.

"He should never have written something like that. Never."

"I know what you mean, Mr. Angelini. I know what you mean. The past is the past. Let the dead bury their dead."

"If I'd known you then, I'd tell them to go fuck themselves."

"Right. Now we both have to trust each other a little bit. There's one copy of this letter . . . my backup, if you know what I mean?"

I wasn't counting the one that I had told Kathleen to shred. Knowing Kathleen, it had already been shredded.

"Yeah?"

"You don't want it to get out because it would be an embarrassment to you. Right now it would be an embarrassment to me, too. This friend of mine is thinking of running for the Senate, right? He'd be involved through no fault of his own, right?"

"Yeah."

"Someday, maybe after we're both dead, the question arises as to whether my father is a criminal or not. Maybe me or my kids want the truth told. Right? So I want to keep the letter and you don't want to run the risk of embarrassment. How do we handle it?"

"Yeah, how do we handle it?" His eyes turned hard again. This was, after all, the moment of truth.

I took a small scissors from my pocket and with what I hoped looked like a surgeon's delicacy as well as flair, I neatly excised all references to him.

I swept up the pieces of paper on the table, put them in his hand, and closed his hand around them.

"I think that solves our mutual problem, Mr. Angelini," I said confidently.

"Yeah, it sure does."

Then, in a move which I had never seen in any of the films, he put the scraps of paper into his mouth and washed them down with a large draught of wine.

The grin back on his face, he stuck out his hand. "I really like you Doctor O'Kerrigan. You're a man of class."

"Thank you, Mr. Angelini. But as a personal favor to me, read over what's left of the letter, just to make sure it isn't an embarrassment."

I pushed in his direction the two pages of Red Hugh's letter, which now looked like someone might have cut dangling paper dolls out of it.

He picked it up, a little too quickly for someone who thought I was a man of class.

He glanced over it and gave it back to me.

"Perfect," he said. "No embarrassment at all."

"A done deal."

"A done deal." He shook my hand vigorously. "It's a pleasure to do business with a man like you, Doctor O'Kerrigan."

"I feel the same way." I shook his hand again. "Remember, you want something from me, anything, you give me a ring."

"Absolutely."

I thought the last was a nice touch. You want free psychoanalysis for one of your grandkids, you call me. I've treated their kind before.

I walked out in the bright sunlight on North Avenue and winced in the glare.

It had been quite a day already. And it was only halfway through.

LEARY

"James, the deal is done."

"What deal?" I asked dubiously.

"With your good friend the Angel. We sorted it out real good at our sit-down. He respects me and I respect him and we worked out a mutually satisfactory solution to our problems. No more problems."

"They will not try to hurt Kathleen?"

"That'd show no respect."

"What was the deal?"

"You don't want to know."

"You're sure Kathleen is safe?"

"Trust me."

"Kieran, you sound just like Humphrey Bogart."

"You do me an injustice, James. I see myself as more the Robert De Niro type."

"I see."

"You forgot how many times I played the leads with Kathleen in school plays."

"I'm afraid I missed most of those."

"That's right, come to think of it. I guess you did."

"So anyway, that's one less worry. I'm certainly grateful to you. I've been worrying about this for years. . . . Do you happen to know how Kathleen found the letter?"

"Searching through papers for her dissertation."

"That damn dissertation."

"She told you about it?"

"I haven't had time to listen."

"Too bad. It's a brilliant piece of work."

"I find that hard to believe. In any case, let me repeat my gratitude. I'm not sure what you did, but I know it must have required extraordinary courage, more than our families deserve from you."

"Forget the past, James. It's over and dead."

The past, I thought, is never dead. It lives on to haunt us.

"Well, I certainly owe you one."

"Oh? Well, I tell you what, James. I'm going to call in my marker right now."

"Indeed?"

"As a personal favor to me—and to yourself and the Church too—get Gerry Greene out of town for a couple of weeks."

"Might I ask why?" I said stiffly.

"You don't want to know. But you'll be grateful to me, I promise you that."

"For how long?" I asked.

"Until the Feast of All Souls."

"That's a most unusual request."

"Put him in a place where he can't move. No questions asked."

Kieran was an odd man, brave but odd. I could see nothing, however, that would be lost by acceding to his peculiar request.

"I'll see what I can do."

"You won't regret it, James. You won't regret it."

After that odd conversation, I told my secretary not to disturb me. I remained in my office for some minutes trying to piece together the puzzle of Kieran O'Kerrigan.

What would happen if Kieran had elected to remain in the city? For as much as he helped at times, he was still chiefly a nuisance. Like it or not, I had the feeling he was back in our lives after all these years, possibly back for good.

KATHLEEN

"Lunch tomorrow, Kieran?" I tried to still my beating heart.

"Uh huh . . . Cape Cod Room of the Drake at twelve-thirty."

"I have work to do on my dissertation. . . ."

"You can spare a few hours. Remember it's my treat. Expensive!"

"I'm a cheap date, Kieran. Always have been. I don't drink. Twelve-thirty?"

"That's right."

"I'll get up early and finish my work quota before I come down."

"Work quota?"

"How else do you think I'm getting it done? Don't you have a work quota?"

"Doesn't everyone? See you tomorrow."

"I love you, Kieran," I said—after he had hung up.

I shouldn't have accepted his invitation. I really shouldn't. We would have a difficult time keeping our hands off one another. Yet I couldn't avoid him completely. We must have a serious talk sometime soon. In the long run we belonged to each other for the rest of our lives. But until after the election, we must be careful. No, we must be more than that. We must put our passion on hold.

If there was a contested primary in March and Brien lost—as I thought he would—that would mean we wouldn't have to wait till November.

I immediately felt guilty. I didn't want Brien to lose.

No, that wasn't true. I did want him to lose. He couldn't stand the strain of public life. He would have a much better chance for happiness if he practiced law and played golf.

But now that his ego was on the line, a loss would be a terrible blow. What would he do then? Go back to drink? Go back to his lover? Go back to battering me?

Just then the phone rang. It was Brien.

"Hi, hon, how's it going?"

"Okay, Brien. And you?"

"Not too bad. Still burning up the links. I wish I could do nothing but law and golf for the rest of my life."

"That might be a good idea."

"No," he said with a laugh. "Too many people are counting on me. But it would be nice just the same."

Who was counting on him besides his parents and James? No one. I couldn't bring myself to say that.

"You should do what you want to do, Brien."

"I know that. . . . Hey, you know I've been doing a lot of thinking down here."

"I thought it was going to be a vacation."

"If you can think on a vacation"—he laughed—"I can too."

"So what were you thinking about?" I was afraid to find out.

"Doctor Beauregard agrees with you. He thinks I'm bisexual with strong homosexual tendencies."

I could hardly believe my ears.

"He thinks that if I could admit that to myself a lot of the pressures would dissipate. What do you think?"

"I'm not your therapist, Brien, but if he's right, there certainly would be a lot of pressures on you."

"Yeah. I figure you're pretty smart and you'd know what to think about that. . . . Another thing he says is that I hate women—not because of my sexual preference, but because my mother pushed me around all my life. What do you think about that?"

"It takes my breath away, Brien."

"Sure took mine away too, but the more I thought about it the more sense it made, you know?"

"Maybe it does."

"So I tell him maybe the reason I get drunk and hit you when the pressure builds up is that I hate you."

I was speechless.

"Of course, I don't *really* hate you. I love you, you know that, even if I guess it's all over between us now. But, like the doctor says, when I explode, maybe I get you confused with my mother? What do you think of that?"

I was crying. "I know you don't want to hate me, Brien."

" 'Misdirected anger' is what Doctor Beauregard calls it. Rage, actually."

"Oh, Brien." I was sobbing.

"Hey, don't cry. It's not your fault. It isn't anyone's fault really. Heck, it's kind of exciting to figure it all out. . . . I wanted to tell you this before I came back because I thought I might lose my nerve."

"I'm glad you did, Brien."

"We'll always be friends, huh?"

"Always."

"Maybe you'll be happy with someone else, like Kieran maybe. He's back in Chicago. He never did marry, you know."

"Brien, it's too early to talk about things like that."

"If you're gay, you're gay, I guess. That's that. Maybe it's not so bad. You can learn to live with it. A lot of guys do. I know that. More than you'd think."

"I'm sure they do."

"You don't have to pretend anymore."

"No, you don't have to pretend."

"I don't mean announce it formally or anything."

"No, of course not."

"And I can get along without it usually. I mean, I have most of the time."

"It might be even easier if you don't have to pretend."

"Just what I've been thinking. . . . Well, I'm not sure about any of this. I'll have to talk to James, but right now it all makes pretty good sense, you know?"

"You haven't told James any of this?"

"A little bit."

"How did he react?"

"You know James. He didn't like it, but the way I'm beginning to feel, he doesn't have to. Look, I'll see you on Saturday evening, right? We can talk more then."

"Right, Brien. Have a safe trip home."

Tears were still streaming down my cheeks as I hung up the phone.

Brien had sounded happy, happier than I had heard him sound in years. Happy and relieved.

I hoped I had said the right things to him. I had done my best. I probably never loved him as much as I did at that very moment. He had shown great courage and candor—to a woman who in his own way he loved very much.

Maybe, after all, we could be friends.

Of course, James and Sheila would do all in their power to destroy his newfound peace, of that I was certain.

And they'd probably win.

LEARY

"You've lost all common sense. I absolutely forbid you to see Doctor Beauregard again. He's filling your head with sick foolishness."

"It all makes sense to me, James." Brien sounded hurt, as if I had ruined his parade or taken toys away from him.

"Only because it seems to promise a way to escape from your responsibilities. A self-admitted gay cannot seek public office in this state."

"Come on, James, you know better than that. Should I give you a list?"

"Rumors."

"Everyone knows they're true."

"None of the men about whom we are hinting has ever come out of the closet."

"I wouldn't have to do that."

"It would be a terrible mistake, even if it were true—and I'm convinced that it isn't true."

"It might be true, James. You know that."

"I'm certain that it's not true."

"There's nothing wrong with being gay, James. It wouldn't be my fault."

"I'm not convinced of that."

"I don't see why you're so upset . . . it clears up a lot for me."

"The idea that you hate your mother is poppycock, Brien—psychological babble of the worst sort. Why blame poor Sheila for your troubles? Her only crime is to have loved you all your life. You'd be much better advised to blame your wife if you have to blame someone."

"Mom has always pushed me pretty hard, James. It's almost like she's running for the Senate instead of me."

"Don't you want to be in public life?"

I expected a quick answer to that question. Instead I waited.

"Yeah, sure I do. But sometimes I wish I could make the decisions myself."

Doctor Beauregard had done a lot more harm than I had suspected. We would have to put an end to his influence before Brien ruined everything—for himself and for everyone else.

"Brien, I've got an appointment with the Boss for which I'm already late. I'll call you back later. Try to remember these truths: your whole life has been a preparation for the campaign that is ahead of us. You have always wanted this campaign, so have your parents. You've made the decision, they haven't. Instead of abandoning your manhood, now is the time to reaffirm it, to carry forward our traditions for which you are the last and the best hope."

"I understand that, James. I don't want to run away from a fight."

"Good. I'll be in touch with you later."

"I think I'll call Mom now and talk some of these things out with her."

"For the love of God, Brien! Don't do that! Not till we talk further. Do you want to kill your mother?"

"No!"

"Then don't discuss these matters with her until we talk further. Please promise me that."

"All right, James," he agreed reluctantly. "I promise."

On the way to my meeting with the beleaguered Boss, I pondered the conversation with Brien. We were in very deep waters. All our plans were collapsing. Brien was losing his nerve. In some deep and fundamental sense, the whole situation was my fault. If I had not intervened in his life repeatedly, none of this would have happened.

Perhaps I could still avert disaster, but what was the point in trying? I would probably end up making a bad situation worse.

That was, after all, the story of my life.

KIERAN

Jean Cummins, pale and distraught, waited at the door of my office.

"What's wrong, Jean?"

"Do you have a couple of seconds?"

"Certainly. Come in."

She sat down and put a small cassette player on my desk.

"On my answering machine. May I play it?"

"Of course."

She pushed the play button. A deep, menacing voice crackled on the tape: "We have disposed of others like you, Doctor Cummins, and we will do the same to you unless you leave our priestess alone. Psychiatrists make very interesting sacrificial victims. Our Master enjoys every one we offer to him. If you want to find yourself stretched out naked on a slab, a knife pointed at your heart, you will continue to interfere with our priestess. But before we sacrifice you, we will offer up your baby. Our Master loves babies."

She turned off the tape.

"Baby?" I asked.

"My little Mary Ellen. She's ten months. Born just before I came here. . . . Do you think it's an idle threat?"

"Probably. Have other therapists in this field received similar threats?"

"Yes."

"Any deaths?"

"No . . . none that we know of. One attempt however, a dubious auto accident."

"No missing babies?"

Tears in her eyes, she shook her head.

"I see. . . . Jean, what does your husband do for a living?"

"He's a computer engineer. . . . He's away at a conference just now. . . . Played linebacker for the Raiders for two years."

"Can you ask him to come home?"

"Of course."

"He should not let you out of his sight for the next week or so."

She smiled wanly. "He'll probably like that."

"And you don't leave this building today until I tell you to do so, understand?"

"Yes, Doctor. . . . You're going to notify—"

"Some of the relevant personnel. Stay here till I come back."

I called Brendan from the Dean's office.

"Wow!" he said. "They're getting awfully arrogant, aren't they?"

"They probably believe in their dark powers. You call me back at my office when the Feds have someone in place out here."

"Absolutely. Keep that woman in your office till I call you back."

"All right."

I told her stories about my training at Beth Israel and made her laugh until Brendan called back fifteen minutes later. The Feds were fast. Brendan said that Jean could go back to her office. A female agent would drop by to chat with her.

"Thank you, Kieran," Jean said when I told her. "I knew I could count on you."

I just hoped she would.

There were two messages waiting for me after the last patient left and I had spent the required ten minutes filling out his hour with an examination of my notes.

I had struggled to wall Kathleen out of the morning—every minute ought to belong to my patients. I had been only partially successful, more successful, however, than, under the circumstances, a man could reasonably expect of himself. I was, after all, in love.

I put aside the notes precisely at the end of the mandatory ten minutes and turned on the answering machine. The calls were from James and from Jean. I phoned Jean first.

"Kieran," she began, "I'm beginning to suspect that you have preternatural powers."

"I deny the rumor."

"The FBI was most sympathetic to my patient. They believed her. They're putting a tap on her phone to monitor the calls and they've promised her protection. I'm simply astonished."

"I thought they might be interested."

"They must be serious about the Satanism problem, at long last. Thank God."

"I'm glad they responded helpfully."

"You knew they would, didn't you?"

"Who, me?"

"Why else would you have suggested that she see them?"

"You don't want to know, Jean. Believe me, you don't want to know."

"I can accept that."

"Good. Keep me informed."

I was on a roll and in love. Kieran O'Kerrigan, the Clint Eastwood of the South Side Irish.

With a beautiful woman waiting for me and a free afternoon ahead of us.

I phoned her brother next.

"Thank you for calling back, Kieran."

James was his most genial self.

"I've acted on your suggestion about our mutual friend. My attorneys were uneasy about such an examination, but I told them that I wanted to be sure that we had solid evidence before we risked a trial. They went along eventually."

I had suggested only that he get Greene out of town. Why was James giving me credit for more than I had suggested? What did he want from me?

"You won't regret such prudence, James."

"Now, I wonder if we could talk about Brien for a moment if you have time?"

"Sure." I had an assignation with Brien's wife in a few minutes, but I still had some time.

"He has been seeing one of the men you recommended—Doctor Beauregard."

"An excellent practitioner, one of the very best."

"Is he really?" James sounded dubious. "Frankly, some of the things Brien tells me about their conversations are very disturbing."

"To Brien?"

"No. To be candid, Brien seems quite pleased, but the comments are, ah, shocking."

"I don't want to intrude in his treatment, James."

"I fully understand. I don't want to either, but I've had a special relationship with Brien for many years. He's almost like a brother. In some ways even more than a brother."

"Yes."

"I am more than a little troubled to learn that Brien has been told that he has a violent hatred for women, and most especially his mother."

"We all tend to be ambivalent about our parents, James."

"So I am told. But I gathered that this was described as more than the usual ambivalence."

I should hope it would be!

"Does it offend Brien?"

"In truth, Brien is less disturbed than I am. But so much is at stake these days with the Senate campaign and all. . . ."

"You realize I cannot speak with either Doctor Beauregard or Brien?"

"Naturally."

Not so naturally: he wanted me to lean on Pete to change his tactics. Come on, James, that will never do!

"So you want my advice to you?"

"Precisely."

"I may be candid?"

"We know each other too well, Kieran, for anything else."

"For the time being, then, leave Brien alone to work things out with Pete Beauregard. Don't meddle, don't intervene, don't try to learn what goes on between the two of them. Listen to what Brien tells you but offer no comment."

"You're telling me to stay the hell out of the relationship?"

He wasn't genial anymore.

"In effect, James, that's exactly what I'm saying."

"That requires tremendous confidence in a doctor I do not know."

"You can check his credentials with others, your own consultants, for example."

"I already have. They give him the highest ratings."

"What more can I say?"

"I appreciate your candor, Kieran." He sighed. "There are so many critically important issues at stake."

"Like the rest of Brien's life."

"Yes, that too. . . . Well, as I say, I appreciate your candor. You are probably right."

No probables, James. But you'll meddle—like you always have.

I thought I saw something at that moment, something astonishing, terrifying, and illuminating, but it was lost in the whirlwind created by the arrival of Brendan McNulty.

"We should have lunch, Kieran."

"Brendan, I already have a date."

"What I have to say will only take a minute—you managed to get Gerry Greene out of the scene, didn't you?"

"Who, me?"

"Yes, you. The Boss called him and told him that they were sending him to a funny farm out in New Mexico till the middle of November."

"Your friends at the Bureau tell you this?"

"Don't ask! . . . But they're delighted that he's out of the picture."

"Did Greene agree easily to the orders?"

"Nope, fought back but caved in when the Cardinal threatened to remove him as pastor. Funny thing about Gerry: he really likes being a parish priest."

"I don't doubt it. You know, the tragic thing is, he was probably victimized as a kid, Brendan. Most of these people are. And maybe, just maybe, if there weren't such walls of silence around this kind of crime, maybe Gerry could have gotten the help he needed before he turned into an abuser himself. It's such a vicious cycle."

Brendan nodded. "So what did you do to James to get him to change his mind?"

"Personal favor."

"It must have been a big one."

"Pretty big."

"Can I ask what it was?"

"You don't want to know. . . . Believe me, Brendan, you don't want to know."

"I'll take your word for it. . . . Well, I'm out of here. Enjoy your date."

"I am planning on it."

I beat Kathleen to a darkened corner booth of the Cape Cod Room by a minute and a half. The last time I had been seduced, more or less. This time I intended to do the seducing. Or so I told myself before she arrived. But when she came in, I realized that she might take the lead yet again.

Every head in the room turned when she swept by, wearing a large black hat and a black knit minidress which fell no lower than midthigh. Her hair was loose and falling to her shoulders. "Stunning" would have been an inadequate word to describe her appearance.

"Kathleen," I whispered as she sat down, "you're gorgeous. Do you know what a stir your entrance just caused?"

It was too dim to see for sure, but if I didn't know better, I'd say she blushed. "You said it would be an elegant lunch, so I dressed appropriately."

"I hope I have been telling you often enough that I love you, Kathleen?"

"I think I have heard that now and again."

"This is not a one-time fling on my part."

"Kieran"—she giggled—"whatever else you may be, you are not a one-time flinger. Neither, as far as that goes, am I. . . . You can order for me the bookbinder soup without the sherry and crab Maryland."

"Without the sherry?"

"On that subject I am a rigorist."

"I'm glad that it's only on that subject."

"About other subjects we'll have to wait and see."

"No, we won't."

KATHLEEN

I told myself when I woke in the morning that it would only be a friendly lunch, nothing more. I renewed that promise in church, more to myself than to God who, I felt, was playing the role of an interested observer for the present.

But when I had finished my morning's quota of work and began to prepare myself for my date with a leisurely shower, I knew that the lunch would be something more than just a friendly conversation.

We would have to restrain our relationship, but not today.

No, not today. No way. Having convinced myself that I could respond to the passions of a passionate man, I must now establish to my own satisfaction that I could be an adequate sexual aggressor. I thought I could, but I wanted to be certain.

In our first encounter I had been sleepy-eyed and unprepared. Not so today. I'd be ready, black lace, minidress; the works.

I'd keep the whole afternoon open. He could have me till suppertime if he wanted.

The look in his eyes when he saw me told me that he indeed wanted.

There'd be lonely days ahead. Memories of this golden October afternoon a week before Halloween would keep us going until all the problems were solved.

I was not prepared, however, for him to begin the work at hand while we were still in the Cape Cod Room.

During the bookbinder soup, mine without sherry and his with, his hand slipped under my skirt, up the smooth nylon on my thigh.

"No one can see us," he whispered.

I glanced around. In truth, no one could see us.

"I'll stop if you want." He began to withdraw his playful fingers.

"No, don't stop. Please. But we do have to eat lunch eventually."

Eventually, we did eat lunch. And an apple tart with heavy cream for dessert.

"Are you coming to my apartment voluntarily or will I have to take you by force?" he asked once we were through.

"I guess I'll come voluntarily."

"It might be awhile before I let you go."

"I guess I'll just have to take my chances." I sighed with mock resignation.

We rode up the elevator discreetly. After all, he was known in the building, and my picture had been in the papers and on TV. No, it was not an affair in which we could engage publicly until a lot of other problems were solved.

He kissed me for the first time in the apartment. Well, that isn't altogether true. I kissed him. And thus we began the game of the day—who could be more outrageous. I think I won but not by much.

He did not give me much time to admire the panorama of the city,
lush and placid under the hazy golden sunlight which clothed it like a
transparent gown which just covered her breasts.

More covered than mine would soon be.

He took off my hat first. The way he did it made it a very suggestive
gesture.

When he began to undress me, starting with my hat, I protested.
"Kieran! You haven't drawn the drapes!"

"The transparent shades"—he unzipped my scandalous minidress—
"are opaque on the outside. No one can see in."

"Are you sure?"

"Positive."

I had never made love in an apartment with the light streaming in
from all sides. The illusion of exposure made me feel all the more
wanton.

We were gentle and outrageous, abandoned and tender, wild and
meek, demure and passionate.

The good Lord had made us for one another, body and soul, and was
now giving us a second chance.

Afterward, as Kieran walked me to my car, I decided that I should tell
him about Brien's call—how Brien had practically given his blessing to
this affair. I also confided in Kieran about Doctor Beauregard's diagno-
sis. Kieran listened carefully to my account.

"Astonishing," he murmured when I was through. "Truly astonishing."

"It's so sad."

"A bad hand, a very bad one."

"What does this mean for his future?"

"It means he has a fighting chance if your brother and his mother
leave him alone. The best thing in the world would be for them to let
him drop this quest for public office. Then I think he'd have a good
chance for a happy, productive life."

"They won't leave him alone."

"I'm afraid not."

"What can we do?"

"I can't do anything without possibly interfering with Doctor Beauregard's efforts. You can support Brien in his decisions. I just don't see
how either of us could make any impression on Sheila and James."

"We can help him by not making things worse."

"By cooling it, Kathleen?"

"For a time. If there is a contested primary, perhaps only till March."

Kieran looked as unhappy as I felt. But he didn't disappoint me.

"As long as it takes, Kathleen, to give that poor man a fighting chance. . . . March, next autumn, whatever."

She nodded solemnly. "I knew you'd agree. That's one of the reasons why I love you so much. You will stay in touch?"

"I'll call you every day."

"Every other day . . . and I forgot to steal your phone number at the apartment. I was, uh, otherwise occupied."

"Were you really?" He pulled out a card which had his three office numbers printed on it. He wrote his apartment number on the back before giving it to me.

"I'll stay in touch," I told him, hoping the tears welling in my eyes wouldn't spill over.

"I love you, Kathleen. This time I'll never leave."

"You'd better not." I kissed him lightly on the lips, then slipped into the Mercedes.

The next few months would be hard. I didn't realize then just how hard.

LEARY

"Have you seen Sneed's column?" Sheila had caught me at breakfast in the Cathedral rectory. I had the *Sun Times* in my hand.

"I've got it right here:

DEM SENATE FIGHT?

*Sneed hears that the Democratic primary in March will certainly be contested. Unannounced candidate **Brien** (pronounced 'Breen' if you please) **Donahue** will be beaten to the press conference by veteran River Forest committeeman **Neil Clifford**. The Dems will have two 'blue-ribbon'*

candidates who might split the white vote and give a black candidate a
fighting chance. Both candidates have lots of the green stuff on their own
with which to launch fund-raising campaigns. Donahue's 'Kennedy' image
may be a liability, given all the dirt about the Kennedy family. Insiders say
that the Mayor will be neutral, but some of his staff think Clifford will
prove a stronger candidate against incumbent downstate Republican Joe
Johnson."

"That bitch!" Sheila exploded.

"Mike Sneed?"

"No—your sister."

"Kathleen?"

"She gets Brien out of town and then goes to her friend Richie and knifes him in the back. You know she's always been opposed to his running. She says he can't win. Now she's trying to prove that to us."

"I hadn't considered that possibility."

Like our father before us, Kathleen had a weakness for convoluted political deals.

"We've got to get Brien back here and put some iron in his spine. He has to stand up to her and prove her wrong."

"A contested primary will be a dogfight, Sheila, an expensive dogfight."

"It's time we finally won a victory against the Daleys."

"Sneed says he's staying out of it."

"And you believe that?"

"Not necessarily."

"I've already called Brien. He's out playing early golf. You call him too and get him back here. We have a lot of work to do."

With Sheila, politics was an obsession. The game was far more important to her than to Tom, who, at this stage of life was content with golf, martinis, and vacations.

She had never liked Kathleen either, a reaction I had not anticipated when I promoted the match.

There was so much I had not anticipated.

Yet she was right that we had to stiffen Brien's resolve. He would never forgive himself if he failed to seize the present opportunity—and seize it forcefully, manfully.

I resolved to call him as soon as I arrived at my office.

KIERAN

I put aside the *Sun Times*. A primary race would tear Brien apart, of that I was certain. So, too, would the general election should he win the primary. If he lost in the primary, at least the battle would be over and he could get on with his work with Peter Beauregard.

Either way, Kathleen and I had our pledge, which we would honor.

I figured it was all right to hope he lost in the primary. It would be a terrible blow but it might finally liberate him from the illusions imposed on him by his mother with the help of James.

In the whole Lenihan, O'Brien, Donahue, Leary crowd, there was only one politician worthy of the name, and she was not running for anything except to be my wife—something she would already have been for eighteen years, had I not lost my nerve.

KATHLEEN

The Mayor was on the phone, as I knew he would be.

"I'm not stabbing you in the back, Kathleen."

"I'm not running for office."

"Yeah, but we owe Brien something just because he's your husband. . . . How am I supposed to say to Neil that he can't run because we owe you?"

"You couldn't do that, Rich."

"It wasn't my idea."

"If you say so, I believe you."

"Now, if you were running . . ."

"No way."

"I understand. . . . I don't know what people over here are saying, but I don't think Neil would be any stronger a candidate against Johnson than Brien."

"If you ask me, neither has much of a chance unless the Democrats find a good presidential candidate."

"You're absolutely right."

"If they offer you the nomination, Rich, take it!"

"No way! . . . Look, if Brien wins, we're solidly behind him. But I've made this rule about staying out of primaries. . . ."

There were various ways of staying out of primaries. The Mayor was telling me that he would stay out of this one in the strictest sense of the word, which was fair enough. We couldn't ask for anything more.

"I understand."

"You'll explain to Brien?"

"I'll try."

I wouldn't be able to convince him, or more precisely his mother, that there was not yet another Daley plot to get them. Nor James, as far as that went.

As if the Mayor and his large clan had the time to waste on such unimportant people as we had become. As we'd always been for as long as I had lived.

BRIEN

Another couple of drinks won't hurt.

I can't believe she'd do this to me. I just can't believe it.

But Mom is convinced and so is James. They must be right.

Daley would never run a candidate against me without her approval. She either suggested it to him or told him it was all right.

What the hell is wrong with her?

Just when I'm getting my life straightened out.
The bottle is empty already.
I'll call room service for another.
Then I'll go home and straighten things out.

PART V

KATHLEEN

"Wake up, damn it."

It was Brien, in blue sports coat and matching slacks, golf clubs slung over his shoulder. He wasn't supposed to be home until Saturday. I had not put the bolt on the door.

The Sneed item! I should have realized that it would bring him home early!

He threw his golf clubs on the floor and grabbed my shoulders. "What are you trying to do to me, bitch!" He jammed a clipping from the *Sun Times* in my face.

"What do you mean . . . please, Brien, you're hurting me!"

The terrible stench of alcohol swept over me. He was drunk.

This time he would kill me.

"I go out of town and you put your friend Richie up to stabbing me in the back, that's what I mean!"

He hit my face with his open hand. I felt a tooth jar loose.

"Brien, that's not true!"

"The hell it isn't! You want me to lose! Eat this!"

He shoved the paper into my mouth and forced it down my throat. I gagged on it and tried to spit it up.

There was already blood on my gown.

"Swallow it, goddamn you, or I'll hit you again and knock out some more of your pretty teeth!"

Choking and gagging, I swallowed it.

"You think you're pretty smart, don't you?" He grinned savagely. "I'm going to give you a lesson that you'll never forget."

He hit me again. I decided that even though I would lose, I would fight back. I dug my knee into his groin.

He doubled up and shrieked with pain. I grabbed a chair and tried to keep him at bay.

"I'm going to teach you a lesson you'll never forget." He faked right, then dove left. The chair clattered to the ground. He grabbed my wrist and hit me across the face with his forearm.

"Please, Brien, don't hit me! You could kill me!"

"Wouldn't that be a shame!"

He tore off my gown and threw me on my stomach.

"Stop whimpering," he bellowed.

"No more, Brien, please," I begged.

My pleading only infuriated him.

He systematically beat me. With one punch he broke my nose. With several more, he knocked out my front teeth. I didn't know it at the time, but another blow broke my jaw. I was in such pain and bleeding so profusely, I was barely conscious for the continued pounding that managed to crack four of my ribs.

Drifting in and out, I heard him laugh insanely. "I've only begun to teach you a lesson you'll never forget. And, damn it, stop whimpering or I'll brain you!"

He reached for his golf bag and pulled out a club.

"See this!" He waved an iron in my face. "It will make mush out of those precious brains of yours. You'll never finish your dissertation now!"

Death, come quickly, I begged God.

"Daddy! What are you doing to Mommy?"

Dear God, it was Maeve! Don't let him kill her too.

Maeve tumbled into the room. Her hair was tousled and she was wearing a blue and gold Notre Dame T-shirt that doubled as a nightgown.

"Get out of here or I'll do the same thing to you."

Maeve advanced relentlessly. That's when she got a good look at me. Just the sight of me made her retch.

Brien grabbed for her shoulder and raised the golf club.

She kicked him in the knee, twisted away, and wiped the vomit away from her mouth.

Brien howled with pain and swung the club at her.

"Stop it, Daddy!" she demanded. "I don't want to hurt you!"

"I'll kill you! And then your mother! Watch, Kathleen, while I brain this brat of yours!"

"Please don't, Brien," I mumbled through swollen lips and a bleeding mouth. "Kill me, not her!" But my words were hardly intelligible.

He grabbed for her again, but all he got ahold of was the shoulder of her shirt. He managed to rip the back out of it with one firm yank. Then he swung the club at her head. She ducked away and his club shattered a lamp, plunging the room into darkness. The only illumination came from the streetlight outside my window.

"Stop it, Daddy." Maeve's voice was cold and implacable. "I'll stop you!"

Maeve's foot shot out, kicking the golf club from his hand. The kick was unmistakable: it was from her repertoire of Taekwondo.

I realized that in his drunken frenzy, Brien didn't stand a chance against my little champion—not unless he struck a lucky blow.

He reached for the club. She kicked it away from him.

"Give up, Daddy," she ordered with unearthly calm. "I don't want to hurt you anymore."

He tried to rush her. She kicked him in the jaw. He fell back on the bed, on top of me. I passed out in pain.

I fought my way back into consciousness. In the dim light of our ruined bedroom, my daughter continued to kick out defensively while her father persisted in charging at her like some crazed, wounded bull.

Somehow Brien, one arm limp, managed to find another golf club, a wood this time.

"Stop it," he bellowed, "or I'll brain your mother."

He swung the club toward me.

With unerring precision Maeve kicked at him. Her foot hit the side of his head with a heavy thud. He spun away from her and crashed heavily against the nightstand next to the bed. His head hit the corner of it as he went down.

That is when, for the umpteenth time, I passed out.

When I struggled up from my dense sea of pain, I saw my daughter standing timidly over her father.

"I think I killed him, Mommy."

KIERAN

I was sound asleep when the phone rang.

"Dot Halder, Kieran. Sorry to wake you. There's been a terrible . . . accident. Brien Donahue is dead."

"Kathleen . . . !"

"Savagely beaten, and I mean savagely. But she's still alive. We've patched her up. She'll be all right, though it will take time. Like you said, she's a survivor. She wanted me to call you."

"Can I talk to her?"

"I'm afraid she can't talk. We had to wire her jaw."

"Dear God! . . . Is she at Little Company?"

"She insisted that we bring her home. I'm here with her keeping her under observation. Father McNulty is here too."

"I'll be right out."

"Yes, I think you should come."

It took me twenty minutes to drive from my apartment to Beverly—in drizzle and fog. I ignored the one-way sign at 87th and Pleasant and roared up to the house on Hopkins Place.

There were a couple of police cars, an ambulance, and two TV vans.

A senatorial candidate was dead, that was news. Killed by his wife? I wondered. Dot hadn't said.

Sheila and Tom Donahue were in front of the house, shouting "Murder" at the camera. I ignored them and rushed to the door.

A woman police officer reached out to stop me.

"Doctor O'Kerrigan," I said.

Her expression softened. "Go right in, Doctor, they're expecting you."

In the parlor was an unlikely assortment of people—a police captain, another woman patrol officer, Dot Halder, Brendan McNulty, and the three kids in jeans and slacks, figures set in stone, and a mummylike figure, swathed in bandages on the sofa.

Everyone seemed grim and pale. Brendan's fists were clenched in fury.

"What happened?" My question was directed to no one in particular, but it was Maeve who answered.

"I killed Daddy," she replied, her face hard as stone. "I didn't mean to, but he was killing Mommy and I tried to stop him. He swung a golf club at her head and I kicked him and he fell. He hit his head against a table and he's dead."

"Maevie!" I threw out my arms. "How terrible!"

She came rushing into my embrace and the other two along with her. The three dissolved into sobs in my arms. I wept with them.

I glanced around the room. The woman cop was crying, her captain had turned away his head, Brendan McNulty was smiling his approval, the mummy raised her thumb in support.

"Open and shut case of self-defense," the captain said. "You should see the room, Doctor."

"And what he has done to Kathleen," Dot Halder added.

I went over to my love, knelt at her feet, and took her hand in mine. She squeezed it tightly, a survivor.

I thanked God for sparing her. I vowed anew to take care of her for the rest of my life.

"Okay," said Dot. "We waited till he came. Now another injection."

Kathleen did not resist.

"Some pills for you guys too," Dot said, turning to the girls. They obediently took the pills.

"I found out who the Satanists' victim was supposed to be," Brendan whispered to me.

"What?" I was as surprised he was bringing this up now as I was by his discovery.

"She's here in the room," he said, nodding at Brigie.

I glanced at the youngest of the redheads. She seemed to have grown a couple of inches since I'd seen her last. She would be the tallest and the most beautiful of Kathleen's daughters, a willowy Irish goddess from Celtic antiquity.

"But . . ."

"It won't happen now," Brendan said grimly. "Obviously. Incidentally . . . one more thing. Some loves by their durability over time and obstacles are very much like sacraments—metaphors that is, for God's durable love for us."

Then James burst into the room, his face white, his eyes wild.

"What have you done to him!" he wailed.

LEARY

Sheila woke me up.

"He's dead!" she moaned.

"Tom!"

"No, idiot! Brien! She killed him!"

"Who killed him!"

"Your crazy sister—who else?"

I dressed and hurried out to Beverly.

Tom and Sheila were talking to TV reporters in front of the house on Hopkins Place.

"The police will try to cover this up," Tom was saying. "But it was murder, cold-blooded, brutal murder."

"Do you know whether Brien's wife or daughter killed him?" A woman reporter jabbed a microphone at Tom.

"They both did," Sheila shrieked. "And Richie Daley and his crooked cops will try to cover it up, but we won't let them. They both belong in the gas chamber."

I rushed up to them.

"Tom! Sheila!"

"Get away from me!" Sheila groaned. "He's dead. They killed him."

"Do you have any comment on this tragedy, Bishop?" someone asked me.

I searched for something to say. "No," was all I could manage.

A woman police officer opened the door for me. I raced into the parlor.

"What have you done to him!" I shouted.

No one answered.

"Who killed him?"

Again no answer, until little Maeve spoke up.

"I did, Uncle James," one of the daughters said. "He was killing Mommy!"

"Nonsense! . . . where is his body!"

"Upstairs." Brendan McNulty pointed at the staircase.

What was he doing here? I would take care of him permanently before this was over.

"I will anoint him!" I hurried up the stairs.

"I already did," McNulty shouted after me.

The bedroom was a shambles, broken furniture, smashed lamps, torn sheets, scattered golf clubs. It smelled of booze and death. I glanced around quickly and became sick myself. Brendan McNulty held my arm while I vomited on the already bloody carpet.

I shook his arm away.

"Where is he?" I groaned.

"Over there, next to the bed."

Brien lay on the floor as if asleep. His face was tranquil, his clothes stained with blood.

"Are you sure he's dead?"

"He is, James. The medical examiner just left. They're going to take his body away in a few minutes."

"I must anoint him."

"I already did, James. He's with God now, what we all want."

I let him draw me away from my lifelong friend's body. I remembered the two of us as four-year-olds running along the sands at Long Beach.

"Is that his blood?" I pointed at the blood-drenched bed.

"No, it isn't, James."

"Whose is it?"

"Kathleen's."

"Whose?"

"It's your sister's blood."

We were standing on the landing at the head of the stairs, a landing on which I had stood thousands of times when we had lived in this house.

"Impossible. Brien wouldn't have done that."

"He was drunk, James. He didn't realize what he was doing."

"Is she dead too?"

The young priest stared at me with a strange expression on his face.

"No, James, she's not dead. She's the one downstairs wrapped in bandages."

KATHLEEN

Larry Murray shifted uncomfortably on his feet. "You will not come to the wake," he said, trying to sound firm. "Nor the funeral."

He was the commodity trader who had married Janet Donahue.

We had no intention of coming to the wake, I wrote on a piece of paper. *Not in my condition.*

Brendan and Kieran were on either side of me. James stood between me and Larry, forever trying to be a mediator.

I handed the paper to Larry. He looked at it and nodded.

Poor guy, he had no taste for this job.

I was dressed in black. A black veil obscured my face.

Various doctors and dentists had been poking and probing me all day. It was imperative, they said, that their efforts begin at once.

"We'll fix you up all right, Kathleen," Dot had whispered. "Good as new. In some ways maybe even a little better."

"I don't care what I look like," I tried to say.

She was the only one who really understood me.

"You don't now, but you will."

"You may come to the funeral Mass, but you will remain in the back so as not to attract attention."

The papers and the television were filled with the Donahues' wild charges of murder and cover-up. The police and the State's Attorney replied that the evidence indicated accidental death during legitimate self-defense. The Donahues accused the Mayor of personally thwarting an investigation.

One of the papers had already printed an editorial asking for a full grand-jury investigation to "clear the air."

I tried to think of what I wanted to write in response to the prohibition of our attending the funeral.

"They'll be in the front row," Father Brendan snapped, "as the principal mourners. Or there won't be a Mass—not in my church."

"Maybe we can compromise some way, Brendan," James pleaded. "Surely there must be something we can agree on."

James had been trying to compromise all day, poor man.

"Stay out of it, James. This is my turf."

My brother lapsed into shocked silence.

"Is that clear, Mr. Murray?" Father Brendan continued. "I grant your parents the right to their grief, but not to their behavior, not as long as I'm acting pastor of this parish. I assume, Bishop, that I still am?"

"Yes, of course," James murmured.

"Go back and tell them that Mr. Donahue will be buried at St. Praxides as the papers say he will. His wife and children will be in the front row. If the Donahues do not want to attend the Mass, that is their problem."

Murray shrugged his shoulders and left.

They would cave in, poor people.

"Megan," Kieran said, "do you guys have a caterer you normally use?"

"Sure, Doctor O'Kerrigan. Three Seasons."

"You'd better call them. There'll be a lot of people coming by this house. Only soft drinks, out of deference to your mother."

"Yes, Doctor O'Kerrigan."

"And, Brigie, will you sing Mozart's *Jubilate* at the Mass?"

"Yes, Doctor O'Kerrigan."

"No one will come by here," I tried to say.

They all turned in my direction.

"She said," Dot explained, translating for me, "that no one will come by here."

Kieran and Father Brendan both laughed.

"You'd better find another black dress and a new black veil." Kieran turned to me. "The one you're wearing is appropriate for a wake. You'll need another one for the funeral."

"Yes, Doctor O'Kerrigan."

They all laughed. For that they didn't need a translation.

Father Brendan and Kieran were right. There was a steady stream of visitors for the next two days. The Mayor and Maggie were the first to come.

James came both days and stayed for a time. He was still shattered and incoherent.

My mother did not come. I tried to care about that, but couldn't. The best that was in her, and that best was very good indeed, had died when Dad died.

On TV that night, the Mayor told the reporters who were camped in front of our house that the request for a special grand-jury investigation was nonsense.

Sheila Donahue demanded on the same program that Maeve be tried, "just like a. e. ."

"Can they do that, Doctor O'Kerrigan?" Maeve asked the newfound hero.

"No, Maeve, they can't. Your grandparents are crazy with grief. They'll get over it."

I wasn't so sure that the Donahues would ever let up. They wanted revenge.

The various doctors who were trying to put me together again insisted on doing their work even before I went off to the funeral Mass. I was so sedated when Dot and Phil Carver led me to the waiting limo that I hardly heard the reporters' questions.

"Did one of your daughters murder your husband, Kathleen?"

"Do you favor a special grand-jury investigation of a possible cover-up?"

"Which child is the killer?"

"Why won't you answer our questions, Kathleen?"

Dot stared right into the camera. "I am Mrs. Donahue's physician. She can't answer your questions because her jaw is wired shut. Her late husband broke it."

Even the reporters gasped. The police had only hinted about my injuries. The media weren't at all aware of how extensive they were.

I continued in a lethargic half-sleep through the Mass. James had wanted to preach, but Father Brendan insisted and James backed off.

He preached about the enormity of God's love. I wept almost automatically.

I did my best with him, I told God. Now it's up to You to take care of him.

BRENDAN

"They don't let up, do they?" Phil Carver shook his head. "And now your brother says that he favors a special grand jury," he said to Kathleen.

"Asshole," I snapped.

"They're all sick with grief," Kieran said.

"I agree, Kieran," the lawyer replied. "But there is a limit to how much slander grief excuses."

"Can anyone challenge a police decision about what they take to be an obvious matter—in the total absence of evidence of a cover-up?"

"No," Phil Carver said, "they can't. Unless the media help them to get away with it. This is a big story. It will all collapse some time, but until then the pressures for a big exposé will continue to build up. 'Unanswered questions,' you know the line."

"What does this do to the children, especially Maeve?" I demanded.

Phil Carver sighed. "Neither the media nor the Donahues seem to care about them."

We were at what had become our headquarters, the parlor of the home on Hopkins Place, three days after the mortal remains of Brien Thomas Donahue had been laid to rest in Mount Olivet Cemetery at 111th and California.

If the facts of what Brien had done to Kathleen would become public, the media circus would collapse. But no one, not even the police, wanted to tell that ugly story.

Kathleen made a noise to attract our attention. She had scribbled something on a piece of paper. *Stop them! For the love of God stop them!*

I nodded. "She wants us to stop them."

"How can we stop them?" Kieran asked.

"Phil, do I understand that every time they open their mouths, the Donahues are engaging in slander?"

"They certainly are. When they accuse Maeve Donahue of killing her father in cold blood, they are speaking falsely and indeed in reckless disregard of the truth."

"I know how to stop them," Kieran said.

"How?" Phil looked puzzled.

"Get the kids in here. I want their agreement."

I went to get them.

Kathleen was undergoing what she called her daily repair work. She was still a terrible mess and wore a veil even with us. That her vanity was returning was, I thought, a good sign.

She also spent an hour or two each day in her room working on her dissertation.

She was a survivor, all right.

Kieran described his plan. It was, to fall into the language of my young charges, totally awesome.

There was silence around the room.

"Maeve?"

"Oh, yes, Doctor O'Kerrigan."

"Brigie? Megie?"

They nodded solemnly.

"Brendan?"

I inclined my head slightly.

"Phil?"

"It will work, no doubt about that."

We all turned to Kathleen.

She stuck out both fists. Two thumbs up. Naturally.

KATHLEEN

We were in a conference room in the offices of Phil Carver's law firm. The media were busy setting up their microphones and cameras. Neither my mother nor James had come. Father McNulty and Kieran were outside the doorway watching closely.

I sat in a chair in front of the blackboard, dressed in my wake dress and still wearing my veil. If anything, I looked worse than I had the first day because the discoloration had spread all over what was left of my face.

"It's going to be all right," Dot had insisted. "In a few weeks you'll be as beautiful as ever."

I no longer tried to say that it didn't matter, because it did matter.

My daughters sat with me, dressed in black dresses and high heels and looking very grown up. Megan had volunteered to read my statement, the other two had agreed that she should.

Dear God, they're so brave. But they're going to need so much help in the weeks and months and years to come. I only hoped I'd be strong enough to help them.

"Very well, ladies and gentlemen," Phil began after clearing his throat. "My client as of this day is entering a suit for slander, asking one dollar in compensation from Thomas and Sheila Donahue for false statements made in reckless disregard of the truth against her minor daughter, Maeve Anne Donahue. Mrs. Donahue."

I stood up as decisively as I was capable and wrote on the blackboard, *I cannot speak because my jaw is wired. My daughter Megan Marie Donahue will read my statement.*

There was a buzz in the crowd.

Megan rose, folder in her hand, and waited for the buzz to stop. She was in her element, spoiling for a fight. As sure as the sun rises in the morning, she had practiced all night in front of a mirror.

" 'I loved my husband,' " she began reading in a strong, clear voice, " 'and I honor his memory. If I now bring some facts to public attention it is to defend my daughter Maeve from charges of willful murder.' "

Megan extended her arm around her sister in a reassuring hug. That was not part of the act, not as we planned it. I couldn't see Kieran's face, but I knew he was grinning.

" 'My husband was a deeply troubled man. The pressures of his life were enormous. Often, it seemed, too much for him. However, he had sought out the help of a very distinguished psychiatrist and was making enormous progress. Only two nights before his tragic death, he phoned me from Florida where he had been relaxing with a week of golf. We had a most loving and affectionate conversation in which he gave names to the demons which were haunting him. I was confident that with time and the same sort of help he was receiving, he would have conquered those demons.

" 'I am not altogether sure what occurred between that conversation and his return to our house. But the demons had returned and taken possession of him. He was drunk. . . . I am told that the alcohol content in his blood was .25 . . . he assaulted me violently. I was afraid he was going to kill me. When the pain from his assault was so great I begged death to come quickly.

" 'I lost consciousness several times. Each time when I awoke he was still beating me.

" 'Then my daughter Maeve entered the room. Brien threatened to kill her. He swung a golf club at her head. Fortunately, she is skilled in Taekwondo and was able to fend him off and to protect what was left of me. At the end, he swung a golf club at my head. She kicked him to protect me. He fell against the nightstand and fractured his skull. Apparently, he died instantly.

" 'You will see from these facts that Maeve, far from being a murderer, is the heroine of this story. She saved my life. If it had not been for her, I would be in Mount Olivet Cemetery and not here. Despite her incredible bravery, she will find it difficult, I am sure, to adjust to memories of the terrors of that night.' "

Megan's voice rose to an angry pitch.

" 'She is a survivor, like I hope her mother is. She will make it. But I will not tolerate any longer public attacks against her character and her heroism. I grieve with Mr. and Mrs. Donahue's grief and for their grief. But their slanders against my daughter must and will stop! Now.' "

I threw away my veil.

The media people gasped.

I let the cameras grind away.

Then I turned to the board and began to write.

KIERAN

The two of them had carried it off perfectly. Naturally. It had been a difficult ordeal as I knew it would be, but it was also, paradoxically, a healthy experience. They had exorcised a lot of demons. In Kathleen's case the demons of a lifetime.

She wrote on the board in best parochial-school script: *In these folders are hospital and police records of some of the injuries I suffered and a few pictures in case you want to examine evidence. In some of the pictures I think I look worse than I do now.*

She turned and tried to smile.

The media crowd laughed nervously.

She erased the board and continued.

I've laid down the ground rules that my daughters are not to be questioned. We'll enforce those rules. If you want to ask me any questions, I'll try to write out my answers.

"Will the doctors be able to save your face?"

She wrote: *Yes. Good as new. Maybe better!*

Another anxious laugh.

"Had you been beaten by your husband before?"

Yes.

"How often?"

She shook her head in refusal.

"Do you hate your in-laws?"

No.

"Will you run for the Senate in place of your husband?"

No way!

"What memories will you carry with you of your husband?"

Of our last phone conversation.

"Do you think he'd want you to tell this story?"

Absolutely!

So it went. We'd won.

Something kind of strange happened at the end. Kathleen's eyes grew bright and she raised her hand as if waving at someone in an empty doorway at the back of the conference room. She glanced at Maeve, who waved too. They both smiled. Neither of the other children seemed to notice.

"What was that all about?" Brendan asked.

"Just now I don't want to know."

I may never want to know.

The Donahues' charges were not repeated. The suit was dropped.

There were, however, no apologies.

I ate supper that night with Jean Cummins and her linebacker husband and admired her daughter, Mary Ellen, and their other two kids as well.

He told wonderful John Madden stories. Jean repeated the FBI's account of the arrest of the Satanists. The Feds were going to throw the book at those sickies—another Manson case, they had told the grand jury. Moreover, as I had expected, the Feds had also seized a huge cache of drugs. More than anything else the "Satanists" were drug addicts whose brain cells had been eroded by all the chemicals which their bodies had absorbed.

Then we talked about the news conference that afternoon. I suppose Jean, smart young shrink that she was, smelled the nature of the relationship between me and Kathleen. She did not, however, express her suspicions.

"What will happen to that woman, Kieran?"

"What do you mean?"

"Will she be able to bounce back from the trauma? She and her children?"

I hesitated. Somehow I had never got around to asking myself that question.

"Maybe, Jean, maybe."

"If you want a nonprofessional opinion," the linebacker observed, "a woman with that kind of courage can bounce back from anything."

I hoped he was right.

LEARY

"Yes, Kieran, I watched it," I replied to his question.

"And?"

We were on the phone. He had wanted to come to my office, but I said that I was not up to a face-to-face conversation.

"I felt terrible grief for the Donahues."

"Not for Kathleen or her daughters?"

"I'm sorry, Kieran. I realize that you must have planned it and I understand your motives, but I feel that they enjoyed the exhibitionism rather too much."

"Those charges had to be stopped, James."

"At the price of ruining poor Brien's reputation, possibly forever?"

"I don't think that happened."

"I do. My mother does. Tom and Sheila do. Aren't our feelings important?"

"Maeve is a heroine, James."

"I'm afraid I find that hard to accept. Surely she could have been more restrained."

He was silent. So I continued. "The charges would have stopped. Tom and Sheila were merely expressing grief."

"The charges had picked up a momentum of their own, James. If there had been a special grand-jury investigation, as you said you wanted, a lot more would have come out. We both know that."

"Perhaps."

"You don't think so?"

"I can't believe that Kathleen would have attacked the memory of her husband."

"You're saying she would have committed perjury? Especially given the medical evidence there is?"

"I can't believe that would have become public."

"And Doctor Halder has detailed evidence that she had been beaten before. The hospital would not hold back such information under sub-poena. What would that have done to his parents, James?"

I rubbed my hand across my face. He had a point; that I had to admit.

"Maybe you're right, Kieran. I don't know. I certainly think you acted in good faith, and perhaps wisely. I trust that time will heal all the wounds. Do call me again in another couple of weeks. I'll be happy to see you at that time. I do not want our friendship to suffer."

Would he eventually marry Kathleen?

I thought that he would. It would probably be an unwise match. Perhaps not. Perhaps they should have been married long ago.

Several days later I read in the paper that Anthony "the Angel" Angelini had died of a stroke. He was, the *Tribune* reported, reputed to have been in charge of fixing criminal-court cases for the Mob for many years.

"Angel" was the name Kieran had used.

So that ended another chapter.

In the same day's paper there was a story of a bizarre arrest by the FBI of a group of men and women who were engaged in a Satanic ritual in a suburban home. They were planning, the story said, to sacrifice the thirteen-year-old daughter of one of the participants to the Devil. The government was charging the whole group with the sexual abuse of a minor and conspiracy to commit murder.

It was all scarcely believable. Yet the carefully selected documents shown on the evening news that night seemed altogether too plausible.

The next day I opened the report from New Mexico on Father Gerry Greene, confidently expecting that he would be given a clean bill of health. On the contrary, they described him as a deeply disturbed man with a sadomasochistic fixation on boys. "A very dangerous individual," they had written.

I was profoundly shocked. Surely there must have been a mistake. I postponed showing it to our lawyers until I had a chance to consult with the Cardinal.

KATHLEEN

"Are you going to marry Doctor O'Kerrigan, Mommy?" Megan asked me.

I was able to talk again. I had even gotten back to working on my dissertation. I still looked kind of tattered around the edges—and skinny—but I didn't need the veil anymore.

"It's much too early even to think about that, Megan Marie."

"WELL, like I didn't mean next WEEK."

"Would you guys disapprove?"

"No," she said. "We wanted to tell you that."

"We'll have to wait and see. I'm not even sure he would want to marry me."

"We think he kind of likes you but is too much of a gentleman to show it."

"Six months at least, Megan—maybe a year—before I even think about such an idea."

"That's all right."

"I know one thing."

"What's that, Mommy?"

"If Doctor O'Kerrigan ever becomes part of our family, the reason will be not because he likes me so much but because he adores all three of my daughters."

"Mo-THER!"

Kieran had been wonderful. He had called frequently, sent flowers, dropped by when he was sure the kids were home, brought them presents—and never once was alone with me. I could tell he was giving me time. Time I very much needed.

KIERAN

"So you have withdrawn from the relationship?" Maggie Ward asked me.

It was after Thanksgiving, which I had not celebrated with the Donahue family because I had not been invited.

"For the time being."

"Lost your nerve or your desire or both?"

"Desire kind of slipped away during all the horrors, to tell the truth. But my instincts say I should give her room now. Space. Leave her alone."

"Psychiatric instincts."

"Chicago political insights."

"In your case, Kieran, I'm not sure what the difference would be."

However, she left me alone on that subject. Instead we wrestled with a countertransference I was experiencing—or thought I was experiencing—with an attractive young woman patient.

In the first week in December, Kathleen called me at my apartment. Out of the blue. I hadn't talked to her since before Thanksgiving.

"Good news, Kieran. The Mayor has offered me an appointment on the Chicago Plan Commission."

"Congratulations! I assume you will accept it?"

"He says my historical credentials will fit in nicely on the Commission."

"I assume that the dissertation is almost finished."

"Before the new year begins."

Definitely a survivor.

"You will accept the appointment?"

"I guess so . . . the money will be nice."

"Money? Is money a problem?"

"Well, we're not starving or anything and I have some money in trust funds from the family. But I have kids to send to college."

"Surely you can borrow on expectations of Brien's will?"

She did not answer.

"You can, can't you?"

"They're contesting the will."

"The Donahues?"

"They still hate us."

"What does Phil say?"

"That they can tie it up in court for years."

"I see."

"That's all right. We'll survive. I don't want any more fighting."

"Would it be out of line for me to ask you to lunch some day during the week before Christmas?"

"I don't think so. Let me get my schedule . . . kind of busy this time of year . . . I'll be downtown finishing my Christmas shopping on the twenty-second."

"At Water Tower?"

"Probably."

"There's a nice little Italian place on Chestnut Street just down from Water Tower. Convito Italiano, second floor above the food shop. Great pasta, and quiet."

"Just lunch, Kieran."

"I understand, Kathleen. That's all I expect."

I called James after she had hung up and suggested that we should have another conversation.

It was time I settled with the last of the demons.

LEARY

I would have to face Brendan McNulty and Kieran O'Kerrigan on one afternoon. They had been right on so much and I had been wrong on so much. Yet I could not bring myself to believe that they had been right on everything.

Moreover, I had to live the rest of my life with my responsibility for telling Brien about the Neil Clifford candidacy. I may have thus issued his death warrant.

Dear God, for this and for everything, forgive me.

"I won't take much of your time, James," Brendan said. "By the way, you look beat. I hope you can get away for a couple of weeks after Christmas."

"I hope to take my mother to Arizona. These have been very difficult times for her, as you can imagine."

"I can indeed imagine."

I would try to persuade Mother that she should reconcile herself with Kathleen. I feared that it would be a lost cause however. The display on television was an affront from which my mother would never recover.

"I must admit that you were right about that pedophile suit, Brendan." I tried to sound generous. "We have agreed to establish a lay review board. Father Greene, as you know, has retired."

"I know."

"The Cardinal wants you to continue your work with the law and, of course, at St. Praxides."

"I'm delighted to hear that."

"Did you have something you want to talk about?"

"Yeah. I've thought about this for a while, James. Finally decided I should tell you. These are transcripts of some of the recordings." He opened a briefcase and removed a sheaf of papers. "The Bureau—FBI, that is—made them of phone conversations from St. Sixtus' rectory and from Gerry's house down the street. The United States Attorney, who gave me permission to show them to you, will confirm them if you call him this afternoon. He assumes that you will shred them after you've read them."

"What are they about, Brendan?" I looked at the stack of papers with distaste. I did not approve of wiretapping, especially wiretapping rectories.

"Basically they show that Gerry's house was to be the site of that little Satanist ritual that almost went down on Halloween."

"So," I said softly.

"There's more." Brendan took a deep breath. "Gerry was the one who called your sister about Brien. He was Brien's last homosexual lover."

"Impossible."

"Still more, James. I'll give it to you straight. Brien ended the relation-ship because Gerry demanded Brigid as the sacrificial virgin."

"What!"

"He was dead serious. Brien, God be good to him, turned him down flat. Then Gerry made his call to Kathleen. It's all in here. Pretty disgusting."

"My God!"

"In a way that call set in motion everything that led to Brien's death. So I hope it's some consolation for you, for all the horror and violence, there was bravery at the end of his life too."

"Have you told this to my sister?" My whole body was trembling.

"Good Lord no. Someday maybe, but not for a long time and maybe not ever."

"You've told Kieran?"

"Sure."

"I would have assumed so. . . . Wait a few moments, Brendan. I will glance through these pages and give them back to you."

I read through them quickly.

They were as he had described them. I gave them back to him. "It will not be necessary for me to call the United States Attorney. You will thank him for me. It was very good of him to make this material available for my perusal."

"Do you believe them, James?"

"What? Oh—do I believe them?" I paused. "Yes, I believe them, Brendan. You were correct. They are horrible and yet they do bring me some consolation."

I sat at my desk, face in my hands, waiting for Kieran. Whatever he wanted to say could not be more chilling than what Brendan had brought me.

I was wrong.

My old friend from long ago, my more recent "reconvert" to the faith, my most recent adviser on Gerry Greene, and my possible future brother-in-law was grim and unsmiling. This was a Kieran O'Kerrigan I had not seen.

"I have three items on my agenda, James. The first is that this absurd contest against Brien's will must stop and it must stop before tomorrow ends."

"Now, Kieran." I extended my hands. "I don't think any ultimata are necessary. I'm sure the various lawyers involved can reach an acceptable compromise."

"No compromise."

"The Donahues are elderly people, Kieran. They need some kind of victory."

"No compromise. They withdraw their attack on his will. Now."

"And if they don't?"

"Surely I need not spell it out, James?"

"I'm afraid you do."

"They owe me, James, for what they did to my father."

"I thought that was finished." I was horrified by his threat. "This is blackmail."

"Only a demand for justice. In lieu of justice for my parents, who are with God, I demand justice for Brien's memory and for his wife and children. I don't think that can be called blackmail."

"You will not accept any compromise?"

"Absolutely none."

"Does Kathleen know of this threat?"

"She does not. If she ever learns of it, she won't learn it from me."

"Do you intend to marry her, Kieran?"

"That's an irrelevant question, James. But to answer it anyway: at present, I have no such plans."

"It might be better if you did."

He paused and smiled slightly. "We will see."

"I'll have to approach this carefully with the Donahues. I don't want to shock them."

"Do it any way you want."

"All right, then. However reluctantly, I accept your demand in the first item on your agenda because I have no choice. I do not approve, but I accept. What is your second demand?"

"No more demands, James. Just two questions."

"The first?"

"Do you think your plot to get rid of me would have succeeded unless a drunken priest had seen me walking by the Regan house?"

"What do you mean?"

"You know full well what I mean: you took the Calcutta money and then paid it back yourself. I was the fall guy."

"That's absurd."

"No, it isn't."

"You can't possibly prove it."

"I don't have to prove it to anyone. You didn't tell Kathleen about my phone calls from New York. You wanted to get rid of me so she would marry Brien. I can tell by your expression that you did it. That's all I need to know."

It was time to tell the truth.

"I meant well, Kieran. I truly did."

"I have no doubt that your motives were good, James. You meant the best for everyone. In the process, however, you fouled up three lives."

"Perhaps I did. I have regretted it profoundly ever since. . . . But I still don't think either of you would have been happy together in those days."

"But now you do?"

"I think that perhaps it will work now."

"I won't debate either point. The former is moot, the latter remains to be seen."

"As to your question, Kieran, you would have been suspected even in the absence of Father O'Connell's report. You were the natural target."

He leaned back in the chair, remarkably self-controlled given the circumstances. "Perceptions are funny things, James. That's the way you perceive it. That's the way I perceived it then. Yet I find that today those who remember the incident—and they are few—perceive it differently. They say that only a very few people thought I had taken the money. The others thought the charges against me were silly and blamed Dave Regan for being careless and boasting about it."

I considered this observation clinically and carefully, as though it were not being made about one of the worst sins of my life.

"That may very well be correct, Kieran. In this life we will never know with any certainty. But might I suggest that it was still beneficial for you to leave Chicago, that indeed your present maturity and eminence in your profession is proof of it?"

"As you say, James, we will never know."

"Would it be out of place to ask for your forgiveness?"

He seemed surprised. "Not at all. Sure, I forgive you, James. All's well that ends well."

He reached out his hand and shook it. Can falls from grace be remitted that easily?

"I appreciate that, Kieran. . . . Will you be buying a house at Grand Beach?"

"Maybe." He smiled. "Who knows?"

"And your second question?"

"It's funny, James. I don't need to ask this because I know the answer. But you need to have someone ask it."

"Oh?"

"You and Brien were, of course, homosexual lovers, were you not?"

I could deny it, lie about it, refuse to discuss it. But what good would any of those responses be? "A long time ago, Kieran. A long time ago. At first it happened before either of us knew what we were doing. Then, later, we had only vague ideas that it might be sinful—wrong, dirty, yes, but not sinful. Then when we found that we shouldn't be doing it, we tried to stop. It required time and effort to do so."

I buried my face in my hands. "I suppose you could say that I led him astray. I seduced him. I corrupted him."

I began to weep.

"That's an overstatement, James. One homosexual relationship during the adolescent years does not make a person gay. Maybe it discloses it to him, but it doesn't cause it."

There was little more that could be said. I was too distraught to continue speaking.

Kieran waited patiently until I regained my composure.

"I'm not making any judgments, James. I leave that to God. Religiously what is important is not your sexual identity, but your celibacy, which I would not dream of questioning. I'm sure you will find sympathy and understanding from God."

I was silent again, striving to pull myself together, still unable to believe that this conversation, this judgment, was taking place.

"You wonder, naturally, whether my friendship with Brien since then was something more than mere friendship. I repeat that there was never any homosexual activity between us after he was married and I was ordained. We never mentioned what had happened when we were young, not once. But, yes, I loved him passionately. I still do."

I began to sob again.

"So, by persuading him to marry your sister, you felt that he would continue to be part of your life."

"I didn't think of it that way," I moaned. "But I suppose that was part of my motivation. I must apologize again, Kieran."

"Not at all." He stood up. "That's it, James."

"I have often thought of resigning, of retiring to a Trappist monastery and devoting my life to penance for my sins. After this conversation, I'm sure I'll do just that."

He turned at the doorway and looked at me, a smile on his lips.

"No, you won't, James. That would be the easy way out. Your purgatory is in this office, not in LaTrappe. . . . And by the way, you should make peace with your sister."

KIERAN

"So you're having lunch with herself tomorrow?"

Brendan was grinning. What did he have up his sleeve now?

We were eating lunch at the Cliff Dwellers, a club on the top of Orchestra Hall. Outside, Grand Park, its trees bare, glittered under new-fallen snow. In the distance, Lake Michigan, framed by the buildings of the Chicago skyline, was ice blue under the bright sunlight.

The color of her eyes.

"The damn kids talk too much."

"I have a point of canon law in which you might find some relevance . . ."

"Oh?"

"The law says that if a couple are marooned somewhere, like on a desert island for example, and there's no prospect of a priest for thirty days, they can exchange marriage vows and validly and licitly contract marriage."

"Interesting enough," I said. "And generous, especially for those on islands."

"Yeah, not that Chicago is a desert island. But there is a solidly probable opinion that the same rules apply if a priest is not only physically unavailable but morally unavailable."

"What does that mean?"

"It means that if for some good and proper reason the couple simply cannot approach the Church for a marriage at a given time, although they are free to marry and it would be wise for them to do so, the island rule might apply."

"What might make it wise?" I tried to pretend I didn't understand what he was saying.

"Healing that cannot and ought not to wait for six more months. Or even three months."

Now his point was clear enough. I felt my face grow warm.

"Oh?"

"So some theologians would hold that public scandal if two prominent people were to marry soon after the death of the spouse of one of them might make a priest morally unavailable."

"Okay, Brendan, you don't have to draw me a map."

"I didn't think I would."

"However, the time is not ripe for such a union."

"Did I say that it was?"

KATHLEEN

I meant it when I told Kieran that it would be lunch and nothing more. If there were ever anything more it would have to wait a long time. There had been too much grief, too much suffering, too much humiliation. I did not think I would ever be ready for sex, not ever again.

With the exception of some minor scars, slowly healing discoloration, and a few persistent aches, I was in reasonably good shape. I had started to run again and even do a little working out with the bars.

Vanity, as Dot said, was a sign of health.

My mind or soul or whatever it should be called was healing more slowly, if at all. My nightmares were terrible and filled with huge golf clubs smashing into my head. My normal waking condition in the morning was cold sweat. Nor did my grief seem to be abating. I mourned my husband. I did not miss the fear of the last weeks of our life together, but I did miss him. I would always miss him. I mourned especially the final possibility of his life from which he had been cheated.

I knew who had done the cheating. They had meant well, by their own lights anyway. I wondered if that was an adequate excuse.

"Don't blame your grandparents," I said to the children. "They wanted what was best for Daddy."

"They wanted what was best for themselves," responded my normally placid Brigid. "And Uncle James doesn't even know our names."

"He thinks all redheads look alike," Megan said bitterly. "Really!"

"Now just a minute, young woman." I spoke with my lay-down-the-law voice. "We are Christians, remember? We believe in forgiveness, don't we? Maybe we can't make everything right with your grandparents and your uncle, but we still forgive whatever they do to us, just like God forgives what we do to other people, right?"

They frowned, stubborn redheads to the bitter end.

"Right?" I repeated my demand.

"Right, Mommy," Megan agreed. "But it's not easy."

"If it's not easy, it's not forgiveness, Megie. You don't labor at forgiving your sisters after a fight, do you?"

"No." She grinned. "Sometimes one of them is a geek and the other a pest, but I love them, so I don't stay mad at them. Right, guys?"

The other two snorted derisively but they did not disagree.

"Forgiveness is an act of generous love." I concluded my sermon. "We do it with a wave of a hand because we love someone or it isn't forgiveness. . . . Do I sound like Father Brendan?"

Then they laughed at me. Which was much better than all of us bursting into tears.

How could I heal the wounds between generations? How to make my children love their grandparents again, especially when my own mother would not speak to me? How could I practice what I preached by forgiving James and Sheila for destroying my husband, just when he seemed on the verge of health?

The kids wanted me to invite Doctor O'Kerrigan for Christmas dinner. They did not, I thought, want him for themselves so much as they wanted him for me.

The image of Kieran in another room in our house at Christmastime was by no means unattractive. But the thought of him in bed with me was too much. I would never be any good with a man again.

So, on the day we were to have lunch the week before Christmas, I dressed in a plain brown skirt and sweater and a brown blazer for my friendly lunch with Kieran on Chestnut Street.

As proof that it would be nothing more than friendly, I told myself, the sound of his voice on the phone did not excite me. Indeed, I was happy to talk to him and to anticipate seeing him again. It had been more than a month since the last time he had come to visit after they had finished some of the painful work on my nose. But the sound of his laughter not only did not stir up any sexual longings, it did not even awaken twinges of love.

Later maybe. And maybe not.

Just before I left to drive to the Rock Island station, the phone rang.

"Kathleen Donahue."

"James, Kathleen."

"Oh?" I got ready for another argument.

"Please forgive me."

"For what?"

"I . . . am not up to specifics at the moment. Later maybe. But you know what I mean."

Time for me to practice what I preached.

"Of course, James."

"For everything?"

"For everything!"

"I love you, Kathleen. I may never have said that. But I do love you. You're a beautiful and . . . brilliant woman."

"Oh, James, I love you too. You're a wonderful priest."

"We need to, ah . . ."

"Restructure?"

"Precisely. Restructure our relationship."

I was crying now. So, I think, was he.

"After this conversation, James," I said tenderly, "it is already well on its way."

"I agree."

It had been easy after all.

Despite the emotional jarring of this sweet, sweet conversation, my good resolutions continued on the ride downtown and my morning shopping efforts. Nor did I experience a single hint of passion when he walked into the Convito Italiano. I was delighted to see Kieran, nothing more. His face was red from the sudden December cold snap and he looked healthy and happy. He did not seem any more interested in sex than I was.

I moved my stack of Christmas presents for the kids off the chair next to me so he could sit there. No point in putting him across the table.

We chatted amiably for a while. Then he approached the important question, "You look fine, Kathleen . . ."

"A little skinny, maybe."

"You'll be able to enjoy the Christmas gluttony more than the rest of us."

"I've thought of that."

"But the important question is, how are you feeling?"

"Better."

"The kids?"

"Up and down."

"Any therapy?"

"Maeve is talking to Father Brendan. Megan is seeing a counselor at school. Brigie . . . I don't know about her."

"They all should be in intensive therapy, Kathleen. You should be, too."

"Yes, Doctor, I know that. The girls want to talk to you . . ."

"It would be very unwise."

"That's what I tell them. They are not convinced."

"And yourself?"

"I'm not seeing anyone either. I know I should."

"Imperative . . . I could make a recommendation."

He scribbled a name on a piece of paper and gave it to me.

"Margaret Mary Ward . . . sounds like one of us."

"Most definitely. Call her."

"Is that an order?"

"You bet it is."

"All right." I put the paper in my purse. "I will."

"Tomorrow. Tell her Doctor O'Kerrigan recommended you. And tell her it's an emergency."

"It really isn't . . ."

"It really is. Now do what I say—tomorrow."

For a fraction of a moment I had the rich feeling of belonging to him. I reached for it and it slipped away.

"I will, Kieran."

"Promise?"

"Promise . . . What's the prognosis for us, Kieran?"

"Uncertain. What happened will always remain with all of you. You can learn to live with it. I repeat, you should all be in therapy."

"There's no chance that you . . ."

"It would never work."

"I know that . . ."

His smile was so kind and sweet, just as it had been on that first day so long ago.

Then, words escaped from my lips which I never intended to say. I was ashamed as soon as I had spoken them: "I guess the whole family wants to seduce you."

KIERAN

"There's nothing wrong with that, Kathleen." My fingers reached out to touch hers. "Nothing at all."

She pulled her fingers away, though not very far. Her chest was moving up and down rapidly, her lovely breasts agitated under her sweater. I could tell she was uncertain and frightened, but she had made a big leap.

She was so very lovely, so fragile, so desirable, so in need of love. My love.

"You said there wasn't much hope for us."

"I said no such thing."

"Well, what did you say?"

"I said what happened would remain with all of you."

"That means there's not much hope."

"Kathleen, that's the therapist speaking. Even he's hopeful. He does not, however, have the last word."

"Who does?"

"The lover." I touched her fingertips again. This time she didn't pull back more than a fraction of an inch.

"What does he say?"

"He says he'll take care of all of you always."

"He does, does he?" She looked at her empty pasta dish.

"I had an interesting conversation with our mutual friend Brendan McNulty."

She looked up shyly and smiled.

"He pointed out that a couple on a desert island who can't find a priest for thirty days can administer the sacrament of matrimony to themselves."

"Everyone knows that." She was studying her pasta dish again.

"He also said that the same thing applied in cases of moral impossibility, like when for some reason it would create scandal if people were married the usual way."

"Everyone knows that too."

"I didn't."

"Well, now you do."

I captured her hand. She didn't pull it away this time.

"Can it be this easy, Kieran?"

"Never easy, but easier, Kathleen."

I rested my other hand on her thigh. She didn't push it away.

"You're not suggesting, are you?" She sounded angry. "That we just sit here in this restaurant and exchange marriage vows?"

"No. I thought we could walk down the street to the Cathedral and do that. Maybe celebrate with a malt at the Ice Cream Studio afterwards. Maybe celebrate all day."

For a few moments she kept her eyes on her empty plate. Then she looked up at me. "I think," she said softly, "that that's the most wonderful suggestion—"

"You've heard all day?" I said, interrupting.

"At least all day." She laughed lightly, but I could see her eyes were glistening with tears—tears of joy, for a change.

And so I escorted the love of my life to the Cathedral to exchange our sacramental vows, finally making good on the promise I had made her so many years ago.

Afterword

Whether there are in fact "Satanic" rituals is vigorously disputed. Therapists like Doctor Cummins in this story, who have dealt with patients who have multiple personality disorders (and similar syndromes) are certain that such rituals occur. Law-enforcement personnel are much more skeptical. For an example of the skepticism of the latter, see Kenneth V. Lanning, *Investigator's Guide to the Allegations of "Ritual" Child Abuse*, National Center for the Analysis of Violent Crime, January 1992. Mr. Lanning, a Supervisory Special Agent of the Behavioral Science Unit at the FBI Academy in Quantico, Virginia, admits the possibility of such abuse but points to the absence of bodies and murder scenes (which cannot be hidden even when bodies may have been destroyed). His position is not unlike that of Doctor O'Kerrigan early in this story.

I have been told by one highly placed criminal-justice official that there are certainly cases of ritual abuse of children by family members in some drug subcultures.

After the first draft of this novel was completed, the pedophile crisis in Chicago became public. While the Archdiocesan bureaucracy's initial response was to deny, cover up, and protect the accused priests, Cardinal Bernardin reacted more wisely. The result was the establishment of a program much like that advocated by Brendan McNulty and Kieran O'Kerrigan—outside review board, second legal and medical opinions, a policy of not reassigning pedophile priests to parish work. The happy ending in this story anticipated the happy ending in reality, much to my surprise.

A.G.